NOT
ANOTHER
ROCKSTAR

Not Another Rockstar

KATE CALLAGHAN

No part of this book may be reproduced or stored in a retrieval system or transmitted in any form or by any means, electronic, mechanical, photocopying, recording, or otherwise without express written permission of the author.

The characters and events portrayed in this book are fictitious. Any similarity to real persons, living or dead, is coincidental and not intended by the author.

Edited By: Ellie Owen

www.callaghanwriter.com

Readers! Please note: this is a stand-alone novel with mentions of trauma, death, grief, cheating, violence, stalking, injury and chronic pain which may be triggering.

Who Knew Falling in Love Could Be So Bloody Dangerous!

After the video of her rockstar fiancé's tragic car crash is released, Phoebe Fletcher is hit with false accusations. Thrust into the relentless media spotlight, the budding artist becomes the focus of obsessive fans, putting both her life and aspirations in jeopardy.

Phoebe seeks refuge with her ex's band, the Brothers of Anarchy, where she forms a bond with the brooding drummer, Axel Adler. She knows fans will tear her apart if she moves on too fast, but Axel's wavering care and encouragement sparks a fiery connection between them.

In the midst of fame, betrayal, and illicit love, Phoebe and Axel must navigate a web of lies and treachery, or risk losing all they hold dear.

Other Books By The Author

YA Dark Fantasy | A Hellish Fairytale Series
Crowned A Traitor I
Where Traitors Fall II
When Traitors Rise III

Towerwood | Novella
Stepmother | Novella

Village of Yule | Interconnected Stand-Alones
The Naughty Or Nice Clause
Tis The Season For Secrets

Village of FoxFord | Interconnected Stand-Alones
Potions & Proposals
Don't Go Breaking My Heart

Romantic Suspense | Stand-Alone
Ms Perfectly Fine
Not Another Rockstar
The Situation Ship

Phoebe & Axel's Playlist

I Knew You Were Trouble | Taylor Swift
Meant To Be | Jared Benjamin
Not Another Rockstar | Maisie Peters
Escapism | RAYE
Hurt My Feelings | Tate McRae
Club Heaven | Nessa Barrett
Getaway Car | Taylor Swift

Scan Me

KATE CALLAGHAN

"Phoebe Fletcher's illustrative paintings, currently featured at the exclusive Hogan Gallery, depict deeply emotional stories in a manner that speaks not only to children but the neglected inner child in every adult. We're expecting many great things from the social media-risen artist in the future."

Lena, her agent, read Phoebe the review from her phone because she was too nervous to read it herself. Phoebe tried to contain her happy squeals—best to be professional, considering how many people were gathered in the gallery to view the exhibition.

"They love the collection?" she asked, peering over Lena's shoulder. It was her first time being reviewed in the paper, and the praise felt too surreal to believe. It felt like she'd finally made it.

"Love it? There are two more paragraphs singing your praises!" Lena beamed, earning a few stares from those around them. "The review has been posted all over social media. Be prepared to be very busy."

"I feel like I can finally breathe again, after months of stressing about all this. I can't believe they love it! I'm so glad I left the commission form open on my website."

Phoebe couldn't wait to get home and check if she had any new commissions or print orders.

She took a deep breath and resisted the urge to burst out in a fit of joy-filled laughter. Probably better not to look like she'd lost her mind, if she wanted these people to purchase her art.

"Has Cillian seen this? When is he getting here?" Lena asked the dreaded question.

She read Phoebe's hesitation in an instant.

"Cillian hasn't turned up? You've been showing for a week, and he couldn't make it for one night? Are you serious?" she whispered as Phoebe placed a red dot on another sold painting.

She'd been worried about the price putting people off, but Lena had informed her at the start of the night that three of her largest paintings had sold to one collector at asking. The best part about having an agent was that she did all the price negotiating. Phoebe was terrible at pricing —she'd give everything away for free if she could.

"After so many years of struggling, I have a sell-out show and an agent to celebrate my success with. Please let's just bask in this moment?" Phoebe pleaded. "Do I want him here? Yes, but nothing can dull my shine right now. I've a sneaking suspicion that Cillian bought the three paintings since he couldn't make it. He mentioned wanting to purchase some art to decorate the villa in Italy."

"You're right. I shouldn't think the worst of him. I won't bring him up again, but you shouldn't let him get away with not being here for you. How many times have you made sacrifices to be at one of his shows or be there to support him?" Lena offered her a glass of sparkling water, since she didn't drink while working.

Phoebe clinked her long, manicured nails against the glass to ease her nerves. She'd had her nails done for the first time for the show, since they were usually stained with paint. Given all the hands she'd be shaking, she wanted to make a good impression—and give her hands a treat for all the hard work they'd done to bring her to this point in her career.

"It's the band's first stadium tour. Him missing one exhibition isn't the end of the world," Phoebe reasoned. She hated to be the girl who was always defending her absentee boyfriend, but she'd been with him long before he was a famous rockstar and understood the stress he was under.

"Judging by how this exhibition has gone, and the beaming faces of the gallery owners, it won't be your last show here," Lena said with a wink.

Even if exhibitions were more stressful than selling prints online, it was great to see the collection appreciated by so many in person.

"He wanted to be here, but he has a show in Munich tomorrow. I couldn't ask him to fly home for my last night. I had no expectations that he'd be here," Phoebe said, organising her remaining prints at the front of the gallery. It was awfully hot despite the late hour, and with the door opening and closing, it was nice to get a breath of fresh air. "The same way he didn't expect me to be at his London show last week because I was getting everything ready for the exhibition." Phoebe tucked a strand of her cropped lilac hair behind her ear as the draught by the door caused some strands to stick to her lip gloss.

"That's different," Lena countered, taking a salmon puff from a passing tray of hors d'oeuvres. "You've gone to countless concerts, and this is your first big exhibition."

Phoebe knew Lena didn't like her fiancé. They'd met briefly before Cillian left for the tour months back, but they hadn't clicked, and his lack of support since hadn't helped.

Not that she needed them to get along. Lena was her agent first and friend second, and she was always professional.

"We're in this fabulous gallery, surrounded by fabulously creative minds, and celebrating my sell-out exhibition. Please just be ridiculously happy for me." Phoebe put out some more cards with her commission details, trying not to let Lena's concerns ruin her buzz. "Tomorrow, when you wake up hungover and I drag you to an early-riser yoga class, you can bitch as much as you want about his failures as a boyfriend."

Fiancé, Phoebe corrected herself. The ring on her finger, an obscenely large diamond that wasn't her style, glared up at her, but his heart was in the right place. They hadn't grown up with much, so he tended to overcompensate. At twenty-six, she hadn't been expecting a proposal. Her art career was taking off, and with Cillian being away for months with his band, Brothers of Anarchy, it felt crazy to think about planning a wedding.

"Fine, I'll stop." Lena gave in. "I'm ridiculously happy for you. With all the money you've made tonight, you'll be able to stop temping."

Lena was the only person Phoebe knew who loved her desk job, though she was rarely at her desk. Public relations meant she spent most of her time wining and dining, attending openings and premieres of the clients she managed.

"You'll be happy to hear I handed in my notice this morning. I'm officially a full-time artist," Phoebe said, still in disbelief. "I didn't have much of a choice, since you've already booked three more exhibitions next year." In the meantime, Phoebe hoped the royalties from this show, commissions and her website sales would keep her comfortable. Once the rent was covered and she could paint all day, she didn't care.

"I'll cheers to that! I'm sure your mum and dad are so proud of you. I didn't see them around?" Lena glanced around the busy studio, alive with small talk. Phoebe illustrated emotions as characters, with scenes to match. She loved listening to what people thought, and seeing if they could figure out what emotion each painting depicted.

"You already missed them. They were some of the first to arrive, but with Dad's bad hip they couldn't stay long," she said.

Just that morning, she'd paid them back for the two years of art school she'd attended. Her professors had called her work childish and doubted she'd ever be a 'real' artist. When she'd decided to drop out after two years, her parents never doubted her decision.

Phoebe had the internet to thank for making her a success. She'd started with small prints, but seeing the large canvases on the walls felt like coming home. For an extra dash of petty, she'd sent some of her professors invites to the opening—which went unanswered.

"I'll have to catch them next time," Lena said. "Getting back to the sunrise yoga, why do we have to get up at the crack of dawn? Why don't we have a late brunch and then go to an afternoon class like regular people?" she suggested, touching up her red lipstick. "I think celebrating should come with a long lie-in."

Lena was blessed with genes that allowed her to remain trim without having to exercise, whereas Phoebe only had to look at a dessert and her body would decide to hold onto it for life. That didn't stop her from loving her sweet treats; she'd learnt to love her curves after years of too much exercise and obsessing over 'good' and 'bad' foods. It did nothing but ruin her mental health, and what's wrong with being pear shaped? Pears are juicy and delicious.

"Because I've a flight to Munich in the afternoon,"

Phoebe admitted, as her phone vibrated in the pocket of her black midi dress. *Is there anything better than a dress with pockets?*

She hoped it was Cillian. Instead, it was her brother, Nick, the guitarist of Brothers of Anarchy or B.O.A for short, telling her he'd left her ticket for their concert at the hotel she'd booked last minute.

"I should've known that he'd make you go to him," Lena said, when Phoebe explained what was going on. "You haven't seen him since he proposed." Lena's moaning was interrupted by a couple asking to buy a print of an illustrated flowerpot with a terrible scowl and flaming petals. Phoebe tried not to laugh as Lena was forced into silence. The customers finished congratulating her before leaving with their purchase. Once they were out the door, Phoebe worried Lena was going to explode as she turned the same shade as her auburn hair.

"He doesn't even know I'm coming—it's a surprise," Phoebe explained. "With the exhibit over, I finally have some time before I have to work on my next collection. I want to spend as much time with him as I can, maybe start planning the wedding. I was thinking Italy, something super small at the villa where he proposed." She was getting carried away, but they had to start planning at some point and her Pinterest board was getting crowded with ideas.

"Italy is a beautiful idea, but there's no rush. You've only been engaged a few months," Lena said, always erring on the side of caution.

"I'm not saying I'm going to fly off tomorrow and elope." Phoebe tried to act as though she hadn't considered it. She'd never been to Vegas, and with their busy schedules, it was an option. If they eloped, they wouldn't have to worry about the press.

She doubted Cillian's fans would be happy with his engagement. It didn't matter that they'd been together since they were fourteen, an engaged rockstar wasn't as sexy as someone attainable. Phoebe did her best to keep her relationship away from her social media; she only posted about her art and the process that went into it. She liked to keep her private life private. But with Cillian and her brother being in one of the world's biggest bands, it was hard to hide in the shadows.

"You'd better not! But if you do, please call me. It'd break my heart not to be there!" Lena gave her a tight squeeze.

"I promise not to get married without you."

As much as she loved the idea of a private ceremony, having Lena by her side felt equally important. She struggled for years to find a trustworthy agent, but she and Lena had been fast friends since they met at an art show last year. Any time she doubted herself, Lena would (metaphorically) slap some sense into her.

"Thank you, and since you promise not to elope, I suppose I can join you at the crack of dawn." Lena released her and put down her glass of champagne.

"I'll bring you a latte with an extra shot," Phoebe promised as they headed over to a group of guests.

The exhibition wouldn't go on much longer now that most of the paintings were sold, but she wanted to do some more mingling to thank everyone for attending.

"Better make it two extra shots!" Lena grabbed another glass of champagne. "Also, I purchased a painting for my parents. They fell in love with the breakfast scene I sent them. It'll go perfectly in their cottage kitchen."

Phoebe stared at her wide-eyed. "You didn't! I would've given it to you. Or made a copy for them!"

"Of course I did." Lena blew her a kiss. "My best

friend and client is a sell-out artist, it's my duty to support you."

Phoebe couldn't argue as they joined the other guests, but she reminded herself to buy Lena a large coffee and her favourite chocolate croissant in the morning.

Morning yoga had been the perfect way to relax after the exhibit. Even Lena enjoyed herself, but that might have been the three shots in her coffee that kept her awake during the asanas. But now, Phoebe's trip was proving to be anything but relaxing. The flight to Munich had been delayed for two hours. The woman sitting beside her stank of old cigarettes, and she desperately wanted to jump in a hot shower and freshen up once they landed. But of course, her suitcase was the last out.

The traffic wasn't too bad, but the hotel had no record of her last-minute booking. By the time she made it to her room, washed off the smell of airplane and changed into a cute outfit, she was out of time.

In the back of the taxi, she tried to focus on her excitement, on how happy Cillian would be to see her, instead of having to wait three weeks until the band travelled back to Dublin. Unfortunately, by the time Phoebe arrived, stadium security had shut the doors. She groaned as she heard the show commencing inside.

Her general admission ticket was useless.

"Sorry, miss, but the concert has already started. Please move along." The security guard dismissed Phoebe in her thick German accent. "You can join the other fans and press gathered at the side entrance hoping to catch the band afterward."

The two hulking security guards gave her a weird look when she didn't move along.

"I'm sorry I'm late, but I'm friends with the band," Phoebe pleaded, rocking on the heels of her favourite silver knee-high boots to keep warm. "I'm sure everyone says that trying to get in, but please call Anita Scott, their manager. She'll let you know who I am," she rambled on, hoping she wouldn't be escorted away like any other deranged fan trying to get in. She didn't want to use the 'my boyfriend is in the band' excuse, but she couldn't wait out here all night. Wearing a short white dress, even with long flowing sleeves, in Munich in February had been a seriously stupid idea. However, she hadn't expected to stand outside the venue very long, or for the temperature to drop even further. With all her bad luck, Phoebe wondered if she should have stayed at home.

"Do you have a backstage or visitor's pass?" the security guard asked, barely looking at her.

"No, I wanted to surprise the band." Damn it—why hadn't she called Anita ahead of time? The whole plan had been stupid. She'd planned on texting Nick to sneak her in so Cillian wouldn't find out, but he was already on stage.

"Who are you exactly? Do you have some ID?"

"Cillian Hunt's girlfriend, and Nick Fletcher's sister?" she informed them quietly. Judging from their bemused faces, they didn't believe her.

The security guard rolled her eyes. "I'm sure you *think* you are. However, all friends and family are required to have a security pass. We need to keep your *boyfriend* safe."

"I wanted to surprise them. I didn't plan on getting here so late. Hold on, I have my ID." Phoebe reached into her tote bag for her purse, but winced when she realised she'd left it in the hotel.

"I forgot my ID, but I can still prove who I am." She scrolled through her Artgram profile and held up her phone to show the guards multiple pictures of her with her brother and Cillian.

"Anyone can doctor some photos. You can leave the premises, or you can go round to where the other 'girl-friends' are waiting to catch a glimpse." The other guard, a bald giant, shook his head. She wanted to smack his condescending face, but her phone ringing startled her. Phoebe frowned, wondering why Anita was calling her.

"Phoebe? What are you doing arguing with security?" The echo of the concert came through the phone.

Phoebe glanced around at the fans gathered outside, but there was no sign of Anita. How did she know she was here?

"Can you help me? Security won't let me in without a pass," Phoebe pleaded quietly, as Security glared at her.

"I'll see what I can do," Anita said, and hung up. She wasn't the type for small talk.

Minutes later, the staff door by the entrance swung open.

"What the hell are you doing out here?" Anita panted, clearly having rushed out. "Why didn't you tell anyone you were coming?

"Told you so." Phoebe winked at the stunned security guards. Though she felt bad for causing trouble.

"She doesn't have an access pass," the female guard informed Anita flatly.

"She's family. She doesn't need a pass." Anita ushered her through the performers' entrance without a second look at the guards.

"Hurry up! I haven't got all night." Anita marched

ahead of her through the concrete maze beneath the stadium. The sound of the band was muffled by the thick concrete walls and long, echoing hallways.

"How'd you know I was here?" Phoebe asked, weaving her way past the staff.

"It's my job to know," Anita said, focusing on the next urgent matter on her phone.

Phoebe didn't know how Anita could walk so fast in her towering heels. There was about ten years between them, and Phoebe often felt intimidated by B.O.A.'s manager's presence. One wrong look from Anita's dark eyes might turn anyone to stone. Then again, she had no choice but to be ruthless in the music industry.

"Some fans outside were live streaming your interaction with security on a fansite," Anita eventually explained. "'*Cillian Hunt's girlfriend banned from concert*' came up on my keyword alerts."

The band saying their goodbyes came through the speakers, and the crowds' cheering followed.

"I didn't think anyone would notice me. Sorry for adding to the rumour mill." Phoebe smiled in disbelief at the band's success. She remembered when they used to perform at their school's cringey talent shows; now they had millions of fans across the world.

Anita glanced at her over her shoulder. "How many women with short lilac hair and a nose piercing do you think are dating the lead singer?"

Phoebe imagined tomorrow's headlines about their alleged breakup, and her trying desperately to get into the concert.

"Sorry," was the only thing to say.

"Life would be dull without a fire or two to put out," Anita quipped as she smoothed a hand over her slicked-back ponytail.

"So much for my surprise trip, the world already knows before Cillian," Phoebe said. "Next time I'll call ahead and spare everyone some trouble."

"I'd appreciate it." Anita's pace didn't ease up. "Between interviews and signings, I don't have a minute to play 'hunt down Phoebe'."

She stopped as they reached a fork in the corridor; one way went on to the stadium stage, the other to the dressing rooms. Phoebe nearly crashed into her back; she wasn't as graceful as Anita.

"Can you find your way to the guys? They should be off stage by now—and please remind them to be in the press room in thirty minutes. I've got to make a few calls to make sure the headlines aren't about you and security outside instead of tonight's concert." Anita didn't look up from her phone or wait for a response before she walked off towards a group of people waiting for her.

Passing doors marked 'Maintenance', 'Security' and 'Equipment', Phoebe dodged out of the way of a cardboard cut-out of August, the band's bassist. She reached the dressing room doors with their taped-on signs showing the band members' names: Cillian, Nick, August and Axel, the drummer, a late addition to the band after the original drummer had decided fame wasn't for him.

She heard Nick's laughter, the same as their dad's, echoing down the hall. She thought about going to say hi, but stopped short at Cillian's door. His post-show routine dictated that he went to his dressing room to decompress before heading to meet the press or fans, so she knew he'd be inside. Checking her lipstick in her phone camera, she tried to conceal her excitement. She took a deep breath, placed her hand on the doorknob and twisted.

"SURPRISE!"

Time stood still, and ice coursed through her veins.

Her smiled disappeared as she tried to process what she was seeing. *Scream, cry or throw up?* Her body couldn't quite make up its mind.

The smell of cigarettes and other smokable substances didn't help settle her rolling stomach. *How out of their minds are they that they didn't even notice me entering the room?* Judging from the half empty bottles of whiskey and champagne: very.

Without thinking, Phoebe stepped into the room, grabbed a vase of sunflowers by the door and threw them at the dresser beside the half-naked pair fucking on the couch, still completely unaware of her presence. The smash of the mirror and the shattering of the vase seemed to do the trick.

"Who the fuck are you?" Cillian snapped, his voice hoarse after hours of singing. It was the venom in his tone, though, that made him sound completely unrecognisable.

Phoebe had never seen such anger in his eyes as when they met hers. Everything moved in slow motion. His bleached hair was plastered to his forehead with sweat, the smile she'd loved so much punctured by two new lip piercings. He didn't even look like the man she'd agreed to marry only a month ago.

"Fuck! Phoebe? What the fuck are you doing here?" Cillian quickly straightened up and zipped his jeans as though he hadn't been caught in the act. An image she wouldn't be able to scrub from her mind.

She wanted to laugh—he made it sound like she was intruding.

The woman didn't show any remorse, glaring at her unashamedly and accusingly. Phoebe recognised her pitch-black hair and smoky eyes: the band's make-up artist, Helen. They'd met half a dozen times; she'd always been so friendly. Maybe her cheery mood had been because she was getting laid—her lack of reaction led Phoebe to believe this wasn't the first time they'd been walked in on.

The desire to throw up returned as she listened to the blood pumping in her ears. If she stayed a moment longer, she wasn't sure who she'd strangle first. Cillian called her name, but it sounded like he was underwater.

She forced herself through the fluorescent corridors, back the way she'd come. None of the staff paid her any mind. They couldn't see that she'd been stabbed in the heart.

Reaching the staff entrance, she heard a rush of footsteps behind her. Someone's rough hand grabbed her elbow and pulled her away from the exit. Rage surged through her.

"Cillian, let go of me!" She didn't care who heard. Hell, she hoped they did. She hoped they knew what a disgusting, pathetic cheat he was. Then it hit her: did everyone know? They'd worked with the same make-up artist for the whole tour. Months!

Her thoughts were silenced when she realised it wasn't Cillian who had a hold of her. Axel's startled eyes searched hers; he stood so close she was forced to stare up at him. It was hard to mistake the two, Axel was taller than Cillian, and older. His breath was heavy—he'd run after her. Was he here to be the voice of reason, to defend his friend?

Axel's shaved hair and constant 'don't fuck with me' expression had a way of making everyone shrink around him. She wasn't in the mood to shrink; she wanted to destroy this whole place like Godzilla on a rampage. Stomp everyone into the ground and roar until her throat bled.

"Phoebe, you can't go out there." It sounded like a command more than a request. His refusal to remove his hand from her arm only fuelled her desire to scream. Why he cared, she didn't know; they'd never been friends. He clearly knew what Cillian had done, and suddenly she felt an overwhelming humiliation that forced her to look away from Axel's searching eyes.

Cillian hadn't locked the door. Did he even care about getting caught? About hurting me? The wave of emotions strangled her.

"Are you alright? I didn't know Phoebe was coming tonight."

Axel had gritted his teeth as he overheard Cillian's consoling words. He watched Phoebe storm down the corridor; she didn't even notice him standing by the door. Glass crunched under his boots as he entered Cillian's dressing room. *So that's what the crash was,* he thought, looking at the broken mirror. Phoebe must have discovered the truth, to leave this much destruction behind her. Axel took a deep breath, furious. She shouldn't have had to find out about Cillian's cheating this way.

"We never should have listened to your promises to end it," he said, staring at the haphazardly dressed pair. "You were never going to confess everything to Phoebe, were you?"

"Now isn't the best time for a lecture," Cillian snapped, picking up a bottle of vodka from the table. Helen didn't look up at him; she just focused on her hands on her thighs.

They'd all hoped Cillian's recent destructive behaviour was due to the pressure they were under, but it was becoming a habit. Nobody in the band had wanted to be the one to tell Phoebe. Nick, being her elder brother, didn't want to get involved in her relationship. August, who thought of Phoebe like a sister, didn't want to pick sides. That only left Axel, and he wasn't the right person to tell her.

"I have no interest in lecturing you, but the least you can do is go after Phoebe instead of standing here drinking like a coward!" Axel grabbed him by his fashionably torn T-shirt with their band's snake logo and shoved him towards the doors.

"Why should I?" Cillian sneered. Axel smelt the alcohol on his breath. He would've knocked Cillian on his ass, but he didn't want to ruin his hands. They were already sore from drumming all night.

"She threw a vase at us! Could've sliced us both up. I'll talk to her when she calms down," Cillian argued, and from the size of his pupils he wasn't thinking clearly.

"You didn't bother to go to her exhibition, and she still turned up to surprise you, only to find you balls deep in another woman, and you're pissed about some broken glass?" Axel was doing his best not to throttle him. When Cillian sobered up, he'd hate himself. A cycle that had repeated after every show this tour. It was getting old fast.

"Don't talk about me like I'm not here. I'm not some other woman!" Helen barked, getting between them.

Axel ignored her attempt to play the victim. "I'm sorry, but has he been dating you for over a decade? Have you got a ring on your finger?"

He didn't blame Helen for falling for Cillian; his charm won everyone over. Cillian was the one who'd broken his commitment to Phoebe.

"Don't speak to her like that!" Cillian got in his face.

Axel shoved him back, before he did something he'd regret. Helen left in a huff without another word; she was used to Cillian's drunken tantrums.

"Where was this protective instinct when it comes to the woman you're meant to love, to marry?" Axel snapped.

Cillian's nostrils flared, but before he could charge at him, Nick appeared in the doorway.

"I thought Phoebe would be with you guys. Anita told me she arrived." The room went silent as he surveyed the damage. "What's going on?" Nick scratched the side of his neck, which was stained red from his last dye job. Like his sister, he preferred coloured hair, and they had the same light blue eyes and high cheekbones.

Cillian dipped his head, staring at the carpet, forcing Axel to explain to Nick.

"Phoebe caught him with Helen. She should be halfway gone by now. Congratulations on ruining your life," Axel said, turning back to Cillian. "How she could even agree to marry such a piece of shit is a mystery I'll never understand."

"Don't play Prince fucking Charming. I've seen the way you look at my girl, you're just pissed that you can't have her."

Cillian swung for him, but Nick caught his fist. Axel rolled his eyes at the accusation—who wouldn't want to be with Phoebe? Talented, smart, beautiful, completely off-limits and wasted on a man like Cillian.

"I thought you broke it off?" Nick asked as Cillian gave up the fight.

"I couldn't," Cillian admitted, pacing by the dresser.

"No one taught him he can't have his cake and eat it too."

"Shut up! Both of you. You want the whole stadium to hear about this?" Nick, always the leader, got between them.

Axel zipped his lips.

"You need to sober up." Nick glared at Cillian.

"Tomorrow, you can talk with Phoebe. Tonight, you need to stay in this room and sleep it off. Alone. There's no point in talking about this when you're drunk."

Axel wasn't surprised by Nick's leniency. He and Cillian had known each other the longest, whereas Axel had only joined the band five years ago. At first, he'd found it hard to bond with people who'd known each other their whole lives, but now he considered them family, and he hated seeing his friend blow up his life.

"Axel, go after Phoebe," Nick ordered. "Take her to your tour bus. We can't let her leave like this, and she shouldn't be wandering around a foreign country alone and upset."

Axel didn't need to be told twice.

"Why should he go to her? She's my girlfriend!" Cillian argued.

"Now you give a shit?" Axel said. The caring boyfriend act had only appeared because Nick was here.

Nick pushed Cillian back, and he retreated, slumping on the couch like some petulant child. Clearly whatever he'd snorted or drunk was draining the fight out of him.

"Go, Axel, I'm trusting you to look after my sister. She won't want me getting involved." Nick and Phoebe had a simple rule when it came to each other's dating lives: stay out of it.

"How can you let him off so easily?" Axel asked. If someone treated his sisters the same way Cillian had, there would be a grave dug and ready.

"Because he isn't in his right mind. Hasn't been for the last few months and we need to support him."

"But she's your sister, and you're defending him."

"And he's like my brother. Do I want to beat him bloody for treating my sister like this? Yes, but this isn't him and this isn't the time to be talking about this. Go."

Axel did as instructed, unable to look at Cillian a moment longer.

Thankfully, Phoebe was in heels, and he was able to catch up to her rather quickly. He hadn't meant to grab Phoebe, but she was about to go out the press exit.

"Cillian, let go of me!" Phoebe growled.

Axel stilled, struggling to find his words as her teary blue eyes stared up at him in surprise. He didn't know how to make this situation better, but he could try not to make it worse.

"Phoebe, you can't go out there."

"Are you here to defend him? Because I don't want to hear it." Phoebe pulled against his hold.

He heard the shouts of the press through the door, waiting for their pound of flesh, and he couldn't let them have her.

"I'm not here to defend Cillian. Nick sent me to make sure you're okay while he deals with him," he reasoned, wondering how she could look so fierce and stunning in the same moment.

"Trust my brother to pick his friend over me," Phoebe muttered, looking at him with eyes brimming with tears. He loosened his grip, not wanting to hurt her.

Cillian was right to accuse him of being attracted to her. How could anyone be around her and not want to be hers? He had kept his distance, for his own sanity and out of respect for her relationship with Cillian, but not anymore.

"Don't be like that. Would you rather your brother be here?" Axel asked. "Besides, Cillian's not in his right mind. I wasn't going to be left alone with him."

Phoebe's small frown made him wish he hadn't added the last part.

"Thought you weren't here to defend him," she said,

and he saw the rage behind her eyes—and that she was a hair's breadth from tears.

"I'm not. Your brother is worried about you, so he sent me to make sure you didn't do anything you'll regret. Don't go out there in this state. You were already seen outside with security earlier, which only drew more press. If you leave like this, they won't leave you alone."

"Good, I'm glad they're out there. I can tell them all about their beloved cheating prick that's disguised as a charming rockstar. He's really living up to the stereotype. I can tell the world that Cillian Hunt is officially single, and they'll be delighted that the wedding is off." Her voice got louder with each word until some people in the corridor stared at them. A glare from Axel moved them on.

"What about August and Nick's reputation? Smear Cillian across the tabloids and you'll take them down with him. Don't let him ruin all they've worked for."

Axel hated using her good nature against her, but he was protecting her from herself as much as he was protecting them. The press would tear her apart and the fans would gnaw at the bones.

Her eyes narrowed with resentment. "Are you sure you aren't worried about your brand?" she snapped, folding her arms. "Surely this would only help the band's image. Bad boys sell rather well."

Axel shook his head. "Couldn't care less about our brand. It's not safe to go out there right now. Come with me to my tour bus and take a moment to breathe. Once the press leave, then I'll bring you back to your hotel myself." He was practically begging—and he never begged. "You don't want to hurt them because that idiot who doesn't appreciate or deserve you fucked up. If you still want to rip him apart in the press tomorrow, feel free, I'll even help you, but give yourself some time."

Phoebe's expression softened, and she rubbed her arms. She must have been cold in that dress.

"I've got plenty of jumpers to warm you up," Axel threw out in desperation, which earned a small hint of a smile.

She quickly concealed it. "Fine, but only until the press are gone. Then I'm getting the first flight out of here."

He led her down another corridor, away from the press and to the private parking lot where all the tour buses and equipment trucks were parked. Axel kept glancing over his shoulder to make sure she didn't disappear. He wasn't the best at comforting, and he was too angry at Cillian to think of nice things to say. He wished his sisters, or his cousin Autumn, were here. They'd know exactly what to do.

Outside, the tour buses were painted with the band's logo: a snake wrapped around a guitar. Axel's was parked at the end of the row beside Nick's, so Phoebe wouldn't have to see Cillian—if he even made it to his bus. Nick would probably lock him in his dressing room to keep them apart.

Axel took his key from his pocket and opened the door.

"Luckily, I cleaned up a little this morning." His attempt at conversation was off to a great start.

He turned on the lights. The only mess was some dishes from his pre-show snack in the small sink and an empty bottle of beer. Phoebe hesitated at the bottom of the steps.

"You don't have to see anyone you don't want to," he reassured her and offered his hand to coax her up the steps. He tried to hide his surprise when she took it without argument.

"Make yourself at home." Axel removed the guitar from the table in the main sitting area. He was trying to learn in his spare time; he got a little stir-crazy when they were driving around Europe.

"Just until the press conference is over," she said, looking awkward in his space. She eyed the multiple packs of hot Doritos in a bowl in the kitchen.

"Do you want some?"

He hated how awkward he was. His sisters loved treats when they were going through a breakup, but maybe this was too soon. She shook her head, putting him out of his misery.

He had to do something, so he gave her a glass of water. She didn't drink it, merely studied it. He'd have given anything to know what she was thinking. He'd never had to deal with real heartbreak—he usually ended things before they ever got too serious—but her watery eyes were breaking his heart.

"You can wait in my room if you want some privacy. There are some hoodies in the drawers under the bed if you're still cold," he said, and she walked through the tiny passage past the bathroom to his unmade bed and sat down. He pulled at the back of his neck, knowing he had to get to the press conference before Anita hunted him down.

"Don't tell anyone I'm here." Phoebe sounded utterly defeated and not her usual chirpy self.

"You got it," he agreed, though Nick already knew. "I've got to go, but we can get you back to the hotel when I'm done."

"Sounds good." Phoebe nodded and closed the dividing partition.

Axel let out a sigh of relief; at least she was safe from the hungry press. He waited there a moment, to make sure she was okay, only to hear her muffled sobs on the other side of the partition. His desire to strangle Cillian returned.

Anita blew up his phone. He didn't want to leave Phoebe, but he doubted Cillian would be attending the conference in his current state. If one band member was missing there would be questions, but if two didn't attend then there would be rumours of B.O.A. breaking up before the sun rose.

THE PRESS CONFERENCE went by quickly, and Axel sat in awe of Nick's professionalism. His secret talents included smiling through trouble. August, at the end of the table, was unaware of the chaos because he'd been at a meet-and-greet for fans with disabilities. Axel envied his blissful ignorance, but he was sure Nick would fill him in soon.

After signing some albums, and offering a quick thank you to fans, Axel returned to the bus. To his relief, he heard no sobs, but the bus was too quiet and the glass of water still sat empty on the table. He exhaled, hoping she hadn't left before he made sure she got back to her hotel safely.

He opened the partition, expecting to find his bed empty, but found Phoebe curled up in his hoodie with his pillow cradled against her body. Her boots were still on, and a box of tissues sat beside her. Axel sighed; her tears must have knocked her out. Carefully, he slipped off her heeled boots, put her tote bag on the floor and slowly covered her with his duvet. Better she was here, and close to those who loved her, than alone in a hotel.

If someone had told him this morning Phoebe Fletcher would be asleep on his bed, with her mascara-stained eyes and purple hair fanned over her face, he'd have called them crazy. However, it was a sight he could get used to.

Shaking away the thought, he closed the divider and got to work transforming the breakfast area into his bed for the night.

The following morning, water dripped down Phoebe's face as she washed away the mascara stains with Axel's array of skincare products. *His shaved head probably gives him a bigger budget for skincare*, she thought, drying her face. At least she no longer resembled a swollen panda.

Closing the sliding bathroom door behind her, she rolled down the sleeves of Axel's hoodie, then found a pair of his grey sweats and pulled them on over her dress. *I hope he doesn't mind*, she thought. *I wouldn't take them if I wasn't so freaking cold!* She'd wash and return them when she could.

He'd probably stayed with the others last night, She hadn't meant to take over his bed, but she couldn't even remember falling asleep.

Axel being a foot taller than her meant the sweats bunched at her ankles, but the oversized set made her feel safe and she enjoyed the spicy tang of his cologne. She had never noticed how good he'd smelt; then again, Axel never got close enough for her to find out. She ran her hands through her hair, unable to believe where she was and how she'd got here. Flashbacks of Cillian's dressing room tormented her and she rubbed her eyes, wishing them away.

After crying herself to dehydration last night, her

thirst drove her to the kitchen. Phoebe opened the divider and stumbled over her bag with a loud curse. She winced as a low groan told her she wasn't alone. Axel sat up in a makeshift bed in the middle of the breakfast area.

"Sorry, I didn't mean to wake you," Phoebe said. As if she wasn't feeling enough already, her brain added embarrassment and anxiety to the mix.

"Too late to be sorry. I'm up now." Axel stretched his tattooed arms above his head.

Confirmed. Axel Adler is NOT a morning person.

Despite having been around each other for the last five years, she knew very little about him.

Phoebe averted her eyes from his bare, muscular chest. *Drumming is certainly a good workout.* Sometimes he'd perform shirtless, so she shouldn't have felt bashful, but she'd never been alone with a half-naked man other than Cillian before.

"I didn't mean to fall asleep here. I only closed my eyes for a second," she said, hoping he wasn't put out about having to sleep on the breakfast table. "Also, I borrowed some sweats, I didn't want to stay in my dress and it's cold." She stumbled over her words, and her brain told her to shut it.

"They look good on you." Axel's yawned words were barely audible as he got up.

She didn't know what to say, and thankfully he filled the silence.

"You fell asleep last night without eating." Axel grabbed the blanket from the pull-out and tossed it onto the cushioned bench beside her. Her stomach groaned on cue.

"Just give me a second to put the table back together, and I'll order us some breakfast," he said gruffly, and when he turned around, she tried not to stare at his broad shoulders.

She didn't have the energy to argue. To give him some privacy, she went back to the bedroom with the navy blanket. To her relief, she heard him turn the heating on. What she didn't expect was for him to appear in the doorway and offer her a cup of tea.

"Thank you." Phoebe smiled softly and took the mug eagerly.

"You said you were cold," he said, placing a handful of sugar sachets in her hand before she had a chance to ask.

"I don't think I need that many." She blushed, nervous about how to be around him. He seemed just as uncertain as he kept his distance, lingering in the doorway with his hands in his pockets.

"The sugar is good for the shock. My mum used to make sweet tea after a bad day."

The detail was far more intimate than she was used to getting from him. She put the sachets she didn't need down beside her and sipped her tea. She felt him watching her like she was going to burst into tears at any minute.

"I should go," Phoebe said, not wanting to overstay her welcome.

Axel scrubbed his hand over his shaved head and glanced over his shoulder to the door as though waiting for something. She hoped he hadn't called the others. She couldn't handle seeing them, certainly not Cillian.

"You should finish your tea first, and one of the security guys has gone to get us breakfast. I didn't think you'd want to eat with the others."

His kindness nearly got her tears going again.

"Can I ask you a question?" she said.

"That's a question."

His black sweatpants hung low on his hips, and she

could make out the tattoo of an angel with a sword on his hip. *Stop staring,* she scolded herself, focusing on her tea. He followed her gaze to his hip and walked towards her. She backed up a little on the bed, unsure of what he was about to do.

"You had a question?" he asked, reaching up over her head to a cabinet. He pulled out a worn-out band T-shirt.

"Have you seen *The Devil Wears Prada*?" she asked, while he shrugged on the T-shirt.

"Yes," he admitted, sipping on his black coffee. The smell was tempting, but she didn't think caffeine would do her any good right now. "I've got sisters. I couldn't avoid rom-coms."

"You know that scene where Stanley Tucci talks about how your personal life going up in flames means it's time for a promotion?" Phoebe hugged the warm mug to her chest as she gathered the courage to express her feelings. She wasn't as close to Axel as she was to her brother or August, so he was the only one she could ask. "Is this the price of my art career taking off? I lose him. I know it sounds ridiculous, but it's like the more successful we each became, the further we drifted apart."

"Don't ever think your success played any part in his actions. You didn't lose him because of your art. Cillian lost you because he's a cheating arsehole who didn't appreciate what he had," Axel said, angry enough for both of them.

Too tired to be angry or sad, a numbness settled over Phoebe. "I think that's the nicest thing you've ever said to me," she said.

"Don't get used to it," he said teasingly. "I just don't want you to ruin any more of my clothing with your tears."

Phoebe rolled her eyes.

"I can drive you back to your hotel once the food arrives. I wasn't sure if you'd want to talk to Cillian first before heading back to your hotel?" he asked, putting his mug in the sink, not meeting her gaze.

He probably feels uncomfortable caught in the middle, she realised.

"I don't want to speak to him or anyone," she sighed, and Axel shifted uncomfortably. "I mean, I'm here, so I'll talk to you," she clarified.

"How considerate of you," he said with a smirk. His strong jaw flexed, and with his shaved head, tattoos and sullen expression, he looked a little frightening. Maybe he liked people to think he was scary so they'd leave him alone, but given he'd saved her from the press last night, let her stay in his bed and borrow his clothes, she knew he had a good heart beneath his hard shell.

"Thank you for talking me out of confronting the press last night. I doubt I would've given them a single coherent quote, and they'd probably have reported that I was hysterical or intoxicated."

Making a scene at a concert only twenty-four hours after her exhibition closed wouldn't have done her any favours, and she wasn't going to let Cillian taint her success.

Axel opened his mouth to speak, but then the bus door opened and she remembered the breakfast he'd ordered. The thought of food brought her some joy. However, the sudden sight of Cillian's beetroot face made her want to jump out one of the tinted windows. Coming face to face with the man she loved so much broke her heart all over again.

"It's been less than twelve hours, and you have my fiancée in your bed?"

Both were startled by Cillian's accusation as he charged

towards them. He was wearing the same clothes as last night and his hair was greasy—he hadn't even washed since he was with *her*.

"First of all, fuck you," she snapped. "Second, even if we slept together, it would be none of your business. We broke up the second I saw you with another woman. You didn't even lock the door."

When Axel stepped between them; she wasn't sure which of them he was protecting. The one person she'd never thought she'd need protection from was Cillian. The thought made her ill—how could this be the man she'd agreed to marry?

Enraged, Cillian grabbed Axel's T-shirt, causing him to drop his mug. Phoebe gasped, but Axel didn't even flinch as the hot coffee pooled around his bare feet.

Yesterday's rage flooded back into her.

"Get off him!" Phoebe barked, shoving Cillian back.

Cillian stumbled back wide-eyed. He didn't say a word as she turned to Axel.

"Thank you for the safe space and the tea, but I'm leaving," she said, refusing to glance in Cillian's direction.

She put on her heels, but she kept on Axel's clothes. Going out in her dress felt too revealing, and she didn't want Cillian to see even an inch of her skin.

"You aren't going anywhere until we've talked." Cillian looked past her, sneering at Axel as though this was all his fault.

They both ignored him.

"Let me call you a taxi," Axel offered, but Phoebe didn't want to stay a moment longer in Cillian's company.

"She's my girlfriend, stop with the Prince Charming act," Cillian barked.

Axel chuckled, not helping the situation. Phoebe stared at them, feeling like she'd missed the joke.

"I'm not your girlfriend, and stop acting like this is his fault." She grabbed her bag, sick of his temper tantrum. "Axel helped me while you were sobering up with your other girlfriend."

She was out the tour bus before either of them could stop her. She heard raised voices behind her, but didn't dare look back.

Walking through the empty parking lot, she wished she'd never come to Munich. *Twenty-four hours ago,* she thought, *I had a sell-out exhibition, I quit my day job and was engaged to the love of my life. Now, I'm trying to escape my cheating ex with a lump in my throat the size of Ireland and I wish I hadn't worn these damn heels.*

Her sadness was replaced with irritation when she reached the booth by the security gate, and the guard looked her over like she was a groupie doing the walk of shame.

"Can you open the gate? I want to leave," Phoebe asked politely.

"Just need you to sign out beside where you signed in." He pushed a clipboard with a list of names through the gap in the protective window.

"I didn't sign in," she said. She could sign out beside someone else's name, but if he checked her ID it'd look suspicious.

The guard's eyes narrowed, and he took back the clipboard. "How did you get into the venue?"

A gargled voice came through the radio on his shoulder. She waited impatiently as he finished replying in German.

"My brother is in the band," she said, "but I didn't come in with them. Does it really matter? Please let me out."

She immediately regretted her tone when he radioed in

German so she couldn't understand. Last night she couldn't get in, and now they didn't want to let her out.

Can I please get back to my hotel without another argument?

A car horn made her jump.

"Get in the car!" Cillian called out through the car window.

Phoebe ignored him and waited for the guard to open the gate. Instead, he sealed the window to his booth, leaving them to it.

"They aren't going to let you out without my permission," Cillian said.

So that's what the urgent radio message was, she realised, turning to face him. *A black Porsche? That's new.*

"I don't want to be in the same country as you, let alone the same car." She crossed her arms over her chest, trying to compose herself.

"Get in the car, you'll be mobbed by fans out there."

Where had this sudden concern come from? He'd just been on a rampage about her sleeping with one of his best friends. The dark circles under his bloodshot eyes confessed how hungover he was, so it made sense he wasn't thinking rationally.

"Why do you care what your fans do to me? You've hurt me far more than they ever could. Holding me here against my will isn't going to make me forgive you. Why don't you go have breakfast with that woman—her name's Helen, right? Show her the sights, and I'm sure soon you'll forget we ever existed. In fact, why don't you give her this?" Phoebe threw her engagement ring through the window, hoping the diamond would do some damage to his smug face.

The booth window reopened. "Is this woman a threat to you?" the guard asked sternly.

"No. My fiancée has a stubborn streak." Cillian's smug smile made her want to scream.

If looks could kill, Cillian would have disintegrated.

"I'm not your fiancée, or your girlfriend. I don't even know you." She turned to the security guard. "This man is bothering me, please open the gate."

"There is quite the crowd out there, sir." The guard ignored her and addressed Cillian. "Are you sure you don't want to call your personal security to escort you?"

"He isn't escorting me anywhere. Open the gate."

"Just get in the car!" Cillian banged on the car door, startling her. "Stop making this man's job harder. If something happens to you then he could lose his job, and Nick wouldn't want you leaving on your own."

"Then why didn't he come?" Phoebe asked. She considered calling her brother, but they'd agreed long ago that they wouldn't get involved in each other's relationships.

"Who do you think sent me to fix this? Please let me explain, and if you still hate me by the time I'm done, you'll be back at your hotel, and you can slam the door in my face."

As much as she hated him, she was tired of his pleading and the security guard's judgemental stares. A twenty-minute drive of his excuses, and then she could pack her bags and leave. Without a word, Phoebe walked to the passenger door, and pulled it open.

"Thank you," Cillian said, motioning to the security guard.

"Don't thank him for forcing me to get into the car with you," she grumbled, placing her bag on her lap.

Despite the early hour, the gate opened to dozens of screaming fans. Phoebe dipped her head to conceal her face, not wanting to be photographed as they drove away from the stadium. Yesterday, she would've been proud to sit by Cillian's side. Now, tears burnt her tired eyes, and she refused to let him or the fans see her cry.

"Are you ever going to look at me?" Cillian asked, shifting gears.

"Why would I want to look at you? It would only remind me of what I saw last night. Of what you did to me, to us!" Phoebe choked back her emotions and focused on the streets outside.

"I'm sorry you had to see that," he said. "I was on a high from the show, and in other ways. We were celebrating, and she was there. It happened so fast, and then you were standing there, and I panicked. There's been so much going on and I feel like I'm disappointing everyone. I messed up, but please don't let this be how we end." His excuses sounded rehearsed.

Though her heart wanted to believe him, remembering how Helen had reacted, like Phoebe was the one in the wrong, made her believe this was more than one mistake. Had he been cheating every time he was stressed or away from home?

"Don't put this on me. You ended us the moment you slept with her. I apologised for you when people asked why you weren't at my exhibit, when you missed my birthday or forgot to call on Valentine's Day. I made every excuse for you, and you couldn't even respect me enough to break up with me before screwing your make-up artist."

"I should've known you secretly resented me," he huffed. "I can't believe you're bringing all this up now. I thought you understood my responsibilities and that I can't always be there."

"This isn't about resentment but respect. I've been there for you every step of the way since we were fourteen. I believed in you when you wanted to give up. I cheered when no one else did—but what I didn't know was that you were too busy partying and cheating to be there for me. You didn't even call me yesterday." She tried not to let her voice crack. "You didn't even lock the fucking door."

"Why are you so obsessed with the door?" he snapped.

"Because you didn't care who walked in! You didn't care who found out. You didn't care that I'd be humiliated, the clueless idiot always talking about how lucky I am to have you and how we were so lucky to find each other. Does everyone know about the two of you?"

"It was only one time—"

"Don't you dare lie, or I swear I will jump out of this moving car."

"It's complicated. You haven't been around, and I didn't have anyone to talk to."

"So it's my fault?" she gasped.

"No, I made the mistake and I've apologised. Why are you making this so hard? I'm trying my best to keep us together." He banged his palm against the steering wheel, and the car shook. She froze in her seat, terrified he'd lose control of the car.

"Keep us all together?" She wanted to laugh, but feared his reaction. "If you love me so much, why didn't you come after me last night? You stayed with her," she said. "Axel had been the one to chase me down when it should've been you, the person I promised to spend the rest of my life with."

"Nick locked me in my dressing room to sober up. I was out of my mind, then I passed out. I didn't know you were with Axel, and he had no business getting involved. I only found out where you were this morning when I met the others for breakfast."

He swerved to avoid a cyclist, and she gripped the side

of the door. With the way he was driving she needed him to focus more on the road and less on her.

"You've no right to be angry at Axel, he has nothing to do with this. If anything, you should be thanking him for stopping me from leaving," Phoebe said as he turned down a narrow street.

"Oh, I'm sure he was happy to keep you company. You're so naive," he scoffed.

She hated his insinuation. "Naive enough to believe you wouldn't cheat on me."

She focused on the sunrise; it shouldn't be long before they were at the hotel.

He took a deep breath. "I'm sorry, I shouldn't have accused you both, but seeing you on his bed in his clothes… I lost my mind, and I don't want to lose you."

His gaze fixed on her, waiting for her to respond.

"Eyes on the road," she snapped.

"I'll spend the rest of my life making it up to you. I wouldn't be me without you. You're my muse." His eyes were on the road again, but he didn't slow down.

"If we were meant to be together, then you wouldn't have needed to find comfort in someone else. Some time away from each other might be what's best for us. You'll have to find another muse."

She tried to keep her calm as he ran a red light.

His nostrils flared. "What about the songs we made together? Without your lyrics, we would be nothing. You can't just give up on us."

Phoebe couldn't believe what she was hearing.

"Is it me you don't want to lose or the songs? I never considered you were keeping me around as a song factory. Is that why you proposed, to make sure you didn't lose your writing partner? It'd make it much harder for me to break up with you if we were married."

"Don't be ridiculous, I love you! We've written together since forever. It has nothing to do with our engagement. I just want you to know how much I love you, how much I need you."

Need me? She had never asked for song credit or payment, and even agreed to keep her involvement from the other members of the band because she didn't want her brother knowing she helped write their songs. But now, it just made their relationship feel like a business arrangement.

"Do you love her?" she asked, not letting memories of the past sway her. "Since Helen looked at me like I was the other woman, she has feelings for you."

"Does it matter?" Cillian rolled his neck like her words irritated him. "You're going to throw away over a decade together because of how she looked at you?" The anger she'd witnessed in the tour bus crept into his words. "You don't know the whole story!" Cillian banged the steering wheel again and again, and she flinched away. She'd never seen him act this way.

"Does it matter? Clearly not, since you threw away a decade together for something you can't even explain. I'll explain for you then: you were drunk, high, missed me, lonely, got caught up, and my personal favourite, she threw herself at you and you couldn't resist?" She was losing her patience. "At least tell me how long you've been cheating. Since we've been engaged or before?" She didn't want the details, but she wanted him to face what he'd done.

"You're putting words in my mouth. Why can't you understand the pressure I'm—"

"Just save your breath. I'm glad she was around to give you the release you needed."

Phoebe's cheap shot earned her the silent treatment. Cillian sped up, and she realised they'd been driving far longer than necessary. There was little to no traffic on the roads this early, and the speed he was doing had her heart hammering.

"What are you doing? You said you'd take me to my hotel," she asked, whipping her head around to watch the hotel disappear behind them. "Please slow down, you're going to kill us!"

He took a sharp turn and clipped a bollard. The car shuddered on impact, but luckily they didn't spin out. She let out a sigh of relief, but it was short-lived.

"Not until you tell me that you can forgive me. I can't lose you," he said, and sped down a narrow lane.

Phoebe screamed as they clipped the curb on the next turn. Blaring horns echoed behind them, and she prayed police would pull them over soon.

"Please pull over, and we can talk. I promise I'll listen if you just pull over."

He ignored her and ran a red light, cutting across traffic at a busy intersection.

"We've never been apart; I can't do any of this without you. I haven't come up with anything for the next album. Writing with you ruined me. Loving you has ruined me. You can't give up on us." Every word was frantic, but she wasn't even sure if he was talking to her.

The tires screeched, and they swerved violently. Phoebe's scream cut out as her head knocked against the window. Disorientated by the blow, she begged him to stop. Cillian locked eyes with her. His lips were moving, but she couldn't hear him. Glass shattered, and she raised her hands to protect her face. The air was knocked from her lungs as she was flung forward, and the seatbelt cut into her. The cry of grinding metal replaced the sound of morning traffic, and then everything went still.

After watching Cillian run out of the tour bus after Phoebe, Axel needed to get some air. He also needed to talk to Nick about why he'd asked Cillian to take Phoebe home, even though Axel had told him last night that she'd made it clear she didn't want to see or talk to her ex.

He headed to Nick's bus.

"How was your night? Did Phoebe get back to the hotel okay?" Nick asked, cracking open an energy drink and passing it to Axel.

They still had one more night to perform in Munich, so the band were waiting around until sound check. Nick's bus was packed with snacks, clothes, scented candles and his own pillows from home. Phoebe's brother never had understood the concept of travelling light. At least they weren't all cramped together in one bus anymore.

August strummed his guitar in the corner, minding his own business. He looked fresh compared to them; his dark curls were tied back in a messy knot exposing his tattooed ear. He offered Axel a polite nod, never being big on talking or drama. It was Axel's favourite thing about him.

"Phoebe passed out before I got back from the signing, so I figured it was best to let her sleep," Axel said, leaving out how Cillian had accused them of sleeping together. "Cillian picked her up about forty minutes ago to bring her back to the hotel."

"Are you kidding?" Nick stood up so fast he knocked over his can.

"Why are you so surprised? Cillian said you sent him?"

From Nick's flaring nostrils, Cillian had lied to them.

"No, I didn't. I wouldn't have let him anywhere near my sister. I locked him in his dressing room to sober up, but when I let him out this morning, he was still drinking his sorrows. He shouldn't be anywhere near a car!" Nick chucked his empty can in the sink.

August stopped playing and listened in, his brows pulled tight with concern.

"He stank of drink, but I thought it was because he was wearing the same clothes as last night."

Axel wished he hadn't hesitated in going after them, but he'd told himself what happened between them wasn't his business. Who was he to interfere when her own brother refused to get involved? Still, he never would've let Cillian drink and drive.

"There is no way he would put her at risk by driving drunk," August mumbled, taking a bite of the breakfast burrito that was meant to be Phoebe's. Axel had brought them the breakfast since he didn't want it to go to waste, and he didn't have an appetite after the earlier confrontation.

Nick pressed his phone to his ear. "Phoebe's phone is going straight to voicemail," he snapped.

"Let's not panic. She's probably back at the hotel and doesn't want to speak to anyone," Axel reasoned. "And Cillian is probably pleading outside her room."

"Neither of them will answer." Nick dropped his phone

on the table. "We should go by her hotel; I know where she's staying. It's not far."

Axel nodded. "I can drive over there and see if everything is okay. They might've pulled over somewhere to talk."

With the mood Nick was in, Axel didn't want him anywhere near Cillian or the hotel in case he made a scene. The situation was hard enough for Phoebe already, and he didn't want them to make it worse.

"No, I should go," Nick argued. "I should've stepped in last night. I never thought he'd be stupid enough to get behind the wheel. What the hell was he thinking?"

"No, stay here in case they come back. She'll need you here. I'll go to the hotel and call you if I find her. I'm sure they're fine," Axel said, forcing himself to remain calm.

Nick's hard stare told him he wasn't buying it. "Fine, but I'm going to keep calling."

"August, can you hold down the fort?" Axel said, not able to meet Nick's eye. "Make sure Anita doesn't find out about this. I'll bring them both back."

"Great, I love running interference. She'll probably make me do an interview." August sighed, but his white-knuckled grip on his guitar revealed his concern. Nick placed a hand on his shoulder as though steadying himself.

Axel left Nick pacing on the phone while August headed off in search of Anita. Back in his own tour bus, he grabbed the keys to his rented car, only to trip over something on his way out.

"You aren't mine," he said with a frown, picking up a purple notebook imprinted with butterflies. "Phoebe must've left you behind." He shoved it into the back of his jeans, figuring it was best to bring it with him.

Not wasting another moment, he put the address for the hotel into his phone and drove out of the lot. It wasn't long before he reached the hotel, and he tried Cillian a few more times as he parked. Still no answer as he walked up the steps to the revolving door. Hopefully Cillian was just ignoring his calls because he was upset about Phoebe staying in his tour bus. But he feared the worst.

Inside the busy hotel lobby, Axel hoped his charm would get him the information he needed. By the marble front desk, he lingered on the edge of the queue, hoping to be spotted. Usually, he never used his fame to get favours, but this was an emergency. Once he saw Phoebe, the elephant sitting on his chest would get off.

One of the younger receptionist's eyes widened as she spotted him, and she promptly waved him over to another counter. He tried to conceal his relief while ignoring the displeased looks from those waiting ahead of him.

"Thank you for seeing me so quickly." Axel gave her his best smile.

"It's my pleasure, what can I do for you?" the receptionist asked, fidgeting with her manicured nails.

"I was wondering if you could give me the room number for a guest, Phoebe Fletcher? She checked in yesterday." He tapped on the counter impatiently, ignoring the growing whispers behind him. He hoped no one asked him for an autograph or a photo—he didn't have time, and he didn't need to feel like a prick on top of everything else.

"I'm sorry, sir, but we don't give out that information," the receptionist said quietly.

"I wouldn't want you to get into trouble, but could I call up to her room? She isn't answering her phone, and I want to make sure she made it back from the concert okay," he said, careful not to reveal his frustration.

"I heard it was a great show—my roommates got to go. I had to work, but I guess I got the better deal." She beamed as she picked up the phone.

He stopped tapping as he waited for Phoebe to pick up. However, the receptionist's smile faded as she put down the phone.

"I'm sorry sir, but Ms Fletcher isn't in." She typed away on her keyboard. "From the details here, I believe the last time her room key was used was last night."

"Thank you for your help," he said quickly, about to leave when she called after him. He winced and turned back towards her.

"Could I get an autograph? My roommates won't believe I've met you, and my little brother wants to be a drummer like you when he grows up." The receptionist smiled nervously, and he didn't want to disappoint her.

"Sure." Axel forced a smile, swallowing his fear long enough to scribble his signature on a hotel notepad. She thanked him, but he was already halfway across the lobby.

Walking back to his car, he checked his watch. It'd only taken him twenty minutes to get here. They could've gone for breakfast, or somewhere else to talk, he supposed, but Munich wasn't familiar to either of them. They wouldn't know where to go, and Cillian wouldn't go off without some of their security.

Axel was about to pull away from the curb when Phoebe's name flashed up on his phone in the holder.

"Phoebe! Where the hell are you? Nick has been calling you, and you aren't at the hotel? Are you and Cillian alright?" he asked frantically, desperate to hear they were okay.

The silence dragged on.

"Phoebe?" he asked again.

"This is Nurse Muller. I'm sorry to call but you were the last missed call on our patient's phone." His stomach dropped as he heard the word 'patient'. "We have a Phoebe Fletcher in the ICU, and we need someone to come and confirm her identity and assist with medical information."

Intensive care unit? He thought his heart was going to hammer through his chest.

He struggled to find the words. "I'll be right there, but she was with my friend, Cillian Hunt. They left in a car together. Is he alright?" It felt like he had swallowed sandpaper as he spoke.

"I'm afraid I don't have any information on the other patient brought in during this time," the nurse said flatly.

He got the name of the hospital and the ward information before hanging up. His hands shook as he gripped the steering wheel and called Nick. Every part of him dreaded telling his best friend that his sister was in the hospital, and that he had no information about Cillian.

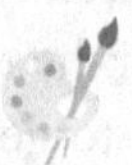

AXEL GOT to the hospital first. They couldn't tell him anything other than that Cillian's car had collided with another vehicle. Being stuck in the waiting room with other families until Nick arrived with August and Anita nearly killed him. Every minute felt like a year, and when the doctor in scrubs finally arrived and brought them to Phoebe's room, the dismayed looks from the nurses as they passed the nursing station gave Axel the overwhelming feeling that it wasn't good news.

"I'm sorry to tell you this, but Mr Hunt was killed on impact when the other car struck their vehicle. Ms Fletcher was unconscious when she came in and will remain under observation in the ICU for the time being. She has suffered a severe concussion, and her right hand required surgery due to severe lacerations. We expect her to wake up when she is ready. She was very lucky to escape such an accident with her life," the doctor said, clutching a tablet to her chest.

Axel held on to Nick as they absorbed the news.

Phoebe's wrist was wrapped, her thumb sutured. Axel's heart broke for her. Nick barely managed to get out that she was right-handed and a painter when the doctor talked to them about her surgery. Axel prayed the injury wouldn't affect her painting. The weight of his guilt forced him to sit down in the armchair by her bed. He didn't care about the nurses' stern warnings for him to leave since it was long past visiting hours. Axel had promised Nick not to let Phoebe out of his sight, visiting hours or not.

Outside her room, Nick and August were talking with Anita about cancelling the rest of the tour. Axel wanted to take Phoebe's hand to let her know he was there, and that she was safe. However, with one hand wrapped post-surgery and the other filled with tubes administering drugs, he could only comfort her by remaining by her side.

"I've got your notebook," Axel told her, gently brushing her lilac hair from her bruised cheek. "You left it behind, but I'll keep it safe for you until you wake up."

He pulled out her notebook from his back pocket and flipped through the pages. He'd been expecting to find sketches. Instead, his eyes widened as he found the lyrics to their songs. Songs past and present, and many, in the final pages of the packed notebook, he didn't recognise.

He stared at her sleeping, bruised body, stunned to have discovered her secret. He ran his fingertips over the handwriting. Some scribbles looked like Cillian's—had they been working together in secret all along? The realisation that Cillian wouldn't write or perform with them again took the air from his lungs.

"Does Nick know about your hobby?" Axel asked her, glancing over his shoulder to Nick.

He didn't know how Nick was holding it together; it couldn't last long. They were all so focused on making sure that Phoebe was okay, no one had really registered the news about Cillian. Nick hadn't stepped foot in his sister's room yet, and Anita had insisted on being the one to identify Cillian. No one argued; they weren't ready to see their friend in that state.

How was Nick supposed to come to terms with the fact that his lifelong best friend had nearly killed his sister because he was stupid enough to drive drunk? Axel scrubbed his hands over his face, hating that the last words he had spoken to Cillian were in anger. Seeing Phoebe in this state contorted his grief with sadness. He wished he'd stopped them, but there was no changing the past.

"I should've made sure Cill was okay this morning. I just lectured him and left," Nick said, numbly, finally walking through the door.

Axel concealed the notebook behind his back. Now wasn't the moment for Nick to discover the truth.

"You can't think like that. He made the choice," Axel said, letting him sit down beside Phoebe.

"Don't say it like that." Nick grimaced. "This wasn't him."

Axel couldn't blame him for his disbelief. They'd grown up together; he never would've thought Cillian was capable of this.

"I don't know what to say," Axel murmured, as if the weight of words might crush them all.

The steady beat of the heart monitor comforted him; she was still with them. That was all they needed to focus on.

"There's nothing to say," August said sadly as he sat on

the end of Phoebe's bed. He stared at her like she'd disappear.

"She's going to be okay," Axel told him.

"She's the best of us." August placed a gentle hand on her leg covered in the rough hospital sheets.

"I can't be here," Nick said suddenly. "I need to call our parents."

He left like someone had lit a fire under his ass. Nick never handled emotions well—not that anyone could get through this situation unscathed. Axel guessed Phoebe had inherited all the feeling genes.

"I'm going to talk to the nurses," Axel told August. Axel wanted to see if he could talk or bribe his way into getting a cot for the room so they wouldn't have to leave her. Focusing on Phoebe cushioned the blow of what they'd lost.

Anita came in as Nick was leaving. Her eyes were puffy, as though she'd been crying. Not that she'd let them see her cry; it was her job to keep their shit together.

"I've cancelled everything," she said, "and done my best to hold off the vultures, but we'll have to make a statement soon."

Axel didn't want Phoebe hearing this, even if she was unconscious. She needed to recover, not listen to the arrangements being made for her dead fiancé.

He took Anita out into the hall. "Did you manage to get through to Cillian's mum?"

"She was devastated." Anita let out a long sigh. "I don't think I've ever heard such noises before. She doesn't want to fly out, so the body will be flown back once the police have wrapped up their investigation. It'll take some time, but it's procedure."

"Are you sure you want to manage all this? We can get

someone else to handle it," Axel offered, wanting to give her an out. She'd already done a lot for them.

"Life goes on, and I'm in charge of making sure the machine keeps going." Anita shrugged it off.

"We aren't a machine. Maybe if we'd realised that sooner we wouldn't be in this position." Her eyes narrowed, and he realised how that had sounded. "Sorry, that came out wrong. I just don't want you to deal with all this, he was your friend too."

Anita shook her head. "I've never treated you like a machine or a product. I think of you as family. None of us could have seen this coming, but it's my job to make sure the show goes on. I owe it to Cillian to be here for him and all of you, now more than ever. If you'll excuse me, I have some calls to make."

Axel let her go. With emotions running high, keeping on at her would only lead to arguments that nobody had the strength for. He rounded the corner in search of coffee for the long night ahead. He wanted to be there when Phoebe woke up, and when they told her about Cillian. Following the signs to the canteen, he found Nick with his head pressed against the cream hospital wall.

"You okay?" Axel asked, even if it was a stupid question. "If you're going to have a meltdown, you're in the best place."

When Nick didn't respond, Axel placed a hand on his shoulder.

"I should've protected them," Nick said.

Nick sank down the hospital wall and placed his head between his knees. Axel sat beside him, trying not to let his own emotions smother him.

He didn't know how long they sat together in the corridor that smelt like bleach and heat, but he knew they'd lost a brother and would never be whole again.

Two weeks later

Scratchy sheets, fluorescent lights and the incessantly beeping heart monitor wore down her patience. Phoebe tried to focus on the officer's questions instead of the itch of tightening stitches running from her wrist to her thumb. Two surgeries, neither she'd been aware of. Nerve damage and tissue trauma, all thanks to her instinctive urge to protect her face during the crash. She didn't care about the pain—her surgeon's advice this morning, "No painting for the foreseeable future," hurt far more.

"Ms Fletcher, we're sorry to make you go through this again, but we need your statement before we can close our case. Can you tell us one more time what you can remember?" the bearded officer asked.

It was disconcerting enough to be confined to a hospital room in a foreign country, let alone have two police officers standing over her asking questions about how her boyfriend nearly got her killed. After the question, the heart monitor beeped, making her feel like she was attached to a lie detector.

"We were fighting. Cillian started speeding," Phoebe explained, repeating the same story she'd told them when she first woke up a week ago. "I told him to slow down, and then nothing. My brother told me Cillian died on impact. The doctors and nurses told me I was lucky." She choked on the last part. 'Lucky, not dead' was a low bar. The driver of the other car walked away with a few stitches, and a nice cheque from Anita to keep the victim away from the papers.

"Mr Hunt's blood alcohol level was twice the legal limit. Were you aware that he was drunk before he got behind the wheel?" The officer's thick accent reminded her how far from home she was.

August, sitting quietly in the corner of the room, was a small comfort, even if he didn't look up from his book during the interview. He'd refused to leave, and the officers didn't argue. Her brother had made him and Axel promise to stay with her. They'd become especially protective after the accident.

"He'd been drinking the night before. I didn't know he'd been drinking that morning, otherwise I wouldn't have let him drive. We were fighting, but him drinking that morning was the last thing on my mind. He has never…" She caught herself. She'd forgotten Cillian was in the past tense now. "He'd never drank and drove before."

"We're sorry to go over this again, but since the car was a rental, we have to file a separate report for insurance purposes," the officer said, jotting down details on a notepad.

Anita will probably pay off the rental company too, she thought.

"You're free to leave the country. Our investigation is closed." The officer closed his pad, as though the worst moments of her life were nothing but a task to tick off.

"Can I have my belongings from the car? My bag, Cillian's things? Do you have them?"

Nick had brought her suitcase from the hotel, but she needed to make sure she had her notebook. If someone found out what it contained, Cillian's legacy would be ruined. Even with all the heartbreak he'd caused, she couldn't do that to his memory. She needed her phone as well. She was sick of borrowing Nick's.

"We collected everything for our investigation. What was recovered we gave to the nurse when we arrived. They'll be returned once we've left." The officer smiled, but his gaze reeked of pity.

"Thank you," she said, rubbing her forehead as a headache crept in. It was time for her afternoon painkillers.

She hadn't been the one driving, but she felt like this was all her fault. If she had stayed home, she wouldn't have discovered Cillian's cheating and they wouldn't have ended up in that car. Axel and Nick had told her repeatedly that Cillian had chosen to drink and drive. Yet her grief settled between guilt and anger.

"We're sorry for your loss," the officer said. "As his next of kin, his fiancée, the body will be released to you."

Fiancée. A wave of nausea caused her to swallow. The thought of being responsible for Cillian's body made it all feel real. The hospital had put her in a cocoon, and with the others keeping her company every second, she hadn't had time to stew in her own thoughts.

"His mum has made the funeral arrangements," Phoebe informed them. She wasn't in any state to help with the funeral of the man who'd broken her heart, only to then shatter it by dying.

"We'll leave you to rest."

The officers left with a sympathetic nod. Moments later, a blonde nurse came in, holding a brown paper bag with an evidence seal.

"How are you doing? I'm sure you're glad to be done with them. I've brought your things and some painkillers." Seeing August, she blushed, and handed Phoebe the bag.

"Thank you, my head was starting to pound."

Phoebe took the painkillers first, then broke the seal. Seeing her bag inside brought her some comfort, but the glimmer of her engagement ring in a clear evidence pouch stung. She guessed Cillian's items were with Nick or Anita. She put the engagement ring in the pocket of her bag, not wanting to look at it.

Her cracked phone was long out of battery. She'd been using Nick's phone to talk to their parents and keep them updated. She hadn't found the strength to talk with Cillian's family yet. Hearing his grieving mum's voice was too much for her to contemplate.

Phoebe frowned. Her notebook wasn't there. The songs for the next album were in it. The last album she'd written with Cillian was gone.

The nurse watched her cautiously. "Are you alright? Is there something I can get for you?"

"There was a notebook. Did the police take anything from the car? It was a purple leather notebook with butterflies?"

"I'm sorry, this was all they gave us." The nurse shook her head as she administered some antibiotics into Phoebe's IV.

What if the guys asked about the album that Cillian promised them? The thought of telling them the truth made her heart ache. She forced a smile, not wanting August to worry.

"Let me get you some tea," the nurse said, placing a hand on her shoulder. "You look pale, and stress isn't good for your recovery."

"I'm fine, I just lost something that was important to us." She tried to stifle her tears.

Us. There is no us, and never will be again.

"You've been through a lot. Why don't we put these things away for now." The nurse helped her put everything back in her bag, but Phoebe held on to her phone.

"Do you have a charger?" she asked. "It'd be nice to use my own phone instead of using my brothers."

The nurse smiled softly. "I can ask at the nurse's station. I'll be back in a bit."

"Thank you," Phoebe said, settling under her blanket. Nick had bought her a soft pink blanket, but the hospital got so hot in the evenings she only used it for comfort.

"I can get you a new notebook." August suddenly got up from his chair.

Sometimes it was tricky to gauge his emotions, but she'd known him long enough to notice when he wouldn't meet her eye. He wanted to talk but was overwhelmed.

"Do you want to talk before the others get back?" Phoebe prompted.

She sensed he didn't want to say it first. He was never a big talker; his music did most of his talking.

"You knew Cillian was cheating on me," she said for him, and he dropped his head to study the grey floor.

He walked to her side and held her good hand, confirming what she already suspected.

"Why didn't you tell me?" she asked.

He'd never been able to lie, so she guessed that was why he chose silence.

"Because we love you," he said gruffly, like it was obvious.

"Then why let me continue believing everything was alright?"

The betrayal cut her deep. Those she'd considered family had kept their mouths shut.

"Because we love him, and we couldn't lose either of you." August kept it simple, which was all she wanted. Cillian had put them in an impossible position, but she wished they'd told her and let her make her own decision.

"We hated him for hurting you, but he was ours," August admitted. It was the closest she'd ever seen him to tears.

"In future, even if you're scared that it'll hurt me, please tell me the truth. Promise me."

He nodded slowly.

"I found the charger." The nurse interrupted them, and Phoebe wiped the tears from her eyes.

"Thank you." Phoebe took the charger.

"Purple or blue?" August asked, abruptly returning to his notebook-hunting mission.

The nurse looked at him, puzzled by his sudden question, before hurrying off to her next patient.

Phoebe was about to say purple, but her last notebook had been purple. She didn't want the reminder.

"Blue."

August smiled as he left, happy to have a task. Phoebe plugged in her phone, and the charge symbol brightened up. At least it wasn't broken.

"Where'd you get a phone?" Axel barked.

Phoebe startled, and the pain radiating up her arm nearly caused her to drop her phone. She looked up, and found him standing in the doorway.

"You scared the hell out of me."

"Sorry." He grimaced. "But you shouldn't be looking at screens right now. Not until your headaches stop."

"The doc said nothing about screens, and the nurse

brought me a charger. She wouldn't have if it was against doc's orders."

"I can't leave you two alone without you bickering," Nick said, appearing behind him with the burgers she'd requested. She couldn't handle any more hospital food.

He exchanged a worried look with Axel.

"Where did you get a phone?" he repeated Axel's question, while putting the greasy paper bags on her table tray.

"What are you hiding from me?" she asked. Nick sat beside her on the bed but didn't do anything to take the phone from her. "Why do you care if I've got a phone?"

Given how the guys were staring at her, there had to be something. She scrolled through all the missed calls and condolence messages. It felt odd scrolling with the wrong hand.

"I'm able to handle it," she lied, barely glancing at the messages she wasn't ready to reply to.

She clicked into Artgram, and her newsfeeds revealed what they'd been trying to protect her from.

"Crazy girlfriend causes accident after breakup." She read the headline numbly. Swiping up, she watched the footage of her trying to get into the concert.

"She's seen it," Anita sighed.

Phoebe hadn't even heard her come in as she scrolled through photos of the crash site. Seeing the crumbled car nearly made her sick. She couldn't remember the accident, or leaving the car. Given the frightful images, she was glad for her memory-eating concussion.

"They want to sell stories, get likes," Anita said, interrupting her thoughts. "They think Cillian was driving you back to your hotel after you refused to leave the stadium. With the footage of the security guards not letting you in, and witnesses at the stadium seeing the two of you fighting at the gate that morning, they've jumped to the conclusion that an argument caused Cillian to crash."

"They aren't wrong—we were arguing," Phoebe said, though it hadn't been because she refused to leave him alone. It was her ending their relationship that caused him to lose control.

"Social media artist costs rockstar his life in fatal accident." She read out another article. 'Rising star in the art world, Phoebe Fletcher, and her childhood sweetheart, Brothers of Anarchy's Cillian Hunt, were involved in a fatal car accident following a sold-out concert in Munich. Sources close to B.O.A. revealed how the couple were fighting before the shocking crash that claimed twenty-six-year-old Hunt's life. Was his failure to appear at Fletcher's successful gallery exhibition the spark that burned down their relationship? Fans filmed Ms Fletcher being refused entrance into their Munich concert despite her own brother being in the band—"

"Stop!" Nick snatched the phone from her. With only one free hand she couldn't fight him. "They're parasites looking for a villain."

"I'm the villain because I didn't die," she snapped, and the room went silent.

"Everything will settle in time, you just need to stay away from social media. Reading all that nonsense won't help your recovery," Anita reasoned. She was gripping the end of the bed so tight her knuckles were white. "I've released statements that the news being circulated is false, and that you were in a happy, committed relationship."

"*I* was in a happy, committed relationship. He wasn't," Phoebe countered.

Anita glared at her. Now wasn't the time for jokes, apparently.

"There were dozens of people who saw us arguing that

night," Phoebe said. "You already paid off the victim, but Cillian's blood alcohol level tells its own story. You can't bribe everyone into silence."

"Already done." Anita shrugged, like it was nothing.

Nick sighed. None of them looked like they'd been getting any sleep.

"What about Helen? The make-up artist?" Phoebe asked, and suddenly everyone found the floor or ceiling very interesting. "An affair with a dead rockstar would be worth its weight in gold in book and movie deals. Don't act like you haven't all thought about it."

"Taken care of." Anita crossed her arms.

Phoebe had to admire her for being so thorough. No wonder Cillian was able to hide things for so long; he had someone in his corner cleaning up his messes.

"Great, so I'm to play the grieving fiancée?" Phoebe asked, hating how easily everything was being swept under the rug.

How was she even meant to do that? God, she hated that she hated him. She hated that she loved him. Nothing felt right; she couldn't just be the sobbing, tragic fiancée.

The others didn't make any of this easier.

"You are a grieving fiancée," Nick snapped. "Despite his mistakes you loved each other very much. This is just your anger talking. This is why we didn't want you to see the news."

"I'm angry with him regardless of what the gossip pages write. Why didn't you want me to see the news, if everything is under control?"

"Because there is a small fraction who believe that you're responsible. They've made threats." Axel broke the hard news with ease, and she appreciated his honesty.

"That's expected—you've all had your fair share of

crazies. Why are you concerned?" Phoebe pressed, not wanting an ounce of truth kept from her.

"*Death* threats," Anita revealed, typing away on her phone. Probably putting out another fire.

"We've had extra security posted outside the hospital, and you will fly back with us for your own protection until this all dies down," Nick reassured her. "Mum and Dad are terrified by what they've seen on the news and online. They've made me swear to make sure nothing happens to you."

"I think you're overreacting to some keyboard warriors." She wasn't going to hide away because strangers who knew nothing about them had an opinion on how they should live their lives.

"We aren't going to risk it," Axel said, picking up August's book and putting it on his lap as he sat down. "Like it or not, you'll be seeing a lot more of us."

"Won't that just fan the flames? Surely we should put as much distance as we can between all of us," she said, noting the dark circles under Axel's eyes. They only made him appear more intimidating. Even though he'd slept in a cot by her side, she still knew so little about him.

"You're my sister, it's my job to protect you." Nick's tone told her his patience was wearing thin.

"We're family, you belong with us," August added firmly. Axel placed a hand on his shoulder, trying to put him at ease.

Axel had an easy bond with August, despite joining the band late. It had always been August and Axel, Cillian and Nick. Phoebe felt a knot in her stomach as she realised how the dynamic of their lives would have to change.

"All we're asking is that you lie low for a short while. It's only for a news cycle or two, until the shock fades," Anita said, her voice devoid of emotion.

Phoebe grimaced at her insensitivity. "Cillian's death isn't a news cycle."

"No one is saying that," Nick interjected, "but we need to focus on keeping you safe, and that's going to require some sacrifices on all our parts."

Phoebe looked at her hand. She'd already sacrificed enough. Glancing up at those around her bed, she saw their troubled eyes. How bad were the threats, to have them all so spooked?

"Remind me to thank your brother for booking such an early flight," Axel groaned. Struggling to keep his eyes open at four a.m., he sipped his black coffee.

"You would've got a better night sleep at the hotel. The doc gave me the all-clear and I'm safe here—you didn't have to stay," Phoebe said, packing up her hospital room.

A few days had passed since they'd told Phoebe about the death threats, and they had kept their promise to not leave her alone. She'd made her feelings clear about said promise.

"Do you have everything you need?" Axel didn't want to argue. He'd been trying to help, but every time he moved, she scowled.

"Yep, I can't wait to leave," she sighed, pulling on her pink hoodie. She managed to get her head through, and he stifled a smile as she wrestled with the sleeves.

"Let me help," he said, not wanting her to hurt her hand because she was too stubborn to ask for help. He widened the right sleeve, and she didn't protest as she slipped her injured hand through.

"Thank you," she muttered, tugging at the ends of her sleeves.

This close, he smelt her caramel perfume, and out of

the hospital gown she looked like herself again. The small scratches on her face had healed, but he knew she still had a long way to go.

She stared up at him, like she was waiting for him to speak. He knew she didn't want them to keep secrets from her, but the only update he had was about him packing up Cillian's tour bus yesterday. August and Nick couldn't bring themselves to step inside, but none of them had wanted a stranger going through his things. After hearing her crying in her sleep last night, he didn't want to make it worse.

Axel's phone buzzed, and he put some distance between them to read the message from Anita. Phoebe went back to packing up her toiletries and he opened the video message. Flashing lights, an ambulance, a crumpled car, a cluster of paramedics pulling open a door—it took him a moment to register what he was watching. The flash of lilac hair made his stomach twist; the paramedics were pulling Phoebe from the car out the driver's side since the passenger side was pinned by the other car. It made it look like she was the driver. Cillian wasn't anywhere in sight. Axel struggled to keep his eyes on the screen as they placed Phoebe's unconscious and bloodied body on a stretcher.

Who the fuck would even take such a video, never mind upload it for the world to see? He tried to remain calm so he wouldn't alarm her. There was no audio, and the video stopped once police moved the gawking crowd on.

He glanced over his shoulder to the bathroom door. Phoebe should never see this footage. The only mercy was that there was no image of Cillian's lifeless body.

He slammed the phone face down as she returned. She lingered by the bed, and he tried not to stare. What if she'd already seen it?

"You can stop looking at me like I'm going to fall apart.

I take it you watched the video of me being pulled from the car," Phoebe said flatly, folding her pink blanket against her chest.

"How'd you know?" He winced, picking his phone up again.

"Because you turned terribly green the moment I came out, and it was the same shade I went when I watched it. My agent, Lena, sent it to me last night because she didn't want me to be blindsided. It's being circulated all over Artgram and ClickClock. Many were kind enough to tag me in the video." She put her blanket on top of her suitcase.

"I'll call Anita," Axel said. "We might be able to get it taken down."

"She already knows. I called her the moment Lena sent it to me." She sighed. "Anita doesn't want to address it. If the world thinks I was driving, then it doesn't matter what Cillian's blood alcohol level was. She's trying to spare Cillian's reputation."

"By setting yours on fire? This isn't right; you shouldn't be blamed for the accident," Axel ground out, wanting to tear into Anita for preying on Phoebe's good nature.

"I'm alive, so I have time to mend mine." She shrugged it off like they were talking about groceries.

"But this is only going to add fuel to the fire, you're already getting threats." He couldn't believe how calm she was. Calm or numb, he wasn't sure.

"Is this why you were crying last night?" He couldn't stop himself. It made sense, now, why she'd wanted to be alone last night, and he was relieved he hadn't listened.

"You heard that?" She flushed, hiding her face as she zipped her toiletry bag.

He nodded. A tense silence settled between them, and there was nothing he could say to ease her pain.

"Let me give you a hand," he offered, and she glared at the pun. "We'll miss our flight at this rate."

Watching her struggle with her organising cubes and bag with one-hand was painful, but it was worse for her. He'd never noticed how stubborn she was before.

"I'm almost ready. You can help me get this stuff in," she agreed. She'd sorted everything into cubes, which was interesting—he was more of a 'chuck it in and sort it out later' type of packer.

It was her first time leaving the hospital since the accident, so he understood why she would be anxious.

"Nick was right about the early flights. Considering the video, we'll need to avoid as many people as possible," he said. "The press will be desperate to get your side of the story."

"I know you all want to protect me, and I'm lucky to have you all as my own personal bodyguards, but you can't lock me away in a tower. The more I hide, the harder they'll try to get to me."

"I was thinking about a house or an apartment—do you know how expensive and difficult it would be to rent a tower?" he said with a smile.

She rolled her eyes and chucked a cube at him. He caught it and packed it with the others. There were still some socks to pack, so he picked up one of the cubes she'd left out.

"Do you have anything else for this bag?" Axel started to unzip it.

"No, not that one." Phoebe tried to snatch it.

"Why are you blushing? Think I've never seen women's underwear before?" He chuckled, and it was nice to have a moment of normalcy despite their setting.

Phoebe grumbled something he couldn't make out and gave up on her packing process.

"Only trying to help," he remarked.

She shoved everything into the case. Clearly, she didn't like him watching her; anytime he got close, her cheeks turned pink. He wished he knew what he was doing that made her so angry. Her nose scrunched up adorably as she struggled with the zip.

"Can I help zip it for you?" he asked, and she pushed it towards him without argument.

"Done." He smiled, taking the case from the hospital bed.

She put her small bag on her shoulder. Neither of them mentioned the tiny specks of blood on the bottom of her bag. It was her bag; she could use it if she wanted. He wheeled her case behind him and gave her a moment of privacy as she hugged her nurse goodbye and thanked her. She had Axel buy a couple of boxes of chocolates for the nurses as a thank you, and everyone at the nurses' station beamed as she handed them over.

"This feels so weird, to be going home without him," Phoebe said, quietly. They hadn't spoken about Cillian, not since she'd asked if they'd known about his cheating.

"We all feel the same, but least we have each other," he said, trying to assure her that she wasn't alone.

She smiled softly, and he noticed her resting her bandaged hand protectively against her chest.

As they reached the main doors, the sound of the crowd and flashing cameras stilled them. The hospital security ushered back those hoping to get a glimpse of them. Axel saw Phoebe's car waiting by the curb; the others were going to meet them at the airport.

He cursed under his breath. "We can go out another exit. Someone must have leaked our plans to the press."

"No, let's just get out of here," Phoebe said, taking a deep breath. "The car is right there."

"Stay close to me." He took her good hand and led her through the door.

Once the sliding doors opened, they were surrounded by their own security. The sea of voices shouting questions merged into a buzz of illegible noise. Axel kept Phoebe close at his back, protecting her from the onslaught as best he could. Security opened the car door for her, and she hesitated, gripping his hand tighter. The fear in her eyes told him their mistake. None of them had considered how getting into a car might affect her.

"You're safe." Axel placed his hand on her lower back. Her eyes met his.

She nodded, and got in the car.

"I'll be right behind you," he said as security closed the door.

The car pulled off, and Axel's own car pulled up. If they'd ridden together, it would've just drawn more questions. He hopped into the back, while security put their bags in the back with the other luggage.

Axel let out a low sigh, only for his phone to ring. The only person who'd ring him at four in the morning was his cousin, Autumn. Being a musician herself, she didn't keep to normal hours. She was the one person who'd understand how they were all feeling.

"Sorry if you can't hear me, it's a circus outside the hospital right now," Axel said, skipping the pleasantries.

"I'm sorry to hear that. I've been watching all the drama online; I can only imagine how hard it's been for all of you. How is Phoebe doing?"

Axel barely heard her over the sound of the crowd banging on his window as they started to pull away.

"As good as can be expected. Being pinned in a car with her dead first love isn't something she can walk off, not to mention the damage to her hand."

"I imagine not, but she has you and the others to support her. It takes a village to heal. Speaking of healing, how are you?" Autumn pried.

"Dealing. Once everyone is home and safe, I'll relax."

"He was your friend too. Make sure you're looking after yourself as much as the others."

"I can love him and still think he was a prick." It was easier to be angry at his friend than grieve. There was too much going on to collapse now. "We're on our way to the airport to meet Nick and August. I'm worried about what's waiting for us out on the other side," he said, as they finally made it away from the hospital. He wouldn't have minded running over one or two of the vultures.

"This stuff online is insane. You're going to need some extra security," Autumn said, reading his mind.

Now they were on the open road, he could focus. Autumn was his favourite cousin. They'd bonded over their love of music, though she clung to her piano while he kept to his drums, and introverted dislike of social settings. Autumn, having been stalked herself, knew how fame could turn nasty.

"We hired extra security for the hospital, but once we get home it's going to be harder to manage. Most of the heat is coming from trolls online—hopefully with time they'll go back to their lives." The news cycle could be cruel, but this time it would play in their favour.

"Please stay safe, I'm worried about all of you. I don't like that someone leaked the video of that crash. The attention will get worse now that people think she was driving," Autumn warned.

"We've suggested she lie low for a while, but I doubt she'll listen. I'm worried about her; she lives alone, now that Cillian is gone."

He hadn't thought too much about what would happen

once they were home. August and Nick were barely holding it together, so he would have to step up.

"What if she were to stay with you? You already share that massive home, I'm sure you have more than a few spare rooms," Autumn asked hesitantly. "It's not like you're strangers; you've known each other for years."

"I doubt she wants to live with three guys, one being her brother—and as an extra bonus, a German Shepherd." Axel shook his head. "She'll want her own space to grieve and heal. They've told her she needs a lot of physiotherapy for her hand before she even considers painting again. I doubt she'll want all of us hovering."

"I wouldn't suggest it if it weren't for the threats, and I'm sorry to hear she's suffering so much with her hand. Maybe that's even more reason for her to stay with all of you. She'll be surrounded by those who care about her. I loved isolating, but then Elijah turned up at the door, and as annoying as he was, he was exactly what I needed to get out of my bubble. Phoebe's grieving not only for her art, but for her first love. Being alone might not be best, but don't force her. I'm sure Nick can get through to her, and August loves her like a sister."

Autumn's logic was sound, but they weren't the problem: he was. Being around her twenty-four seven would certainly complicate the situation and his feelings.

"I'll think about it, and talk it over with the guys. Nick might not want to have his sister around the house," he reasoned, trying to give himself an out. "How's your life going? We haven't talked in a while."

"I'm fine," Autumn said, giving little away about her own struggles.

"I'd expect nothing less," he teased, and he heard her sigh. He'd seen in the news that her stalker's trial had concluded recently. He wanted to ask, but he didn't want to press her to talk about something she wasn't ready to discuss.

"If you need anything, just call. I'm sending you some tickets to my next showcase this summer," Autumn said. She hadn't done a live performance since the trouble with her stalker, and it was great to hear she was performing again. "Bring Phoebe along—it'd be good for everyone to have something to look forward to."

"I'm sure she'd love to come, and thanks for the free tickets. Before I forget, tell Elijah that August has some notes about the last game he created."

"I'm sure he'll love that. Just send him an email, and cc me—I want to see his reaction." Autumn chuckled, delighting in her fiancé's critics. They loved to wind each other up as much as they loved each other.

The sound of a dog barking in the background interrupted her.

"Sorry, I've to go. Now that Brinkley knows I'm up, I'll have to walk her or she'll pounce on Elijah," Autumn said, and the barking settled. "Look after yourself and each other. Call anytime, and please give Phoebe my number if she needs someone to talk to. Overcoming traumatic events is a talent of mine."

It was a relief to have Autumn to turn to. He made a note to repeat her offer to Phoebe. They'd met briefly at a B.O.A. concert years ago, but he doubted she remembered.

"Will do, I'm sure she'll appreciate the offer. While I have you, did you get the engagement present?" he asked, having had it shipped express.

"It arrived this morning! We love it, but with everything going on you really didn't have to! The painting is gorgeous, please thank Phoebe for us. Elijah and I just have to agree on where to hang it."

Seeing how Elijah brought Autumn out of her shell made Axel believe in the healing powers of love. "It was already arranged, and I'm sure Phoebe will be happy it's found a good home," he said quickly. They were pulling up to the airport. "I've got to go," he said as his security opened the door for him. Up ahead, Nick was helping his sister at the drop-off point. Phoebe didn't know that Axel had bought one of her paintings, and he didn't want Autumn wondering why he was keeping his support of her secret.

"Talk soon!" Autumn's goodbye was masked by the barrage of questions and flashing cameras waiting for them. He pulled down his cap.

The others waited inside the doors, and luckily the paparazzi couldn't follow them past security. Having a moment to breathe, Nick and August went to get a drink in the private lounge while Axel followed Phoebe to the bookstore. Even if she had two security guards with her, he wasn't leaving her alone.

After ten days stuck at home with no company and nothing to paint, Phoebe realised how quiet her apartment was. Usually, she'd be too busy painting to notice the silence, and she was so used to Cillian coming and going at all hours—before he started touring, anyway —that she couldn't help waiting for him to walk through the door. Nick had tried to get her to stay with them, but after being trapped in the hospital where her every movement was watched, she wanted to be in her bed and have her own shower. Midway through her second bowl of cereal for the day, she contemplated if she'd made the right decision. The hospital had refused to give her any more of the 'good' painkillers, so she'd been numbing herself with hours of trashy soap operas and takeout. She was starting to leave an impression of her body on the couch cushions. Eat, sleep, ice her wrist, do her physio, rest, shower, eat, sleep—taking care of herself had become a full-time job.

Her phone buzzed on the coffee table and she leapt to answer, hoping it was Lena with news about her next show. Even if she couldn't paint right now, she had enough work in her studio for at least her next two scheduled shows. The collections would be smaller, but even the chance to be around paint again felt like breathing fresh air after choking.

It wasn't Lena.

"Oh, my girl, Nick told us about what happened at the airport, but we've just seen the video on the Facebook," her mum rattled off quickly, and she regretted answering. "I'm glad Axel gave security a good earful, I always thought he was a good egg, pardon the pun. How are you coping?"

"I'm fine, please don't watch that stuff. It was only a few eggs, nothing a shower couldn't fix. Since I can't paint, I've been sleeping mostly. The pain in my hand and the physio exercises have me worn out, so I don't have time to worry about what people think of me online." She thought talking about being tired might get her mum off the phone faster.

Lena had called when she first got home and warned her to stay away from social media, so she hadn't known the footage of her being egged outside Dublin Airport had gone viral. The message online was clear: she was the reason that Cillian Hunt was dead. Thankfully, she was too tired to feel any rage, grief, or the injustice of it all.

"You're right to focus all your energy on healing and getting back to your art. Be sure to get some rest and get out for some air. We wanted to come and visit you and your brother, but it's all been a terrible shock to your dad's heart. I do feel terrible, but I don't think we'll make it to the funeral."

Her parents had had Phoebe and her brother later in life; the generational gap meant they liked to sweep it under the rug rather than face hard emotions.

"Are you sure? His mum will miss you," she said, surprised they weren't going to attend considering Cillian had been a part of all their lives for so many years.

"We've called Maureen to let her know and sent some flowers. We'll come up once everything has settled. It's been hard for us, given all the media attention. So many loved him, I doubt our absence will even be noticed."

Phoebe didn't argue; she wasn't going to force them to attend.

"To think we were only planning your wedding, and now a funeral. It's heart-breaking and you don't deserve half of what they are saying about—" Her mum cut herself off.

"What aren't you telling me? Have the press been contacting you?"

"Nothing for you to worry about. The dog shelter got a few calls, but it was just the pushy press being nosy and some upset fans. A stern warning, and they haven't called back," Mum said in a dismissive flurry.

Phoebe sat up abruptly, knocking her pillow off the couch. She'd seen the online vigils for Cillian, seen the comments and shares from celebrities and fans mourning another great artist gone too soon, despite barely knowing him. The grief and outcry was expected, but she was not prepared for her parents to be targeted by aggrieved fans. It was a mercy that news of his cheating hadn't been leaked and that his 'girlfriend' had kept quiet.

If her parents weren't going to the funeral, at least she wouldn't have to worry about them finding out the truth.

She hadn't told them about the accident in detail. They thought she'd only had some stitches and a concussion. They'd never believe in a million years that their golden boy future son-in-law would drink and drive. Why tell them and ruin their memory of him?

"I'm so sorry, I never expected you to be targeted." Phoebe struggled to mask her upset.

"I don't want to hear you blaming yourself. You loved each other dearly and this was a tragedy," Mum said softly.

"Please tell me or Nick if you get any more calls or letters." Phoebe started pacing, needing to use up her adrenaline. She wished she had never got on that plane, never got in that car with him.

"Don't worry about us, we're able to handle ourselves. Anyway, we've closed the shelter for a few days. We're long overdue a holiday, and we have someone watching the dogs. Once the funeral is over, I'm sure things will settle down and you can all be left in peace."

Glancing around her small apartment, Phoebe thought a little less peace might be nice.

"Make sure you and your brother look after each other. Family comes first, and we're here if you need us. Come home any time. Even if we can't be with you in person, you always have us in your corner."

"Love you, Mum. Make sure Dad stays away from the news."

Phoebe hoped they wouldn't receive any more harassment. Her dad had already suffered two heart attacks in the last five years, and she didn't want all the hate online to increase his stress.

"I'll do my best, but you know how he worries," Mum said. "I'll let you get some rest, and make sure to keep up with the physio. I'm sure you'll be back painting in no time."

Phoebe wished she had her mother's unwavering optimism as she stared at her scarred hand.

After hanging up, curiosity got the better of her and she looked up the video on her laptop. On the screen, Phoebe's lavender hair stood out amongst the crowd of fans—the band's fans; they certainly weren't hers. She cringed as she watched herself turn when her name was shouted, the carton exploded as it hit Axel walking behind her. He got the worst of it since the carton rebounded off him and splattered on her. He'd been kind enough to help her wipe the egg out of her hair. The bands' security quickly blocked the bystander's camera. The last thing they caught was Axel arguing with one of the security guards, while the rest of the band bundled into the waiting cars.

Keys turned in the door, and Phoebe closed her laptop. She half expected Cillian to walk in with pink roses, her favourite, as he did when he came home from every tour. She felt a rush of overwhelming sadness as she remembered he wouldn't be walking through the door again.

"I've got your groceries, and I'm never picking up your birth control again," Nick said, removing his baseball cap. "I'm your older brother, and I'll take a bullet for you, but never again."

Phoebe chuckled, delighted by his embarrassment. "You insisted on helping—and speaking of discomfort, you've been ignoring Mum's calls?"

"With cancelling the rest of the tour and speculation about the next album, I haven't had a chance to call her back." Grimacing, Nick put the groceries down on the kitchen table behind her sofa.

"She sends her love," Phoebe said, putting her laptop on the table. "Did you know they were being harassed?"

Nick hesitated, scratching the back of his head. "Anita told me Mum called her about the threats. They've filed a report with the police just in case."

He'd already dealt with it. Of course their parents went to him first. He was the eldest, if only by two years.

"I thought we agreed no more secrets?" She raised her eyebrows as he unpacked her groceries.

"Sorry, last time," Nick promised, tossing over her

favourite salt and vinegar crisps. She was getting better at catching things with one hand. "Thank you for covering for me with Mum. Speaking of avoiding people, I couldn't take being at home a moment longer." He reached into her fridge for an energy drink, a habit they both shared. "Axel is locked up in his basement. I think his drumsticks have become surgically attached to his hands. August is wandering around the place like a lost puppy, and Bart won't leave Cillian's bedroom door. No one is used to being this idle, and I'm beginning to agree with Anita about pushing ahead with the next album."

"Without Cillian?" she asked, realising that only two of the four OG members remained.

"I don't want to do it without him, but none of us want to disband. Moving forward might be the best way to heal," he said, sounding unsure.

She wondered how long it would be before he discovered there were no songs for the next album. She swallowed her secret, feeling like a hypocrite. They'd promised to stop keeping secrets.

"Don't rush into anything," she said. "Maybe wait until after the funeral before making a decision."

"You're right—the others think the same. I think I just want the distraction. Anyway, Cill's mum wants me to pick out something for him to be buried in. I can't even open the door to his room, never mind go through his things to look for the songs he was working on."

"I'm sorry, I wish I could do something to help."

Phoebe doubted he was sleeping, given how he chugged the energy drink.

"I hate to ask this, given how everything happened. Did Cill ever mention what he wanted in case he…" Nick drifted off, collapsing beside her on the couch.

Phoebe swallowed the golf ball in her throat. "We were

too focused on building our future. You know him, he never liked to think anything could go wrong."

Nick scrubbed his forehead as a silence filled the space between them.

"I'm sorry I didn't tell you." His apology tumbled out. "I'm sorry I didn't tell you about Cillian's cheating. I never wanted you to find out like that."

She cradled a pillow to her chest. "Let's not." She didn't have the energy for this conversation.

"I want to say that I'm sorry," Nick said, staring at his hands. "I should've gone after you that night and made sure you got back to the hotel. I didn't think you'd want me to get involved. I thought Axel would be the best person to help you out, and they would've killed each other if I left them alone. I didn't expect Cillian to keep drinking."

"I accept your apology, but you couldn't have known what would happen. We all agreed you'd never have to pick sides, to ensure our relationship wouldn't get in the way of the band's future. What happened wasn't anyone's fault." She patted his shoulder, and he finally looked at her. She hated seeing him so torn up. "You were trying to protect me, and even if you'd told me, I don't know how I would've reacted. Maybe I would've forgiven him or given him another chance. There's no point in focusing on what could've been. Besides, I'm glad you sent Axel after me. Otherwise, I would've made an arse of myself in front of the press. Even if I hadn't been there that morning, Cillian could've still driven the car."

"I hate that Cillian put me in a position where I had to lie to you. I swear that he promised he was going to end it with her and tell you." Nick dragged his hands through his fire-engine red hair, and she was amazed it didn't get tangled in his rings.

"I believe you."

"I'm sorry Cillian accused you of…" Nick couldn't finish. She guessed Axel had told him what happened on the bus.

"Nothing happened between Axel and me."

"I just want to know if there is anything about that night that I haven't been told. With all the press, I want to make sure there aren't any more surprises before the funeral." Nick downed the rest of his can.

"Nothing happened," she assured him, sure that the notebook with the songs she'd written had been destroyed in the accident. "I fell asleep, and Axel slept on the pull-out bed. Cillian saw us talking and made some drunken assumptions. He wouldn't let me leave unless I got in his car. He told me that you'd sent him to bring me home."

Nick clenched his jaw, angry that Cillian used him as an excuse that nearly cost her life.

"You know what happened next."

She left out that they'd argued about the music they'd written together. With the notebook lost and presumably destroyed in the crash, there was nothing to tell.

"I'm sorry for bringing it up again," he said, and she shrugged it off.

"I suspect Anita wanted you to double check?" she asked, knowing their manager had been putting out fires left right and centre since that night.

"None of us can handle any more surprises," he confessed.

"What's done is done, let's just focus on the future."

Phoebe let out a long sigh. She put her arm through his and rested her head on his shoulder.

"Next person you date, please don't pick my best friend," he quipped, breaking the tension.

"You don't have to worry about that! I don't plan on dating for a *long* time."

"How are you really?" he asked.

"About as good as you," she said, staring at her hand.

"Have you thought any more about coming to stay at the house? We've got plenty of rooms, and it's not good to be here alone."

"We talked about this," she groaned.

"You talked, and I listened, but I'd feel a lot better if you'd stay with us."

"I'll think about it," she said. She *was* lonely—not that she'd admit it—but there were so many memories of Cillian in that house. She didn't want to be constantly reminded of the man she missed as much as she despised.

"Fine, I tried." He raised his hands in defeat, and started for the door. "Call if you need anything, and don't go out alone unless it's for physio. I mean it! Otherwise, I want you to have some security with you."

Phoebe rolled her eyes. "I don't need security, and I'm not in the mood to go out anyway."

Hopefully, after the funeral everyone would forget about her.

"Call Mum back!" she called from the couch as he opened the door.

He smirked. "The first chance I get."

She knew that meant never.

T he others hated it when Axel drank orange juice straight out of the carton, but he was so thirsty he finished what remained in a few gulps. He stared out the kitchen window; it was already dark out. His hands ached from the hours he'd spent in the basement playing. Since he couldn't hear the TV blaring, he guessed August was in the game room at the other end of the house. Bart, their four-year-old German Shepherd, hadn't come scratching at his door, so he must have still been posted outside Cillian's bedroom door upstairs. It looked like he'd eaten his breakfast, at least.

"If you keep drinking August's orange juice, he's going to poison it," Nick said, coming in from the garage.

"I'm not worried. We can't afford to lose another band member." Axel broke down the empty carton and tossed it in the recycling.

"Not funny." Nick glared at him, the same evil eye he shared with his sister. Except Phoebe was much sexier when she was mad.

"Any luck with Phoebe? Has she thought anymore about moving in?" Axel asked, wiping the sweat from his neck with his T-shirt. The house was big enough for all of them. They'd bought it together during the pandemic so they could still release music. After two years, they'd got so used to living together they'd never moved out.

"She's going to think about it, I didn't want to press the issue. She didn't say, but she must be lonely in the apartment. Judging from how clean the place was, she's bored out of her mind without her painting."

Axel saw the worry in Nick's eyes as he took two beers from the fridge. He wished Phoebe wouldn't be so stubborn. With nine bedrooms, two recording studios, Axel's basement (no one could stand his drumming at four a.m.), and August's game room, none of them had to be around each other if they didn't want to be.

"You told her about your parents?" Axel asked, having heard him hotly debate the topic with Anita that morning before he'd left to run Phoebe's errands.

"Sadly, my mum beat me to it. Mum's worried about Dad's heart, so they aren't going to come to the funeral. Not that I blame them. It's going to be a shitshow with all the media. I don't want Phoebe to attend, but there's no way she'd sit it out," Nick said, taking a seat at the counter as Axel took some burgers from the fridge.

"Regardless of what happened, she loved Cill and needs closure. We all do, and if she didn't attend, it would only feed speculation," Axel said.

Nick had been helping Cillian's mum with the funeral arrangements, and Axel knew Nick was best left alone until he asked for help, no matter how much he was struggling. Until then, he'd back him from afar.

"It's not the media I'm worried about. Phoebe's not only grieving Cillian—I'm worried about her hand. The physio is obviously painful, and the thought of her dealing with it all alone is—" He cut himself off, and Axel could see how helpless he felt.

"Let's get through the funeral and be there for Phoebe

in whatever way we can. We made a mistake not telling her about Cillian, but we can make it up to her by being there for her now." Axel patted his friend's shoulder, hating what he had to ask next. "Cillian's mum called while you were out, and Helen is named in his will. She'll be at the will reading at his mum's house."

Cillian's mum had insisted on hosting the others in his childhood home. Hopefully it would be too packed for Phoebe to notice Helen's presence.

"What was Cillian thinking? Why would he put her in his will? What else wasn't he telling us?" Nick picked at the label on his beer. "I'll have to tell Phoebe at the funeral, I don't want her to be blindsided by Helen being there. We can't stop Helen from coming or it could cause a scene that would only add to the feeding frenzy."

"We'll keep them separate for as long as possible. By the time the reading takes place most of the guests will have left. August and I can run interference," Axel said, almost happy to have something to do on the dreaded day.

He'd been cooking up some burgers while they talked. Nick wasn't sleeping, but Axel tried to keep them fed. Nick had always bordered on lanky, so he couldn't afford to lose any more weight. Axel didn't mind cooking; like drumming, using his hands relaxed him. It also kept a sense of normalcy in the house. They owed it to Cillian's memory to hold it together at least for a couple more days.

"What? Like lock them in separate rooms?" Nick chuckled, taking out the burger buns from the cupboard.

"If we have to." Axel clinked his beer against Nick's. "Speaking of have to—you need to get some sleep. You're going to burn out at this rate."

"Sleep sounds good, but Cill's mum wants me to write a eulogy," Nick said as Axel handed him a stacked burger.

"She'd asked us all to do one, but August and public speaking…"

"I can find Cillian something to wear, and August can stand with us while you speak," Axel assured him.

Out of habit, he'd cooked four burgers instead of three. He considered tossing it before the others saw it, but that felt wrong. Instead, Axel made the extra burger and left it on the counter where Cillian used to sit. Nick stared at it and cleared his throat. They shared a moment of silence, eating as though their friend was still with them.

"What about the suit he wore to last year's Hotify awards?" Axel asked, once he'd finished.

"Should be fine," Nick agreed, wiping his mouth with a napkin.

August came around the corner from the sitting room having smelt the food.

"I'll figure it out. August, you want to give me a hand?" Axel asked, as August took a plate.

"No." August sat in front of the TV by the dining table that separated the sitting room and kitchen.

Axel didn't ask twice. That was the most August had spoken since they had got home—he didn't like that Phoebe wasn't staying with them. It was a start, and his eating felt like a win.

On the second floor, Axel hesitated at the end of the hallway. He fought the urge to knock on Cillian's door before heading in, and his chest tightened as he walked inside. Cillian had been extremely sensitive about his privacy, which made sense considering all the secrets he had.

He tripped over the box of Cillian's belongings from the tour bus at the end of his bed. The room was rather musty, and he opened the curtains and windows to air it out. Not wanting to linger, he found the collection of suits in the walk-in wardrobe by the wall of trainers. Cillian's awards suit: he wore it for every award event for good luck. Axel smiled to himself; hopefully it would bring him luck in his next life. He put the suit bag on the unmade bed before searching Cillian's collection of T-shirts for his favourite Beatles Abbey Road one. Finding it, he slipped it under the jacket in the suit bag and placed a guitar pick inside the pocket, only to find a flask inside. The memory of them sneaking drinks in during reward shows choked him, and he rubbed the tears from his eyes.

Axel sat on the bed to compose himself and picked up their group picture from the opening of their very first tour. Phoebe was on Cillian's back, while August lay out on the street in front of them. Nick had Axel in a chokehold, and Anita had taken the shot. The best days of his life. Before the band's original drummer left, he'd been a freelancer hopping from band to band, but joining B.O.A. had felt like coming home. They had little to no money, shared one bus and lived on takeout.

Wiping a stray tear with the back of his hand, he set down the picture. Lost in his memories, he accidentally dropped it down the back of the bedside table.

"Hopefully the glass isn't broken," he muttered. Reaching down, he eased the frame out carefully only for it to get stuck down the side of the bed. He gave it a shove, and the frame popped out along with a black leather notebook. He flipped through the pages, noticing how similar it was to Phoebe's. Except, instead of finding song lyrics, he found diary entries that dated from the beginning of last year.

He shouldn't be reading this. He should give both journals back to Phoebe and mind his own business—but he hesitated. What if what was written inside only hurt Phoebe further? Maybe he should do a quick scan to make sure first.

He felt his conscience shaking his head, but he flipped to the final entry, to make sure it wasn't Cillian professing his undying love for another woman. He set aside his morals and started reading.

I'M GOING TO TELL PHOEBE. THE LADS IN AA SAID THAT I SHOULD COME CLEAN. THAT IF I'M SERIOUS ABOUT MY SOBRIETY I NEED TO STOP SABOTAGING OUR RELATIONSHIP AND CONFRONT MY MISTAKES. I DON'T KNOW HOW TO TELL HER, I LOVE HER SO MUCH, AND I HATE MYSELF FOR WHAT I'VE PUT HER THROUGH. IF I'D TOLD HER SOONER ABOUT THE CHEATING, THEN THINGS WOULDN'T HAVE GOT SO OUT OF CONTROL. HOW AM I SUPPOSED TO TELL HER THAT I'M GOING TO BE A DAD? HOW CAN I EVEN BE A DAD WHEN I CAN'T LOOK AFTER MYSELF?

FUCK, NICK WILL KILL ME, AND I DON'T BLAME HIM. I PROMISED HIM THAT I'D LOOK AFTER HER, THAT I'D NEVER BREAK HER TRUST. HE PROMISED NOT TO TELL PHOEBE ABOUT THE CHEATING IF I CAME CLEAN, BUT HE DOESN'T KNOW ABOUT THE BABY. I CAN'T FIRE HELEN TO KEEP THEM FROM FINDING OUT, BUT I'VE ALREADY MADE SURE SHE AND THE KID ARE SET UP. I FEEL LIKE THE SHIT-

TIEST PERSON ALIVE. ONCE THE TOUR IS OVER, I'LL TELL PHOEBE. I'LL TELL THEM ALL EVERYTHING.

THE WORST PART IS THAT SOMEONE ALREADY KNOWS. THEY'RE TAUNTING ME. SOMEONE LEFT A BABY GROW IN MY DRESSING ROOM WITH A 'WORLD'S BEST DAD' SLOGAN. I THOUGHT IT WAS AXEL, BUT IF HE'D FOUND OUT ABOUT THE BABY, HE'D MAKE ME CONFESS. THERE IS NO WAY HE WOULD TELL PHOEBE, HE WOULDN'T WANT TO BE THE MESSENGER THAT BREAKS HER HEART. I SEE THE WAY HE LOOKS AT HER, LIKE HE'S WAITING TO SWOOP IN AND BE THE FUCKING HERO. MAYBE I SHOULD LET HIM. SHE DESERVES BETTER.

FUCK, THE PARANOIA IS DRIVING ME CRAZY, AND ANITA WON'T STOP NAGGING ME TO FIX IT. I WOULD IF I FUCKING COULD. WHAT IF THIS SOMEONE TELLS PHOEBE BEFORE I GET THE CHANCE? I CAN'T LOSE HER; I CAN'T LOSE ANY OF THEM...

AXEL SLAPPED THE NOTEBOOK SHUT. He wasn't surprised by Cillian's accusations about his feelings for Phoebe, but Helen's pregnancy felt like a gut punch. So that was why he couldn't end it with her.

He couldn't bring this to the others; there were too many unanswered questions, and with the funeral in two days, he couldn't drop the bomb now. He hoped Helen would keep it quiet, but then it struck him.

The will reading. Now it made sense why she was

attending. Cillian might've been a prick, but he would make sure his kid was looked after.

He grabbed the suit and closed Cillian's bedroom door behind him. In the safety of his basement, he placed Cillian's journal in his bedside drawer with Phoebe's notebook. He stared at the closed drawer and contemplated whether he should give the books back to Phoebe, but this was not the week to do it. Unlike Cillian believed, he didn't delight in being the bearer of bad news, especially not when it was going to hurt those he cared about most.

W ith heavy rain and grey skies, it was the perfect day for a funeral. Once the coffin was in the ground, they all bundled into their cars in a sea of black umbrellas and went on to Cillian's mum's house. The door was left open for visitors to come and go as they pleased. There were plenty of corners to hide in, but Phoebe couldn't escape the sympathetic smiles. They only made her angry. The cold caused her hand to ache, and her painkillers were wearing off as she stood in the cramped hallway.

"I'm so sorry for your loss. I can't even imagine the heartbreak you must be feeling," Cillian's cousin Martha said, but Phoebe couldn't stop staring at the spinach stuck in her teeth. "We were so looking forward to your wedding —you were perfect together. I can't believe you aren't going to be part of our family."

She sniffled, and Phoebe offered her a tissue from the table by the stairs.

"It's a loss for all of us."

Phoebe tuned out the rest of her condolences, looking to the couch where Cillian's mum sat with a tissue pressed to her nose as her extended family comforted her. They talked in hushed tones, and her throat tightened when she recalled the last time she'd seen his mum. It was when they'd told her about their engagement. The urge to turn around and bolt down the hallway became overwhelming.

She interrupted Martha's rambling. "If you'll excuse me, I've got to check on my brother."

"Yes, please do whatever you need." Martha's sudden embrace stilled her. "Look after yourself. We're all thinking of you, and please know we don't believe a word the press is saying. We know you wouldn't have done anything to hurt Cillian."

Phoebe clenched her teeth to stop herself from biting Martha's head off. Walking away down the small hallway, she kept her head low so no one would stop her to offer their condolences. The crowded kitchen stank of pre-made casseroles and cakes, and nearly brought her breakfast back up.

Out in the garden, she didn't care about the rain. Down the side of the house, she heard August playing to keep his mind busy in the garage-slash-rehearsal space. It had been their hangout since Cillian's thirteenth birthday, when he and Nick first decided they were going to start a band.

Opening the door, she expected to find the comfort she needed. Instead, Phoebe froze as she came face to face with Nick and Helen.

"I'm not leaving!" Helen barked, shoving past Nick. Her voice reached a pitch only dogs could hear.

What the hell was she doing here? Phoebe hadn't seen her in the church. From August's guilty expression as he sat with Axel on the thrifted couch in the corner, she suspected they'd been keeping them away from each other.

She didn't have time to speak before Helen got in her

face. "He loved me. We were together for six months, but he couldn't tell you. He couldn't leave you until they released their next album. We both know why he couldn't."

Phoebe's stomach dropped. Had Cillian told her about their songs? Luckily the others were too caught in all the other horrid stuff she was spouting to take notice.

She couldn't think with Helen continuing to rant in her face. *Shut up, shut up, shut up! Today isn't about you!* Phoebe clenched her fists.

"Everyone is talking about *poor Phoebe*—you killed him. He wouldn't have been in that car if it weren't for you, and my child wouldn't have lost their father. We were going to be a family."

Phoebe's blood ran cold as the sobs dissolved the anger in Helen's words. Axel was between them in seconds.

"Aren't you going to say something?" Helen snapped as she tried to get around him. "Did you even love him at all? You didn't shed a tear at the church, not even at his grave."

An unsettling calmness overcame Phoebe as she punched her. Helen yelped, holding her hands to her nose. Axel and August didn't make a move to intervene, too shocked to speak.

Helen stared at her with wide, watery eyes. Phoebe wasn't sorry, because now that Helen had shut up, she could breathe, and deliver her message.

"Cillian's mum wants you all to come in and share some stories." Phoebe excluded Helen from the invitation. "A little warning would've been nice," she said to the others, before walking out.

She shook out her left hand. Even if it hurt, it felt fucking fabulous. Today wasn't the day for Helen to say her piece.

Listening to stories praising Cillian wasn't something

she could tolerate after the altercation, and she found herself upstairs in Cillian's childhood bedroom. There were still the same movie posters on the wall, his collection of vinyl. His mum hadn't changed a thing; it felt like stepping into a time capsule, seeing the photos of them on the walls from their school days. Her hair was longer, and Cillian didn't have any tattoos or piercings yet.

She opened the wardrobe doors and pulled aside some of the clothes he'd left behind when he moved out. Her heart sank as she saw 'P+C 4eva' written in sharpie. She ran her fingers over the fading letters on the navy wall and thought of Helen's accusations: *Did you even love him?* He was her best friend before he was her boyfriend. She had loved him for nearly half her life, and maybe that was long enough. She wasn't grieving for the man he'd become but for the Cillian she used to know.

Was he really going to end it? What was the point in proposing if he'd been seeing Helen for so long? She sat with her back to the closet wall, the symbol of their past above her.

"Phoebe?" Axel had found her. They had never been close, but he had a calmness about him that she appreciated.

"If the others sent you to get me, there's no way I'm going downstairs to reminisce. I'm afraid of what I might say. His mum doesn't know about the cheating, and I'm not going to spoil the memory of her perfect son."

"I'm not here to make you do anything, and I think you broke her nose," Axel said, sitting on the floor with his back resting against the bed so they were facing each other.

"It wasn't like it was the original." She didn't care about sounding petty. "Questioning someone's grief is low."

"I'm not judging." He shrugged as his eyes flicked to the writing above her head.

"His mum will be pissed that we drew on the walls," Phoebe mused, wondering if she would pack up his room. "She could paint over it; our forever is over."

"How's your hand?" Axel asked, masterfully changing the subject.

She wished people would stop asking how she was.

"The exercises are helping, even if they hurt like hell," she said, looking forward to having a little more mobility.

"I meant your punching hand." He smirked, moving to sit beside her in the small wardrobe. He looked good in all black, and his collar hid most of his neck tattoos.

"It's fine. Throbbing, but fine. I can't believe I punched a pregnant woman. I've never hit anyone before, I've never even wanted to hit anyone before." The word 'pregnant' stung, but there was no avoiding it. At least she knew why Helen was at the funeral. They couldn't not invite the mother of Cillian's child.

"I think you get a pass today. She shouldn't have accused you of not caring."

"Was she telling the truth? About the baby?" she asked, resting against his shoulder, wanting to be close to someone who didn't look at her with pity.

"Yes." Axel brought his knees up to his chest. She noticed his Doc Martens, and wondered if they could be deemed suitable funeral attire. Cillian would've appreciated the rebellion. "We only just found out, and Nick was going to tell you once the guests left."

"Before the will reading? Because she's in the will?" Phoebe put two and two together.

Axel nodded, and she appreciated his honesty.

"I can't tell you whether he loved her or not. He never spoke about her like that. Not with me anyway. To be honest, we assumed it was over when you got engaged.

Cillian said he was going to stop drinking. He wasn't himself when he was drinking."

"Once is a drunken mistake, six months is an affair." It was a relief to speak openly with him. "I still can't believe Cillian proposed knowing he'd got her pregnant. Makes me sick."

"We wish he'd told us how much trouble he'd got himself into. We knew he'd messed up, just none of us expected it to be this bad. But I do know he loved you in his own fucked up way," he said, fidgeting with his skull cufflinks.

"You're being oddly comforting. Why haven't we talked like this before?" Phoebe stared up at him, and he chuckled.

"I'll take that as a compliment—and because Cillian didn't like it if I got within five feet of you."

"Yeah, he wasn't your biggest fan," she admitted.

He nodded knowingly. "I wasn't his either, but I still miss him."

"Me too," she confessed, picking up a shoebox full of old photos. Instead of taking them as she'd planned, she placed them back under his clothes in the corner.

"You don't want them?" Axel frowned.

"The man in those photos no longer exists. I'm beginning to think I lost him long before the accident," she said. "That Cillian never would've cheated on me. I was his world; we were a team. At the beginning, he'd call me on tour and fall asleep with me still on the phone. He flew home after a concert in Korea because I had the flu and was stuck in bed. The man in the car… he was just a shadow." Her heart tightened as she confessed her feelings to the one person she'd least expected to be her comfort.

"Touring, fame—the pressure can twist even the best

person," he said. She hadn't heard him speak about what they did this way before.

"You seem pretty normal," she said, "except that you're allergic to smiling, interviews and social media." He was the only one in the band who refused to be online.

He shrugged. "I was older when I met the lads."

"Only by five years. You're hardly ancient." She nudged him, and he rolled his eyes.

There was a hint of a smile, and as sexy as his brooding demeanour was, there was a kindness in his smile that made his eyes light up.

"On the road, five years is a lifetime. I'd toured with solo artists and other bands to get my start. Anita thought I'd be a level head since I'd already had my wild years."

"You were wild?" she said with a smirk, never having even seen him drunk. There'd only been a couple of beer bottles in his tour bus, unlike the others who thought every night was a party.

"You've no idea." His eyes met hers, and something giddy stirred in her. It made a nice change from the heart-break and upset.

She wanted to know what his wild meant. *Girls, booze, drugs?* She'd never thought much about his past. Maybe his quietness wasn't him being cold or rude; maybe he'd felt out of place since she had known the others since school.

"I think we've been gone long enough," Axel said, offering her a hand.

She sighed, bracing herself to return to the accusing stares and sorrowful glances. He helped her up, and she stared at their joined hands. A spark she'd never felt before rippled through her, and from the way his brow creased, he felt the same. With only inches between them, her eyes drifted to his lips in the tense silence. He didn't pull away, and she became curious to know what his red wine-stained lips tasted like.

He cleared his throat. "Stop looking at me like that, Bee," he said softly.

He'd never called her Bee before. It felt too intimate, but she wanted to hear it again.

"I don't know what you're talking about," she said as he tucked a strand of lilac hair behind her ear, just like that night in the tour bus.

"Yes, you do," he rasped. His fingertips grazed along her jaw, her neck, as though he was trying to memorise every inch.

Her breath caught as he drew near.

"I'm sorry," he said suddenly, snatching his hand away like she'd burnt him.

"We should go downstairs," she said, but neither of them moved. Eye level with his chest, she stared up at him, seeking answers. He let out a deep breath, lost in thought, but when her eyes met his, his gaze darkened.

"Fuck it," he cursed, and pinned her to the wardrobe door. He crushed his lips against hers, hungry and exploring.

She moaned as he pulled her flush against his hard body. She lost all ability to move, to think, to breathe—there was only him. Trying to steady herself, she rested her hands on his chest. The rush of his heart told her they were both nervous, this wasn't the time or place, but the taste of his lips ruined her self-control. His touch, the comfort of being held, brought tears to her eyes, and the last thing she wanted was to cry.

"Axel? Phoebe? You up there?" Nick's voice froze them both in place.

Phoebe covered her mouth with her hands, not sure if she was going to laugh or cry.

"We should get back," Axel said, but his grip on her didn't loosen. Nor did she want it to. She couldn't remember the last time she'd been kissed like nothing mattered more than her.

"Grief waits for no one." She brushed off the gloss from his full lower lip. His eyes widened at the gesture. She blushed in disbelief—why was she so comfortable touching him?

"Why?" Axel asked, breaking the heavy silence as they reached the top of the stairs.

"Why what?" Her heart was beating so fast, she couldn't bring herself to look at him.

"The kiss."

"I wanted you to, and Cillian will be turning in his grave."

"So, it was to get back at him?" he asked.

In fact, Cillian hadn't even crossed her mind. That scared her more than if it had just been about getting revenge.

"It wasn't the only reason. Does that bother you?" Phoebe asked, unsure of how to process what had happened between them. If it wasn't for revenge, then why?

"Happy to be of service." He shook his head, placing his hands in his pockets, and they headed down to join the remaining guests in the living room.

"You both okay?" Nick asked.

"Just needed a minute." Phoebe forced a smile, trying to hide her shame.

"Cillian's mum wants you to say something before everyone leaves. Most of the people here would've attended your wedding, so she thinks they'd like to hear from you." Nick shuffled uncomfortably as he relayed the request.

"Everyone would understand if it's too much," Axel reassured her, but it was the final step, her goodbye.

"A few words couldn't hurt, and once everyone leaves, we can get to the will reading and call it a day."

They watched her solemnly and stayed close.

Cillian's mum smiled at her warmly as she walked over. The guests turned, and Phoebe fidgeted as the mourners stared, waiting for her to speak, but she was momentarily enraged by Helen sitting on the couch consoling Cillian's mum. Finding out about her son's child and other woman would bring her a new level of grief. Phoebe wished they'd put off the will reading, but if Helen was involved, ripping off the band-aid might be best for everyone.

"I want to thank all of you for coming and helping us celebrate Cillian's life," she began. "I've loved Cillian for most of my life. Before he was my boyfriend, my fiancé, he was my brother's annoying best friend, and I was the younger sister with a helpless crush. The more time we spent together, and much to my brother's irritation, we became inseparable. I can't pinpoint the day we fell in love, or even the day we started dating, because we just were. That was how I expected to spend the rest of my life, with him. Sadly, it wasn't to be. Not because of the accident, or his untimely passing, but because he was having an affair. What's a ten-year relationship compared to a six-month affair? Not only was he with another woman when he asked me to spend his life with him, but he'd also got her pregnant.

"I feel like a fraud, because I'm sure you were all expecting to hear from the person he wanted to make a life with. The truth is, that's not me. The man I loved died long ago, and like my love for him, I can't pinpoint the day or the hour it happened. The Cillian I loved and grew up with, cried and laughed with, wasn't the man that nearly killed me. Today I buried a stranger, and the future I thought we were going to have together. Now, I think you should all hear from the woman he was building a future with, the woman who's carrying his future."

Phoebe raised her glass to Helen and downed the champagne as the room stared between them blankly.

"That was a beautiful speech." Cillian's mum, Maureen, embraced Phoebe, after most of the guests had said their goodbyes.

Of course, Phoebe hadn't said what she wanted; she couldn't hurt the guys or his mum like that. Instead, she had told the room what they had wanted, needed to hear, and when she'd raised her glass to his memory there wasn't a dry eye in the house.

"I'm sorry to interrupt, but if I could get everyone in the office we can do the reading of the will," Mr Murray, the lawyer of Cillian's estate, said politely.

They weren't done yet. Anita had made the band write their wills when they first started to gain traction to prepare for the worst-case scenario, but Phoebe had no idea what was in Cillian's will. She had always believed he had left everything to his mum. His mum, who was alone now, she realised. Her heart grew heavy.

Nick, August and Axel followed Maureen and Phoebe into the dining room off the kitchen. There was no office in the small two-storey home. Despite Cillian's protests, his mum had never wanted to move to a more luxurious home. As a single mum, she had lived frugally, and wanted to remain in the house where she had raised her son.

They all sat around the table, and Phoebe noticed Helen lingering by the door. At the head of the dining table, Mr Murray laid out some papers, and cleared his throat.

"Before we get started, Mr Hunt made a recent change to his last will and testament. I'll read the entirety of the will, and should anyone have an issue, I ask that you wait patiently until the end so that we can get through this as quickly as possible."

Everyone nodded in agreement.

"The most recent addition: Mr Hunt awarded five million euros and his penthouse apartment on West 23rd and Main in New York to Ms Helen Lycett."

Phoebe clenched her teeth and kept her eyes low to conceal her emotions. His mum stared at her, while the others looked anywhere else.

"There must be some mistake," Maureen started, but Phoebe rested her hand over hers.

"I'll explain later," she said quietly, not wanting to do this now. Her wrist ached, and she realised she was clenching her bad hand.

Helen remained quiet, but Phoebe noticed her hand placed defensively over her tummy. Despite Phoebe's hurt, this woman was pregnant with Maureen's future grand-child, so she hid her disgust for her sake.

Having heard what she needed to, Helen left the room.

"Mr Hunt awarded one million euros and the recently purchased villa in Amalfi, Italy, to Ms Phoebe Fletcher. The deed to the Dublin studio apartment you currently reside in will also be transferred to you," Mr Murray said, looking as uncomfortable as they all felt.

The villa in Italy? He'd mentioned buying it after he'd proposed, but her apartment was a complete surprise. She'd been renting for years—when the hell did he buy it?

"There must be some mistake," Phoebe argued, breaking the rules. "I've rented my apartment for years. I know my landlord."

"Cillian didn't want you to worry about the rent going up, or your landlord selling it out from under you, since you live across the road from your art studio. He bought the apartment over two years ago, and your name is already on the deed," Mr Murray explained.

"She's been paying rent on an apartment she already owns?" Axel asked, and everyone turned to look at him, surprised by his sudden outburst. He sank back into his corner.

"Nick, did you know about this?" Phoebe asked her brother, sat across from her.

"Not a clue." Nick shrugged.

So Helen wasn't the only thing he'd been lying about. Were the secrets ever going to end?

"The money you've been paying in rent has been put in a high-yield investment portfolio," Mr Murray informed her.

"How much is in it?" Phoebe asked, trying to do quick maths of how much rent she'd paid into it. She knew nothing about stocks; she would keep her money in her mattress if she could.

Mr Murray riffled through another envelope of papers until he found what he was looking for. "A little over three hundred thousand. The investments are rather volatile, but Mr Hunt didn't mind the risk."

"Except it wasn't his money to risk."

Nick nudged Axel into silence.

"I'm sure he was only making sure that you were looked after," Maureen said. "He always worried that you didn't have a safety net in case your art didn't work out." She didn't mean to sound condescending, but to hear that

Cillian had such little faith in Phoebe's art career felt like another betrayal.

"We can pull the funds whenever you like and put it into a savings account, should you wish," Mr Murray added, but she wasn't sure what to do with her newfound fortune. She had never had more than a thousand in her savings account before. Even with her success, she had only started making a profit on her art this year. Even then, she had been putting it back into her work, renting her studio and supplies.

"The rest of his financial estate and properties are to be left to his mother, Maureen Hunt, to be handled as she sees fit."

Phoebe tuned out for the final details. The band retained the rights to his image, voice, music and masters, which made moving forward a lot easier for them. She heard Anita practically sigh in the corner.

After all was said and done, Phoebe asked the others to leave so she could explain to Cillian's mum exactly who Helen was. She tried to keep it short and sweet, but the words burnt her tongue like she had eaten a spicy pepper and washed it down with sour candies.

She took some comfort in not being interrupted as she explained how she'd found out. Maureen didn't utter a single word, only stared at the burning candle in the centre of the table. It was a lot to digest, burying your son and gaining a grandchild in the same day.

Phoebe noticed Helen lingering by the door, looking rather green, still with a protective hand over her tummy. Maureen followed her gaze.

"I don't believe a word of it," she snarled suddenly, as though seeing Helen made it all real. "My son would never betray you. Even if he made a mistake, he would've told me. I understand why he might not have told you at first—he would've been terrified of losing you. All he did was talk about your future together, you were his everything. Always have been, and now I suppose you always will be."

"I wanted to believe that too, but it's true. If you've any doubts, you can request a paternity test. However, the guys believe her, and from what she has said herself, they were together for months. It wasn't a mistake," Phoebe said, needing her to understand so she wouldn't have to keep repeating the details.

Helen looked like she was about to burst into tears. A bruise was forming nicely where Phoebe had struck her, and Phoebe was mad at herself for losing control, but the balls on this woman were astonishing. But she had a child to provide for now. Cillian's child. For their sake, Phoebe swallowed her pride.

"Cillian is gone, but his child will be born in the next few months," she told his mother. "You should know your grandchild. He would've wanted to make sure the child was looked after. I don't doubt that the child is his, or he wouldn't have put her in his will."

"How can you be so calm? How long have you known about her? About the baby?" Maureen asked, as though accusing her of wrongdoing.

"I only found out in Munich."

"Before the accident." Maureen paled.

"Yes. I learnt about their…" The word 'relationship' choked her. "…situation when I went to their last concert. I only found out she was pregnant today," she finished, wishing she was anywhere but here.

"I don't know what to say." Maureen leaned on the table. Such a shock wasn't good for a woman in her sixties.

"There's nothing to say," Phoebe said, numb to it all.

"My Cillian wouldn't have done this! How could he be

so careless, so cruel—and after how his father treated me. Cheating is the last thing I'd expect from him."

Phoebe hated seeing her like this.

"I wish I had answers for you. I'm still processing everything. But you should give Helen a chance, for the sake of his kid." She didn't want to be the bigger person, but the baby was innocent, and given that Cillian didn't have any siblings, it was the last thing Maureen had of him.

"I don't think I can stand to look at her."

"Give it some time," Phoebe said, unable to fathom how she was defending the woman who had altered the course of their lives.

"How can you be so forgiving?" Maureen snapped, looking for someone, anyone to take her anger out on.

"I'm hurt, angry, disgusted, but I can't yell at him, or throw things, or find out why he did what he did. He's gone, and we're here to make the best of this shitty situation."

"I'm so sorry." Maureen's tone softened and tears glazed her eyes. "You've been like a daughter to me, and to see you treated so breaks my heart. I'd give him a good going over with a wooden spoon if I could."

When their eyes met, they both laughed, only for gentle tears to follow. Maureen had been threatening them with the wooden spoon for most of their lives, but she had far too gentle a constitution to ever act on it.

"Just talk to her, if and when you want to," Phoebe said, taking Maureen's hand. From the corner of her eye, she saw Mr Murray hand Helen an envelope.

"I don't think I can bear it today."

"No one expects you to. Mr Murray will have her information when you're ready," Phoebe assured her, and Maureen nodded slowly.

"You're more forgiving than I. When Cillian's father

left me and started a new family, I couldn't get out of bed for a month. I swear I could've set him on fire."

"Cillian is the one who broke my heart. She's only guilty of falling in love with him."

Phoebe knew how charming Cillian could be. They'd spent so little time together since the tour began, and he hadn't texted or called as much as he used to. Days would go by before they checked in with each other. She'd thought his tour anxiety had lessened, but he had found someone else to comfort him.

"You think she loved him?" Maureen asked, interrupting her thoughts.

"She came to his funeral and faced all of us, alone."

Phoebe's words took a moment to settle in.

"Maybe I should say hi," Maureen said eventually, smoothing her hands over her black skirt.

Phoebe nodded, and Maureen kissed her cheek before leaving the table.

Phoebe took a moment to catch her breath. She didn't care what Cillian had left Helen. If anything it was the only considerate thing he'd done.

"Are you expecting a sainthood in your next life?" Axel said from behind her chair.

Phoebe jumped as his words brushed her ear. "Were you eavesdropping?"

The will revelations had distracted her from thinking about their kiss. He took a seat beside her and scooted closer; she had the overwhelming desire to do it again.

"I didn't mean to. I was hiding behind the door that connects this room to the sitting room," he said gruffly, as though that were a rational thing to do.

"Why were you hiding?" she asked, trying not to stare at his lips.

He twisted a snake-shaped ring on his finger. "One of

the cousins is a big fan, and she keeps following me around asking for my number. This place is too small to hide."

"Poor rockstar can't handle all his adoring fans," she teased.

Axel's expression hardened as she tried to deflect. "Don't change the subject. Why'd you help Helen?"

"I didn't."

Axel distracted her by resting his hand too close to hers. His pinkie finger brushed hers, and suddenly she felt like she was the cheater. She placed her hand on her lap, and he smirked, knowing exactly what he was doing. He wasn't going to let her escape without an answer.

"I helped Cillian's mum." Phoebe rose from her chair and pushed it under the table. "I don't want her to miss out on knowing her grandkid because of her loyalty to me. I didn't do it for Cillian. I did it because she deserves something good after all this."

"You really are too good for him." Axel sighed and walked her to the front door.

"I did feel guilty about her nose," Phoebe admitted, trying to make light of it.

He smirked, and the way he was looking at her made the world feel a little less daunting.

She wasn't sure whether to be glad when Nick called him away, but she took the chance to escape to her apartment, which she now knew she owned. It suddenly felt like everything in her life was tainted by Cillian's secrets.

February turned to March, and Phoebe's new routine was forming nicely. After her post-therapy nap, she walked to her art studio across the road from her apartment. She couldn't paint yet, but she had some prints to package from her website and being in the studio with all her supplies and work made her feel safe. Despite her therapist's advice, she was still napping during the day to help combat her insomnia—her nights were haunted by the recurring nightmare of Cillian reaching for her as paramedics pulled her from the crumpled vehicle. Though, last night, she had dreamt of another event that frightened her, this time involving a beautiful set of red lips and dark eyes. She hadn't mentioned Axel—or his lips —to her therapist because she was too busy celebrating her physio telling her the mobility in her thumb was improving faster than anticipated, and it shouldn't be long before she could start working on holding a pencil or paintbrush again.

As she reached into her bag for her studio keys, a call from Axel lit up her phone. She wanted to share the good news, but she hadn't spoken to her brother or the others since the funeral two weeks ago. She'd been avoiding their calls, especially Axel's. He was taking up enough of her thoughts already. Now wasn't the time for complicated romances.

Her foot crunched on glass on the front step outside the abandoned bookstore turned art studio. She startled, noticing the smashed-in window panels in the front door, which hung ajar.

Why the hell would someone want to break in? She didn't have cash inside, and even if her paintings had tripled in price since the accident thanks to the onslaught of media attention, large canvases wouldn't be easy to take or sell.

Carefully, Phoebe pushed open the door with her sleeve in case there were fingerprints. She flicked on the studio lights, and her blood ran cold. The intruder hadn't been interested in stealing her work, but destroying it. Slowly, she approached her last unfinished commission. The original sketch was of a fire-wrought figure in pink overalls blowing glass over a furnace. A glass artist had commissioned it for their workshop, but now, the word 'IT' had been streaked across the canvas in neon green. Taking a step back, she saw the paintings on the red brick walls were sprayed with 'SHOULD', 'HAVE', 'BEEN'…

She nearly slipped on the paint spattered wooden floor, where she found the final message. 'YOU'.

"You've got to be fucking kidding me?" she muttered to herself as her bag slipped from her shoulder. How could one of Cillian's fans go so far?

The paint on the floor was still wet, which meant whoever did this wasn't gone long. Reaching for her phone to call the police, she heard a scuffle coming from the back. She froze, terrified they might still be here. Ruining a canvas was one thing, breaking and entering another, but the threatening message left her trembling. From her toolbox by a stack of new canvases, she grabbed a box cutter and followed the sound through the small hallway to the storage room and kitchen. The light in the hallway had gone out months ago, and she suddenly regretted not getting it fixed sooner. There was a back door in the kitchen, so she hoped all she had heard was the intruder leaving.

"Come out! I've already called the police!" Phoebe yelled.

She swung open the kitchen door, brandishing the box cutter, hoping to scare off any intruder. Instead, a silhouette advanced on her. She lashed out with a loud cry. A curse and loud hiss caused her to jump back. She opened her eyes to find Axel holding his forearm and cursing wildly.

"Axel? Why are you lurking around my studio in the dark?" she yelled, only to notice the blood on the box cutter.

"Why do you have a knife?" Axel growled, holding his arm.

"You scared the shit out of me!" she said, forgetting about apologising. "It's not a knife, it's a box cutter. And I was scared because you broke in! Did you see the spray-painted message?" Not that she owed him an explanation.

He glared at her like she was the one breaking and entering. "I didn't break in! Nick said you'd probably be here; I was coming to check on you since you aren't answering our calls. When I arrived, the door was open and the window smashed. I came in through the back in case the person was still here," Axel said, examining the cut on his forearm. She had sliced through his jacket to his arm. Not bad, given she couldn't use her dominant hand. Moving around him, she turned on the kitchen light to get a better look.

"Sorry, I panicked, can you please sit down at the

counter? I've got some plasters under the kitchen sink and some disinfectant. I don't think I've ever washed this." She put the box cutter down by the pink kettle. She had plenty of plasters since she always nicked herself putting together canvases.

"It's a scratch, but if you insist," he said, and rolled up his sleeve. Blood seeped from the thin slice but the tattoos hid the damage.

"I do. I don't need fans thinking I'm trying to kill another band member. If they hear that I cut you they might go from spray paint to burning the place down."

"You saw the new posts?" he asked while she grabbed the first aid kit from under the sink.

"You mean the ones accusing me of using his death to make money because people have been reselling my latest collection at triple the price? I'm well able to make my own way without him." She felt better getting it off her chest.

"I'm sorry you had to see that. We hoped you hadn't." He looked at her like she was spiralling. Phoebe heard 'we', but the look in his eye told her '*me*'.

"Did the others send you? Sorry I didn't answer a few texts and calls, but you didn't need to send in the cavalry. Speaking of cavalry, I should call the police," she said, dabbing the blood away from the wound with cotton wool and some disinfectant.

"I sent myself, and don't worry, I called the police when I first arrived. If you'd have answered your phone, you'd have known that," he said as she took his hand in hers. He held her hand tighter as she secured the dinosaur plaster.

"Big baby, it doesn't need stitches." She smirked. "The cartoons really go with your tattoos."

"Really brings out my bad boy persona." He pulled down his sleeve.

"Thank you for calling the police. I got distracted by the mess. I never expected someone to go this far."

"They should be here soon," he said, taking a seat across from her.

The silence threatened to drown her as the space filled up with all they wanted to say.

"Can I ask if you've been avoiding me since the funeral? Is it because of what happened?" he asked, cutting to the point.

This is why he came here, not because I hadn't been replying, she thought, remaining on the other side of the kitchen table.

"It wasn't because of what happened between us," she said, putting the bloody cotton wool in the bin. "I needed some breathing room and I've been focusing on my physio and keeping up with my orders to distract me from all the chaos online."

When she turned around, her eyes landed on her purple notebook in his hand. Instantly, she forgot about the spray paint, the break-in, even their kiss.

"Why do you have that?" A cold sweat caused her to shiver. "I thought I lost that in the accident."

It was the only remaining evidence that she had helped write their songs. She wondered what the fans who hated her would think of their precious Cillian if they knew he had been taking credit for her work for years. All the lyrics they quoted, screamed at concerts, sang in the shower and tattooed on their skin were hers, not his. Well, theirs.

"I came here to tell you that we need each other." Axel put the notebook on the paint-splattered table beside them. The kitchen was the best place to mix paints, even if it made the room look like a Jackson Pollock painting. She listened. "You clearly need protection, and the band needs songs. Anita is trying her best to hold off the label, but they want to use all the publicity to their advantage." Axel's words dripped with disgust.

"Death is free advertising. But why come to me? Everything you need is in there." Phoebe scoffed, putting the cap back on the disinfectant. At least the police were on the way so Axel couldn't stay long. She wanted to start cleaning up the mess outside.

"Because you left this in my tour bus that day—"

She cut him off. "I didn't write them alone. The lyrics, yes, but Cillian did the arranging with you guys. Keep the notebook, use it as you please." She backed away like the notebook was a weapon.

"Were you ever going to tell the band you've been writing their songs?" he asked, following her until she backed into the fridge.

'Were you ever going to tell me my dead fiancé was cheating on me?"

He took a deep breath at that.

"Sorry, that wasn't fair," she said. They had all apologised enough.

"I think him taking credit for your work is worse than cheating," Axel added, giving her some space as he went to stand by the sink.

"Spoken like a man who has never been in love." She crossed her arms over her chest, and he waited for her to continue. "I didn't want the credit. Seeing him happy on stage, singing our songs was reward enough."

"Loving you would've meant giving you the credit you deserved," Axel huffed, putting his jacket back on. "If we'd known, we wouldn't have given Cillian so many chances. The reason we thought he was acting out, drinking, partying, was because of the pressure the studio had him under to produce a new album, but it was you writing them this whole time."

"Have you told the others?" Phoebe said, afraid of what he would say.

"No, but can you tell me why you had it that night in Munich?"

"I wanted to surprise him with the finished songs. It took me longer than expected to add the final touches because of my art show," she confessed, and it felt good to tell the truth. "I didn't realise the toll it was taking on Cillian. This was the only time he relied on my input so much."

"He was partying it up while you were doing his work for him," Axel scoffed, his leg bouncing.

"Can you stop making this worse? I hate him enough at the minute already," she snapped.

"Sorry, but I've got to tell the others. They deserve to know, and I won't continue this lie. Nick would kill me if he found out that I'd kept this from him."

"They're grieving, you can't put this on them. Why can't you leave it alone?" she asked, not wanting him to complicate her life any further.

Axel hesitated. "I won't tell them for now, but we have to tell them at some point. Cillian doesn't deserve to have us lying for him anymore."

Phoebe couldn't argue. Though she wondered if he was being so hard on Cillian because of his own grief. They had never been super close, but after five years living in the same house and being on the road together, they had a brotherly bond—and that didn't always mean they had to like each other.

"How can you be okay with someone, anyone, using your work?" he asked softly. "What if someone was copying your artwork and reselling it?"

There was no point in discussing something he couldn't understand. She went to him and took his hand.

"Please just use the songs, I don't care what you do with them. I don't want anything, please just take it, and think of it as a gift. Happy birthday and Christmas," she added, trying to get him to accept it so they could move on. "It's only one more album, and if you don't take it, then you'll have to face Anita with no songs. You've got enough to deal with without having to come up with a new album. Just say thank you."

Axel studied their joined hands. He stared at the long scar along her thumb, and he let out a sigh. "I can't say no to you. So, thank you," he conceded, putting the notebook back inside his jacket. "But you have to agree that we will tell them?"

She nodded eagerly. "Not now, but soon."

Axel took her breath away as he kissed the back of her hand. The feel of his lips against her sensitive nerves made her light up—he wasn't grossed out by her scar. She turned his hand, and much to his amusement, kissed his palm, calloused from years of drumming.

"We've shook on it, so no take backs," he said.

"No take backs." She released him as the electricity became too much. "The last thing to do is to clean up. You've bled all over my floor." She grabbed a towel to clean up the droplets.

"Remind me to never surprise you again," he grumbled.

"Are you going to help?" She tossed him a rag. "I don't want the police coming in and seeing the blood."

"The police are the least of our concerns," he muttered under his breath.

The sound of footsteps echoing down the hall interrupted them. The police had arrived. Voices called out their names.

"Maybe we shouldn't have called them," Phoebe fretted, putting the towel on the counter. "I don't want the break-in to get leaked to the press. Getting the police involved only draws attention." She was afraid of what the headlines would be. That, and she had her own plans to find out who did this.

"Someone broke in, and they deserve to be punished. This is about your safety. Even if it gets leaked, the intruder might get spooked and back off," Axel said, resting his hands on her shoulders. She stared up at him, knowing he was right.

Axel guided her out of the kitchen, and they found two stern-looking police officers looking over the studio.

"Axel Adler? You called about an intruder?" the officer with red hair and a long beard said, squaring his shoulders as Axel shook his hand.

"Yes, thank you for coming," Axel said. "I got here about thirty minutes ago, and I noticed the broken window in the door. I went around back to see if I could catch the person, but they were already gone."

The officer looked to Phoebe. She felt that was her cue to continue.

"I noticed the door, and came in to turn on the light. That's when I saw the threatening message on the canvases and the floor," she added, feeling like she was back in the hospital in Munich being questioned. She had seen enough uniforms to last a lifetime.

Thankfully, the red-headed officer didn't seem to care who he was interviewing as he took down the details of the break-in. It was the female officer with a pixie cut who offered them her condolences, and that damn slanted smile that made Phoebe want to roll her eyes.

"Do you want to go to the hospital?" the redhead asked, looking at Axel's torn jacket. "Did the intruder injure you?"

"No, I don't," he said firmly. "As I said, whoever broke in was already gone."

"How did you get injured?" The officer arched a brow.

"I cut him," Phoebe admitted, not wanting to draw out the interview any longer than necessary. "It was an accident, I thought he was the intruder. The light is out in the hallway to the kitchen, and I couldn't see that it was him."

"Right, and you don't need medical attention?" the redhead asked again, while the other officer examined the door.

"Phoebe already took care of it," Axel said, holding his arm.

"Has anything been taken?" the male officer asked Phoebe, taking notes on a tiny pad that looked comical in his large hand. The woman had moved on to taking pictures of the ruined artwork.

"No, I don't think so. They slashed some canvases, and graffitied my work," she explained. "Put the paintings together and it spells out 'it should have been you'."

"Have you received any threatening messages prior to this?" he asked, looking up when she hesitated. He looked between them like he already knew the answer.

"There has been some negative media attention about me recently. Mostly just internet trolls." Since the officers were fans, she didn't need to elaborate.

The officer nodded solemnly, like he understood.

"My agent, Lena, is handling my social media at the minute so I'm not sure of any specific messages or threats."

Axel scowled as she brushed over the topic. She wasn't going to mention the calls her parents had received.

"Have your agent take screenshots of the accounts and the messages, in case they delete their accounts or things escalate," the officer instructed.

"Judging from the state of her studio, things have already escalated," Axel interrupted.

Phoebe pulled at the corner of his jacket, not wanting his tone to get him in trouble.

"I understand you're upset, but you need to keep a level head," the officer said, closing his pad. "We'll find who did this." He looked between them. "What is your relationship?"

Phoebe didn't like the implication in his tone, the way his gaze shifted between them as though they were guilty of something.

"She's my best friend's sister," Axel said gruffly. "Why does it matter?"

"Sir, I'm only trying to get a better understanding of the situation. These are routine questions," the officer said curtly. "Ms Fletcher, do you live with anyone?"

"No—I live alone, in the apartment building across the road." Phoebe wondered if 'escalating' meant they'd come to her home next.

The officers glanced at one another solemnly.

"Given that you live across the street, I'd suggest you stay with someone for the time being," the man said. "Better to err on the side of caution, given your notoriety and connections."

"Is that necessary? I doubt whoever did this even knows where I live. My studio is publicly listed for clients," she argued, feeling Axel's heavy gaze on her. *This is exactly what he wanted. Ammunition to get me to move in.*

"We can't force you to follow our suggestions, but it wouldn't be hard for people to find out where you live. If you decide to remain at home, here is my number. If you hear or see anything or anyone strange, please don't hesitate to call," the officer said.

"Thank you, I will." Phoebe doubted if there was

anything to be done. At least no one was hurt and everything in the studio was insured.

"And I'd suggest you install some cameras. We'll request the street cams, but their view won't be perfect." The female officer smiled tightly.

"I'll get on it," Phoebe said. "I have to change the locks and have the door fixed anyway."

"Right, well, we'll leave you now and contact you again if we have any updates or questions," the officer finished, having taken photos and prints from the door.

Phoebe was amazed they left without asking for Axel's autograph, though the bearded officer had looked like he was on the verge of asking before his partner called him away. Once the officers were gone, Axel helped her collect all she needed to take home from the studio without complaint. She accepted his help gratefully as she wanted to get out as quickly as possible. He carried the boxes outside and waited for her while she pulled down the rarely used shutter. She had never thought she would need to use it. She bolted it with a padlock, hoping that would prevent anyone getting in again.

"I can help you pack up what you want to bring back to mine. I brought my car with me, so pack as much as you like," Axel said, helping Phoebe with her boxes up the stairs to her apartment.

"I'm not going back to your place. I've got the officer's number, and I'm not going to be run out of my own home." She paused on a step to take her prints from him and tuck them under her arm. Though she was relieved he'd insisted on seeing her to her door, she didn't want to let on that she was afraid that the person who'd broken in might be waiting for her.

"Fine, then I'll stay with you," Axel said, like him staying in her apartment was no big deal.

"Sorry, I only have one bedroom, and the couch isn't long enough for a man of your size." She stared up at him defiantly as he blocked her path.

His eyes darkened, and she tried not to let her gaze settle on his lips as he leaned in closer. "I don't mind sharing a bedroom, if you don't."

"If you think seducing me is going to make me give in, you're sorely mistaken."

"I was talking about taking the floor, but I can work on the seduction if you prefer," he teased.

"You're infuriating," she said, ducking under his arm.

"Now you know how I feel. I'm supposed to be at the recording studio right now, but I can't leave because you refuse to see reason."

Phoebe rolled her eyes and continued up the stairs.

"Don't roll your eyes at me! I'm only trying to help, and more importantly, keep you safe."

Turning to face him, Phoebe slipped on the step. He dropped the boxes of paints and prints to catch her. Face to face, she noticed the flecks of green in his eyes, and his sweet, smoky cologne tempted her to forget what they were arguing about.

"Why are you so insistent on helping me? Is it guilt for letting me go that day? Because you don't have to feel guilty—I made my own decisions, so please free yourself." She tried to shove him, but she'd have had more luck shoving a brick wall.

"Don't push me away," he grumbled. "This has nothing to do with guilt. I need you to be safe, and the longer you ignore me, the more insane I get. I haven't stopped obsessing over that kiss. I came to find you today not because you were ignoring us, but because I needed to see you." He held her close, and the desperation in his words tightened her chest. She didn't know what to say; her lips parted but no words came out.

"You're looking at me like you did that day." He caressed her cheek, running his thumb along her jaw. She blushed, nervous under his intense gaze.

Unable to stop herself, she wrapped her arms around his neck and pressed her lips against his. She gasped as his hand slipped into her hair, and the taste of him overwhelmed her.

"Bee, please come home with me. I need to keep you close."

He moaned, gripping the back of her neck as she bit him in rebellion. He liked to call her 'Bee', so she might as well sting.

"Don't ruin the moment. Just kiss me," she ordered.

He gripped her hips, pulling her against him harshly. There wasn't an inch between them. He deepened the kiss as she groaned. His smile against her lips made her giddy, loving how he responded to her. His hard body pushed her up against the wall, and she dropped the prints, not caring as they fell on the staircase. She fisted his jacket, trying to steady herself as she reached up on her tiptoes.

She'd never acted this way, like all the anger was pouring out of her and turning into something much sweeter. His hand travelled down her waist to the hem of her skirt, squeezing her thigh as he feasted on her neck. He invaded her senses, and her hand slipped under his T-shirt and he gasped as she explored the smooth planes of his body. She forgot where they were as she felt his rough hand reach under her skirt between her thighs.

"You had to be wearing tights. I want to tear these fucking things off," he rasped.

She rested her head against the wall to brace herself, wishing he'd stop teasing her mercilessly. The sound of footsteps echoing up the staircase reminded her how exposed they were. Axel stilled, then put her skirt back in place. She blushed, removing her hands from him, and tugged playfully at his T-shirt. Luckily there weren't any cameras in the stairwell.

"You need to go," Phoebe panted as he tipped her chin up to face him. She didn't want him to go. He let out a long exhale, and she hoped he wouldn't argue.

How could something feel so right but be so wrong? He wasn't only her brother's best friend, but her ex's frenemy, and she couldn't get enough. Those dark eyes, and strong hands—he was the opposite of Cillian's boy-next-door charm.

Phoebe distracted herself from her thoughts by picking up the prints they had dropped.

"I won't push you to move in, but if anything happens… call me or the guys, please," Axel said, helping her clean up the mess without prompting.

"I promise." She glanced at him, unable to suppress her smile when she caught him staring.

They walked to her door in silence. She wished she knew what he was thinking.

"Can you do me a favour?" she asked as he placed the boxes inside her apartment. "Don't tell Nick about the break-in before I do? I don't want him to worry."

"And you swear that you'll tell him?" he countered.

"Cross my heart. If I tell him now then he'll be the one dragging me back to your place, and I need some time to think," she said, needing some time to process.

Axel put his hands in the pockets of his black jeans. "Fine, I'll give you twenty-four hours, because if they find out that I let you stay here alone after what someone did to your studio, Nick and August will shove my drumsticks where the sun doesn't shine."

"Shake on it?" she asked, wanting his word. Trust didn't come as easy as it once had.

"Don't trust me?" He arched a brow as he stared at her hand.

"I'm having trouble trusting anyone at the minute."

"You can trust me." Axel took her hand gently, careful not to hurt her.

"Be safe, and please call me, for anything," he said, kissing her hand. It was becoming a habit.

"You have my word." If she didn't let him go now, she wouldn't. He smirked as though reading her thoughts.

Phoebe closed the door before she was tempted to invite him back inside. It was the perfect boundary they needed. She chewed her lip as she watched him hesitate outside the peephole before heading back down the stairs.

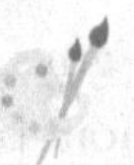

ONCE AXEL HAD LEFT, Phoebe put her art prints on the couch and opened her laptop on the coffee table. She had neglected to tell the police and Axel about the nanny cams she had installed in a painting hanging by the entrance to the studio. She had every inch covered; given the threats, she wasn't going to leave herself unprotected. A few days after the funeral, Lena had helped her install them because the insurance company demanded more security given her increased notoriety. They hadn't got around to installing an alarm system yet—it was an old building and it would be a big job that required rewiring. None of the contractors they had called had had any time in their immediate schedules for the project, no matter how much they offered to pay.

Phoebe scrolled through the footage while she iced her hand. She was trying to rely less on the painkillers and stick to ice. The spasms had increased because she had been clenching her fist.

"Show me your face," Phoebe muttered to herself, squinting at the screen.

She scrolled to the time of Axel's arrival and watched him walk around the back. She scrolled back in time, wishing she had installed some automatic lights to come on when someone entered the studio, because the streetlamp outside wasn't helping.

"There you are," she muttered as a hooded figure

appeared on the front steps. They looked around before breaking the window to let themselves in. "Clever enough to hide their face, and wear gloves."

Clenching her jaw, she watched the intruder tear up her studio, ruining canvas after canvas. She ran her hand through her hair as hours of her work disappeared before her. *So much for having enough paintings left over for my two remaining shows. Four of my largest canvases gone—I'll just have to fill up the space with smaller works. Maybe Lena was right about considering cancelling the next two shows...* but she didn't want to let the trolls win. Her leg bounced as she waited for a glimpse of something that would lead her to the person responsible.

"Turn around, show me that face," she pleaded, watching the intruder leave.

The idiot couldn't help but glance back at their own masterpiece.

"Bingo." Phoebe smiled.

Zooming in, she got a better look at his blurry face. He was probably in his early thirties, pale and eyes a little too far apart. There was nothing familiar about him. It was incredible to her that someone she didn't know could hate her so much to risk getting in trouble with the law.

Once she got a screenshot of his face, she watched him walk back to a red jeep and drive off without a care in the world.

She called the band's head of security for help identifying the intruder. "Olivier? It's Phoebe. Sorry to call you, I know it's late."

"Hi Phoebe. No need to apologise, I was just getting in from a job. Is everything alright?" She heard traffic in the background.

"Could you help me find someone?" she asked, not

wasting any time with small talk. "I have a picture but it's blurry, and a picture of their jeep."

Olivier was the only one who could help her without having to reach out to the police. She wanted to look the person who'd done this in the eye and dare them to spew their hate to her face. Only a coward hid in the shadows.

"Are you in trouble? Is someone harassing you?"

"Nothing to worry about. Just a small incident at the studio," she said, removing the ice from her frozen hand. She flexed her fingers as she added the screenshots to an email.

"Okay, if you say so," he said hesitantly, but he didn't ask anything more. "Send me the photos and I'll reach out to some people."

Olivier wasn't one for conversation, but he had been protecting the band since their first headline concert and there was no one else she trusted more. She couldn't imagine how he felt losing Cillian. He would never have let them through the gate that day in Munich, but he had been on leave.

"I'm sending you a photo. Could you see if you recognise him from any of the fan signings or concerts? I know you keep a file on the crazies. If you could check, I'd really appreciate it."

"Got your email. I'll message you when I have something."

She cheered silently. "Thank you. Could you keep this between us? I don't want Nick to worry about nothing."

"Alright, but do *I* need to be worried? I can have someone watch the apartment." When they had left the airport, he had suggested getting security for her building, even if it was just someone driving by from time to time.

"No, that's not necessary. I just want to find them," she

said, and Olivier muttered something she couldn't make out.

"Right, I got the email you sent. I should have something for you soon."

He hung up with a quick goodbye. Phoebe stared at the culprit on the screen and smirked.

"I've got you now."

Three days of wandering around her apartment, waiting for answers, had her itching to create. She dealt with stress by painting, and this was the longest she had ever gone without a paintbrush in her hand. Without it, she felt like she might crack; she couldn't count the number of times she had checked her phone, waiting for Olivier to call. She had run out of things to clean, and even packed up Cillian's belongings. She kept their photo albums, donated some clothes and sent the rest to his mum. Her confidence had taken a dive since the funeral and she felt guilty for not having checked in on Maureen, but she didn't feel right calling. Phoebe didn't want to hear about how she was getting to know her grandchild's mother.

After Axel had talked about staying at hers, she realised how the space still felt like *theirs* instead of *hers*. She wasn't doing anything wrong by having a man in the apartment, but with Cillian's things around, it had felt like she was. It was time to make the space hers again.

She had decided to pack up her studio. Even with the locks changed, it didn't feel safe to go there. Lena agreed and sent movers she trusted to help.

As Phoebe was putting her breakfast dishes in the sink, her phone finally rang.

"Hello? Phoebe?" Olivier asked as she fumbled it in her desperation to grab it from the couch.

"Yes, yes! I'm here," she said, without a shred of subtlety.

"I've got the information you're looking for. I'm sorry it took me a few days. The man's name is Gunther Sheen. He attempted to get in to see you in the hospital in Munich, but security turned him away. Security got his details after he kept hounding nurses for information."

She couldn't believe this stranger had tried to get into her hospital room.

"Do you have any other information?" she asked, hoping for an address or a place of employment. She could track him down online, but Olivier was one step ahead.

"Gunther tried to get access to the hospital in Munich by showing a work ID for LouderTech, explaining that he worked for the band and had business to discuss. Apparently, he works with them?"

"LouderTech? The music production company?" She frowned. Their office was only a thirty-minute drive from her apartment. "Didn't they organise a festival Brothers of Anarchy headlined last summer?"

Maybe he'd met the band and got a little too attached? Wouldn't be the first time.

"Metal and Gunpowder was the festival, but he's rather low on the totem pole to have any close interaction with the guys. LouderTech received several VIP tickets for the concert in Munich and other European dates, but it's hard to know who the passes went to or if he was one of them."

Phoebe knew it wasn't strange for B.O.A.'s management to give out tickets to companies they worked with, wanted to work with, or celebrities. *Maybe Mr Sheen came to the hospital to offer his help in a time of need in hopes of getting closer to the band and when he was turned away, he got angry? He broke into my studio to vent?*

"Axel told me about the break-in." Olivier disrupted her thoughts. "If you want me to send someone over to watch the apartment or the studio, I can. I kept my promise not to tell the band about the pictures, but I hope you aren't planning on doing anything stupid."

Phoebe put Olivier on loudspeaker as she ordered a taxi. "He shouldn't have worried you. I'm going to pass on the information to the police." It was only half a lie. "I'll be fine, and thank you again for your help."

"Look after yourself. We're here if you need us," Olivier assured her, and she hung up before guilt got the better of her.

Looking at herself in her bedroom mirror, she knew she wouldn't get into an office building in her sweatpants and fluffy headband. She threw on a granny square jumper and jeans with her white trainers, but tying the laces took her longer than she cared to admit. Some mascara and lip gloss helped her pass as an employee, or at least an intern. She packed a sports bag with a few necessities and hurried downstairs to the waiting taxi.

All through the ride over to the LouderTech building in the heart of the city, she considered turning around and giving the information to the police. However, when the driver pulled over into the taxi rank just down the street from the offices, she found herself getting out. She was sick of people doing whatever the hell they wanted and getting away with it.

A pretty smile got her through the initial security barrier without a second glance. The weight of the paint can in her bag was uncomfortably heavy on her shoulder, but she tried to walk as naturally as possible. Though her lilac hair had faded, she was terrified one of the employees heading into work would recognise her, given how much she had been in the press. Luckily, this was the last place they would expect her to be, and no one batted an eye.

Her heart pounded as she slipped into the underground car park through the delivery entrance. After the morning rush, the staff car park was painfully quiet, but she couldn't chicken out now. She couldn't paint, but Gunther Sheen was about to learn how creative she could be. At the end of the second row, by the elevators, the sight of his jeep made her giddy. The shiny, bright red paint was free of scratches or dents, begging to be destroyed.

From her sports bag, she pulled out the bucket of yellow paint. It was a bit of a struggle getting it open, but revenge spurred her on. Her physiotherapist would have been proud of her for pushing herself.

She could have smashed the windscreen, popped a tire, but that all seemed too obvious. Standing in front of the car, she made sure no one was around before she pushed the bucket of paint up onto the roof. Luck was on her side when no alarm sounded. *We're off to a good start.*

Hopping up onto the bonnet wasn't easy, and she fought back a loud curse when she leaned too much pressure on her right hand. Still, she got on the roof, putting some nice dents in the metal work. She wobbled a little and grabbed the crowbar she'd rested on the windshield wipers.

Windscreen or sunroof? She asked herself. *Let's go with the sunroof. Why ruin such a pretty paint job?*

Channelling every inch of rage from the past weeks into one good swing, she shoved the crowbar into the sunroof. *My god, does it feel good to hit something,* she thought as adrenaline rushed through her.

The sound echoed off the concrete, and she cringed. She froze, waiting for someone to come running. When no one arrived, a nervous chuckle escaped her. *The gods must think he deserves this,* she decided. It took two hard swings to hear the satisfactory crackle of glass falling into the front seat.

Perfect! She smirked, taking a long, deep breath of petrol-scented air. She barely even felt the pain in her hand, but she feared its return once the adrenaline wore off. She would have to make this worth it. Staring through the destroyed sunroof, she admired the interior. A pop of colour would make all the difference to the black leather and brushed suede trim.

"Least the yellow will complement the red exterior."

She picked up the tin and poured the thick yellow paint inside. Long streams of paint bounced and spattered against the chairs and dash, filling every nook and cranny, soaking into the carpet and finishings nicely. She made sure the mess was contained to the car; she didn't want anyone to have to clean up her revenge. When the last drop landed, Phoebe considered the deed done.

Her shoulders relaxed as she went to get down, only for the glare of headlights to blind her. Her hand shot up to protect her eyes. She was surprised how calm she felt. She didn't care about getting in trouble; she was content with her destruction. Her luck had to run out at some point.

She squinted in the harsh light, and put the empty can down on the roof.

Phoebe stared at him like a deer caught in the literal headlights.

"Are you out of your mind?" Axel didn't bother parking before getting out.

She swayed, surprised. He cringed, afraid she would fall off the roof, but in the dimly lit garage, destruction looked good on her.

"Morning Axel, fancy seeing you here?" Phoebe said, kicking the paint can into the car as though trying to hide evidence.

"Olivier told me I might find you here, but not on top of the jeep with a crowbar in your hand." He sighed, walking around the jeep to stand under her just in case she fell. "I should've tossed you over my shoulder and dragged you back to my house the other day. I'd hoped with some time, you'd come to your senses and accept our help. Instead, you put yourself in more danger by going on a revenge rampage. Still, I'm impressed you managed to get up there."

"How'd Olivier know I'd be here?" she asked, twisting the crowbar in her hands as she ignored his rant.

"Get off the car, Bee. We're leaving before you get arrested."

He wished her vengeful spirit didn't turn him on so much.

"I'm not going to be arrested. How'd you know I was here?"

"Olivier had someone from our security team posted outside your apartment, and when I got there this morning to check on you, they said you'd left in a taxi. All it took was a call to Olivier to find out what you were up to."

He stepped closer, and her smile widened.

"Ah ah. Another step and I take off the side mirror," she threatened. "I'm a big girl, Axel, I can take care of myself. If I wanted you involved in this, I would have called."

"I can see that." He backed off a little. "Olivier told me that you'd promised to pass on the information about the intruder to the police."

"Given their attitudes at the break-in, I don't think what happened at my studio was high up on their list of priorities, and I wanted to send Mr Sheen a clear message: leave me the hell alone."

"I suspected you were coming here to confront him, maybe get him fired."

"I don't want to get him fired. He destroyed my work, so I thought I'd give his jeep a custom job." She would have sounded rational if it wasn't for the yellow paint dripping out of the doors. "We saw how much he loves neon, so I thought yellow would be the best choice."

"Okay, you've had your fun." He offered her his hand. "Let me help you down, and we can get out of here before we are arrested."

"I'm not done yet." Phoebe picked up the crowbar.

Smashing up the car would attract too much attention. It wouldn't be long before the sound drew security.

"Look at the gearbox—it's probably not ever going to

run again. It's ruined, let's go," he reasoned, but she shook her head.

"Bee, get off the car and let's go!" Axel smacked his hand on the hood in frustration.

"Careful." She pointed the crowbar at him. "Those hands are expensive, and I wouldn't want to be accused of harming another band member."

"Have you been drinking? This isn't like you."

Or maybe all that bottled-up anger was finally coming out.

"Maybe this is the new me. A me who is taking back control."

He scrubbed his hands over his face and took a deep breath. "Sorry, I didn't mean to shout, but can you please come down? You can do as much destruction as you want, but you being up there is making me nervous."

Phoebe's expression softened, and he thought she was considering it.

"What the hell are you doing to my car?" a man interrupted, appearing behind them.

Given the wide eyes and rigid expression, this was the owner of the vehicle. His thick, rosy skin meant he either drank too much or spent too much time in the sun. Axel winced under Gunther Sheen's astonished gaze; he didn't like being gawked at.

"Making a masterpiece, Mr Sheen." Phoebe bowed, drawing Sheen's attention. Axel tried not to enjoy her theatrics. "Since you like my artwork enough to break into my studio, I thought I'd gift you a personal commission."

"You're a fucking lunatic. I'm calling the police," Sheen barked, reaching for his phone in his beige corduroy trousers. "Axel, Mr Adler, you should get away from her. She's deranged."

Phoebe let out a howl of laughter. Axel wished they'd left when they had the chance.

"You don't have to call the police, we can settle this," he said, not wanting this splashed all over the papers tomorrow.

"Axel, butt out, or your car is next," Phoebe warned.

Axel raised his hands in defeat, but he didn't move too far from her. She shot him a look that read, *Aren't you a knight in shining armour?*

"Please go ahead and call the police," Phoebe said with a smirk, stepping down from the roof to the bonnet. Her rage kept her steady.

Sheen hesitated with his phone in hand as he realised the position he was in.

"Why the hesitation? Call the police." Phoebe looked to Axel, telling him she knew he wouldn't. "I'd love to tell them that I've found the person who ruined my studio. Threatened me, stalked me, the list just goes on. Damage to your car? I'll get a fine, and a slap on the wrist, but the cost of what you did to my studio and the threats—that's a far more serious charge."

"You've got no proof." Mr Sheen's nostrils flared.

"I've a wonderful shot of you admiring your destruction as you left the gallery. If the police find out, at best you'll be forced to pay me back. It'll cost you far more than replacing or fixing your jeep." Phoebe jumped down onto the concrete.

Axel stared at her proudly.

"Fucking bitch," Sheen snarled, squaring up to her. Before Axel could get between them, Phoebe swung the crowbar, planting a shot between Sheen's legs. An agonising groan escaped him as he fell to his knees. Axel cringed, but figured a good crotch shot might make him think twice about trying to intimidate another woman.

"I'm so sorry, the nerves in my hand are messed up," Phoebe said. "Sometimes it has a life of its own."

Axel knew she was lying. He leaned against his own car, letting her have her moment before he dragged her back to his place and didn't let her out of his sight.

"Sadly—what was it you said, it should have been me who died in the accident? Well, it wasn't, and to redo the work you destroyed, I'd feel the pain you're feeling now with every brush stroke." Phoebe crouched down to get a better look at Sheen's twisted expression. Seeing her get so close to the man who had hurt her made Axel nervous.

"If I can apologise, then I think you should be able to. Now, we can both consider ourselves even, and we can go our separate ways." She glanced over her shoulder, and winked at Axel, who couldn't hide his bemused smile. He didn't dare intervene. This was her battle, and she wanted to take every inch of satisfaction she could from this piece of garbage.

"Still nothing to say?" Phoebe sighed, staring down at him on the ground. "I'm disappointed, but I can be the bigger person. If you ever come near me, my studio, my family or friends ever again, you can forget about being able to bring any more self-entitled pricks into the world."

There was a long pause. Axel got the feeling this guy wasn't used to women getting the best of him. Axel thought he was in love.

"Agreed?" Phoebe said sharply, putting her crowbar in her bag.

Mr Sheen nodded, but made no attempt to stand.

"Great. I wish I could say that it was lovely to meet you, but I'm glad we could come to a fair resolution."

Phoebe started to walk away, and Axel wished she would get in the car so they could put this all behind them.

However, a vicious laugh echoed from Sheen as he got to his knees.

"You're so clueless," he sneered. "I was paid to do it, and now I think you deserved it." Sheen clutched his crotch, glaring fire at her.

Phoebe shot a look at Axel that made his stomach twist.

"What do you mean you were paid? By who?" she asked, while Sheen smiled smugly, like he had won.

"I don't know and I don't care. There was an envelope on my desk with five grand in cash and a note with instructions. It was easy money."

"Do you still have it? The instructions, the envelope?" Axel asked. Phoebe went silent behind him, pacing back and forth.

"No, I'm not an idiot," he scoffed. Axel begged to differ. "I trashed them. Once it was done, I got another envelope of money."

"Why did you try to get in to see me in Munich?" Phoebe asked, and Axel's ears perked up—this was news to him.

"I was trying to get the scoop, to get information, and none of the band would leave your side. When I got home, the envelope was on my desk. Sorry, but you're nobody compared to them." He didn't get to finish before Axel grabbed him by his shirt and shoved him against his jeep with a yelp.

"Don't you dare talk to her like that. You've just cost yourself a job. I hate singing, but I'll make sure to sound extra pretty when I make sure no music company, PR firm, or McDonald's hires you ever again. I hope you enjoy that money, because it's the last you'll see for a while. I suggest you go back upstairs and pack up your desk. By the time the elevator dings, you'll be blacklisted from every company that matters."

Phoebe rested her hand on Axel's back, settling his rage. "Let him go, he isn't worth it."

"You ever speak her name, or even think about her, I'll rip your tongue out," Axel warned him, his blood hot with rage.

"I'm not the one you should be worried about," Sheen said. He slid down the jeep when Axel released him.

Axel made sure not to turn his back on him on his way back to his car.

"You might want to crack a window before driving," Phoebe said to Sheen as she took Axel's hand. "I wouldn't want you to pass out at the wheel from the fumes."

Axel stared at her, silently thanking her for calming him down before he'd done something he wouldn't even regret, but would have resulted in him having to call Anita to bail them out of jail.

"Close your mouth, or you'll catch flies," she teased.

"Sorry, I was wondering who you were and what you've done with Phoebe," Axel said as she walked to the passenger side of his car without argument.

"Nobody messes with my art, or the people I love. My dad raised me to finish the fight," she said as they got in the car. "Please take me home," she asked, sinking into the chair.

"Absolutely. Nick is getting the spare room ready for you."

There was no way he was letting her go back to her apartment. The break-in at the studio might not have been her last straw, but this was his.

"And why is my brother getting a spare room ready for me?" He felt her staring at him.

"Because you decided it was a good idea to go after a crazed fan who was paid by God knows who to trash your studio. We've lost Cillian, and the last thing we want and need right now is to be worried about you. So, you're going to stay with us until we can figure out who's behind this."

"You shouldn't believe a word he said," Phoebe said, securing her seatbelt. "I bet he was lying. Just a coward's way of trying to frighten us, keep us paranoid."

"Lying or not, you're coming back to the house with me."

"Do I have a say in this?" she asked as they left the car park.

"You have a say in whether you want to pack or if I'll have to do it for you."

"And if I say no?" she huffed, and he noticed her rubbing her scarred hand in the same spot where he got carpal tunnel after a show. After all the exertion, he guessed it had to hurt. Now that the scar had healed, he made a mental note to give her some of the herbal wraps his acupuncturist gave him when his wrist wanted to give up mid-tour. They were magic.

"Are you listening to me?" Phoebe waved a hand in front of his face, interrupting his thoughts.

"If you don't come willingly, then I've been instructed to take you home." He shrugged.

"I've got my own home where I'll be perfectly safe."

"Home is where your family is. Nick and August are your family. What you did today left us with little choice. Please don't make this harder for me, I'm only following orders, and there is no way you're going back to your apartment with this new information—your brother would kill me."

Unable to reach a middle ground, they fell silent. The drive to the house that overlooked the Irish Sea felt like an eternity. Axel dialled in the code at the gate, and they drove through. Much to his relief, Phoebe didn't try and jump out before it closed. They turned down a short driveway lined with bushes to protect them from paps trying to pry. They reached the garage doors and Axel hit the button on his keys to open it.

"I'm not getting out of the car," Phoebe said, and he wished she wouldn't be so stubborn.

"Suit yourself, you can stay here. I must warn you that it gets awfully cold in here at night. There's a blanket in the trunk if you want to make yourself cosy." Axel climbed out of the car, not up for an argument. She would come in eventually.

"I don't need to be here," she said through the window.

He hesitated on the stairs that connected the garage to the house. "It's only for a little while." Before she could argue, he added, "Come inside or I'll tell Nick about the jeep incident."

Phoebe's eyes narrowed. "You wouldn't dare."

"Try me," Axel said, opening the passenger door.

Phoebe groaned, but finally got out of the car. Then she froze. He followed her gaze, and cursed internally. Cillian's car. She hurried into the house without a word. He pulled at the back of his neck; he had forgotten how many reminders of Cillian were in the house. However, right now her safety trumped her feelings.

When Axel reached the kitchen, August was standing by the sink doing the dishes, looking confused.

"Where'd she go?" Axel asked him.

"Guest house," August said, pointing to the gardens.

He huffed. Was she going to make him chase her? The thought made him happier than it should have. She was a welcome distraction from the others' grief and his own, and she was wearing those jeans that hugged in all the right places.

The garden was empty, but the sliding door to the guest house was open. The glass house's windows tinted as the day wore on, and it had the best view on the property except for Nick's balcony on the second floor.

Axel shivered at the cool breeze coming off the sea below. He closed the sliding door behind him and walked through the open-plan guest house and down a short corridor to the pool room. The smell of chlorine greeted him, the water reflecting off the mirrored roof. It was one of his favourite places because while you were swimming, you could look out on the sea for miles. He was also too chicken to get into the cold sea during the winter.

"I'm not in the mood to play hide and seek," Axel said, walking past the two loungers.

He heard Phoebe's laugh, and then she pushed him into the pool. Water shot up his nose. At the surface he coughed and smacked the water while she stood on the ledge, laughing.

"That's what you get for following me." Phoebe smirked as he pulled himself up onto the ledge. He ran his hands over his face, but he was soaked through.

"Get in the house." He had run out of patience, and her smile quickly faded as he approached her.

She scowled. "You don't give up, do you?"

"Not in my nature." He grabbed her hips and pulled her over his shoulder. She groaned and struggled, but he held tight.

"Don't you dare toss me in the pool," she snapped, and the fear in her voice amused him. There was no way he would, not with her wrist still healing.

"I can walk." Her words came out raspy as she wore herself out struggling.

He didn't respond, afraid he would say something he would regret. When they made it back inside, August was still by the sink. His pierced eyebrow creased as he stared at them. Axel's jeans were plastered to his legs, and his T-shirt pulled out of place as she grabbed at him in protest.

"Have a nice swim?" August asked, and Axel glared at him. His feet squelched against the carpet until he made it to the bedrooms on the second floor.

"Put me down, Shrek!" Phoebe barked, and her voice echoed off the high ceilings.

"If you keep struggling, we'll both go down the stairs." He smacked her butt, and she pounded those adorable fists on his back.

"Touch my butt again, and you'll be glad those hands are insured." Holding her legs with one arm, he opened the spare bedroom door and dropped her on the bed.

"You didn't seem to mind my hands on you the last time we saw each other." He smirked, and she muttered something he couldn't make out.

She looked at the room hesitantly. They had made it up so she wouldn't have to be near Cillian's room; it was a blank canvas just for her.

"Nick had our housekeeper make up the bed with purple sheets, and your favourite snacks are by the night-stand in case. There's even a mini fridge with water and icepacks for your hand." Axel stepped back. "Nick should be home soon, and you can tell him about your adventure. Then we'll decide, together, what our next steps will be."

He was glad for the distance between them. Anytime she got too close, his willpower waned, and he forgot that she was his best friend's sister and his dead friend's ex.

"As nice as all this is, I can go back to my place and we can talk about next steps tomorrow." She tried to get past him, but he wrapped his arms around her and pinned her to his chest.

Staring into those eyes, he loosened his grip. She didn't move. Her eyes drifted to his lips, and the tension turned to something else. The curves of her body melted into his, and the damp patches on their clothing only increased the heat between their bodies. She diverted her gaze from his, and he lifted her chin, afraid she was plotting something.

"One night. The room is already organised for you. Whatever you need is in the bathroom, even clothes in the wardrobe," he said, watching the fight leave her. After the morning she'd had, the adrenaline couldn't last forever.

Her hand grazed his. "I'll stay if you do."

Her words stunned him. She swallowed as his touch trailed from her chin to her neck. "I don't think that's a good idea." Axel clenched his jaw as her lips parted. He had never wanted to kiss someone more in his life. Just one taste, and he would leave.

"You brought me here, you can't leave me alone." She tilted her head towards his, and it took all his will to step away from her. The tiny crease between her brows made him want to regret his decision, but it was for the best.

He moved to the door, leaving her standing in the middle of the room. "I can't."

"Why? Afraid you can't control yourself? Maybe I should go back to my apartment." Her words were barely a whisper. He didn't want to leave her, but she was using his desire against him.

"Sorry to disappoint you, but keeping you safe matters most to me. I'll have to learn to control myself. Get changed out of your damp clothes—and after this morning's event, you should probably ice that wrist."

He closed the door and locked it, taking the key. If she

really wanted to leave, there was another door through the bathroom that led to the hall.

"Damn you!" She kicked the door as her seduction failed.

He rested his hand on the doorknob, wanting to go back inside, but he wasn't going to let her use his feelings for her as her reason to leave.

F or two weeks Phoebe slept, letting the world and her problems slip away. She didn't want to admit Axel was right to insist on her moving in, even if he was. Once she'd reluctantly talked to Nick and the others about her staying for the foreseeable future, the adrenaline she'd been surviving on fled, leaving her exhausted. All she could do was sleep. She only left her room for food—not that she was hiding from Axel. Okay, maybe she was.

With a clear mind, she couldn't believe how reckless she'd been going to LouderTech alone. Confronting a grown man injured—yes with a weapon, but he could've easily overpowered her. The thought of him being out there, and that someone had paid him to do her harm, set her on edge.

Each day, though, the ache of grief eased little by little, sinking deeper under the surface. Questions only popped in when the silence got too much. *Was he tolerating my love for the sake of the band?* was a thought she couldn't escape. *Lena was right about the missed birthdays and exhibits.* She didn't want to believe it, but the last-minute cancellations and one-word messages all added up.

Phoebe stared at the engagement ring sitting on the sink. She couldn't toss it or sell it, but it felt like a lie, meant to keep her caged while he lived his life freely. Now she felt caged by her paranoia; she didn't want to believe what Sheen had said about being hired to ruin her studio. However, she'd been wrong about Cillian, and now she was forced to consider if someone was trying to ruin her and her relationship with the band.

An unknown number appeared on her phone, vibrating on the glass shelf below the bathroom mirror. Panic swelled in her chest. Who would be calling her from a private number? She answered; it might be the police calling about her incident with Mr Sheen.

"Hello?" Phoebe said, hesitantly.

"Ms Fletcher?" A soft Italian accent greeted her instead, and her shoulders relaxed. It wasn't some journalist or troll. "My name is Rowena. We haven't met, but Mr Hunt's lawyer gave me your number. I was hired to look after the villa in Amalfi. I'm so very sorry about the accident, but I was wondering how you would like the villa to be maintained and if you'd like me to stay on, as I believe ownership has been passed on to you."

Phoebe didn't realise Cillian had hired someone to keep the place up when they weren't there. She put the call on speaker as she got ready.

"Yes, please stay on if you can. I'm not sure what needs doing, and it might be a while before I can get out there," Phoebe said as she moisturised her skin, paying close attention to her scars. "How much do I owe you? I'm sorry if you haven't been paid; I can make up for whatever's owed to you."

"Please don't be sorry, Mr Hunt already paid for the year. I take care of the grounds and the house. We are a small village and I live down the street, so I keep an eye on the place. I was dusting this week, and I was wondering if you'd like me to pack up any of Mr Hunt's belongings. I wasn't sure." Rowena hesitated, and Phoebe understood the woman's discomfort. Talking about a dead employer to his ex-fiancée wasn't the easiest conversation to have.

"Don't worry about his belongings, just keep doing what you're doing, but thank you for the consideration. I'll try and get out there soon." Phoebe flexed her hand; the scar tissue made her skin feel tight and uncomfortable.

"As you wish. If there is anything you need, please ask," Rowena said kindly while Phoebe riffled through the numerous suitcases she'd been living out of on her unmade bed. Last week, Lena had packed up most of her clothes and things. The others were afraid that if she went back to her apartment she wouldn't come back. Seeing how upset her brother had been when Axel told him about Sheen, staying was best for everyone.

"Thank you. Maybe if you could find some packing boxes. I can pay you for them, if you send your details," she asked, finding a pair of mint green sweats and pulling her white T-shirt over her bralette. She felt the fine scratches on her chest and shoulders where the glass had cut her, and shook away the unpleasant memories.

"I've already been paid expenses for the year, so it's no trouble. When you're coming send me a list of groceries so I can stock the fridge for you," Rowena offered.

Phoebe appreciated her kindness, but she wasn't sure if she was ready to return to the place where she and Cillian had planned their future.

"Thank you, I'll be in touch," she said, and closed her bedroom door behind her.

When she hung up, she contemplated selling the villa. She could use the money to buy her own place, maybe a house with her own studio. Her thoughts were cut short by the sound of her name coming from the TV downstairs.

Downstairs, she hovered in the kitchen doorway so the others wouldn't turn off the news.

"In entertainment news, we have a shocking update in relation to the death of Brothers of Anarchy frontman, Cillian Hunt. The studio of his long-term girlfriend and established artist, Phoebe Fletcher, has been vandalised, ruining a collection of works scheduled to be shown in Buckland's Gallery next month. Reports from a source close to the band and Miss Fletcher claim that the break-in was done by a disgruntled fan. We hope that fans can give the band members and Ms Fletcher some space and privacy during this dark time." The glamourous anchorwoman offered a condescending smile before moving on to the next piece of gossip.

Luckily the break-in wasn't news to any of them, but they still grumbled about it hitting the news.

"Some space and privacy, while reporting on every single one of our movements," Phoebe said, alerting the others to her arrival. She picked up the control by the microwave and turned off the TV.

"If it isn't Sleeping Beauty. We were beginning to wonder when you were going to join us." Nick got up from his stool at the counter and squished her to his chest. He was far taller than her—much to her annoyance—and she struggled to breathe in his embrace.

"Breakfast looks good," she said, pushing her brother away.

August pushed a plate of pancakes towards her. "I made your favourite, just in case you came down."

His thoughtfulness almost made her burst into tears. Being so emotionally raw was a new experience.

Axel cleared his throat as he sat on the counter by the oven with a loaded bagel in his hand. August glared at him, and Phoebe noticed his dark circles had lessened since she'd last seen him; she wasn't the only one getting some sleep.

"Okay, my idea, but Axel made them," August confessed, biting into a slice of bacon. Nick had told her Axel's love language was feeding people. It was the reason they had no need for a chef.

"Thank you." Phoebe glanced at Axel, who hid behind his breakfast. She hated to admit that he was right to bring her here.

"Don't mention it, I'm just glad you're out of bed." Axel hopped off the counter while the others put their dishes in the sink. "I was beginning to think I'd have to kiss you to wake you up," he whispered as he brushed past her. Thankfully the others didn't hear.

"Would that make you my true love?" she said with a smirk, and he winked. Falling for another rockstar wouldn't be good for her health, but flirting wasn't off-limits.

"What was that?" Nick asked, looking between them.

"Nothing." they said in unison.

Nick frowned, but luckily Anita coming in distracted him.

"Phoebe, nice to see you are up and about, but we were in the middle of something," Anita said, picking up a green smoothie from the counter that looked like freshly mown grass.

"Sorry to interrupt," Phoebe said. The atmosphere felt strained, now Anita was back. "I can take my food back to my room."

"No, you should stay. You should have a say in this as well," Nick said, and Axel suddenly walked out of the kitchen.

"Axel! We aren't finished discussing the concert!" Anita called after him.

"What concert?" Phoebe asked. Wasn't it too early to be thinking about performing again?

"I'm coming back!" Axel shouted down the hall, and Anita turned a shade of stressed-induced purple.

"I don't know how we could perform without Cillian, and it's far too soon to replace him," Nick argued. "The fans would be furious. Axel replaced our last drummer, but that was a completely different situation."

"No one is talking about replacing Cillian," Anita said. "You could fill in. You are one of the original members, and the fans will respect your decision to lead."

"Do you want to sing lead?" Phoebe asked her brother, not caring what the label or Anita wanted.

"I don't have much choice, none of us want to disband," Nick explained.

Phoebe's gut churned; disbanding felt like another death.

"We certainly aren't considering disbanding," Anita countered. "The label thinks a concert in honour of Cillian's passing would help calm the situation. Give the fans something to focus on and look forward to. With all the bad press recently, we could all use a boost of positivity."

"It's only been a couple of months?" Phoebe said. "Isn't it a bit soon?"

"The concert wouldn't be for another few months," Anita said, clearly having already talked it over with the label since she was pushing it so hard. "No one is asking for miracles. It's just a small concert, twenty thousand tops, to commemorate Cillian's memory and give the media something to chew on."

"Are you sure you're ready for that?" Phoebe asked August and Nick, who didn't look enthused by the idea. Phoebe sat at the table by August, who offered her a weak smile.

"The concert would be a nice way to honour him, but

that's not the whole proposal," Nick said, crossing his arms.

"They want another album," Axel said, returning.

Phoebe choked on her pancakes when she saw her notebook in his hand. August slapped her back, but it wasn't food caught in her throat.

Nick downed his orange juice. "An album we don't have because Cillian didn't finish, or if he did, we can't find any trace of it."

"The album shouldn't be a problem." Axel placed the purple notebook on the island in front of everyone.

Phoebe wanted the tiled floor to open and swallow her. Axel glanced at her as she shook her head, begging him not to say anything. She couldn't believe he hadn't talked to her about this first. August got the notebook before she did, flipping through the pages. His scowl confirmed his suspicions.

"This isn't Cillian's handwriting." August stared at the lyrics of a song on their last album. Phoebe couldn't meet his eye. Nick stared over August's shoulder, and she knew he would recognise her handwriting; she had a childish habit of putting circles on her i's.

"Care to explain?" Anita asked, tapping her foot impatiently.

"I think Phoebe is the only one who can," Axel said, not giving her an out.

She wished she'd never got out of bed that morning. However, her conscience told her she had to face the music at some point. Axel had given her weeks, but she'd kept putting it off, and now they were out of time.

"We wrote them together," Phoebe admitted.

"You've been writing our songs?" Nick stammered.

"There is no point in lying," Axel said to her as she hesitated. "I think we've all had enough lies, and we can't move forward if we don't start being completely honest with each other."

"Yes," she confessed, feeling a weight lift from her shoulders. "But only for the last album, and we still worked together on it. It wasn't entirely me."

They all gawked at her like she'd grown a second head.

"You're like a walking media disaster. Anything else we need to know? Any lovers in the wings or other secret talents that might blow up in our faces?" Anita ranted, her face turning a nice shade of red.

"Back off," Axel cut in. "Phoebe's work has been making you, us, money for years and she hasn't expected a thing in return. You—*we* should be thanking her, because without her now, we are finished."

Nick's nostrils flared, looking like he wanted to punch something. Probably Cillian, but it was too late for that.

"You've been writing our songs?" Nick stammered, taking the notebook from August. "How could you not tell me? I'm your brother!" He slammed the notebook on the table. "We promised not to get involved in each other's careers. I accepted your relationship with him, but you've been doing this behind my back for years! When did this start?"

"I don't know, but it was after you were already signed. Cillian was struggling and I just helped," she said, hating the look of betrayal in her brother's eyes. "Over time, it became a habit. I never wanted to lie about it, but it felt so harmless, and it's only words—you guys did everything else."

"I don't know what to say. I don't know whether to be angry, grateful or pissed that Cillian kept this from me." Nick ran his hands through his hair. "When did you find out about this?" He turned to Axel.

"The concert in Munich," Axel confessed. "I found the notebook in my bus after they'd left."

"I'd come to surprise Cillian with it that night," Phoebe added, and the room drifted into silence.

"Okay. Here's what we are going to do," Anita said, taking charge as she always did. Phoebe wished she wouldn't micromanage them so much. "We need this album, so we'll continue as normal." Anita turned to Phoebe. "Next album, you keep your hands off. We can bring in some songwriters, if necessary, but the fans don't need to know about your past involvement."

"The whole point of this concert is to honour Cillian and help with the negative press," Axel countered. "Maybe telling the fans that Phoebe's the reason they have all the songs they love might help bridge the gap."

"Or those who already blame me will think I'm trying to take credit for his work," Phoebe pointed out.

"Enough," Anita huffed. "There is enough chaos right now. We don't need any more surprises, or the label will skin us alive. We need this next album to make back all that was lost with the cancelling of the tour."

"You can have the songs, but I don't want anyone to know I wrote them," Phoebe said, not wanting to be accused of stealing the spotlight or tainting Cillian's memory. She couldn't win no matter what she did, so staying out of it was best for everyone.

"Good, and can you promise to lay low between now and the concert?" Anita asked. Phoebe hated her condescending tone. Still, she was trying to stop their ship from going under.

"I haven't left the house except for physio, I can't get a much lower profile than that," Phoebe pointed out. She had no power over what the media did; she'd never realised she could be everywhere and nowhere all at once.

"I know you're doing your best, but the news about your studio has kicked everything up again," Anita said.

"This is bullshit," Axel muttered under his breath. "Secrets have done nothing but cause this mess in the first place."

"I don't want the credit. Like I said, we wrote the songs together. Consider it my parting gift." Phoebe looked at the notebook that contained the last remnants of their relationship.

"If she doesn't want the credit we shouldn't force her," Nick argued. "It's only one more album. Then we can take some time to figure out next steps."

"Exactly. We just need to get through the storm and then we can reassess," Phoebe said. "Now isn't the time to drop another bombshell on the fans."

August nodded. "I'm with Phoebe."

"Is this what you really want?" Axel asked Phoebe.

She nodded.

"Fine, we can get started on producing," Nick said. "The concert can be a way of saying goodbye to Cillian and for the world to get a chance for closure. I'll just have to sing and play, and Axel, you'll have to support more on vocals."

Axel grumbled a little but agreed.

"Good." Anita beamed. "I'll tell the label the concert is on, and that we'll announce the new album the same night, in Cillian's honour." She couldn't hide her satisfied grin. Of course she couldn't—she loved getting her way. "Getting back to normal is best for everyone."

They all exchanged a look. Nothing about this felt normal.

Anita was too busy gathering her things to notice their hesitation.

Lying low meant the most exciting part of the day was deciding what colour sweatpants to wear. Today was an old grey pair with some paint stains, which only increased Phoebe's desire to start painting again.

Wandering out into the garden for some fresh air, she found Axel playing fetch with Bart, the ever-energetic Shepherd, who brought her the tennis ball as soon as he saw her. He had only stopped whining outside Cillian's bedroom door since they had put one of Cillian's T-shirts in his bed to help cheer him up. He had started eating again and wanted to play. Phoebe's heart warmed to see him getting back to his happy self.

"Lena sent over everything from the studio the other day. I was wondering where my paints are," Phoebe said, taking the slobber-covered ball and tossing it across the gardens.

"Are you sure you're ready?" Axel asked as Bart brought the ball back to Phoebe.

"Good boy!" She rubbed Bart's ears and threw it for him again. He took off, tail wagging happily. "I don't know if I'll ever be ready, but I was wondering if there is a room I can set up my easel in. I was going to ask Nick but he's out in the studio and I didn't want to disturb him."

"You don't need one," Axel said, as Bart dropped the ball at his feet. She frowned, wondering why he was acting so dismissive.

"I can use my bedroom, but you've got so many free rooms, I didn't think it'd be a big deal."

"I didn't mean you can't have a room. I meant you already have a space." Axel grinned as he tossed the ball for Bart, who disappeared into the house with it, not wanting to give the ball up anymore.

"Okay, I'm not following?" Phoebe crossed her arms over her chest. It was far colder than expected, even for the early spring.

"We were going to save this, but since you're asking." Axel started walking down the path to the guest house. There was plenty of space inside, so it made sense they'd store her stuff in there. Then again, the last time she'd been there, she'd pushed him in the freezing pool.

She hesitated at the door. "You're not going to toss me in the pool, right?"

He chuckled, which didn't inspire much confidence.

"Tempting, but not this time." He winked, and she followed him inside.

They had transformed the living space into an art studio. Of course, it still smelt like chlorine, with the pool being in the other room, but she beamed like a child of Christmas morning.

"This is…" She didn't know what to say. Her easel was set up in the corner by the glass wall overlooking the gardens on one side and the sea on the other. Shelves with her brushes and paints had been installed on the wall behind. They must have done this while she was playing Sleeping Beauty, she realised.

"If you want to change anything around, feel free,"

Axel said. "I can help or ask the others, so you don't hurt your hand."

"This is perfect." She couldn't stop smiling.

Blank canvases of every size sat against a blue suede couch. Her smile slipped when she noticed, above the double sinks with her stained glass jars on the washboard, two paintings hanging on the white-bricked walls.

"That's two of the paintings from my show." She struggled to find the words as she stared at the illustrations.

"Since we couldn't be at your show, we wanted to support you." Axel shrugged like it was nothing.

To see the walls decorated with her work made her feel like she was back in her studio. They reminded her of what she had achieved and what she could do again in time.

Before she could stop herself, she wrapped her arms around Axel. He stilled, only to relax into her embrace.

"Thank you," she said, all teary-eyed. His chin settled into her shoulder, and she didn't want to let him go. "This is the best present I've ever received."

She couldn't wait to get started; having such a sunlit beautiful spot to work in would make it worth the pain. She would just have to ice her wrist a little longer tomorrow.

"I know you didn't want to be here, and lying low sounds a bit like house arrest, but I hope having your own space out here, you can feel at home," Axel said, when she finally released him.

"Thank you again," Phoebe stammered as he headed for the door. "It's perfect."

"It was a team effort, and with all you've done for us— the songs…" He paused. "We wanted to give you a slice of home."

"Like the pancakes?" she asked, seeing that he had a

habit of doing something nice for her and then framing it as a 'team effort'.

"Have fun," Axel said, and she swore she saw him blushing as he left.

AFTER HOURS of sketching out ideas, the sound of Phoebe's pencil hitting the floor was beginning to drive her crazy. She kept on dropping it, her grip strength limited. She gave up on sketching for the day and curled up on the couch and scrolled through her phone to find some inspiration, only to drift off. A hand on her shoulder startled her from her dream.

"Let me go!" Phoebe hit out before she realised it was Axel, but he pulled her against his chest to prevent her from injuring either of them. The heat of his body radiated into hers as she pushed against his hard chest.

"Are you sure you want me to let you go?" he asked, loosening his grip. She didn't pull away. Her heartbeat quickened, and she hated how her body betrayed her. She wanted him to touch her, to stay close. Her desire outweighed her guilt, and it felt so good to be wanted, even if she shouldn't be wanted by him.

As though he could read her mind, his eyes drifted to her lips, as she leaned against him until his lips crashed into hers. All thoughts of resistance evaporated as she tasted his lips. She arched her back, getting closer. His lips broke away from hers, and she sighed as his kisses travelled down her neck. Wrapping her arms around him, she clawed at his muscular shoulders. As he returned to her lips, she met his passionate kisses with her own. Out of breath, their chests rising and falling, his hands settled on her hips, and he pulled her onto his lap. She could feel his desire for her. His hard body tested the last shred of her willpower.

"We need to stop," she panted, and he rested his forehead against hers.

Both tried to catch their breath. Phoebe thanked him silently for his momentary restraint. Finding the will to resist, she slipped off him. His eyebrows creased, confused by her sudden withdrawal. She couldn't face those eyes that transfixed her.

He smiled as her stomach grumbled. She had been so distracted by her sketching, she had forgotten to eat.

"We ordered food, there's a pizza waiting for you," he said. "I just came to get you."

She smiled anxiously, sensing the discomfort the sudden halt in their steamy activities had caused in him. "Pizza sounds perfect."

She hadn't realised how late it was until she saw the dark sky. Axel led the way to the house, and she was careful to keep her distance so the others didn't notice the tension between them. The clock in the kitchen told her it was almost midnight as she chugged a glass of water. August was asleep on the couch in the sitting room with a few empty beers and old episodes of The Simpsons on the TV. Axel grabbed two pizza boxes from the marble island.

"I can carry this up to your room for you," he offered kindly.

She hesitated. "I'm not tired. Think I'll stay down here for a while."

"Nightmares?" he asked, and she wondered how he knew. "When I came in to check on you, you were crying."

"I can't even remember what I was dreaming about, thanks to your sudden interruption." Phoebe rubbed her eyes, sure she looked like a red-eyed panda.

"If you insist on staying up, come with me." He stopped at the door to the basement when he noticed she wasn't following. "Don't worry, I'm not going to chain you up in the basement." He smirked. "Unless you ask me to."

"I'm only following because you have my pizza held hostage."

She reluctantly followed him down the steps. Curiosity got the better of her; she hadn't been in his room before. His man cave smelt like him, and it was surprisingly tidy. His drums were in the corner by the bed, and his collection of CDs was impressive. She especially liked the Britney Spears album sitting by ACDC. She wondered if it was organised by preference.

"You can't have a collection without the Queen of Pop," he said, taking the album from her hand and placing it back on the shelf.

"You've got me here. Now what?" She crossed her arms over her chest.

"Now we eat. Sorry it's cold. We didn't want to interrupt you out there, but I was worried you'd overdo it the later it got." He sat on the bed and put down the pizza boxes. "Pepperoni for you, extra cheese and pineapple. Though I strongly believe pineapple has no place on a pizza."

"More for me then," she said, picking up a large slice.

Bart brushed against her legs at the side of the bed, staring up at her as he begged for a taste. She peeled off a slice of pepperoni and he happily lapped it up.

"How'd you get on out there?" Axel asked, and she wiped her lips with a napkin.

"Better than expected, but I sketched a little too long and started to lose grip strength. I'll start again tomorrow," she said, loving the tangy sweetness of the pineapple.

"It'll take time to heal." Axel moved to his desk. His

sweats hung low on his hips, and she could just make out the tattoo under his torn band shirt.

Phoebe watched, amused, as Bart rested his paws on the bed and took the slice Axel left too close to the edge.

"Bart!" Axel grumbled, and the Shepherd happily scurried away up the basement steps. Axel shook his head and sat down beside her.

"Hopefully this helps." He distracted her with a single-use ice pack. "I use them for my carpal tunnel. Drumming has its own side effects."

"The things we do for the things we love," she said, accepting it. "You know, if you keep doing such nice things for me, you're going to spoil your image."

"If it means you'll keep letting me do nice things for you, then fuck the image," he said, and she forced herself to turn from his gaze. He wasn't even trying to hide the way he felt about her.

"Where's Nick?" Phoebe hoped the ice pack would cool her emotions along with her aching hand.

"Still in the studio. You don't have to worry, I brought him his food." Axel fidgeted with his crust, clearly annoyed by her deflection.

"Thank you for looking out for them," she said. He seemed to be the glue in the group.

"I need them as much as they need me," he confessed, pulling at her heartstrings.

He put aside the boxes once they finished eating, and she considered going back to her room.

"You can stay, if you want," he said. "The bathroom is just through there, and there's water in the drawers beside you."

She considered it, but she didn't know if he was expecting more from her than she was ready for.

"Nothing will happen, except you might get a good-night sleep," he said, as though reading her mind.

She didn't want to be alone, but… "And if the others find me sleeping in your bed?" She glanced at the stairs.

"The door has a lock, and you can leave whenever you like," he said, giving her an extra pillow.

"Just for a little while," she conceded, and the bed dipped a little as she climbed beneath his blue sheets. He snuggled down beside her, and she burrowed under his arm before she even thought about it. He turned off the light beside him, and she felt his chest rising and falling with ease as she rested a hand on him.

"Can you tell me something?" she asked.

"Like what?" He rested his arm behind his head, and she glanced up to see his eyes closed as though already used to having her in his bed.

"How'd you get into drumming?" She picked at the logo on his T-shirt as she rested her head on his chest.

"Making me the main character of a bedtime story? You'll inflate my ego."

"I don't think that's possible."

He squeezed her tightly, and she squealed.

"Where should I begin?" He sighed. "Once upon a time, there was a boy called Axel, who hated school. He struggled to pay attention in class, and his test scores sucked. He loved art and music and skipped class to smoke in the bathrooms. He had a hard time making friends, and this led the boy to get into some fights. His single mum couldn't afford therapy, and no other school would take him because of the bad grades and fighting. So, his sisters all chipped in what they could and bought him a drum set for Christmas. Having a place to put all his anger, he stopped fighting. However, his grades still sucked, and he left school at seventeen, before doing his final exams, to work in some dodgy bars and play for whoever would let him."

The steady sound of his heartbeat and the hum of his voice allowed her to drift. The thought of sleep no longer stirred her anxiety, and she tucked his duvet beneath her chin.

"He moved from gig to gig and lived out of a suitcase with his drumsticks in his back pocket. Then one day, he got to join Brothers of Anarchy, and he found his home. What he didn't know was that this new home came with a woman who he couldn't escape. She was everywhere he turned, her smile, her eyes and lavender hair. He always wanted to be around her, but she wouldn't give him the time of day because her heart belonged to another. He kept his distance, because having her in his life, even if she never knew how much she meant to him, was enough."

"I like your sisters." Her words got caught up in a yawn. Half asleep, she struggled to stay awake as he stroked her hair.

"Me too," was the last she heard of his story before sleep took her.

LENA: Dropped off your mail with the
security guy. He's one hell of a silver fox.

PHOEBE: I'll tell Olivier you said so. Thank
you! I'm sorry to make you do such a minor
task, I feel like I'm under house arrest here.

LENA: I'm sorry I haven't been able to
come over more. I've been up to my eyes. I
do have some good news! I've had the new
alarms installed in your studio, along with
extra cameras that I can see from my
phone. I can send you the link so you can
keep an eye on it, but no one is getting in,
so it's one less thing for you to worry about.
How's the painting coming along?

PHOEBE: Don't worry about it, you've done
more than enough already. It's different,
simple sketching is taking a lot longer.
Hopefully with time, it'll become easier.

LENA: Take all the time you need to heal.
My phone has been ringing off the hook
with people looking for commissions.
Whoever said bad press is still press was
right. There is no pressure, I've got a
waiting list for you a mile long.

. . .

Phoebe wanted to be excited, but anxiety crept up her spine. *What if I can't fulfil the commissions? What if I can't paint like I used to?* The thought pestered her. Maybe she could, but certainly not at the same speed.

She tried to twirl a paintbrush around her fingers the way she used to, only to drop it. Its clatter against the tiles reminded her to consider carpeting the pool house turned art studio. At least she didn't have to worry about the studio being broken into again. One less thing to focus on.

> PHOEBE: And they are okay to wait? I can't even give them an ETA.

> LENA: Are you kidding? The longer the wait the greater the anticipation. Your health comes first, and I've got everything handled on my end, so please don't worry about a thing. I've already informed the two galleries for the next showings that the collections will be smaller and more exclusive. We'll work around what you have, and if you can add one or two more, then great. If not, it's no big deal. Your healing is most important.

PHOEBE: Thank you for understanding! I don't know what I'd do without you in my corner! The guys were kind enough to set up a studio for me, so hopefully having a safe space will be inspiring, and my physio has given me the all clear to start painting. It's just about managing the pain and making sure I don't overdo it. I never knew there were so many types of pain. Some days it's like a gnawing, others it's numb like pins and needles, or my personal favourite, lightning sparks from my thumb to elbow when I grip a paintbrush too hard. I just need to find the balance between rest and work, that's the sweet spot.

LENA: I wish I could click my fingers and take it all away, but all I can do is make sure that you're looked after. It's my job to handle your battles and keep the stress off your back. I'm your frontline, and if you want to cancel the next two shows, we can.

PHOEBE WANTED TO CRY. Even having the option to cancel helped her anxiety subside. But with all that had changed recently, she didn't want to sacrifice any more. She wanted to celebrate her work and be surrounded by people who appreciated her work for what it was and not for who she was or her connections.

PHOEBE: Thanks for being so kind. I don't want to cancel after working so hard to get those slots in the first place. We can work with what we have, and I can work on a commission or two in the meantime.

LENA: Whatever you want! I'm here. X

. . .

PHOEBE TOOK off her headphones when Bart jumped down from the couch and welcomed Olivier, the head of security, with sniffs. His black trousers were covered in dog hair in seconds, but he didn't seem to mind and welcomed the cuddles.

"Your mail," Olivier said, walking into the pool house. "Lena sent some over from the studio."

She thought about Lena's silver fox comment. Olivier was barely over forty, but his dark hair was threaded with silver and grey. Probably the stress of his job.

"You didn't have to bring it. Lena texted me, I would've come to get it." She took the few letters and a small brown package while he rubbed Bart's ears.

"No trouble at all. Gives me time to stretch my legs. Lena left it at the front this morning, so I wanted to wait until you were up," Olivier said. "Your friend is interesting."

Over the years, Phoebe had never seen him look nervous. Lena must have been her usual flirtatious self. Olivier was all about quiet, order and routine—Phoebe tried to suppress her smile as she imagined him trying to figure out Lena, an extrovert to her core who wasn't shy of saying what she thought.

"I'll tell her you said so," she said, wondering if there had been a spark between them. There was about eight years between them, but nothing could stop Lena when she set her eyes on someone.

"I don't mean it in a negative way—she is unique." He stumbled over his words. *This guy was in the military for over ten years, and Lena made him nervous.* Seeing him sweat made Phoebe's day.

"Sir, are you blushing?" she teased, and he clenched his jaw.

"Goodbye, Phoebe," he said, and left with Bart following close behind.

Olivier's interruption was welcome; it was good to take a break. When she was creating uninterrupted because the others were busy producing their album, she barely thought about the pain in her hand.

In front of her easel, there were no other thoughts to bother her. Nothing about the person who might've hired Sheen to break into her studio and then leaked it to the press, or the fact that she couldn't sleep without Axel Adler's arms wrapped around her. Somehow one night had turned into every night. Even if he drove her crazy, there was a calmness about him that eased her grief.

Picking up her mail, she distracted herself from thoughts of Axel and his bed. She eyed a brown box marked 'fragile' and ripped open the tape. There was string confetti sitting on top, and she felt a welcome rush of excitement. It wouldn't be the first time she'd received a gift from a fan of her work, but all she'd received recently was hate. She moved the confetti aside.

"Fuck me!" Phoebe hissed, snatching her hand away. The box fell from her lap, and razor blades popped out from beneath the confetti.

"What is wrong with people?" she hissed, pressing her finger to her lips. She tasted the tang of blood. It was only a couple of small nicks, but they hurt like hell.

Crouching down, she picked up the blades and sealed them back in the box. She didn't want to leave them in case Bart came back and hurt his paws. She checked the postage label, and there was no return address or name.

If it wasn't shipped, then someone must've left it at the studio personally, she realised. *There's no way Gunther Sheen would go so far to get back at me for damaging his car. He wouldn't be stupid enough, given the evidence I have against him, but if it wasn't him…*

She had no idea. She couldn't even check the nanny cams like she had the first time—Lena had removed them when she packed up the studio.

Bart's barking interrupted her thoughts as he returned to find her kneeling on the ground. She wondered if he sensed something was wrong.

"Quiet," she whispered, trying to soothe the distressed dog circling her. "I'm okay, let's go look for some plasters."

Letting out a long exhale, she took some reassurance in the fact that the sender didn't know she had moved. With the blades safely in the box, she noticed *'You've Never Deserved Him'* handwritten inside the lid. The message sent a chill down her spine, and she wanted to get rid of it asap.

I should take the studio address off the website and use a PO box instead, she thought, walking into the kitchen. *It's not like I'm going to go back to that studio anyhow.* She found the plasters in the spice cabinet, which was the last place she looked. Bart didn't leave her side as she cleaned and wrapped her fingers. She was about to chuck the "fan mail" in the bin when the TV caught her eye. There was a video of her outside the concert, the news banner reading: 'Breakout artist's collection triples in value after near fatal accident with boyfriend Cillian Hunt.'

Was this why she'd got the package? Because a news headline had triggered a fan? Her lilac hair shone out of the screen, and given the rise in hostility, she decided it was time for a change. If they weren't going to stop talking about her or taking her picture, she'd make herself harder to spot. She took out her phone and texted Lena to see if she could bring her some box dye when she got a chance. She didn't think Olivier would know what to look for, and she didn't want to interrupt the guys in the studio. Given the headlines, Anita certainly wasn't going to do her any favours, so she only had Lena.

She rubbed Bart's ears and waited for Lena's reply. She had never thought it would escalate to the point where she was afraid to go outside.

Later that evening, Phoebe's butt had gone numb from sitting on the bathroom tiles while she waited for the second box dye to take. Luckily, Bart kept her company; the Shepherd laid his head on her feet as though trying to keep her still. She left the door open so they didn't suffocate from the fumes.

"What are you doing?" Axel found her in the main bathroom. She needed the bathtub to dye her hair.

"Doodling." She glanced up from her notebook. "I don't want my hand getting too stiff."

"I was talking about the plastic bag on your head."

"Dyeing my hair. Going to a salon wasn't an option, given that I'm supposed to be lying low." She put the sketchbook down on the black tiles beneath her.

"Do you need some help?" Axel asked, and she wished he wouldn't be so kind and helpful because she was growing terribly fond of him. Staring up at him, she couldn't believe how handsome he was. The crazy spider tattoo and shaved head usually kept people away from him, but his individuality only drew her in.

"I'm not sure you know much about dyeing hair," she teased.

"Because I shave my head?" He arched a brow, running a hand over his stubbled scalp.

"Why do you shave your head? You've looked like you just enlisted ever since we first met," she asked. August was always growing out his hair and her brother dyeing his, while Axel remained the same.

"Why are you changing your hair? I thought you liked purple," he said, not giving anything away.

She couldn't tell him the reason she was changing from her favourite colour to a muddy brown was because of the weaponised mail. She hoped the package had been sitting in her studio awhile, and it wasn't a sign of things to come.

"Deflection looks good on you. I forgot you don't like to answer questions. You prefer to come across as the mysterious, silent type of rockstar," she said, hoping if she got under his skin he would leave her alone.

"Certainly got your attention," he quipped, picking up one of the box dyes back by the sink.

"Thank you for your offer, but I'm fine. Please close the door."

Axel did as instructed, closing the door only to trap them in together. Luckily, she had opened the skylights so they wouldn't suffocate from the smell of dye. He sat between the double sinks.

"I meant close the door on your way out. I've got to wait for the timer to go off; the hard part is already over," she said, hoping this second round of dye had covered the spots she'd missed. It'd taken far more time than normal to get it completely covered, but it was done now.

"You could have asked for help. You shouldn't really be doing this alone; you've been locked up in the pool house and we don't want you putting that hand of yours under too much pressure."

"I already iced it twice today and did my physio exercises. No need to worry," she said, even though she appreciated his concern for her. He'd been kind enough to let her sleep in his bed and keep it a secret from the others for more than a few nights. It was becoming an unspoken arrangement, and even though she started every night in her own bed, she tossed and turned until she padded down the basement steps to find he'd already pulled the duvet over on what was becoming her side.

"'Brunette Babe' was the one you settled on?" He read the label, distracting her from her thoughts.

"I didn't think I was a bombshell blonde, and ruby red would mean twinning with my brother," she reasoned, looking at the collection on the bathroom floor. Red was a nightmare to maintain and wouldn't help with the 'lying low' concept.

"I wanted something different, and when I leave the house, the paps won't be able to spot me so easily."

She'd tried to walk to the shop around the corner from the house a couple of days ago for some sanitary pads and ice cream and ended up on Beefeed's website in an unflattering shot. She hadn't even got home before she was tagged in a repost titled 'Bereaved girlfriend of rockstar lets herself go'.

"I thought you were out with the others." She tried to move the conversation on. "Thought you had an interview photoshoot for the concert once you were done at the studio?" She'd heard Anita give them their schedule the previous night. They'd wanted to take some time off to grieve, but Phoebe wondered if it was better for them to work a little since they weren't used to sitting still.

"We finished up early, and I only just got back and came looking for you. August and Nick have gone out for food. Text them if you want something back from the Chinese."

Phoebe groaned. "Must be nice to sit in a restaurant and eat without being hounded or threatened. I wish I could've gone with them," she said. She hadn't got out of her sweatpants in days.

"No, you don't," Axel sighed. "They aren't in the best mood after the studio session, being in there only reminds us of what's missing. I came home to take Bart for a walk. When he didn't come, I figured he was with you."

"I don't think you're going to get him to go. He's keeping me company in case the box dye gods attack," she said, having been unable to get him to budge. "I was worried about how the fumes affect dogs, but he barked incessantly when I closed the door on him."

"He's never been a fan of closed doors." Axel rubbed Bart's head as the dog looked between them like he knew they were talking about him.

"I'm getting cold. Can you please leave so I can finish?" Phoebe said, forgetting she was only in her sweatpants and a triangle bralette that left little to the imagination. His gaze lingered on her like he wanted to do much more than help.

Her alarm went off, breaking the tension.

"Let me help, and you'll be done faster," he offered, getting off the counter. "In fact, let me help you, and I'll take you to dinner."

"Dinner? Me and you? Do you want Anita to murder us?" She frowned, removing the bag from her head and putting her sketchbook by the sink so it didn't get wet.

"Fair point," he mused. "But Anita doesn't need to know, and you want out of the house. With your new hair, no one will notice."

"They'll notice you," she said. It was hard to miss him.

"You'd be amazed by my disguises," he said. "The

decision is yours. Let me help, and you get a dinner out of the house."

She hesitated, thinking how nice it would be to get away.

"Okay, I accept."

"Good," he said, trailing his hand down her arm, making her shiver. "Now bend over."

"Axel! Really?" she snapped.

"Bend over the tub, so I can wash the dye out of your hair," he clarified, and she wanted to wipe his smug smile off his face. She rolled her eyes; he was enjoying this too much.

She knelt on the floor and leaned her head over the tub, wanting to get this over with as soon as possible.

"How's the temperature?" he asked, threading his fingers through her hair. She wondered if he was trying to fill in the silence.

"Perfect," she sighed, not sure if she was talking about the water temperature or his gentle touch.

"You've still got some purple spots," he told her, breaking her enjoyment of the moment.

"I couldn't really reach the back," she groaned.

"It's not noticeable, nobody else is going to be getting this close to you."

The spots didn't matter; she was too distracted by his fingers in her hair. She'd forgotten how nice it was to be taken care of. She was glad the water dripping down her face concealed her tears.

"What'd you do to your fingers?" he asked, noticing her hands gripping the tub.

"Just a few scratches," she said flatly, not wanting to tell him about the package or the message within. She didn't want to lie, and technically she *was* scratched. She wanted to wait awhile, find out when the fan mail was delivered, before she said anything. No point in worrying everyone if it was nothing.

"I think that's the dye out," he said, placing a warm towel on her shoulders. She wrapped it around herself, embarrassed to be wearing so little.

"Thank you," she said, relieved that she hadn't had to do it herself. Her hand wasn't aching any longer, thanks to the rest. She was still figuring out her limits, but dyeing and doodling had been a bit much for one day.

In the mirror behind Axel, she glimpsed the deep brown hair she hadn't seen since she was a teenager. It made her feel like a different person.

"What's the next step?" Axel asked.

"I just need a break, my neck is killing me."

"While we wait, can I see what you were doodling?" he asked, taking a seat beside her against the bathtub.

She turned the notebook towards him to reveal a sketch of a thin paintbrush decorated with delicate flowers.

"Is that a tattoo?"

"Maybe." She shrugged.

"I didn't know you like to design tattoos."

"I was just playing around. Trying to work on my control since my hand shakes when I try and do fine details. It's not like I'd ever get one." She didn't like how defensive she sounded. So what if she liked tattoos? She hoped he won't notice that she'd taken inspiration from the one on his ribs. She'd seen it in the garden when he was with Bart watering the flowers. Two drumsticks crossed with a band of flowers, except she'd used paintbrushes for her own version.

"Why never?"

Bart snuggled between them, like he was jealous.

"Maybe one day, but Cillian never liked them."

He frowned. "I was there when he got his sleeve."

"He didn't like them on girls." She couldn't meet his eye as she said it.

He nodded slowly.

"Why would that stop you? Your body, your choice."

"It wasn't like I wanted one desperately, so what was the point in arguing over something that I wasn't set on? Relationships take compromise."

It only took his death to realise how much she had compromised.

"I don't think it's considered compromise when he got all the tattoos he wanted but didn't give you the same freedom."

"You've never been in a long-term relationship." She didn't want to argue with him, and it wasn't him she was mad at. She was mad at herself for letting Cillian treat her as less than him for so long.

"Maybe not, but I sure as hell would never tell a woman I loved what she could or couldn't do with her body."

"If I tell you that yes, I want a tattoo, will you drop the subject?" she said, wanting to end the conversation about what he did or didn't do with women's bodies. He'd done enough to hers to make her question her sanity.

They never talked about their intimate moments. They carried on as though nothing had happened, and that was how she liked it, because right now she couldn't handle complicated, and he was a red flag with 'complicated' written in bold.

"The artist who does mine is currently doing a residence in Italy. She's usually booked out a few months in advance, but I'm sure she'd be delighted to work with you on it," Axel offered eagerly. "She loves collaborating with other artists."

"Just because I doodled a tattoo doesn't mean I want to

run off to Italy to get one," she said, though given the mail she'd received today, getting out of town felt like a good idea. She thought about Rowena at the villa, and packing up Cillian's belongings. She might be able to kill two birds with one stone.

"Why not?" Axel asked.

"One, a tattoo is a big decision. Two, Anita told us not to get into any trouble, and us boarding a plane together going to Italy, one of the most romantic destinations in the world, isn't going to help put out any fires."

She stated the obvious, but he didn't seem convinced.

"Is that an invitation?" he said with a smirk.

She was about to argue when he waved it off. "It was only a thought, a chance to get out of the country, away from the press and the fans. Breathe in some of that ocean air and take some time to yourself. Anita did tell you to lie low, and leaving the country is the best way to do that."

Phoebe chewed her lip. A little weekend trip might be just what she needed, and she could sort out the villa while they were there. And it might give her the inspiration she needed to start fresh.

"I did promise you dinner," he added, nudging her a little. "It would be a lot easier to have dinner in a beautiful Italian restaurant where no one would even suspect to find us."

The thought of being able to walk around with little notice felt too good to pass up. If the person who'd sent the package was looking for her, maybe some time away would be safest for everyone.

"Okay! I'll go. I've got to go to the villa anyway—the housekeeper Cillian hired wants me to go through our things," she explained, or more like barked, because Bart's ears perked up in alarm.

Axel beamed, and she'd never seen him smile like that.

He turned a little so she couldn't see his expression, but she could sense how happy he was.

"I'll make a call. When do you want to leave?"

"As soon as possible."

He hesitated for a moment before reaching into his hoodie pocket for his phone. "Pack a bag, and I'll call us a car."

"You're seriously coming with me?" she asked.

"I can't let you have dinner alone in Italy. Besides, I keep my promises."

"What will we tell the others?" she asked, wondering how they could explain going away alone to a romantic destination.

"Like you said, you need to sort out the villa and I'm going to help you. My schedule is the freest since August is needed in production and Nick has to work out his vocals. They can't argue," Axel reasoned, and his plan sounded like it might just work.

"And Anita?"

"Doesn't need to know," he said firmly.

"Agreed."

Axel started heading for the door, and she reached out to stop him.

"Wait!" She chuckled at his eagerness. He probably felt as housebound as she did. "You haven't finished washing my hair," she pointed out.

He paused, and nearly tripped over Bart.

"Right, bend over." The command hung in the air, and she couldn't contain her laughter as Bart looked between them. She'd never seen Axel blush before.

"Again? Really? Get your mind out of the gutter," he said, as she handed him the shampoo and conditioner.

She could barely keep still at the excitement of getting out of the house.

"I can't believe we're flying coach. We're supposed to be keeping a low profile," Phoebe groaned, sinking deeper into her snug airplane chair as the flight attendant informed them of the emergency exits and where the life jackets were.

"I didn't think you'd be such a snob," Axel said with a smirk.

That wasn't what she meant.

"I'm not, but it's a miracle someone hasn't realised who we are." She didn't know how Axel sat so relaxed; she kept waiting for someone to ask for a picture or an autograph. Maybe throw another carton of eggs at them.

"You'd be amazed what people don't see when they aren't looking."

"I love that your idea of being a master of disguise is wearing sunglasses and a baseball cap that has B.O.A.'s logo on it. Maybe you were a spy in a past life," she teased, keeping her voice low so those behind couldn't hear them.

"You wanted to leave as soon as possible, so I grabbed the last-minute seats. This was the earliest flight to Naples I could get, and if I'd tried to take the plane, Anita would've found out and then it would be her we'd be worrying about."

"You're right, but we might as well be sitting on each other's laps."

In the past, she didn't mind economy, but the person beside her didn't have any arm or leg space etiquette and all six-foot-something of Axel was taking up the rest of the space. She felt like she understood how the sausage in a hot dog felt.

"Feel free to hop on at any time." He smiled, patting his thigh.

"Like that wouldn't draw attention."

His long legs took up half of her space, but at least he had switched and given her the window seat. She hadn't even had to ask.

"Fame is an illusion. Act normal, and ninety percent of the time you get treated like you're normal. We made it through security with only a few lingering looks, so you can relax now." Axel settled into his seat while her nerves stood on edge. "It'll be the fastest three hours of your life."

She thought about telling him about her recent "fan mail"—he would be more concerned too, if people were sending him gift-wrapped razor blades. She shook away the thought; she wouldn't punish him for what he didn't know.

"Stop telling me to relax. It's my face plastered all over the news and headlines, it's my presence that's likely to cause us trouble. You are the beloved drummer and I'm the pariah."

"You aren't a pariah, and with your new hair, no one will blink at you," he assured her.

"Except for the woman at the gate who eyed my boarding pass and passport a little too long for comfort."

"Refreshments?" An attendant interrupted them as he passed their row.

They both nodded.

"Two tequilas and orange please," Axel asked.

"It's not even twelve o'clock," Phoebe said, not being one for day drinking.

"If I can't tell you to relax, then I can help you do so." Axel took the drinks from the attendant and handed one to Phoebe.

"What do I owe you?" Axel reached into his back pocket for his wallet. Phoebe caught the steward checking over his shoulder. "On the house. It's a pleasure to have you fly with us." He winked knowingly. "I hate to ask, but if you could sign this for my boyfriend, he'll just die." He offered Axel a napkin and a pen.

While he signed, Phoebe downed her drink. The sweet, tangy orange juice masked the burn of the tequila.

"Thirsty?" Axel eyed her empty plastic cup.

"Parched." She took his from his tray table and tipped it back.

"Better?"

"Much."

Wanting to distract herself, she focused on their plans once they landed.

"We can stay in the villa in Atrani—booking a hotel will only draw attention," she reasoned, after the interaction with the attendant. "We'll have more privacy, and it's only a thirty-minute walk to Amalfi. I don't want to give Anita a reason to kill us."

"Are you sure? Won't that be a bit difficult? A lot of fresh memories," Axel asked, but what he meant was: was she okay staying in the place where Cillian had proposed?

"I have to face the place at some point. I need to go and figure out whether I want to sell the place or not," she said, still unsure if she wanted to keep the reminder of a time when they'd been so happy. "It'll be easier with you around to keep me company."

He'd be the perfect distraction. Cillian had made her feel on edge and that was the excitement she'd thought she loved, but with Axel, she felt calm, at peace. It was unsettlingly different, but he was exactly what she needed right now.

"Just say the word and we can get out of there," Axel said. "If you change your mind, I've booked a hotel."

"Just one room?" she asked. They hadn't kissed since that night on the couch, but they had slept together every night since.

"I booked a suite, so two rooms," he explained, as though the thought had never crossed his mind.

She blushed for presuming, given their unspoken sleeping arrangement at home. *Maybe I'm the one getting carried away with my feelings, and he was just trying to be a good friend.* She didn't know whether he was being respectful or if he was waiting for her to make the first move.

Given the early flight, Axel fell asleep with ease while she fretted over her feelings. Who knew tequila only fuelled her ability to overthink.

THE DRIVE from the airport to the villa had taken a little over an hour, not that Phoebe noticed. She woke with her head on Axel's shoulder. After escaping the airport in Naples without incident, she had drifted off in the safety of the hire car. Seemed the tequila only hit her when they landed.

"You're drooling on my favourite shirt," Axel said.

"I don't drool." Phoebe bolted upright, staring out at the coastline. The sun had started to set as they had driven along the highway running the length of the Amalfi Coast.

"I'm only teasing, and I'm surprised you didn't wipe out on the flight. The stress of being on the plane wore you out and the tequila probably helped. Two in the air is four on the ground," he said, as she brushed off the embarrassment of having fallen asleep on him. It wasn't the first time, and she doubted it would be the last.

Staring out at the beautiful views, they spent the rest of the drive in silence. The smell of the salt in the air and the sight of the town of Atrani tucked snugly between two mountains was the change of scenery she needed. Though she'd never thought that when she returned to paradise it would be with Axel.

When they arrived, there was no parking, so they walked up a small pathway and more than a dozen steps to get to the villa tucked into the mountainside. Phoebe took the key from the envelope and opened the small gate. She felt worlds away from home, and the sight of the villa filled her with both excitement and trepidation, haunted by fond memories.

"Phoebe?" Axel asked, and she realised she'd frozen in the hallway looking at the photos of them all together. It seemed like another life.

"Sorry, I was thinking of all that needs to be done." She forced a smile and headed down the stone hallway and through the arch to the kitchen. Rowena had kept her promise and stocked up the fridge and presses.

"Are you sure you're happy to stay?" Axel eyed her warily as though she was about to burst into tears.

"Perfectly," she said. "I'll feel better once I've finished getting everything organised."

Regardless of what had happened with Cillian, she loved the quaint ocean-view villa.

"Remember to take some time to yourself while we're here," Axel reasoned, but she couldn't relax, not when she was surrounded by the happy memories that now felt so tainted and distorted.

She nodded, taking down some of the more intimate couple photos from the wall.

"Do you want some help? You shouldn't be doing this alone," he asked.

"I'll get through things faster if I don't have to explain. Could you put my bags in the last room at the end of the hall? The room on the right has a nice balcony, if you want it," she said, giving him the guest room. She'd stay in what was going to be her art room; it was once a guest room, but they hadn't got around to removing the bed. She was also being greedy and taking the big balcony. Axel could have the mini one, but at least it was a room with a view. She didn't want anyone staying in what had been her and Cillian's room until she'd packed up what was in there.

Thankfully, Rowena had left the boxes she'd wanted, so she didn't need to take an unnecessary trip into town. While she packed up Cillian's belongings, Axel kept himself busy working away in the garden by the pool, so they weren't stepping over each other. She needed some space to digest.

As she opened Cillian's wardrobe, the scent of him nearly brought her to her knees. She pulled out the T-shirt he'd worn when he proposed, and remembered she still hadn't decided what to do with her ring. Throwing it in the ocean felt like a waste and selling it didn't feel right.

She threw out all the nonsense that didn't need to be shipped home. She'd spent the whole afternoon sorting his from hers; she didn't want Axel witnessing the life they had shared. It felt too personal, and having her someone go through her dead boyfriend's stuff felt a little too twisted. She had to do it, for closure, to say goodbye to a future she would never know. A future she wouldn't have had even if he had lived. She wasn't sure which hurt more.

The only remaining evidence he had ever been there was the group photos she'd kept up. Though the shadow of the pictures of them as a couple lingered in the paint. Without the signs of him overwhelming it all, she wanted to keep the place. It could be an escape for all of them. She loved the privacy, and the view was incredible. It would be a nice place to paint in between shows.

Axel was floating in the clean pool as she finished labelling the last box. The leaf catcher lay filled by the pool, and she smiled, grateful for his help. When the trees shook off their leaves, Cillian had always complained or waited until the pool cleaner came, even if only for a couple of leaves.

"Let me help you." Axel surprised her by appearing behind her.

"It's fine, it's the last one," she said, trying to lift it, but her hand gave way. She cursed, shaking out her wrist. She waited for him to say 'told you so', but he just picked up the box and gave her a moment.

"Thank you," she said, as he reappeared after putting the box with the others.

"Happy to help. Do you want an ice pack or some painkillers?"

"No, I'm okay, it was just a spasm. I did too much and now it's a little numb. I can ice it later," she told him. "Sorry I interrupted your swim." She massaged her hand as they walked back to the pool.

"Please don't apologise. I'm here if and when you need me," Axel said, standing by the edge of the pool. "Not just for my good looks."

She rolled her eyes as he dived back into the pool. "I didn't realise so much time had passed. This is the last box;

I want to get his stuff back home. Cillian moved more stuff here in anticipation of being here more often. I didn't know he'd put together the art room for me." Saying it aloud threatened to break her. How could he be so kind and considerate in one breath and disdainful and selfish in another?

"I saw that when I was putting away our bags," Axel said, and she walked over to the lounger closest to him. "The room facing the ocean with a balcony. He wanted you to be able to sit out and paint, instead of being crammed in the guest room."

"You knew about it?" Phoebe asked.

"We didn't always get along, but we did talk," Axel said, like she was doubting their friendship.

"I didn't mean it like that. He was always anxious about you around me," she confessed. "I didn't think he'd talk to you about me. August treats me like a sister, and Nick is my brother, but you always kept your distance. It made him nervous."

"What do you mean?" He frowned, and she shuffled a little, wishing she hadn't brought it up.

"He didn't like how you looked at me, or acted around me." She shrugged. "I thought he was paranoid; you pretended like I didn't exist."

"He was right to be." His words were barely audible as he dived into the pool, giving her the impression he didn't want to talk about her ex.

She had dwelled enough on the past for one day. It was dangerous to linger on old memories for too long.

"Are you going to join me or just keep gawking?" Axel asked, resurfacing. She swallowed as she watched his muscles ripple.

"I wasn't gawking." She focused her attention on the stone tile around the pool, because she had, in fact, been gawking. It wasn't right to be so obsessed with the contours of someone's body.

"A dip would be nice after all that work," he said.

"I don't have my swimsuit on," she said, still in the same pale blue midi dress she'd travelled in. That, and she was more than a little sweaty.

"Live a little," he pressed, swimming over to the edge and resting his forearms on the ledge.

Her hand could probably benefit from some water therapy, and the cool water would be nice after working so hard. Without a second thought, Phoebe stripped off her dress, leaving her in her baby blue bralette and matching undies. His eyes widened, taking in every inch of her, and she concealed her flush by jumping into the pool. The salt-water pool felt like a breath of fresh air.

She playfully splashed up as she came up for air. Axel circled her, reaching for her hips. She giggled, trying to escape his grasp. He knew how to shift her focus, so she noticed the world around her instead of the small things.

Phoebe let him catch her, and he held her close. She melted against the heat of his body, captivated by the scent of salt on his skin. His lips brushed hers, and she gasped, her parted lips an invitation. The sound of birds chirping and the emerging stars above made her feel like they were the only two people in the universe.

"I don't think you should overwork that hand. Let me help you to the shallow end," he said, and gripped her thighs.

She nodded, brushing her hair from her face as he walked her to the edge of the pool. An ache grew deep inside her, and she squealed as he lifted her onto the pool's edge with ease. His eyes raked over her body, and she'd never felt so seen. She was scared of how much she wanted him to see her, wanted to be with him. His hands rested on either side of her thighs, and he kissed each knee as he slipped her legs over his shoulders. Butterflies fluttered in her lower belly, and she shivered.

"It's chilly," she said as his lips ran along the inside of her thighs.

"Don't worry, I'm going to warm you up." His gaze darkened, and his hands went to her hips, hooking his thumbs into her underwear.

"Lie back," he instructed with a wicked smile.

She lost all ability to speak as he kissed a droplet from her knee, and then the other, until she gave in. With a nervous smile, she rested on her elbows, watching him intently. His lips brushed the salty droplets from her inner thighs, and his hands prevented her from closing her knees. She'd been so focused on the heavenly sensation of his lips on her skin to think. The cool air brushing her sensitive skin only heightened the pleasure as his fingers slid over the seams on her underwear before he eased them down her thighs. His eyes tracked hers as she chewed her lip to silence her moans.

"Make all the noise you want, no one can hear you." His devilish words ruined her.

His shoulders pushed her thighs wider apart, and she gasped as the cool air brushed her core. She lay back as he trailed his tongue along her inner thigh, teasing until finally he made her his. She gasped; he was impossible to resist, and his heady groans as he savoured her heightened the pleasure even more. Her breath came out in gasps, and he pinned her hips down as they moved on their own.

"It's too much, please," she groaned, gripping his shoulders.

She couldn't stand the waves of pleasure coursing through her as he licked and sucked until her back arched off the stone border of the pool.

"Ride my tongue, Bee," he ordered, holding her hips as she writhed against his mouth.

"Be a good fucking girl and come for me."

His gravelly command undid her, and his fingers replaced his mouth, drawing out her pleasure until she didn't know where reality began and dream ended.

"Now that's the perfect way to end the day," he said, kissing her thigh. Spent, she gasped for breath, like she was drowning. She stared down at him, and his hazy, self-assured smile only made her want more.

"If only every day could end like that," she sighed as he eased her underwear back up her thighs and kissed each knee before easing her back into the water.

"Your wish is my command." He winked.

Exhausted, she wrapped her legs around his waist and rested her cheek against his shoulder. He walked them out of the pool and up the garden. He set her down once they reached the sliding door. Her legs felt like jelly as he stood behind her, kissing her shoulder. He followed her inside, keeping her close, his hands on her waist, and it felt as if they'd been doing this their whole life. The realisation of how comfortable she was with him made her freeze. It felt so natural, too natural, and it suddenly terrified her.

"I'll be up in a minute." She let go of his hand, and he paused on the staircase.

"Are you okay?" He frowned, tucking a strand of hair behind her ear. It eased her fear, and she didn't want to let him go, but she had to find her balance.

"I just want to get some water."

"Don't be long." He kissed her tenderly before he headed upstairs.

Phoebe took a moment to catch her breath and turn off the lights in the house. She brought some snacks and water to his room, and found him lying on the bed with his arm tucked behind his head, completely out of it. She couldn't blame him for being so exhausted—*she* was exhausted, and he'd done most of the work. She turned off the light and covered him with the light sheets to let him sleep.

After showering and slipping on one of his T-shirts, the bed dipped as she climbed in beside him. He rolled over and unconsciously tucked her in close. She smiled at his sleepy frown. Gently, she traced the tattoos on his ribs, unsure of how anyone could be so beautiful. The balcony door was open, giving them a perfect view of the calm ocean and bright stars. She wanted to freeze this moment.

"We're here." Axel stopped, and Phoebe nearly walked into the back of him.

"I don't think this place is open. Are you sure she gave you the right address?" Phoebe frowned, looking up and down the cobbled street and its quaint, brightly coloured shops. He understood her confusion since they had walked past other, more welcoming studios after their pasta feast for lunch—he wanted her well-fed before her first tattoo, and the restaurant down the street from Claudia's studio had the best lasagne in Amalfi.

"Claudia likes to keep her pop-up studios discreet," Axel pointed out. "She never stays in one place for long." He stood by the painted black door. "You can find her studios by the all-seeing eye symbol drawn in gold pen along the doorframe."

The small shopfront with blacked-out front windows and no name didn't look all that inviting. It would be easy to pass the studio without even knowing what was inside, assuming it was abandoned and waiting to be rented out.

Sensing her nerves, Axel took Phoebe's hand, and knocked on the door.

She peered over her shoulder. "All the other shops have

flowers by the door and brightly coloured awnings—a blacked-out shop is the opposite of discreet."

"I like this woman; she says what's on her mind." A woman with a pink buzz cut, many piercings and a mischievous smile opened the door. Unique, striking with a hint of terrifying—from Phoebe's wide eyes, she loved it. Axel had known they would get along.

"Claudia, I didn't expect you to be awake this early," Axel said, giving her a quick hug.

Despite the late hour of the afternoon, Claudia looked like she had just rolled out of bed. Another woman in a purple dress and blushed cheeks joined Claudia in the doorway and kissed her tattooed cheek. Axel winked at Phoebe as the two women said a quick goodbye.

"I wasn't, I haven't been to bed yet." Claudia watched the woman walk down the street with no shame. "I'm being terribly rude—you must be Phoebe. I've heard many things about you."

"From the band?" Phoebe asked.

Axel knew Claudia was trying to make him nervous. He didn't want Phoebe to know how much he talked about her artwork.

"Who else? They're among my favourite clients." Claudia smiled, glancing at Axel, who focused on the new artwork on Claudia's wall. Phoebe stared at the many prints hanging over the old fireplace. This homage to so many artists must have been heaven to her.

"I thought you'd be best to do Phoebe's first," Axel said, following them both into the studio, "since you've done all our tattoos."

"Except for August, who refuses to let me anywhere near him." Claudia pouted.

"Don't take it personally. He hates being touched, let alone by needles," Phoebe assured her, taking a seat on the pink chaise by a giant tank containing a multitude of exotic fish.

"Since we were in the area, I thought we would stop in and inconvenience you," Axel said, sitting on the stool by the tattoo bench.

"No inconvenience at all. How long have you been in Amalfi?" Claudia asked.

"Only a few days, we had some things to sort out," Phoebe said. Axel sensed she didn't want to give away too much information since everything they did at the minute had a habit of turning up in the press.

"Well, I'm honoured to make your list. It can't be that long since I've seen you—London? You got a snail on your ankle after the show?" Claudia's bleached brows pulled together as she tried to recall. Axel rolled his eyes, not all too fond of the memory.

"A snail?" Phoebe asked, glancing at his ankles, which were luckily covered by his socks. It wasn't like she hadn't seen his tattoos when he was naked, but he preferred to keep her focus elsewhere in those moments. Even thinking about her by the pool yesterday made him want to jump into the ocean to cool down.

"Because he's always the last one on stage," Claudia answered for him, distracting him from his fond memories.

"It was a bet," Axel sighed, not elaborating.

"I got to fly first class, free champagne. I nearly messed up the fine lines." Claudia walked through the open-plan studio to a small kitchen area and got some ice out of the freezer. She cleared her throat, and Axel knew what she was about to say but wished she wouldn't.

"I was sorry to hear about Cillian, poor idiot. You never know when your time's up." Claudia's condolences came out with a puff of smoke from her vape.

"You missed the funeral. Nick said he called you." Axel

had been surprised she didn't attend, but she had sent a beautiful flower arrangement to the house.

"I had a show that couldn't be moved, and I have to pay rent here and for the London studio, and with the divorce eating into my assets, I can't turn away any job."

"I thought you and Martha were amicable?" Axel asked, trying to change the subject when he noticed how Phoebe shuffled uncomfortably at the mention of Cillian's funeral.

"We were, until she decided to ask for my vinyl collection."

Axel chuckled as Claudia made them a round of iced teas.

"Anyhow, on to brighter topics. I hear you're a virgin." Claudia handed them their iced teas with slices of lemon.

"A tattoo virgin," Axel clarified, loving how Phoebe blushed and stammered through an incoherent response.

Phoebe glared at him. "Right."

"A perfect canvas! And you're an artist yourself. I've seen your stuff, but I was so sorry to see what that arsehole did to your studio. I can't imagine dealing with that shit." Claudia picked up her tablet.

Axel choked on his iced tea, interrupting her.

"You okay?" Claudia asked, patting him on the back.

"Swallowed the wrong way," he lied, but he didn't want Phoebe to think about all that had happened back home right now.

"I'm taking a break, and I can always redo what was ruined." Phoebe brushed over the topic. Axel raised his eyebrows—she had left out her revenge plot.

"I like your style. Rise above it, it'll be tomorrow's news soon enough," Claudia said, sitting down beside them.

It was a relief to think that all the hate being directed at Phoebe would soon be forgotten, but the thought that the world would move on just as fast from Cillian's death, his loss to the band, left a pit in his stomach.

The thought of seeing his friend on one of those 'Ten celebrities who died before their time' lists made him wince.

"Sorry about her," he said to Phoebe. "She has the subtlety of a hammer meeting a nail."

Claudia frowned, like she didn't understand what she had said wrong.

"Right, are you ready to get started? I got the sketches you sent me, and I think something like this should work?" She turned the tablet to show them the sketch of a blank canvas resting on a fine-line easel with florals and leaves wrapped around the wooden legs. Two tins sat at the base, leaking paint. "I know you said you liked Axel's drumsticks in the email, so I wrapped the legs of the easel with some flowers, but if it's too matchy-matchy, I can rework it."

"Don't you dare change a thing, it's perfect."

Axel turned to Phoebe, who was beaming from ear to ear. He was taken aback by how willing she was to have such a similar tattoo to his own. He didn't care—if anything, it triggered a possessive streak in him he didn't know he had. He was half tempted to tattoo 'mine' on her upper thigh and make it official, but this was subtle, like a secret between the two of them.

"It's so delicate, I love it!" Phoebe zoomed in on the image with the biggest smile he'd seen on her since before that night in Munich.

"Where do you want it?" Claudia asked, printing out the stencil.

"My ribs," Phoebe said, pointing to the same spot where Axel had his drumsticks. He tried to conceal his joy but failed miserably.

"It's a bit more sensitive than places with more fat," Claudia warned.

"I can take it." Phoebe flexed her hand, and he hated how much pain her injury caused her. He wished he could take her pain away, or even share it so he could understand its weight.

"That's what I like to hear." Claudia interrupted his thoughts, preparing everything required on a silver tray. "This design is about the size of my palm, so it should be about three to four hours, given the fine details. We can take a break whenever you want."

"She can hold my hand if it gets tough," Axel offered as Phoebe removed her t-shirt to reveal a pink bikini top that made him want to forget about the tattoo and bring her home. Phoebe scrunched her nose at him, like she knew what he was thinking. He winked, and she shook her head.

Once the stencil was placed, and Phoebe finished squealing about how much she loved it, Claudia got to work while he watched anxiously from the side. Phoebe took the sit like a champion. It was only after the third hour that she took his hand.

"You're all finished!"

Claudia added the second skin to protect the tattoo for the first couple of days. Axel helped Phoebe hop off the bed, and she hurried to the long mirror in the corner.

Thankfully, she didn't seem fazed at all after her first sit. He had never cared so much about another person's welfare before. He constantly wanted to check how she was, if she was in pain or in need of a hug. He wasn't sure how long they would have before Anita caught on and tracked them down, so he wanted to make every minute count.

"I love it! Thank you so much for taking the time to do this," Phoebe said, wrapping her arms around Claudia. Seeing her so happy made his day.

"My pleasure. It's not often I get to do such delicate work, since these tough guys like their bold lines and darker themes." Claudia nudged Axel.

"You have to let us treat you to dinner," Axel offered, wanting to thank her for squeezing them in. She was always booked out years in advance, and she had done this as a favour. He didn't want her to think he was taking advantage of their friendship.

"Please join us?" Phoebe pleaded while Claudia tidied up her station.

"I would love to, but I've got a date. When I get home, we can all go out together. It's been a while since I've seen Nick," Claudia said, with a small smile that spoke of her not-so-secret crush. He'd known she'd bring up Nick; she always brought up Nick.

"I'm sure August and Nick would love to have you round to the house," Axel said.

"How much do I owe you?" Phoebe asked, putting on her T-shirt.

"Not a cent. It's taken care of," Claudia said, waving them off.

"No, you can't do that," Axel insisted.

"Don't argue with me, Adler. I have a gun with lots of needles, don't make me use it. It'll make me feel less like a terrible person for missing the funeral if you let me do this for you," Claudia said, pouting.

Axel sighed, and gave in. "I wouldn't dare argue."

"Please let me tip you," Phoebe pleaded, opening her purse. "You did such an amazing job combining the sketches I sent."

"I won't accept it." Claudia closed Phoebe's hand around the cash. "How about tickets to your next show? That would be thanks enough."

"Consider it done, and a discount on whatever piece you like."

Phoebe thanked her again, and Axel gave her a quick hug as she walked them to the door.

After saying their goodbyes, they walked down the street to the restaurant Claudia had recommended. Axel longed to hold Phoebe's hand, but settled for an accidental brush here and there in case they were spotted. At this hour, the dinner rush was starting, so chances of being noticed were higher.

"I don't think we'll be able to get a table," Phoebe said.

Claudia must've sensed their need for discretion—the restaurant was a tiny hole in the wall, with candles and flowers on the tables.

"Claudia has a standing table; she's allergic to cooking."

"I know the feeling," Phoebe said, as they sat outside under a tree.

The candlelight made it feel like a date. Luckily, Phoebe filled the silence before he had to think of a topic.

"I might've noticed that Claudia mentioned Nick a couple of times, what's the story there?"

"She's had a crush on him for years. They like to play cat and mouse with each other," Axel said. Claudia always found a way to get what she wanted—Nick didn't stand a chance.

Phoebe grimaced. "Gross, I don't want to hear about my brother playing anything with anyone."

Once they had finished ordering, he made sure to change the topic. "Why the blank canvas?" he asked.

"For a fresh start, a new chapter. I was thinking about how the canvases were ruined and decided to think of it as a chance to start again," she said, sipping her sangria— virgin sangria, since alcohol isn't good with new tattoos. Then she moved on to the breadbasket. "I think the adrenaline woke up my stomach."

He passed her the butter before she inhaled the fresh bread.

"Since I answered your question, can I ask why you chose to tattoo a spider crawling up your neck to your head?" she asked as she passed him a piece of buttered bread. He'd eat anything she gave him.

"It's not something I talk about much, but I figure, since you trusted me to take you on this trip… A spider represents accepting one's fate or destiny. It's a reminder that no matter how much I try to control my life, at the end of the day we have very little control," he said, sipping his beer.

"Why on the side of your head? I mean, I like it, it suits you—not that I know what you looked like without it," she rambled adorably as her cheeks flushed.

He put down his fork and hoped he wasn't about to ruin their nice dinner.

"Alopecia." He decided to rip off the band-aid. "Believed to be caused by the stress of my dad bailing when I was younger. It's a lot better now, easier to hide since I got my eyelashes and eyebrows back."

"How come you never said?" she asked gently.

He rubbed his thighs, feeling vulnerable. "I do shave my head, but mostly because it grows in patches that aren't very sexy," he confessed as their plates of pasta and an assortment of seafood and steak were placed on the table. They had over-ordered, but the long day made them hungry.

"You said it was because your dad left?" she asked, cutting up the juicy steak.

"I was about fourteen when it started falling out, which was around the same time. Not sure, it's an autoimmune thing. My immune system attacks my hair follicles, like those follicles are a threat," he explained briefly. "It's not really known why and there isn't a cure."

"I'm sorry you had to go through that." She offered him some of her steak like it would make him feel better, which it did.

"I told you about my sisters and the drums, my fighting in school. I fought because I was bullied a lot because of it. I tried to cover it up with caps when it started to go patchy, but shaving it was easiest," he said, picking at the calamari.

"I'm glad you defended yourself."

He loved how passionate she was. "And I wish I was as imaginative with my vengeance as you."

"I'm glad you had your sisters, but I'm sorry that you felt that you had to keep it from us."

"My symptoms have lessened over the years; I have my eyelashes and eyebrows, and that's enough for me. Siobhan, my sister, developed symptoms as she got older. She loves her assortment of wigs. She rocked a buzz cut for a few years, but as I got more famous the media hounded her, especially if she came to shows." Axel tried not to let the anger seep into his words.

"I can't imagine how that must have felt for either of you. I wish I could've kicked all their butts for picking on you," she said, and he smiled at her scrunched features. He didn't doubt she meant every word.

"I'd have loved to have such a fierce protector," he said, and kissed her palm, forgetting where they were.

"Don't tease. I may be small but I'm scrappy, especially when it comes to those I care about," she said, holding onto his hand. Her assurance made him love her more than he already did.

"So that's why you picked that spot for the spider, because of the lack of control." Her eyes settled on his tattoo.

"I decided to embrace it. As a man, losing our hair can be a sensitive topic."

"And a giant spider is a good way to say fuck off," she added with a smirk.

"Precisely." He smiled, and helped her finish the steak.

"Thank you for telling me." She rested her hand over

his, only to remove it when a waiter came to take their plates.

"Thank you for listening." He noticed her fidgeting. "Is there something on your mind? You're studying your wine glass."

"There is something I've got to tell you, but before you freak out, it might be nothing and I didn't tell you or the others because it might be nothing, but since you're being open with me, I think I owe you the same honesty." She rubbed her hands on her thighs, and he tried not to panic.

"Okay, I promise I won't freak out or interrupt. Please skip to the point before I have a heart attack." He wiped his lips with his napkin and gave her his full attention.

"Before we left, Olivier gave me my mail from the studio. There was a package, I thought it might've been from a fan of my work." She hesitated.

His eyes narrowed, waiting for the shoe to drop.

"I opened it, and there were confetti strings…" She trailed off.

"And?"

"Razor blades," she admitted, picking at the plaster on her finger.

Axel put his hands on his head and took a deep breath so he wouldn't react.

"You promised not to react," she whispered, leaning in close. He was very aware of the others in the restaurant and remembered to remain calm.

"Sorry, yes. Not reacting, I'm cool." He glanced at her plasters, remembering seeing them the night he had helped her dye her hair.

"That's how you cut your fingers," he breathed, taking her hand.

"I didn't say anything because I thought that the package might've been there a while. Could've been dropped off by Sheen before the break-in, I hadn't checked my mailbox for weeks, and it's big enough for parcels," she explained. He hated to see her stressed.

"I'm not mad, but I wish you'd have told me. We could've given it to the police."

"I wanted to, but how do we know it wasn't the police who leaked what happened at the studio to the press? If the person who sent the fan mail wants attention, then we shouldn't risk it getting leaked. I wanted to wait and see if it was mentioned in the press before I said anything. Then we'd know for sure that the same person harassing me is the same person leaking the news." She paused as a waiter filled their water glasses.

"We need someone we can trust, and I think I might know a person," he said, thinking of Autumn, who'd had a detective work her own stalking case last year. "I can make a few calls and we can get to the bottom of this, together. Have room for dessert?" he asked, hoping something sweet or chocolatey would cheer her up.

"So I didn't ruin your appetite?" she said sadly.

"Not in the least." Axel wanted to reach across the table and wrap her in his arms. Instead, he settled for passing her the dessert menu. "On to more important matters—chocolate lava cake or tiramisu?"

"Both?"

"Just when I thought I couldn't want you more."

God, he loved it when she blushed.

With the bill paid, they were the last people at the restaurant, and Axel still wished the night wasn't ending so soon. Phoebe waited outside in the quiet street, and he rested his hand on her lower back, guiding her away. The evening air was still balmy, and under the full moon, he wanted to end the perfect day with a kiss. However, it was a risk he couldn't take. Instead, he took her hand as they walked.

They were just another couple out for an evening stroll. Both were enjoying the silence and the night when a blinding flash surprised them from behind.

"What the?" Phoebe stilled, clutching his hand tightly. Her hand was getting stronger.

They both turned to see a group of photographers catching up to them. Axel's gut sank as he realised they must've been spotted, and their location sold.

"Shit, we need to run!" Axel pulled her into a narrow alley.

"How the hell did they even know where to look?" she asked, but he was too busy trying to figure out how to get out of there. "Then again, the hostess was looking at you funny."

"Doesn't matter now. We have to get out of here before we get swarmed."

When they came out of the other side of the alley, Axel noticed a bike leaning against a tree, and grabbed it before he could think any better of it.

"Get on," he said.

"Are you crazy? You can't steal someone's bike."

"I'll return it tomorrow. We don't have time to argue, and we can't run all the way back to the villa," he argued, putting his leg over.

Phoebe grumbled a little in protest, but she took his hand and got on behind him. Thankfully, they got away, followed only by the shouts of those desperately trying and failing to catch up. Phoebe clung to him as they made their way back to the villa. He only hoped none of the photographers had got a clear shot, or what was supposed to be a break for her would turn into a nightmare.

ONCE THEY WERE SAFELY inside the villa, they stumbled into the kitchen.

"Anita is going to kill us both if they managed to get a decent shot." She paced in front of the fridge. He hated to think how cute she was when she was stressed.

"All they got was two people walking down the street," Axel said, trying to ease her panic as he rounded the counter. "Though I'm not sure we were completely innocent," he teased, trying to lighten the mood.

She glared at him, only for them both to erupt into laughter at how ridiculous the situation had got.

"I'm just kind of hungry. Must have been all that

running." Axel came up behind her and rested his hands on her hips. She leaned into his touch with a gentle sigh. Music to his ears.

"I think there's some ice cream in the freezer," she said.

"Not sure ice cream is what I'm craving." He kissed her shoulder, pressing her up against the fridge.

"Oh really?" She turned around and rested her arms on his shoulders.

"You're just what I'm craving." He loved making her flush, and she nudged him playfully.

Phoebe tasted like sangria. Her lips were soft, and she did this thing with her tongue—*there she goes again.* He reminded himself to take his time, to not get her naked in the kitchen.

Phoebe leaned back in his arms to study him.

"I can hear you thinking."

Her hands on his chest, her face flushed from their fevered kiss.

"I don't want to move too fast; I didn't plan this trip for sex," he said, wanting to make sure she was ready.

"I want this, and I know you don't just want sex, which only makes me want you all the more." She gripped his T-shirt, pulling him closer.

"I've wanted you for so long, I'm not going to screw this up, so we go at your pace." He dipped his head and pressed his lips along her neck.

"The only thing you'll screw tonight is me." Her breathy words tested him.

His hand slipped around her nape and he kissed her until she flushed pink. She slid her hands down his chest and placed his hands firmly on her hips. Her short skirt killed him as it rose up on her thighs so easily. He tried not to think how easy it would be to take her on the kitchen table. She shrieked when he grabbed her around the waist.

"This skirt is very distracting." His lips skimmed her collarbone, and he kissed the outline of her bikini through her T-shirt.

"Your dessert is under it." She smirked, and her hands slipped under his T-shirt.

His muscles tightened as she teased the edge of his jeans with her fingers. He groaned, sucking lightly on her lower lip. Phoebe's fingernails bit into his shoulders. Cupping her ass, he lifted her onto the table. Her skirt rode up her delectable thighs, and he stepped between them, recalling how good she tasted.

"We should go upstairs," he rasped, growing harder by the second.

"Dessert in bed sounds good."

"Tell me if I'm moving too fast."

"Not fast enough."

She flushed, and she reached behind her neck and undid her bikini top. He watched in awe as she slipped it out from beneath her T-shirt and chucked it aside.

"Your wish is my command."

Her heels dug into his thighs as he lifted her off the counter.

"Don't drop me," she said as they reached the stairs.

"I've got you," he said, meaning for now and forever as he held her tight. The questioning look in those beautiful eyes dented his heart. He could hear her thinking, wondering if she could trust him, if she could give him her heart.

Even if it took time, he was a patient man. Her lips trailed along his jaw, sucking his neck, and he gripped her thighs tighter. She gasped as he pressed against her, and shifted her hips, her way of getting revenge. Her every movement against him made him want to beg for relief. A few tugs here and there and she would be naked and at his mercy.

They reached the closed door to the bedroom they already shared, and he didn't dare cross the threshold without permission.

"Are you sure?" he asked, reminding himself that this trip was for her, and he wanted her to experience only what she desired.

"As I've ever been." She pressed her lips to his, demanding and exploring.

They only had so much time alone together, and with her permission he wasn't going to waste another second. His lips never left hers as he kicked open the bedroom door. She squealed as it banged against the wall. He hadn't meant to use so much force, but right now all he cared about was getting Phoebe Fletcher in his bed and screaming his name. He sat them on the bed with her legs wrapped around him.

"What do you need?" he asked, lifting her T-shirt above her head.

His hands slid up her thighs, and she stood for a moment as he eased her underwear down, her hands braced on his shoulders. He trailed his lips along her abdomen and ribs, careful to avoid her fresh ink.

"I still want dessert," she teased, sinking in front of him.

He watched her, his hand sinking into her hair at the back of her head as she undid his jeans and pulled off his boxers. She licked her lips, and he thought he'd lose control. The sight of her on her knees did unholy things to him, but she was worth damnation.

"Shit, that's—"

He loved how she stared up at him as she took him in her mouth. As much as he didn't want her to stop, and wanted to savour every moment of her lips on him, he wanted her more. With a pained, regretful sigh, he pulled her onto the bed beside him, knowing he wouldn't last much longer, and there were many things he wanted to do to her before he lost control.

"I was enjoying my dessert." She smiled devilishly. "You should know better than to get between a woman and sweet things."

"You're going to ruin me," he said. "Come here." He positioned her to straddle him as he reached for a condom from his bag by the bed and rolled it on. "You're so ready for me."

Watching her rise up on her knees, he gritted his teeth as she gripped him.

"I think you've ruined me for anyone else." Her words were music to his ears.

She sank slowly as he held tightly to her hips. Together they savoured every second of sensation. He held her close as she started to rock against him. Her impatience and the way her head fell back in ecstasy melted him. His mouth on her neck, jaw, lips caused the most delicious moan to escape those rosy lips. She pushed on his chest, and he lay back, letting her take control as she rode him. A slight sheen of sweat covered their skin, and his abs flexed with every rotation of her hips.

"Give me those lips." With a palm on her nape, he pulled her close, claiming her mouth with his tongue as they moved at the same leisurely pace, lost in each other. When she gasped, he covered her breasts with wet kisses to bring her closer to the edge.

"I think I'm in love with your breasts," he told her, dragging his teeth over her hard peaks. Her moans made him fall deeper.

"You should, they're your biggest fan."

Her giggle turned into a moan as the combination of

sensations—him inside her—was becoming too much for both of them. He ground his pelvis against her with each shift of her hips, sending her over the edge. Axel whispered in her ear as she came down—how good she felt, and how he loved watching her use his body for her own pleasure. The orgasm keeps going, steamrolling over them.

"Fuck, Phoebe, I love feeling you come around me."

Her reply was an incoherent string of words. He watched her explode around him, never wanting to forget how beautiful she was in this moment. She arched against him; her nails sank into his shoulders as she cried out his name. She shivered, and he held her flush against him as he came so hard everything disappeared except the feel of her pulsing around him. Every muscle in his body tightened and tremors overtook him until he had nothing left to give but a low groan into her neck. Melting into each other, in a collection of satisfied, heavy breaths—he didn't want the moment to end.

Axel lifted her chin up from his shoulder, forcing her to look at him, and kissed her tenderly, groaning through his final thrust. Her eyes snapped open as he rolled her onto her back, because he had to see those bliss-filled eyes staring up at him. He landed on the mattress, taking her with him, not ready to let her go, until he rolled over gently and eased away from her.

"I don't think we should leave this bed until we fly home," he said, kissing her head.

"Excellent, sleep, tired." She was clearly too exhausted to speak in full sentences.

He laughed as she snuggled into him, already half asleep as he ran his fingers through her hair. A few minutes passed and he was sure she was out cold. Carefully, he reached for his phone on the floor and set an alarm for their last day, wanting to make the most of it before they returned to reality. After turning off the light, he eased his arm under her, and she slipped her leg between his and rested her head on his chest. Caught up in her sweet, post-orgasm blissful sleep, he rested his hand over hers on his ribs and kissed her hair.

I n the middle of the night, Phoebe rolled over to see Axel sitting out on the balcony with a cigarette lit and his head hung low. She wrapped the bedsheet around her body.

"Are you okay?" she asked, padding over the cool tiles to kneel in front of him, so he would be forced to look at her.

"I'm sorry." Axel sniffled, putting out his cigarette in the ashtray on the table. It wasn't like him to smoke. He offered her a small smile, but she saw his bloodshot eyes, and knew he had been crying. "I didn't mean to wake you. I woke up and didn't realise where we were, and I was dreaming we were all in the studio together," Axel explained, his head in his hands.

"The grief can sneak up on you. It's perfectly normal." She rested her hands on his knees, letting him talk. It was the first time he had spoken about his feelings since the funeral.

"It's not just about him, but grieving the future we all expected to share. The tours we played, the hours of practice just for fun. Even the arguments, I miss fighting with the arse." He rubbed his eyes and smiled softly, which only broke her heart further.

"When I woke up, I felt like an elephant was sitting on my chest," he continued. "Nick had texted me earlier to say they've been flying through production on the new songs. I realised when he said 'us', that no longer included Cillian. Usually, Cillian would message me complaining about me not getting involved enough with the process, but when I did, he'd be insufferable with all of us. He was a pain, but I miss him." His leg shook, and she ran her hand over his thigh trying to soothe him.

"Shit, sorry, I shouldn't even be saying all this to you." He placed his hand over hers and gently pulled her up onto his lap. He kissed her bare shoulder. "I was just having a pity party. I'm fine, probably the wine at dinner."

"I'm glad you're talking to me. You don't have to hide your feelings from me, ever. I need you to tell me everything if this is going to work. I don't want you to hide anything from me. How you feel is valid and I won't judge you for it." Phoebe cupped his face in her hands. "And please don't apologise, you've nothing to be sorry for. Cill was your friend, and just because you didn't always see eye to eye doesn't mean you didn't care about each other. What happened between him and I had nothing to do with you. You've every right to grieve, and I want to be there for you, just as you've been here for me," she said, realising he must've been hiding his grief to be present for her.

"Are you sorry about us, about last night?" she asked, wondering if he was having second thoughts.

He pulled her closer, putting her at ease. "Never. You're the greatest thing to ever happen to me. Even before..." He kissed her, and her heart bloomed. "You've been my light since the moment I met you. I could never regret what's happening between us."

"But do you feel guilty?" She rested her forehead

against his. "I don't want you to feel like you're betraying him by being with me."

"No, I don't. We didn't plan this, and who's to say things wouldn't have turned out this way eventually? We can only focus on what's happening." He met her gaze. "Do you?"

"Maybe, for being so happy so soon? But not because I found something with you. You're different, we're different," she confessed, wanting to be honest.

"Different is good." He picked up her scarred hand and kissed her gently.

It felt like a weight had been lifted from her shoulders. They were together because they wanted to be, not because of revenge, guilt or grief. Maybe he was right, and they would have ended up together in the future regardless, maybe in a less unfortunate series of events. As she watched him stare at the stars reflected on the quiet sea, she wondered if he was her silver lining.

"I couldn't agree more."

They watched the stars for a while until she took his hand and led him back to bed. Curled up together, they talked about everything and anything until the sun started to rise, and they finally drifted off.

I *had sex with Axel Adler!* Phoebe sat up, her body aching from their late-night sex-capade. She stretched her arms above her head, feeling the pull of the second skin on her tattoo. Forty-eight hours, and so much had changed. She ran her hands through her hair, brushing the strands from her face as she noticed Axel's side of the bed was cold.

"God, I'm starving."

Phoebe's grumbling stomach forced her out of bed. The sun beaming in through the sheer curtains reminded her of their plans to spend their last day at the beach.

The second skin masked her new ink in the bathroom mirror, and as much as she wanted to peel it off, she'd have to wait another twenty-four hours before she'd get to see it properly.

After a quick shower, she'd just finished drying her hair when she heard knocking. She'd figured Rowena might stop by. She tossed on a pair of denim shorts and Axel's T-shirt from the bedroom floor and she started to head downstairs, but froze at the top of the staircase when she saw Anita thrusting a tabloid into Axel's chest. What the hell was she doing here?

"Are you out of your mind? Coming here and letting

yourselves be photographed on a cosy night on the town?" Anita snapped, storming through the front door.

"Nice to see you too, Anita, please come in."

"Read this. There's going to be nothing nice about this visit."

"'Brothers of Anarchy's deranged fan sends a box of razor blades to the ex-girlfriend of the late Cillian Hunt after she moves into the house with remaining members.'"

Phoebe's stomach dropped listening to Axel read the cover. She waited for him to follow Anita into the kitchen before tiptoeing down the stairs to listen in.

"Where's Phoebe? She needs to be a part of this," Anita barked.

"She's upstairs, sleeping. I'll tell her when she wakes up," Axel said. "Why is confronting her important? Phoebe didn't leak this to the press. She was scared and didn't want us to overreact. You told her to lie low, but even leaving the country didn't even make a difference."

Axel's defence of her only made her fall harder.

I was right—the media could've only found out if the person who sent the package leaked it themselves. Phoebe shook her head in disbelief. She'd hidden the evidence in the recycling bin, and that was sure to be long gone now. *I should go out and explain,* she thought, but she tugged at the hem of Axel's T-shirt. Anita would have a heart attack if she realised they were together.

"Lie low?" Anita scoffed and pulled out her phone. "I think you're trying to make my job difficult. Having dinner at a romantic restaurant, in public? The paps got some cosy shots of the two of you. You've gone viral! If I left my alerts on, my phone would explode."

Phoebe heard Axel pacing. "It isn't any of your business what we do or where we go. If the media want to take pictures of two people having dinner, then let them. We shouldn't have to hide," he countered. "We've done nothing wrong, and acting like criminals is going to make us all look like we've something to hide."

"In the court of public opinion, giving your dead bandmate's ex and best friend's sister smouldering stares during a candlelight dinner will get us all crucified. To top it off, you ran off hand in hand."

"She was wearing heels; I didn't want her to fall." Axel's joke made Phoebe wince.

"After everything I've done for you, why must you sabotage us like this?" Anita snarled.

"I thought you'd be happy. The increased press coverage will mean more ticket sales for the remembrance concert you pushed so hard for."

"Or the fans will boycott said concert because you're disrespecting your recently deceased friend by shacking up with his girlfriend."

Phoebe couldn't bear to listen any longer. She didn't regret anything about their trip. Why should she consider Cillian's feelings in death when his pregnant girlfriend was currently moving into his apartment in New York? With Axel, she felt truly wanted without being asked for anything in return, and she refused to feel guilty about it.

"You're crossing the line. Go home. We don't need to be managed," Axel said coolly.

Phoebe hurried up the stairs when she heard footsteps approach.

"If you were, maybe we wouldn't have ended up in this position," Anita argued, reaching the door. "Also, the police came by the house. They were curious to know why you'd both left during the investigation. And that there was no evidence of another person at the studio except for you and her."

No evidence. She wasn't surprised—Sheen had worn

gloves in the video—but did the police think she'd made it up? Phoebe wished she'd given them the footage. Then again, she shouldn't have to fight to be believed.

Axel muttered a curse under his breath. "Are you accusing us of something?"

Not wanting to hear any more, Phoebe hurried back upstairs. She wondered if she'd been hoping for too much, for one weekend with the man who was slowly healing her heart.

In the bedroom, Axel's phone rang. *Autumn*. She recognised his cousin's name, a famous concert pianist, who no doubt was calling about his name being all over the internet once again.

She picked up the phone.

"Axel?" Autumn asked.

"Sorry, it's Phoebe. We met briefly at your concert last year at the Royal Albert Hall," Phoebe said, not expecting her to even remember the encounter.

"I thought that was you. Hi. Is everything okay?" Autumn's concern came in a rush. "There was an international dial tone?"

"We're in Italy, we wanted to get away for a little bit." Phoebe stumbled through the explanation, closing the bedroom door. "I can have Axel call you back."

"No worries, I was only checking in. I saw that he was away, and there were some pictures of the two of you, but I really called to ask how you're coping?"

"I'm fine." Phoebe spoke too quickly to sound sincere.

Autumn chuckled a little. "Sorry, I don't mean to laugh. I used to say the same thing a lot. You don't have to pretend with me."

Phoebe hesitated before confessing.

"Pretty shit."

She flexed her scarred hand, tight from having

neglected her exercises. "Getting away has helped, even if all I want to do is paint the views. Feels like my skin is itchy, like my body is craving paint. Sounds stupid, but…" She didn't know how to finish the sentence, but thankfully Autumn did.

"It's not easy when an injury takes you away from the thing you love. I've had first-hand experience in that department. I would literally play on anything, a table, my thighs, and just imagine the music in my head. Not being able to play felt like a part of me had been torn out. Like a jigsaw missing a piece, and nothing else fit."

"I couldn't have put it better myself. Painting has always been my outlet, so I've had a little too much time to think. I've managed to get some sketching done—my physio thinks the muscle memory will help with the nerve damage—but it doesn't feel the same as before." It felt so good to talk to someone else whose pain had threatened to take them away from what they loved. From their oxygen. Without it, life felt wrong, flat, or just empty.

"Adjusting and accepting a new normal is the hardest part, but the most important thing is to be kind to yourself." Autumn didn't talk of silver linings, or say that everything would be okay; she was honest about the reality of healing, and it was what Phoebe needed to hear.

"Can I ask you something? And if it's too personal, please don't feel any pressure to answer." Phoebe sat on the edge of the bed.

"I'm an open book. You can thank Elijah for that."

Phoebe got the feeling that Elijah was the emotionally expressive one in the relationship. They were an adorable couple, yet complete opposites. Even in the brief time Phoebe had spent in their company, she'd seen how completely devoted they were. Elijah checked in on Autumn while she rolled her eyes, but Phoebe knew she was looking out for him in the corner of her eye. It was refreshing to see. Cillian used to abandon her in a crowd, citing how important it was to "mingle".

"How did you handle the guilt after your accident? I don't even know if guilt is the right word, but seeing the video footage posted on social media… I don't know why I survived and he didn't. The car was so crushed. Sometimes the tightness in my chest gets so bad I forget to breathe." Phoebe tucked her knees under her chin, unsure if she was making sense. But since Autumn had survived her own life-altering accident as a teen, she was the only one she could think to ask. If Autumn could survive a stage collapsing while she was performing and still get back to playing, then it gave her hope that she could overcome her own struggles.

There was a brief silence, and she winced, worried she'd said too much.

"I didn't handle it for a long time, but then I realised that surviving gave me a second chance, and I didn't want to waste that. It'd be a disservice to my friend who passed, and myself, if I didn't live. My back injury reminds me never to forget that no matter how bad the pain gets, I have to be kind and patient with myself," Autumn said. "But it took years. Some days I want to curl up and disappear, and I do, but now I reach out to those I love and trust for support. You have to listen to your body as much as your head and heart, because both can be great deceivers."

"Thank you for being so honest—and curling up and disappearing sounds pretty good."

Phoebe stared at the long scar that ran from her thumb to her wrist. It ached with every movement and clenched fist.

"I can't imagine the weight of your emotions right now. You lost the person you loved, twice—once when you found out about the cheating, and then in the accident. You also lost something you love, or at least the ability to do it with previous ease. Give yourself some grace, and time. If I could give you any advice, lean on those around you. Don't push them away."

Autumn's sincerity meant a lot to her. Autumn owed her nothing, but her words were worth everything.

"I was happy to hear that you're living with Axel and the others," she continued. "Being around people can feel suffocating when you're dealing with pain and recovery, but don't be afraid to need them."

"Axel's been my miracle." Phoebe guessed from her tone that Axel had already told her what was happening between them.

"I feel a but coming," Autumn probed softly.

"I'm afraid of how much I care for him. Everything's happening so soon—what if I'm subconsciously trying to cling to something good?"

Phoebe cringed to reveal her worst inner thoughts. Autumn was his cousin after all, her loyalty would lie with him, and she'd just confessed to the possibility of using him.

"Axel is a grown man; he wouldn't do anything he didn't want to. You've got to let him decide what he wants. He refused to leave your side at the hospital until you woke up. Your brother and August called me to convince him to leave. Don't be afraid to lean on those who love you, no matter who it is," Autumn assured her. "It's easier said than done. It took me finding a six-foot game designer in my kitchen to learn that depending on others isn't weakness. If you're worried about using him to fill some void, then you probably aren't."

Phoebe hadn't known about Axel not leaving her side in the hospital. Was it a guilty conscience for letting her leave the tour bus? Not that she needed his permission to do anything, but she understood how he could feel that way.

"Are you sure you aren't feeling guilty about the possibility of having feelings for someone else so soon after losing Cillian?" Autumn read her mind.

"Why should I feel guilty when he was fucking his make-up artist for six months?" She hated how harsh she sounded.

Autumn sighed. "Because feelings don't make sense. You can be angry with someone and still love them. You never got to talk about what Cillian did or resolve the situation on your own terms. It's only natural to grieve a future you'll never have with him. Now you're seeing Axel in a new light, and maybe Axel is highlighting some uncomfortable truths. New relationships have a way of doing that." Autumn put it lightly. "Given all you've been through it's understandable that you're scared, nervous, confused. Just be honest with him and, more importantly, yourself."

"What was it about Elijah that made you so sure?" Phoebe asked. Even if Axel was completely different from Cillian, she wanted to make sure she didn't repeat or wasn't repeating any bad habits.

Autumn chuckled. "Because he was there."

"So, it was a proximity thing?"

"Yes and no. He never left when things got hard. Instead, he leaned in, and I'd never had that before. As much as I pushed, he wouldn't budge. He saw my scars, both emotional and physical, and refused to waver."

Phoebe thought back to that night when Axel had helped her with her hair, let her sleep in his bed without question, and went to war with Anita for her. *He hasn't wavered.*

"Axel is like that," she said. "I can't shake him."

Autumn sighed. "He has always been so self-assured and determined. He was one of the few people who convinced me to get back on stage after so many years away from the piano."

"Cillian was jealous of that," Phoebe told her. "He could be insecure, and worried what people thought of him, no matter how much praise he got. That's why my love wasn't enough. Ever since Axel joined Brothers of Anarchy, he's been himself. Steady. And it used to drive Cillian crazy."

There had been more than one occasion where Cillian had tried to convince the others to replace their new drummer, but Nick and August wouldn't allow it.

"If you're worried about using Axel to get back at Cillian, don't be. It doesn't matter how you got together, but how you feel now."

Phoebe wished they had talked sooner.

"I don't know how I feel about anything but him, and it frightens me."

"It's normal to experience a longing for intimacy when you've lost such a big part of your life. Don't punish yourself for seeking comfort in others. Don't think too hard. Elijah is constantly telling me not to think so much. It makes me want to slap him, but he's right, even if I don't let him know that," Autumn told her. "If you take the lust out of it, how does it feel to be with him?"

"He makes me feel calm. It's like I can feel my shoulders relax at the mere thought of being in his company."

"That's a good place to start, focus on that. I think you could do with some calm."

Phoebe silently vowed to follow her advice, and not punish herself for enjoying the time they were spending together.

"Also, I wanted to thank you!" Autumn said suddenly.

"Thank me?" Phoebe frowned, letting her knees drop as their conversation washed away her fears.

"For the painting! Elijah and I finally agreed the hallway is the best place for it. The characters are spot on! Me, the black cat. Elijah, the golden retriever. Brinkley loves it too. She probably thinks it's a painting of her and not her owners. It's by far our favourite engagement present," Autumn explained. "I asked Axel to send on our thanks and I sent a card, but I sent it to your studio. With everything going on, I wasn't sure if you'd get it."

Having been distracted by the bladed fan mail, she had forgotten about the rest of the mail.

"Thank you for sending a card. I haven't got to my mail yet, so it's probably sitting in the pile by my bed. I'm glad you love the painting, and I'm sure it's delighted to have a place in your home. Congratulations again on the engagement," Phoebe played along, covering for Axel.

"It's been great talking to you, but I've got to head out to rehearsals. Call me when you're home, maybe we can get a drink and talk more," Autumn said.

"I'd love that." Phoebe beamed, eager for some proper girl talk.

"Great, give Axel my love."

Autumn was gone before she could say goodbye. Phoebe dropped the phone and lay back in the soft sheets. She had no idea Axel had bought and gifted one of her paintings. Then, she bolted upright. *Axel was the collector who bought the three paintings at my last show. The two paintings in the pool house turned studio, and the third was a gift for Autumn and Elijah.*

"Phoebe? You up?" Axel knocked on the door.

"Yep, you can come in." Phoebe smoothed out the sheets. "I'm decent."

Could he be any more adorable? He had seen every

inch of her, and still knocked before coming in. He gave rockstars a bad name.

"That's a pity." He shot her a wink as he walked in, and she rolled her eyes.

He appeared unfazed by his conversation with Anita, but she wouldn't press him about it. She wanted to wait until he was ready to talk.

"Have you seen my phone?" he asked, and she picked it up from the bed.

"Autumn rang." She handed it to him. "I hope you don't mind that I answered."

"Why would I mind?" He leaned in and kissed her good morning. He tasted like oranges, and her insides got excited.

Cillian used to get so mad at me for even glancing at his phone, never mind answering it. Another red flag I ignored.

She reminded herself of what Autumn had said and promised herself to stop comparing them.

"I'll call her back." Axel failed to mention the fact that Anita had come to bark at them. "I was thinking we could head to the beach now before it gets too hot. Soak up the sun before we catch our flight tonight."

"Sounds perfect. I'll be ready in a few minutes."

"Wear this." Axel passed her a clean T-shirt from his suitcase with holes all over it. It looked like a dog had got to it. "It'll be loose, so it won't rub the tattoo and it'll keep it out of the sun. Trust me when I say sunburnt tattoos aren't fun."

"I think you should help me; my hand is kind of sore." She pouted, and lifted her arms.

"Happy to be of service." His grin made her weak in the knees. He lifted off her T-shirt and replaced it with his, but not before gently pressing his lips to her ribs above the fresh ink. "Why do my clothes look so much better on you?"

She swatted at him, trying not to blush.

"Shoo. Go get ready or we'll never make it out of the house," she ordered.

He raised his hands in submission.

"Since we're going to the beach so early, what will we do this afternoon?" she asked, as he went to the bathroom to put on some sun cream. Watching him, she wished she was the one applying it over his smooth muscles. Getting a grip on herself, she focused on grabbing her things. "Should I bring a change of clothes?"

"The plans I have for this afternoon involve no clothes at all." Axel came up behind her and kissed her neck tenderly.

She turned around and rested her hands on his shoulders while his settled on her waist. His thumbs brushed beneath the end of the T-shirt, and her muscles tightened at his teasing touch. She rose on her tiptoes and tasted his magnificent lips. He returned her kiss with equal fervour until she was breathless and all thoughts of the beach were forgotten. He eased away from her with a groan.

"Beach," he stated.

"This afternoon can't come soon enough," she muttered, and collected the rest of her things before they headed out.

On the soft sand, Phoebe lay beside him in a tiny pink bikini that forced him to contain his caveman instincts, but it was a good distraction from Anita's early morning visit. Watching Phoebe read one of the free books left in a small stand by the entrance to the beach, he wished he could be as relaxed as she was. She rolled onto her front, and he felt her studying him.

"Autumn thanked me for the engagement present. It was very generous of me," she teased, and he pulled his cap over his eyes.

"I had to get them something, and Elijah calls her his black cat. When I saw the painting on your website, I had to snatch it up."

"And the other two?" she asked.

That was enough to get the truth out of him. "You heard me talking to Anita, didn't you?" Axel sighed, reminded of Anita's warning to get his feelings for Phoebe under control or he was going to ruin all of them. She'd seen the receipts for the paintings in his accounts and accused him of trying to buy her love. Couldn't have been further from the truth, since Phoebe hadn't known he bought the paintings—well, until now.

"What does Anita have to do with the paintings you bought?" Phoebe played with the sand at the end of her towel.

"She accused me of trying to buy your love," Axel admitted, hating how Anita had insinuated that he was out of line by loving Phoebe because of Cillian. She was her own person, and he wasn't going to let anyone treat her like she was anyone's property.

"That would be impressive, considering you didn't even tell me," Phoebe laughed, taking it better than expected.

"So, you didn't hear the end of the conversation, but I take it you heard the rest?" He lay on his side and played with the strings on her top. She'd removed his T-shirt, but her tattoo was safely concealed by his shadow.

She nodded. "I didn't want to interrupt, and I figured making an appearance would've made the situation worse."

"Why didn't you say something sooner? I'm sorry you heard that; she was out of line," he said. "Us being together is making her anxiety hit the roof. She doesn't want it getting leaked, but she has no right to question us." His mind kept drifting to the tabloid he had tossed in the bin. "Thank you for standing up for me. I know you think of her as a friend. I don't want to be the reason you're fighting." Phoebe's book flopped closed.

"You never have to thank me. I don't care if the whole world judges us so long as you're happy. All I'm worried about is whatever I did to be lucky enough to be with you now," he said.

"You're so cheesy." She wriggled up a little to kiss him. "I wish this trip didn't have to end," she breathed, and he couldn't agree more. The beach was so crowded no one cared who they might be, though his tattoos had caused one or two kids to stare at the 'scary' man.

"I don't want this trip to end either," he confessed, putting his arm around her so she was on his chest watching him. He got the impression she was trying to read his mind.

"I don't think we have a choice. I don't want us to face Anita's wrath if we extend it a few more days."

He tucked a strand of hair behind her ear. "I don't want to ruin our perfect day with thoughts of tomorrow. Reality is the last place I want to be," he said, wondering what would happen between them when they got home.

"One last glimpse of reality—I couldn't find the tabloid she gave you?" Phoebe asked.

"You saw that? I put it in the recycling. I didn't want you to see it."

"Can you tell me? I don't want to be surprised when we get home."

"The story mostly talked about our cosy dinner. The headline was about the fan mail, but very little was said about it, only that you'd been sent 'hate' mail." He wasn't going to hide anything from her, but he wasn't about to repeat the crass and tactless words the media used to defame her.

"I should've said something sooner. I figured it was that Gunther Sheen guy getting back at me for ruining his car. Some men can't handle being bested by a woman," she said. "The person who sent it clearly leaked it. They don't just want to hurt me; they want to destroy my image and career and my relationship with all of you."

"We can go to the police when we get home," he said. "We don't want to be accused of hiding evidence, even if you're the victim."

"What about the first story that was leaked? The break-in? Only the two officers knew, so it was either one of them or Sheen."

"I'm leaning towards Sheen. I don't think the police would risk their jobs over a couple hundred for the story," he reasoned.

"Sheen said in the car park that he was paid off, but the cash envelope and instructions were waiting on his desk when he got back from Munich. Sheen left Munich only two days after the accident. I wasn't even awake, my survival hadn't even been confirmed, and the video of the wreck hadn't been leaked. How could the sender of said envelope have known?"

"So, you're saying, the person who paid Sheen, assuming he was even telling the truth, knew the accident was going to happen?" Axel tried to follow her stream of thought. "Could someone have messed with his car? Cillian was the only one driving it. But no one knew you were coming, so was he the target? If they wanted him dead, why be angry about your survival and destroy your gallery?"

"This sounds insane. The rental company would've said in their report if something was wrong with the car for the insurance." Phoebe sat up, wrapping her arms around her thighs.

"Not necessarily. With Cillian's blood alcohol level and all the press, everyone was eager to wrap up the case quickly," Axel admitted. Had they let someone get away with murder, and now that person was targeting Phoebe? "The anger towards you could be because you weren't meant to be there, but then the message in the gallery said 'it should have been you', which would make you the target then. My brain is starting to hurt." Axel rubbed his temples.

"We need to talk to Sheen, see if he lied about trashing the envelope and if he still has it. If the accident was planned, and they wanted to blame me by leaking the footage of the wreck and paying off Sheen, then the envelope would have been sent either just before the accident or the day of at latest," Phoebe said, and he could tell she'd been playing this repeatedly in her mind. This was just the first time she was confiding her suspicions.

"Why would someone want to kill Cillian?" Axel asked. Even if Cill had had a bit of an ego and loose morals, it didn't make sense that someone would hate him enough to kill him.

"I don't know, but we need to find Sheen and see if he was telling the truth about being paid off before we lose our minds on conspiracy theories. And if he doesn't feel like being forthcoming, I still have my crowbar," she teased, but the worry in her eyes told him how afraid she was.

"Let's avoid violence, so we aren't the ones who end up behind bars."

"Fine, but is it bad that I prefer them focusing on the fan mail rather than a picture of us at dinner last night?" she asked, staring up at him as she leaned against his chest.

"Yes, because a photo of us together at dinner doesn't risk these precious fingers." He kissed her fingertips. "I could kill the person who sent those blades."

"Don't worry, they're insured." She smirked.

"Really? That was smart of your agent," he said, not understanding why she looked so amused. As an artist, musical or not, it was reasonable to insure what made your living in case of accident or injury.

"I was teasing, because yours are." She swatted at him, but he caught her hand.

"It's no teasing matter." He placed his palm against hers; his dwarfed hers. "I think they're both equally important."

He didn't like that she had got rid of the evidence, but

he understood her panic, given Anita's attitude towards her since the gallery was broken into. He wished he had been there when Autumn called, so he could have asked about her detective friend. He would call her back—he had been too distracted when they'd got back from dinner to do it then. He was sure it was all just Sheen messing with them, but he wanted to be safe rather than sorry.

"On a scale from one to fifty, how likely is it that we're going to receive a scolding when we get back?" Axel groaned, soaking up what sun he could, wanting to memorise the sound of the crashing waves for when the others took a chunk out of them when they got home.

"How about we stay here? Throw our phones in the ocean and disappear from the world." Phoebe scrunched her toes in the sand. "We could bury ourselves in the sand, where no one cares who we are. Fame fades—it wouldn't be long before people forgot to care."

"We could," he tested, knowing her conscience wouldn't let her. Not when her brother would see the photo of them, and the news about the hate mail.

"What about the band? You don't want to leave the band, do you?" she asked, sitting up a little.

He knew August and Nick's hearts would be broken if he left.

"They'd survive without me, and they can come and visit us."

"Us?" She arched a brow.

"Sorry, I..." he stammered, not wanting to frighten her off.

"I like the sound of us," she interrupted, resting her head on his chest. "But you love playing, and I know how much you care about the others. No matter what happens between us, I'll never stand in the way of your dreams."

God, if he didn't want to throw her over his shoulder and take her home.

They stayed curled up together beneath the beach umbrella listening to the waves and enjoying the peace for as long as they could.

A nita sent a car to pick them up at the airport; Axel didn't doubt she was making sure they didn't "accidentally" miss their flight. He did his best to hide his irritation—they weren't children to be wrangled—but he didn't want an argument the very moment they stepped on Irish soil.

By the time they reached the front gate of the house, it was nearly two a.m.

"We're home." Axel kissed Phoebe's hair, and she yawned awake, having used his thigh as a pillow. He'd learnt she couldn't sleep on planes, but the car was no problem.

"Did you get any sleep at all?" she asked, eyeing him sleepily. Her falling asleep on top of him was beginning to become a habit he thoroughly enjoyed.

"No, I couldn't stop thinking about what we discussed at the beach, but I'm glad you got some sleep."

"You make it easy, being such an excellent pillow," she said, resting her head on his shoulder.

With the partition separating them from the driver, Axel tipped her chin up, and he felt her breath catch as his lips brushed hers. He kissed her long and hard, his hands tangled in her hair, as they made the most of the time they had left.

He had never felt as vulnerable with anyone as he had that night on the balcony. Her comfort in that moment meant more to him than anything, and he hated the thought of having to hide their feelings now that they were home.

"What was that for?" she asked, running her thumb along his lower lip. He would never tire of her touches, or her lips. His fear was that he would crave her to the point of putting himself in an early grave.

"I won't be able to kiss you like I want to once we get inside," he whispered, while the driver removed their bags from the boot.

"I didn't think about that," she groaned, resting her forehead against his.

The driver opened the back door. "Sir, where would you like the bags?"

"Don't worry about it, we'll take them in," Axel said.

They were welcomed home by the echo of music blaring from the house. They'd been too lost in each other to notice the rager going on in their home.

"I'm going to kill Nick," Axel snarled, climbing out of the car. He helped Phoebe out after him and noticed her cringe at the sight of people staggering in and out of the house.

"Could've been August?" She tried to cover for her brother.

Axel arched a brow. "August only attends parties held in his own home because there's no escape."

"You're right, but they're probably just blowing off some steam," she reasoned, but he didn't let go of her hand as they walked into the house. He didn't care if anyone saw; with the threats against her, who knew who was lurking in their house or the grounds.

"What the hell happened here?" he grumbled, walking into the crowded house with Phoebe close at his back.

Music pounded against the walls, and every countertop was littered with bottles and cigarettes. No one even noticed them arrive, but as they walked through to the sitting room, Nick stumbled through the crowd towards them. Axel could tell he was far past the stage of being reasoned with.

"Welcome home!" Nick grabbed Axel and kissed his cheek. Phoebe chuckled at the sight, but he wasn't amused.

"How could you throw a party? Did you not talk to Anita about the threats against Phoebe?" Axel shrugged off his friend, only for him to wrap his sister in a hug, pulling them apart. Nick was too drunk to notice they were holding hands.

"Anita yapped on about you two heading off to Italy, I didn't pay much attention to the rest. What harm is there in a little party? We're alive, so we should celebrate. Well, *I* wanted to celebrate—August is sulking with some girl in the hot tub out back." Nick swayed as he spoke.

Axel glanced at Phoebe, who looked a nice mixture of annoyed and amused.

"Do you know half of these people?" she asked Nick, overwhelmed by the sea of unfamiliar faces.

"Why do you care? Neither of you were here." Nick picked up an open bottle from the piano and slugged a stranger's beer.

"That's disgusting." Phoebe wrestled the bottle from her brother. He soon gave up the fight.

She turned to Axel. "You get everyone out of here, and I'll get him to bed."

"I don't want to go to bed," Nick groaned, wrapping his arm around his sister's shoulder. "Come have a drink with me, and you can tell me all about your trip."

"I'm afraid packing up the villa wasn't all that exciting, and I think you've had enough to drink," Phoebe said, while Axel helped him up the step to the stairs so he wouldn't trip and land flat on his pierced face.

"Party poopers! The night is only getting started!" Nick yelled, and everyone cheered.

Axel didn't even recognise half the people there. He guessed word had got out, and Nick wasn't checking at the door. Neither was Olivier—Nick must have given him the night off to host this mess. It was probably Nick's way of dealing with the stress, given the threats against his sister, but that didn't stop it from being irresponsible.

"You can party all you want, but I brought you back a present from Italy," Phoebe told him. "It's upstairs with our bags."

Axel tried to hide his amused grin; Nick could never resist gifts. She didn't need to tell him twice as he headed for the stairs.

"How could he be so careless, letting people come and go like this?" Axel muttered to himself.

Someone tried to grind on him as he walked through the makeshift dance floor. He rolled his eyes and reached the speakers. His eardrums thanked him as he turned off the music.

"Party's over." Axel shouted, standing on the expensive coffee table that was now stained and marked with burn marks. How could they have done so much damage in such a short amount of time?

There was a burst of boos and a few curses, but as soon as he turned on the lights, the protest dissipated as everyone started to leave. Seeing the mess left behind, and the red wine stains all over the cream couch, he ran his hands over his head. The cleaning lady came on Fridays, but he figured they could use a hand cleaning up. He texted her to see if she could come in early the following morning to help sort out the mess. He offered double her pay for the inconvenience.

With the inside guests filtering out, he just had to deal with those in the gardens. He slid open the patio door. The heaters were on, and the hot tub bubbled around the corner by the BBQ patio.

He found August in there with not one but two girls. He wasn't paying them much attention, but it was clear they were happy to be sitting with him.

"Please tell me Nick locked Cillian's door?" Axel asked.

August ignored his question and grabbed a bottle of vodka from the side of the hot tub.

"You good?" Axel prompted, wanting to make sure he wouldn't drown if left unattended.

"Are you?" August asked coherently, taking a swig.

"Fair enough."

Axel was far more concerned about any curious eyes sneaking into Cillian's room, or worse, taking some souvenirs for themselves or to make a quick buck off.

"Come and join us, there's plenty of room," the bleach blonde asked with a chemically induced pout.

"Another time, and I'm afraid the party's over. Ladies, if you wouldn't mind?" Axel nodded to the door, but they snuggled closer to August. The more he drank, the less he minded physical contact.

"Don't worry, they can stay with me," August said, and the women giggled.

They were sober enough to make their own decisions,

and Axel had enough to deal with already. On the way upstairs, he texted Olivier to come over and secure the house and the grounds to make sure no one else was lingering. He guessed Olivier had already had his suspicions about what was going on, because a few seconds later he replied that he was on his way.

Axel cursed when he saw Cillian's door wide open. Two people were in Cill's bed.

"Get out!" Axel barked, and the couple startled.

He flicked on the lights and watched them scurry for their clothes before hurrying out. Luckily, Axel had Cillian's journal in the basement. If someone had got their hands on his personal thoughts, he didn't even want to think what they would do.

Axel locked the door behind him and reminded himself to yell at Nick tomorrow when he was hungover. Taking a deep breath, he walked down the hall to see how Phoebe was coping.

He found Nick with his head in the toilet while Phoebe sat on the bathtub rubbing his back.

"How's he doing?" Axel asked.

"I can tick seeing my brother's stomach lining off my bucket list," Phoebe said grimly.

"I'm sorry, guys. The house just got so damn quiet." Nick's words were muffled by the fact he was resting his face on the toilet seat. Axel tried not to enjoy his misery.

Phoebe glared at Axel, pleading with him to sympathise. He clenched his jaw, resisting the urge to yell or laugh. Given that he had been glued to Phoebe and that August wasn't the most comforting person to lean on, leaving him might not have been the best move.

"It doesn't matter now. Let's get you to bed," Axel said, helping Nick up.

His friend groaned as he helped him to bed. Phoebe removed his shoes and covered him with a blanket. They left a bin by his head— not that it mattered, since they would have to get the carpets cleaned anyway. They closed the door quietly so Nick wouldn't wake up.

Axel lingered in the hallway. He knew he should go downstairs and clean up a little; his suppressed anger would make sleeping impossible.

"Nick passed out, and August is distracted. You could stay with me for a little while," Phoebe hinted, backing up towards her own room.

Who am I to deny such an irresistible request?

"I should go downstairs," Axel said, but didn't move.

"You should." She closed the gap between them.

"I need to clean up, and make sure no one left anything burning." He didn't know if he was trying to convince himself or her.

"Sounds reasonable," she replied, running her hands down his chest.

"Fuck it." Axel took her face in his hands and kicked her door closed behind them. She squealed, and he gripped her thighs, wrapping them around his waist.

She startled, clinging to him. "Someone could hear."

"Like you said, Nick's out cold and August is busy with his own guests," he said, trailing kisses along her neck. He pressed her up against the door, only to feel something slick on the door.

"What is that?" she asked, pulling at her T-shirt as it clung to her back. He eased her down and saw his hands were covered in a red, sticky substance.

"Son of a bitch," Axel snapped, and pulled her behind him. He flicked on the lights, revealing what was dripping down the door.

"'Leave, bitch.'" The words escaped Phoebe's lips flatly,

as though she were reading an item from a grocery list. "Hardly original."

"Is it blood?" he asked, daring to say it aloud.

"No." She observed the words closely. "Paint, I can smell it. Spray paint. It must be Sheen."

"We've got cameras, we can see who came in here," Axel said, ready to catch this prick.

"There was probably a hundred people coming and going, and my door wasn't locked."

Axel wondered how she could be so calm, if it was just the shock or, worse, she was getting used to the hateful comments.

"Oh crap! It's all on my clothes. This is one of my favourite T-shirts," she muttered, pulling at her top to see the spray paint splotches.

He was more worried about her than the clothes. He would buy her every T-shirt in the universe if he could get the person who was behind this to stop—if it was just one person.

He rubbed his hands over his jaw, trying not to overreact. Getting upset would only stress her out, and they had been home less than twelve hours.

"We should've put a stop to the hate months ago. The moment it was suggested that you were the driver, we should have protected you." His stomach tightened. "We've failed you."

Phoebe took his face in her hands, forcing him to look at those big eyes. "Please don't talk like that. You didn't fail me. If any of you had come out and refuted the video, it would've just sparked a debate. There is no winning, and you could never fail me. You've made the last few months tolerable and made me feel safe when I thought the world hated me. Even if it does hate me, I still have you."

"Are you trying to flirt with me to stop me worrying about you?"

"I'm thinking if I bat my eyelashes long enough you might stop frowning. Or maybe you want to join me in the shower and help me wash off the paint?"

"As enticing as that sounds, I have to make a call. You hop in the shower, and I'll be waiting when you come out," he said. The sight of the blood-coloured paint covering her terrified him.

"To who?" she asked.

"Someone who can help us." He didn't want to wait until morning.

"It's the middle of the night, and we aren't going to solve who did this now." She had a point, but they had waited long enough. He didn't want to worry Autumn by disturbing her so late, but she'd understand his desperation.

"I can't talk you into waiting, can I?" she asked, turning on the bathroom light.

"Afraid not."

He took his phone from his back pocket. While he dialled, she grabbed some clothes.

She hesitated. "You won't leave, right?" Fear tainted her soft voice.

"Not going anywhere," he promised, sitting on the bed as she closed the bathroom door.

Elijah answered Autumn's phone gruffly. "Axel? It's late, Autumn is asleep. Is everyone okay?"

"Sorry to disturb you both, but it's you I wanted to speak to. I didn't want to wake you up, but it's urgent," he said quickly.

He heard movement, and guessed Elijah was leaving the room.

"Go ahead, I'm awake now. Brinkley will want her

morning walk now that I'm up."

"I don't know where to start, but you've seen all the harassment Phoebe's been getting on the news? Autumn probably told you the situation."

"Autumn has shown me some of it—she's been worried about the two of you—but I'm not sure how I can help."

"You had a friend help with Autumn's case, right? With the stalker? Would he be able to help us figure out who's targeting Phoebe, if it's one person or more? We got back from Italy tonight, and Nick threw a party. Someone painted 'leave bitch' on the back of her bedroom door."

Elijah let out a long sigh.

"Michael. He's the detective that helped us, but he's on holidays for the next couple of weeks with his husband. However, I can reach out to his old partner, Isaiah Rivers. He's trustworthy and wouldn't mind looking into your case off the books."

Axel wasn't going to be picky.

"If you trust him, so can we. We were talking to two officers after the studio break-in, but then it was leaked to the press. I don't want anything else getting leaked."

Water was running in the bathroom. He walked to the door and heard faint sobs from within. His heart broke as Phoebe concealed her hurt.

"Isaiah is discreet. He wouldn't share information with anyone unless necessary," Elijah assured him.

"Thank you, and I'm sorry again for calling so late."

"Don't be, I know what you're going through. You're doing the right thing, reaching out," Elijah said, but Axel hated to have brought up memories of their own experience. "Call us if you need anything else."

"I will. Hopefully all this will be over soon. I want to bury whoever is doing this alive."

Elijah chuckled. "Call if you need help with the body."

"I knew I liked you," Axel said, knowing he meant it.

"I've got to go before Brinkley wakes Autumn up. Tell Phoebe our thoughts are with her. We're here if you need anything," Elijah assured him again before hanging up.

Axel couldn't thank Elijah enough for his support of both Autumn and now Phoebe. Autumn had been harassed, threatened and deceived by someone close to her, and it terrified him to think that someone close to them could hurt Phoebe.

Elijah texted him Isaiah Rivers' number, and he wanted to ring right away, but waking a stranger in the middle of the night and asking for favours might not be the best first impression. Before he did anything, he wanted to make sure Phoebe was alright with his plan first.

Phoebe came out in her lemon-print shorts and matching T-shirt, her eyes red from crying.

"You're not staying in this room. You don't have to stay in the basement, but you can pick any other room but this one," he said, not wanting her to have to look at her door all night.

"The basement is perfect." She didn't argue, merely walked into his arms and rested her forehead against his chest.

Having her space violated like that, there was no way she was going to be able to sleep. Nor was he going to leave her alone for a second. He kissed the top of her head and grabbed her pillow before bringing her down to the basement. Once Phoebe was tucked up in his bed, he told her about Isaiah, and they agreed to seek out his help first thing.

In the morning, Axel made sure Olivier kept all the camera footage from the last twenty-four hours and did a thorough sweep of the house for any cameras or listening devices that could have been installed. They hadn't taken the threats seriously enough, and he was going to make sure no one got within five feet of her without being fully vetted.

"The foils really make your eyes pop. Maybe you should've gone for silver." Lena plopped herself down in the empty salon chair beside her while Phoebe waited for the box dye to be stripped from her hair.

"Sorry, I didn't even notice you come in. I was half asleep." Phoebe swivelled in the chair to face her friend. Lena's own hair was styled to perfection. Phoebe was beginning to think she rolled out of bed perfect.

Despite being home a week, every night since Nick's party, she'd woken up in a sweat, terrified someone was breaking in. Booking an early hair appointment had been the easiest way to avoid people, but she wanted to die whenever a Brothers of Anarchy song came over the radio during the application. The desire to make a run for it was only quashed by the anxiety of having to cancel an appointment when she'd already arrived. Thankfully, her stylist was more concerned about the layered box dye in her hair more than who she was.

"I thought you fixed the sleeping problem?" Lena asked, being the only person she'd told about her and Axel.

"Being with Axel helps, but we're still waiting to hear from Isaiah, a detective friend of Elijah's, to find out if Gunther was up to his old tricks or if this was someone else." They had called after the spray paint incident, and thankfully, Isaiah had been eager to help.

"Has he given you any updates on leads?" Lena asked, tapping away on her phone, the queen of multitasking.

"He is reaching out to the media outlets who were the first to release the stories about Cillian and I. So far, he's learnt that the tips were all sent in anonymously, or the outlets are refusing to share their sources. The sender didn't want money, which makes me think it wasn't Sheen, since he admitted he broke into the studio because he was paid."

"Not much to go on without a name or a money trail." Lena shook her head. "I've tried to reach out to some of my contacts to get their sources. I got one or two bites from friends, but fake email addresses were used to send the footage about the accident and the studio break-in. If you try and email them back, it doesn't go through.

"If you want a career change, you'd make a good detective," Phoebe said, grateful for her help.

"Nobody hurts my clients, especially not my friends." Lena rested a manicured hand over hers. "If they don't want money, why the hell are they bothering to go to all this trouble?"

"To hurt me. Axel and I were thinking that if it *is* Sheen and, like with the studio, someone paid him to leak the articles and videos, he wouldn't need to be paid by the outlets."

"That's if Sheen was telling the truth. That person would have to trust him a lot, and they could be working together either way."

Phoebe hadn't considered that.

"There's one way to figure that out. You've sent stuff to LouderTech before, right?"

"Contracts and the like, sure." Lena shrugged. "Why?"

"How tight is their security? If someone sent an unmarked package, would it be accepted?"

"No way, it must be registered, addressed and signed for. Even couriers must sign in and out, otherwise it doesn't make it past the mail room. I made that mistake of leaving a contract at the front desk without signing for it," Lena said.

So, had Sheen been lying?

"Sheen said that an envelope of cash was waiting on his desk when he got back from Munich," Phoebe told her. "Could someone have got into the building and left it there without raising alarm bells?"

"There's no way someone would be able to do all that and remain unseen," Lena said, looking unsure. "Unless the person who left the money worked for the company. They'd be able to get into the office and leave anything on someone's desk with little notice. They'd be caught on camera, though, which would be one hell of a risk.

"If you want, I could try and bribe someone in security?" Lena offered, sounding rather excited. "Getting you what you need would only take a little grease. Find out once and for all whether he's lying or not. I'd only need a copy of the footage from that week."

Phoebe wasn't sure. "Getting involved could get you in trouble, and LouderTech was an account you worked so hard to get. With Isaiah looking into things, he might not appreciate you messing with the investigation."

"I could send Isaiah a copy of the footage, then I wouldn't be withholding evidence," Lena argued.

"I can't ask you to do that," Phoebe said, though she got the impression that even if she warned Lena off, she was still going to investigate.

"Don't ask. Consider it done." Lena was up and tapping

on her phone. "I have to love you and leave you, because your paintings have arrived at the Reid Gallery for your show this weekend. This space is perfect for a smaller collection, and the gallerist is very excited to work with you. We are going to get everything organised today, and then if you want to stop by tomorrow, we can make sure you're happy."

"I can come by in the morning to help with the hanging arrangement, and I can grab one of the guys to help me bring over some boxes of prints and stickers for the front desk," Phoebe offered.

"Last time, are you sure you want to go ahead with this? I can still cancel, and the gallerist would completely understand."

"Olivier is going to help with security and only those invited or with a ticket can come in, so I think we're safe enough," Phoebe said. She wouldn't let the trolls win. This was her dream, and she wasn't going to see it go up in smoke.

"Okay, I just wanted to triple check. If you're happy, so am I. I'll see you tomorrow."

After a quick hug, Lena was out the door. Phoebe wanted to run after her and tell her not to mess with LouderTech, but with all the foils in her hair, she couldn't. She wished she had kept her big mouth shut, but also counted her blessings to have Lena on her team. She almost felt sorry for whoever was behind this—Lena could be merciless.

"Ready to rinse?" the hairdresser asked, standing behind her in the mirror with a cheery smile.

Phoebe never should have dyed her hair in the first place. No one could force her into a corner. If they wanted to come for her then let them.

"Ready."

Phoebe took a deep breath, feeling as though she was readying herself for battle. The first step: no more hiding.

ARRIVING HOME with her lavender hair restored, Phoebe left Axel's favourite pecan and white chocolate cookies on his bedside table as a thank you for all his support. She chuckled as she heard him singing in the bathroom, as he struggled to recall the lyrics of the songs she had written.

Phoebe tiptoed to the en-suite door. She had never heard him sing before, not without the others. She opened the door a crack to hear him better. The door creaked; she winced, and he stopped.

"Care to join me?" he asked, unashamedly peering his head around the shower curtain.

She resisted temptation. "You can sing?" she asked, stepping into the bathroom and closing the door in case someone came down to the basement.

"And your hair is purple again!" he exclaimed.

"I decided I'm not going to hide anymore. It took a team to get the box dye out of my hair, but I feel like myself again." She swished her hair from side to side.

"I love it." Axel leaned out of the steamy shower and kissed her.

"No distracting me with those lips." She backed away, leaning against the sink. "Why didn't you put yourself forward for vocals? You never said a word when we discussed Nick taking over lead vocals."

"Because I'm happy on drums, and I keep my solos for the shower. I don't mind giving you a private show though." He reached for her, but she dodged him.

"You're going to get me all wet," she groaned.

He stepped out of the shower and wrapped a towel around his waist.

"I don't care, come here."

He followed her out into the bedroom. As tempting as he was, she didn't want to have to wash her hair again.

"I care, and you're soaking wet," she said, trying to hide how much she loved that he was as obsessed with her as she was with him.

"Funny, it's usually the other way round," he said with a wink, as he backed her up against the bed.

"Axel!" she squeaked, covering her flaming cheeks. Her knees buckled as they hit the mattress.

"I love how you say my name," he teased, leaning over her on the bed. Kissing her neck, her shoulders, as she squirmed. He pinned her arms above her head and settled between her legs.

"It tickles," she said against his lips as the droplets from his skin landed on her. The smell of his orange body wash made him even more irresistible. She was beginning to wonder if she'd ever tire of his caresses; he showed no sign of tiring of hers.

They were interrupted by his phone, and his disgruntled groan made her laugh.

She squirmed out from beneath him and tossed him his phone. He paused, eyeing the box of cookies. "You got me cookies?"

"I know how much you love dessert," she said with a smirk, only for his smile to drop when he looked at his phone.

He settled close to her as he answered, putting it on speaker.

"Axel? Hi, it's Isaiah. I wanted to give you an update. I've talked to the officers who were looking into the break-in, and I managed to find Sheen. I tried to get through to Ms Fletcher, but there was no answer. If you'd like to wait to discuss it together later, I can call back."

Phoebe shook her head, glad Axel was with her.

"She's with me now," Axel told him. "I have you on speaker."

"What did he say?" Phoebe asked, nervous about what Sheen might have said about the damage she did to his car, even if it was deserved.

"Nothing he didn't tell you. That he was paid to break into the gallery and report it to the media. His own company leaked the incident, and they have confirmed that he was paid and don't believe any law was broken," Isaiah explained.

Axel frowned at her.

"Not breaking any law? Sheen ruined thousands of euros worth of artwork," Phoebe raged.

Axel took her hand, calming her so she didn't clench her injured hand.

"I'm afraid LouderTech's legal department is stating that you paid them. That the break-in was a publicity stunt. When I spoke to the police, they said they received the same information from LouderTech's legal team. I'm worried that you could be charged with filing a false report. If you weren't aware of the stunt, then we will need to prove it."

"Proof? How about that I was in a coma when the money was left on his desk? This is insane. What about the camera footage?"

"I'm afraid I'll need a warrant, and even if I got one, I'd say it's long gone by now. I don't think they care whether Sheen is telling the truth or not, they are just protecting themselves," Isaiah said. She didn't doubt it. "LouderTech is supplying Mr Sheen with legal aid. He is also saying that you destroyed his jeep as a threat to keep him quiet about your involvement."

"Framing Phoebe must be part of his plan," Axel said. "He comes up with a story to say that he was paid, and now the person behind him is Phoebe. There is no way Phoebe would ever pay someone to break into her own studio. Her work is a part of her, it would be like me setting my drums on fire."

"I understand your frustration, but I'm afraid Louder-Tech have supplied the investigating officers with security footage of Ms Fletcher entering their underground parking on the day his jeep was vandalised, which backs up Sheen's version of events. The officers had their own suspicions, given the substantial insurance payout on her work. Since Ms Fletcher took out the claim only a few months before the break-in, it doesn't look good. I'm not accusing her, but it's why you haven't heard from them."

So that's why they weren't giving us updates, Phoebe realised. *I'm their key suspect.*

She rested her head in her hands, not believing this was happening.

"My agent took out that policy because of the show I had before Munich. The gallery insisted that I have substantial coverage, given the notoriety. Why would I destroy work that I could have easily sold?"

"Someone is orchestrating this to make you look guilty," Isaiah told her. "Sheen was contacted through a burner phone and paid in cash, so he can point the finger at you. If there is someone behind Sheen, they're too good at covering their tracks. If you're called in by the investigating officers, do as they ask, but do not say a word without a lawyer, and ask them to call me. Given the press attention, they are looking to wrap this up quickly."

"Did you get any prints off the fan mail package we

gave you?" Phoebe asked. She had dug it out of the recycling as soon as they had got back from Italy.

"Only yours, your manager's and the head of your security. There was no postage or customs stamp, which means it was left at your studio personally. I'm afraid it doesn't help you offer the officers another culprit."

"Great, so the media sees me as a villain, and now the police are going to prove it," Phoebe said.

"Don't lose heart, I'm looking into a few loose ends. I'll update you when I know more." Isaiah didn't sound all that hopeful.

Phoebe let out a long sigh. "What about my show this weekend? Should I cancel?"

"Our security team is going to be attending, and it will be invitation and ticket only," Axel explained. She knew he didn't want her to have to cancel, but she didn't want any of them to be put at risk.

Isaiah hesitated, putting them on edge.

"No," he said eventually. "This might be a good opportunity to draw whoever is doing this out. Sheen might be a lackey, but with the guaranteed media coverage, whoever is harassing you might not be able to resist attending. A small gathering, in a tight location—we could see who stands out." It sounded risky. "I can be there and help your security keep an eye out," he offered.

Axel looked at Phoebe, waiting for her thoughts.

"If you think it's a good opportunity, I can't say no," she said, wanting to catch Sheen, or whoever it was that wanted her life ruined, before she ended up in cuffs.

They hung up, both deflated. Still, she had some hope that Lena might pull through with the footage from LouderTech—unlike Isaiah, she didn't need a warrant.

"Axel! We have reservations in an hour!" Nick yelled down the basement steps, interrupting their tense silence.

"Sorry, I'm only just out of the shower, but I finalised the last two songs. I sent you the recordings, you can listen with August while I get ready," Axel shouted back, clearly trying to stop her brother from coming downstairs.

"No need, I already sent them on to Mike to finish the production. Once he adds your solos then we're done with the album," Nick said cheerily.

Phoebe was sure the three of them had been sleeping less than her while working on the album, but at least they could channel their energy into something. Painting at such a slow pace was only adding to her frustrations.

The sounds of footsteps interrupted her thoughts, and panicking, she hurried into the bathroom. They weren't ready to tell anyone about the two of them just yet. She just hoped she hadn't left any visible evidence that she'd been sleeping down here every night.

She listened at the door like a guilty teenager.

"Any news from Isaiah?" Nick asked. "It's been a few days."

"No luck with prints on the fan mail, but he's working on some leads," Axel told him, cool as a cucumber.

"Who the fuck could do this to her?" She hated to hear her brother so upset. "That fucking party, I let them into the damn house. Anita gave me such a scolding that night, but I didn't want to listen. I didn't know about the fan mail; I didn't think the threats had become so real."

"It's no one's fault, this is a fucked-up situation. We'll figure it out—it'll just take time, and she has all of us behind her," Axel assured him.

"I'm glad she has you. I know you've never been close, but you've been a good friend to her since everything fell apart," Nick said. Phoebe cringed. If only he knew how good Axel had been to her. Now she had an idea of how her brother must've felt keeping secrets from her for Cillian.

"I don't know how to comfort her, or even talk to her about any of this," Nick continued. "I feel like all this could have been avoided if I'd just told her what Cillian was doing. This all started with Munich."

"You've got to let go of the guilt. It's going to eat you up, and none of us can change the past. Right now, we can only focus on making sure she's safe, that's it," Axel said.

She hated the weight her brother was putting on himself. He wasn't to blame; they were all in a no-win situation, then and now.

"You're right." Nick's voice softened. "Once we find this prick, I swear I'm going to string him up by his feet and treat him like a piñata."

Phoebe rolled her eyes. Nick liked to play tough, but he was really a big teddy bear.

"I'll bring the bat," Axel chuckled.

"Have you seen Phoebe? I texted her about dinner today, but she hasn't said whether she's coming tonight or not," Nick asked. "August said she was going to get her hair done, but I figured she'd be back by now since she left so early."

"We wouldn't have this album without her, so we can't celebrate without her," Axel said. "I'm sure we can convince her to join us."

Phoebe already had every intention of going. She wasn't going to let anyone stop her from living her life, especially not when it was such a big night for all of them. August had booked the whole restaurant, but considering how much he hated crowded rooms, she guessed it was for his benefit instead of her protection.

"Good luck with that." Nick sighed.

"I'll think of something," Axel said, and she hated the smugness in his voice. "She's probably in her room."

Once the coast was clear, Phoebe tiptoed out of the bathroom.

"I hate lying," she said.

"I didn't lie, this is your room," he said with a cheeky grin.

She rolled her eyes at his annoyingly cute statement when she was trying to be serious.

"I should hurry. We've got a celebratory dinner to get to," she said. She hadn't even decided what to wear, and her concealer was in desperate need of touching up since all the stress was causing her to break out. She was beginning to think she should buy stock in pimple patches.

"Go up the back staircase and you can beat your brother."

She hated sneaking around, but they had enough to deal with right now, so she padded upstairs. She had only just closed the paint-stained door behind her when her brother knocked.

After enough Chinese food to feed an army, they all sat around the dinner table listening to Nick raise his champagne glass in a toast to Phoebe. She gripped Axel's hand resting on her thigh as her brother thanked her for helping make their dreams come true. She didn't feel like she deserved so much credit, but it did feel good to be acknowledged and get to celebrate with them.

"To put an end to my emotional rambling, we have something for you," Nick said, taking something from under his chair.

"You didn't have to get me anything," Phoebe said, but she unwrapped the square with a stupid grin.

"It's a mock-up of the album case." August nudged her excitedly.

She turned it over and saw the list of ten songs written on the tail of a coiled snake.

"It's beautiful. You should all be proud of yourselves," she said, only to freeze when she saw the fine print. Under 'songwriter', it read 'Phoebe Fletcher' beside 'Cillian Hunt'. The work they had done together, immortalised.

He deserved to be honoured. He'd been her inspiration, and those few weeks spent creating this last album were memories she would always cherish. Those moments with him, writing in the sun, his proposal, had been magical. She wanted to remember him as he was in those moments, carefree and so full of passion and love. It was like they'd placed a manifestation of her heart in her hands.

"You didn't have to do this, but thank you. I know Cillian wasn't perfect, but he loved all of you, us, and he'd have given anything to see this finished. This can't be easy for any of you, especially with the upcoming concert and all the harassment, but I'm so happy to have you all in my life and I wouldn't change it for the world."

She wiped her tears. If she didn't get a hold of herself her mascara would be halfway down her face.

"Yes, we did have to do this," Nick said. "This was long overdue, and this is the first step towards a fresh start for all of us. Cillian will always be a part of us, and we can honour him by standing by each other and giving him the best send-off at the concert."

They toasted to new beginnings. For the first time since Munich, Phoebe felt like everything was going to be okay. That was until they left the restaurant and were immediately accosted with blinding flashes and deafening shouts. Phoebe struggled through the crowd of photographers.

"Back up!" August growled at a pap who got too close to her.

"Phoebe! Ms Fletcher! What do you say to the person who burnt down your exhibit? Are you going to press charges? The gallery refused to comment, but this is the second time your art has been targeted." The fragmented questions were pieced together from many voices.

"What are they talking about?" Phoebe asked Olivier, who was protecting them.

He didn't answer, too focused on getting them to their cars.

Axel took her hand while the others protected her from the onslaught of questions. She wanted to stop him, to ask what they were talking about. *A fire? A gallery? We've only been at dinner for a few hours. How could something have happened in such a short time, and how had the press found them?* Only those in attendance and their security had known about their reservation at the Golden Elephant tonight.

Axel bundled her into the back of the car and slammed the door with a muffled curse. Nick and August got in the car behind them, and Phoebe glanced out the back window to see them pull off safely.

"Fucking vultures. Someone at the restaurant must have leaked our location," Axel said, climbing in beside her.

The driver pulled away from the curb, careful not to hit any of the paps surrounding the car as they tried in vain to snap a shot through the tinted windows. Phoebe checked her phone and found Lena's many missed calls and messages. Not wanting to be interrupted with any more bad news, she'd turned it off for their celebration, and instantly regretted it.

"Is everything okay?" Axel asked as she put the phone up to her ear.

"It's Lena. She left me a couple of voice messages."

"I'm so sorry, but the Reid Gallery caught fire. I didn't want you to hear it from the media first. Please call me back. When I'm finished here, I'll come over." Lena's panic sent shivers of dread down Phoebe's spine.

Swallowing the news, she wished she hadn't eaten so much. The image of her last remaining paintings going up in flames sent a violent spasm through her hand, and she dropped her phone.

"I need to go to the Reid Gallery!" Phoebe called out to the driver, who quickly turned the car in the opposite direction without argument. She fumbled for her phone, making sure the volume was up high so she didn't miss another call.

"Phoebe, what's going on?" Axel asked, and she wished he'd gone with her brother.

"There's been a fire at the Reid Gallery, and I need to be there. They've got the last of my paintings for next week's show. Lena's there, I need to know she's okay," Phoebe fretted, hoping no one was hurt, and that the gallerist hadn't taken her works out of the protective crates.

"It's not safe," Axel argued. "This might be related to the fan mail—"

"I'm going. You can either get out or come with me." Phoebe didn't mean to snap, but she was on the verge of screaming or crying and wasn't in any mood to argue.

Axel quietly sat back and zipped his lips. Phoebe's hands shook, and he took her hand in his, nearly breaking her last thread of composure.

TWENTY MINUTES FELT like twenty hours. The flashing emergency lights told her they'd arrived. At the busy scene, Phoebe hurried out of the car when she spotted Lena, wrapped in a blanket and talking with a firefighter. The rancid, burnt air forced her to stop short and stare at the busted gallery window and the blackened edges around it and the doors.

She walked into the ruined building. Axel didn't try to stop her, but she felt him following.

"This can't be happening…" Her lip quivered when she saw the charred canvases on the gallery floor.

The rustic gallery, with its low-hanging lights and high beams, was unrecognisable. Heat still radiated from the walls, and she tripped over a ruined canvas. She stared in shock at the ashen piles all over the floor. *Are they mine?*

"I'm sorry, but you can't be in here, it's not safe." A firefighter placed his hand gently on her shoulder, startling her. He apologised, but she couldn't speak as he guided her outside. Moving past the police and firefighters, her legs felt heavy, like she was wading through water. A small crowd had gathered by the fire engine and police car.

"Lena will have answers," Axel said, resting a hand on her back. His calming voice broke her out of her trance. Unsure her legs wouldn't give out, she followed him.

"We have your report. We'll be in touch if we have any other questions," the firefighter said to Lena before greeting them with a polite nod.

"Phoebe? You didn't have to come! Tonight was your celebratory dinner. I was going to stop by once we were done here," Lena said with a sad smile, but from her teary eyes, Phoebe knew she appreciated her coming.

"I had to come. I'm so glad you're okay," Phoebe stammered, smelling the smoke on her. "You didn't tell me you were in the gallery when the fire started."

Lena deflected, turning to the firefighter. "This is the artist—it was her work that was inside," she said, like he needed to know. Phoebe figured the fire was more important than her art.

"I'm sorry for your loss," the firefighter told her. It sounded ridiculous, considering the damage that had been done to the building and what could've happened to her friend.

"I'm just glad you're okay." Phoebe gave her a hug, and Lena sank into her like she needed it.

"I should've waited to call, but I was worried you'd find out from someone else."

Lena looked ready to burst into tears when Phoebe

released her. Phoebe glanced at the small crowd with their phones out and instinctively tried to move away from Axel, but he stayed glued to her side. She shot him a warning glance, but he refused to move without a word, so she gave in.

"How did this happen?" Phoebe asked, desperate for answers.

Lena took a deep breath before she started. Phoebe had never seen her so rattled. "The gallerist and I were trying to figure out the layout for the show. To see if we needed to make an interior change, and where we'd put the bar."

"And?" Axel prompted impatiently. Phoebe nudged him; considering how shaken up her friend was, she was allowed to ramble.

Lena stared at their joined hands, distracted. She gave Phoebe a knowing look before getting back to her story.

"Something smashed through the window, and then everything was on fire," she said. Her nails dug into her silky shirt as she crossed her arms. "It all happened so quickly. The gallerist has already left for the hospital to have her burns treated. She was closest to the window. Her arm got singed, but she's okay."

Phoebe's heart pounded at the thought that someone had been seriously hurt. Had the gallery been targeted because of her? Her thoughts were cut off by the firefighter.

"From the shards we found, it was most likely a glass bottle filled with accelerant." Behind him, his team were sealing off the building. "It explains why everything went up so quickly. The paints are flammable, which helped the fire spread. Your friend was lucky to get out with such minor burns."

"You got burnt?" Phoebe's legs went numb, looking at

Lena like she was about to crumble into ash.

"Just my fingers. I tried to save at least one of your paintings, but it got so hot that I dropped it," Lena said sadly.

"Oh my god, how could you put yourself at risk like that? A painting can't replace you." She wrapped her arms around Lena, afraid she could've lost her.

"But it's all gone! I'm so sorry, Phoebe. I should've divided the collection, it was the last of your work."

"Don't apologise, you couldn't have known this was going to happen." Phoebe didn't want Lena to blame herself for someone else's evil actions, but thinking of the last of her finished pieces going up in flames made her heart ache. Now there was nothing left of her work from before the accident. Her hand screamed as she made a fist so tight she thought her nerves would fry.

"The gallery has precautions to protect work from fires and a sprinkler system, but given the violence of this type of arson, it was intended to harm and destroy," the firefighter explained.

"We'll find out who did this," Lena assured Phoebe. "I've given my statement to the police, and they're already looking into it."

The police? Phoebe thought, uncertain. *Are they going to blame this on me? Will I be framed for this, like the break-in?*

All that work… Phoebe looked at her aching hand and knew she wouldn't be able to create such a volume of work again anytime soon.

"I have nothing for another show." Phoebe's thoughts slipped out.

It felt like her career was over before it began.

"Even if you did, I think it's best for everyone we put a pin in any more public shows," Lena said.

They should have cancelled this morning when they

had the chance. Phoebe felt like she needed to sit down as she absorbed the information. All those years of work, and she'd only had one successful show.

An officer approached them. "You can go now," he told Lena. "There's nothing else we need from you."

She thanked him, and he left with the firefighter after promising to keep them updated with any developments. Phoebe shook her head; she'd heard that promise before.

"Could you take me home?" Lena asked. "I don't want to drive."

"You don't even have to ask," Axel said, and Phoebe offered her a reassuring smile.

They walked back to the car in silence, the tang of the smoky air stuck in her throat. After a quick text from Axel, the driver pulled up, and Axel got in beside him. Lena climbed in the back first, and Phoebe went to open the other passenger door, but froze when she spotted Gunther Sheen in the crowd of phones. At first, she thought her eyes were lying to her, but then the headlights of the car highlighted him. He wore a navy baseball cap and a dark jacket, but she knew it was him. Her stomach dropped, and rage replaced her sadness.

This arsehole burnt down the gallery and hung around to watch the show. It's been him all along. Toying with us.

Phoebe slammed the door on Axel and Lena and started towards Sheen. He hadn't noticed her singling him out from the crowd. By the time Axel caught on and called after her, Phoebe had tackled Sheen to the ground. He grunted as he hit the pavement, and the crowd around them divided quickly.

"Why would you do this?" she screamed in his face.

His eyes wide in sheer terror, Sheen shouted for help. She grabbed him by his collar. He didn't fight back, which only infuriated her more.

"Why can't you leave me alone?" Phoebe wasn't going to let him play victim, to turn this on her. Some startled shouts and screams came from the observers as she shook him. She kept him pinned. She wanted him to hurt, and the white-hot rage killed her fear and the pain in her hand. She balled a fist ready to strike, and howled as she was ripped away from him.

"Get off him!" A cascade of orders rained down on her, but she couldn't let him get away.

"Don't let him get away with this again! He's the one who did this," Phoebe shouted over the sea of voices. Axel had hold of her, while another officer got between her and Sheen.

"Are you listening to me? Don't help him!" Phoebe barked, watching in disbelief as a firefighter helped Sheen up and quickly scanned him for any injuries. Sheen refused an ambulance when the firefighter asked. *Give me a few more minutes with him, and I'll make sure he needs that ambulance.* She wanted to laugh at the care he was shown. She didn't care about the cameras on her. Sure, this was probably being live streamed—her only regret was being forcibly removed before she did any real damage.

"Phoebe, please," Axel pleaded with her. The haze started to lift as she heard his comforting voice. His eyes locked with hers, forcing her to look at him. "Take a deep breath."

She hadn't realised she wasn't breathing.

"Arrest him!" Axel shouted at the officers.

"Calm down, sir! We've no cause. If anything, we've cause to arrest her for assault," the officer sneered.

"Arrest me, but please arrest him too," Phoebe snarled, wishing she'd wrapped her hands around his neck. "He's the one who set the fire, who broke into my studio, who has been harassing me!"

"Think what you want, but I didn't set the fire," Sheen argued, shaking his head violently. He didn't deny her other allegations.

"Then what the hell are you doing here?" Axel barked, and the officers got between them.

"I got a text to come here. I didn't know who it was from, but I was curious," he said, fumbling for his phone.

"You're a shitty liar," Phoebe shot back. Once again, he was blaming some secret shadow to cover his tracks. "You get a random text, and you just show up somewhere that happens to be a gallery showing my work?"

"When money's promised, yes." Sheen's smug reply nearly sent her back into attack mode.

"What the hell is wrong with you? You did this for money? You could've killed someone. Were you going to try and pin this on me like you did my studio? Why can't you get the fuck out of my life!" The words burnt her lungs. What the hell had she done in this life or the last to be tormented like this?

"No! I would never hurt anyone. When I got here, the fire had already started. I'm the one who called the police," he explained, pointing to the officers, who were listening in. "I helped your friend get out, and how do I know you didn't pay me for the studio? I don't know who did."

"Maybe you get off on this! Being the hero after nearly killing them. No one else was involved, this is all part of your sick game!"

Axel held her tightly, and she was glad he was there, or she would've torn Sheen's eyes out.

"If you didn't do this, show us that envelope from the first time, or the text you got to come here."

Sheen shook his head. "I burnt it as instructed. I'm not saying anything more without a lawyer."

Phoebe let out a long sigh. "You burnt the evidence that could prove another person was involved?"

He didn't get a chance to respond before the officer in charge of the scene grew tired of the back and forth.

"I don't know what is going on here, but you all need to calm down! Or you'll be arrested. This is a crime scene, so act like adults," the officer barked, and the crowd around them backed up.

Sheen took his phone out of his jacket.

"Do you have any evidence this man set the fire?" the officer asked Phoebe.

"No." Phoebe gritted her teeth.

"You wanted proof? See for yourself. The text came in after the fire had already started, and I called the police." Sheen showed them a text from an unknown number, and a call to emergency services. The officer handed him back his phone, swallowing Sheen's story.

"You could've sent that to yourself from another phone." Phoebe repeated her suspicions, hate rising from her gut. "Calling the police doesn't mean you didn't set it."

The officer stared at her like he wanted a reason to cuff her.

"Are you going to arrest me?" she asked, wanting to get out of there before she did something she regretted.

"Are you pressing charges?" the officer asked Sheen sternly.

Sheen hesitated, and she thought she saw a hint of worry in his eyes.

"No. This is all a misunderstanding." Sheen shook his head.

It was Phoebe's turn to grab Axel's sleeve before he struck him.

"You're free to leave the scene," the officer instructed Phoebe and Axel.

"You can't believe him!" Phoebe pleaded, but it fell on deaf ears.

"We will investigate and come to our own conclusions. Now, if you don't want to be arrested for obstruction, please leave, and we will contact you," the officer said, not giving them an option.

She hated to leave and let Sheen slip through her fingers again. She could only hope that he'd messed up this time, that he'd left some trace of his involvement behind. She needed to know if he was lying about helping Lena.

Lena waited in the car, and from her pale expression, she had watched the whole scene.

"Is everything okay? I've never seen you go off like that?" she asked as Axel and Phoebe reached the car, a safe distance away from Sheen.

"That's Sheen, talking to the officers. He was in the crowd, watching," Phoebe said, putting on her seatbelt.

Axel didn't say a word, and she worried that he would hop out of the car and beat the answers out of Sheen if they didn't leave soon.

Lena glanced out the window to where Sheen was still with the officers. "Him? That's the guy who broke into the studio. He helped us get out. The door got stuck and he busted it in so we could escape."

"Are you sure?" Phoebe asked, needing to be certain. Shock could distort things.

"I'm positive! We wouldn't have got out without him," Lena said, as shocked as she was.

What if his target was the art and when he realised people were inside, he didn't want to add murder to his charges? Phoebe considered, and she felt Axel watching her in the mirror. She closed her eyes, trying to calm her mind, but the sight of her charred canvases on the ground invaded every inch of her peace.

After making sure Lena got home safely, they arrived through the front door to find Nick and August waiting for them on the stairs. Phoebe glanced at Axel. Having spent the drive from Lena's in contemplative silence, they hadn't decided on how they were going to tell them.

August didn't give them a moment to breathe. "What's happened?"

Bart circled them as though sensing something was wrong. Unsure she could explain, Phoebe rubbed Bart's ears, in desperate need of some fluffy snuggles to calm her nervous system.

"Someone set the gallery for Phoebe's next exhibition on fire. They destroyed her paintings," Axel revealed.

It was a gut-wrenching sentence. Lena was irreplaceable, but with her hand still healing, so were her paintings. *Whoever did this got what they wanted: my career is stalled indefinitely,* she thought as Bart checked on Axel before settling on the stairs where he could keep an eye on all his herd.

August's shoulders sagged, and Nick punched the wall by the door. Phoebe winced; they couldn't afford any more injured hands.

"What the fuck is wrong with people?" Nick said, shaking his hand. "How bad is it? Was it intentional?"

"There's nothing left," Axel confirmed. "The gallery is just char, but luckily no one was injured."

"Not exactly unscathed though. Lena got some burns on her fingers and the gallerist had to go to the hospital for some burns to her arm." Phoebe filled in the blanks.

"Fuck." August said it best.

Phoebe nodded. "My point exactly."

August sat beside her on the stairs and rested his hand on her shoulder. He said nothing, but so much at the same time.

Someone buzzed the intercom.

"Are you serious? What does he want?"

Nick answered the phone. There was a moment's hesitation as they stared at him.

"No, let him in." Nick hung up, staring at them blankly. "Gunther Sheen is here. Olivier held him at the gate, but he said there is something we'll want to hear."

"He's either truly insane or narcissistic to walk into a lion's den," Phoebe said, too blindsided to be pissed.

She didn't have time to gather her thoughts before August opened the door and Sheen stood in the doorway, looking small.

"Thank you for letting me in."

"Say what you came to say before we don't let you leave," Axel said coldly.

Phoebe could barely see Sheen past the wall of men in front of her.

"I want to start by saying that I'm here to help. What happened earlier was crazy, and I never wanted to get wrapped up in arson or potential murder. I think whoever sent me that text wanted you to find me there, so that they could frame me." With his pasty complexion, Sheen looked like he was about to pass out, but given the death stares from those who loved her, he had every right to be afraid.

"But you're doing such an excellent job of framing me," Phoebe said.

"That was LouderTech covering their asses; they saw my car and I was backed into a corner. I was trying to save my job, and they were trying to save themselves a lawsuit," he said. "Seeing how devastated you were at the scene, how you attacked me, I knew it wasn't you orchestrating this. When you asked about the envelope earlier, I lied about burning it. With all the police and cameras around, I didn't want whoever's doing this to come after me for snitching. I kept it just in case."

Phoebe didn't need to verify his conclusions—of course she wasn't deliberately destroying her own career.

"Smart enough to cover your own arse in front of the police though." Axel took the plastic-bagged envelope from Sheen and handed it to Phoebe.

The envelope was blank. She wanted to cry in frustration; they'd hit another dead end.

"This is useless. There were no delivery details— whoever gave this to you had access to the building," Phoebe said. They knew the sender had access to Louder-Tech, but they were none the wiser as to whether the envelope had been placed on Sheen's desk before the accident.

"I'll confess my part, so you can trust me," he started. "I came to the hospital in Munich because I thought if I was there for all of you then I could convince my boss to give me your account. I've long been a fan, and I was pissed when I was kicked out of the hospital and your agent treated me like I was the scum of the earth. When I got home, I was angry and I got involved in something that I didn't fully understand because I needed money," he explained. "But I'm sorry."

"You're only saying this because you're scared."

"I can be sorry and scared," Sheen admitted. "I was blackmailed into going to the gallery tonight."

He opened his phone, and Phoebe got up to stand between her brother and Axel. A video of Sheen breaking into Phoebe's studio stared back at them, filmed from across the street and at a much better angle than her own nanny cam footage.

"There are also photos of me getting kicked out of the hospital in Munich. I think they're trying to pin this on me. If I didn't turn up at the Reid Gallery tonight, it was going to be leaked. I didn't want to call the police, but when I saw the two women inside and the place going up in flames so fast, I couldn't just watch. I never signed up to hurt anyone."

"How can we trust this isn't some scheme you've cooked up?" Phoebe asked.

"You can't, but I had to tell someone about the blackmail in case something happens to me. I'm sorry for the part I played in this, but this is getting too dangerous, and no money is worth the risk. If you need me to go to the police, I'll do whatever you want. I don't know what this person is capable of."

An awkward silence settled over the group. It was a risk even hearing him out, but it seemed like whoever was behind this was tying up loose ends: first trying to frame her and now going after him. With the studio gone and her work destroyed, what else was there to take from her? Her life? Those she loved? Lena and the gallerist could've been killed if Sheen hadn't intervened…

"We have a detective you can talk to." Phoebe decided to take the gamble.

"If you're serious about helping, come back tomorrow, but if this is some ploy to get close to us, then we're the ones you should be afraid of," Axel said, making sure he stayed between them. Phoebe hadn't even considered that might be Sheen's motive.

"I can come by first thing in the morning," Sheen said a little too eagerly.

Phoebe worried that they were playing into his hands. She didn't trust him, and from the others' hard expressions, they didn't either. However, he was the only one who could prove she wasn't behind this.

"No, you can meet with Isaiah and me at Isaiah's office," Nick interjected, keeping him out of the house. Seeing him fill Cillian's role as the leader was a comfort.

"I can do that," Sheen said with a nod.

With the plan arranged, Nick walked him out, and they were all happy to see the back of Sheen as Olivier made sure he left the property.

"I'm going to bed," Phoebe announced, unable to handle any more discussion for one night. They were trying to help, but their anger and upset wouldn't bring back her work.

"Are you okay?" Nick asked. "I know you're not, but are you sure you want to be alone? We can all sleep in the sitting room if you want company."

"I love you for being willing to sleep on the couches for me, but I'll be fine." Phoebe glanced at Axel. Being alone was the last thing she wanted, but now wasn't the time to tell them about their relationship. "Besides, they got what they wanted, destroyed my work and reputation—all that's left is murdering me in my sleep."

The others stared wide-eyed at her, not appreciating the joke.

"If I don't laugh, I'll cry," she sighed, hating their sympathetic smiles.

"Get some sleep. We can talk about all this when

you've had some time to process," Nick said solemnly, and she wanted to say something reassuring, but she couldn't muster any false positivity. She flexed her hand, and the pain reminded her how long it was going to be to get her career back to what it was. Probably long enough to sink back into the void she'd spent years trying to climb out of.

"Goodnight," she said.

She wished she could've climbed straight into Axel's bed, but she trudged back to her own room.

After hours of tossing and turning, she gave up. Anger, disgust, upset and fear coiled like a snake around her body. Her stalker had taken her safe space, her work, and she wanted to scream but no sound would come out. She tiptoed downstairs and saw the light still on in August's game room. She made sure to avoid any creaking floorboards as she made it to the kitchen. Carefully, she opened the basement door and locked it behind her.

"Bee?" Axel whispered, turning on a light as she padded down the stairs.

As soon as she saw him, her world crumbled, but he was the world she needed. She knew then that she loved him, even if she wasn't ready to say it.

Afraid she'd burst into tears if she said a single word, she climbed into his extended arms. She thought about all that had been taken from her, and terror forced her to hold him tight. He was the last thing she loved they could take.

"I'm here, you're safe," he whispered, cradling her against his chest. It wasn't her safety she was worried about.

"I can't lose you," she sobbed quietly as he held her and stroked her hair.

"You won't."

"Sheen never showed?" Phoebe asked.

Axel couldn't believe Sheen had played them.

"Did you try to call him?" Phoebe continued, and he hated the worry in her voice.

"The number was out of service." Axel hesitated on the basement steps as he heard Nick's sharp tone coming from the kitchen.

"Fucking liar. We shouldn't have trusted him," Phoebe said, and Nick scoffed.

"Sheen isn't the only one who's been lying."

The comment caught Axel off guard. Phoebe didn't reply, and Axel's stomach dropped.

"Cat got your tongue? Anything you want to say to me?" Nick asked his sister.

Axel regretted sleeping in so late. He hadn't set his alarm—since Phoebe had climbed into his bed in the middle of the night, he'd figured they could both use a lie in. With Nick going to meet with Isaiah and Sheen, he'd thought they wouldn't be caught.

"Other than 'Did you eat the last of the cookie dough?' Because I remember hiding a tub in the freezer." The sound of ice crunching told him she was going through the freezer.

"No, that's not it. As your big brother, I don't want to talk about this. In fact, I don't even want to know, but given all that's going on, all our sanity is hanging by a thread. I didn't expect to learn you've been lying to us," Nick lectured.

"You're being weird." Phoebe tried to brush him off.

"We agreed no more lies, and last night I saw you going down to the basement," Nick said sharply. "Sneaking around is beneath you, and I don't know if this is some fuck you to Cillian, or the world or a quarter-life crisis, but sleeping with Axel?"

"I'm not having a quarter-life crisis! What I do and where I sleep is none of your business. I say this with love, big bro, but keep your nose out of my business," Phoebe stated.

Axel wanted to back her up, but this was a conversation between family. Still, he stayed close in case she needed him.

"It is my business when it affects all of us. You went to Italy with Axel without telling any of us—just snuck off— but we were understanding."

"I told you I went to clear out the villa," she pressed, and Axel smirked. It wasn't a lie; they had cleared the villa. He did hate that they'd been lying since then, though.

He cursed himself that they hadn't been more discreet, but with her nightmares, he wasn't going to let her sleep alone, and since his room was furthest away from the others', it only made sense that she stayed with him.

"That's not all you did! You've been sleeping in Axel's room since you both got back from Italy," Nick said accusingly, and Phoebe went quiet. "Anita showed me the pictures she bought from the paparazzi. You both looked very cosy. I suspected Axel had feelings for you when he wouldn't leave your hospital room and when he kept volunteering to check up on you. I never thought he'd act on his feelings—and you should be careful. I thought you said you'd never date another rockstar again."

Axel wasn't offended; Nick was just being protective of his younger sister. Nick had told him he didn't want her dating another rockstar, which was understandable given how the last one had treated her. Not to mention how the public would react to them being together. Thankfully, Anita had thought to purchase the photos, so there hadn't been any press coverage, but Axel still couldn't understand how they'd been found so quickly.

"My feelings for Axel have nothing to do with Cillian," Phoebe argued. "I didn't do this to spite him. I think we both know I lost Cillian a long time ago. We were clinging to something that didn't exist anymore."

"So, you aren't denying it? You're with Axel?" Nick huffed.

"I'm happy. Can't that be enough?"

Axel listened to her pacing.

"Not when it's only going to result in heartbreak."

Nick's words stung; he had no intention of breaking her heart. He was far more concerned with her breaking his, but any memories they'd made so far would make the pain worth it.

"Why do you think Axel will hurt me? Do you have so little faith in all your friends?"

"Depends on whether you're planning on dating all my friends," Nick snapped.

"I know you're upset, but that was uncalled for," Phoebe said. "We didn't plan this, and we didn't tell you because we were worried how you'd react with everything going on. Clearly we were right."

"You can't keep dating my bandmates."

"Don't make it sound so bad," she snapped.

"How do you want me to make it sound? How do you think the media will react when they find out?"

"I don't care about the media, I only care about all of you." Phoebe's words came out in a frenzy. "I never wanted to do anything to hurt you, but I love him. I don't know how he feels, but please don't ruin the one thing in my life that's going right."

She loved him. Axel's eyes widened as she said it. He couldn't remove the grin from his face. They hadn't even said that to each other. He wanted to burst through the door and wrap his arms around her, but knew he should let Nick adjust before he tackled his sister with kisses.

"You love him? This is serious?" Nick's tone softened.

"I do, and I really didn't see this coming. You have to believe the last thing I wanted was to fall for another rockstar, but he is so much more than that. I know you're worried about how the world will react and you want to protect me, but no one is going to find out until we all want them too," she explained.

"You're both going to be the death of me, but I can't do anything about who you love," Nick grumbled. "I suppose you could have picked worse, and I've suspected his feelings for you had been going on for a while, so I know he genuinely cares for you. This is probably my fault for insisting you move in with us—but still, promise me no more secrets."

Axel felt his shoulders drop for the first time. He wanted his friend's acceptance.

"No more secrets," Phoebe promised.

"Are you sure you have to be in love with Axel? There isn't anyone else?" Nick asked.

"Sorry," Phoebe chuckled.

Axel opened the basement door and found Phoebe hugging her brother. Nick tensed when he first saw him, but then his expression softened, silently telling him it was okay.

"I hate to interrupt this bonding moment, but keep your paws off my girlfriend," Axel said, and Phoebe looked around her brother to stare at him. He winked, and she blushed as she realised he'd heard everything.

"Fine, but remember that older brother trumps boyfriend," Nick said, releasing her.

"She's your what?" August asked Axel, returning from his run with a box of donuts.

"My girlfriend," Axel answered plainly.

"Finally! I was beginning to wonder how long it'd take you to come clean," August said, putting the box on the kitchen table.

"You knew?" Nick asked August, who shrugged.

"You didn't? Phoebe's been going down to the basement for weeks. Axel holds her hand any chance he gets, and he follows her around worse than Bart." August took a glazed donut. "I just wanted to see how long it would take them to admit it. Now that's out of the way, I got jam and sprinkle donuts. Sorry Phoebe, they were out of Oreo."

The others just stared at him. Axel had been worried about August's reaction most of all, but he seemed the least bothered.

"Why are you staring at me? Did you not want donuts?"

"Donuts are great, thank you." Phoebe walked over to him and kissed his cheek.

"We're good?" Axel asked Nick as Phoebe grabbed a donut.

"Break her heart, and I break your legs," Nick said sternly, wrapping his arm around Axel's shoulders.

"I'll even give you the baseball bat to do it," Axel said, sure that day wouldn't come.

"But I should probably be thanking you, for loving her. It's good to see her happy about something, and I'm glad she has you to protect her," Nick sighed, looking at Phoebe smiling as she sat with August.

"She has all of us in her corner. We aren't going to let anything happen to her," Axel assured him.

"I know, but I wish Sheen had shown up this morning. Isaiah said he's going to go by his place and see if he can find him, try and get him to open up without any of us around to intimidate him," Nick said, revealing more to him than he had Phoebe. "He'll be by when he knows why he didn't show up. I don't know how much more bad news she can take."

"She's tougher than all of us. You should have seen her go after Sheen at the gallery—she's a fighter, and once we find out who's doing this, I'm more afraid of what she'll do to them," Axel said, trying to ease his worries.

Nick let out a long exhale, but didn't look convinced.

"Promise me that if anything happens to me, you'll protect her," he said.

Axel rested his hand on his shoulder. "Nothing will happen to any of us. We're going to figure this out, and one day this will all just be a bad memory."

Colour came back into Nick's cheeks, and Axel hoped he'd brought him some peace.

"Evening. Please come in." Phoebe said, opening the door for Isaiah, anxious to find out what he'd learned from Sheen.

"Thank you. Sorry I couldn't come earlier," Isaiah said, his shoulders heavy. His stubble had got further on its way to a beard since the last time they'd talked in person.

"Please don't apologise, we understand that you're busy," Phoebe said. "We've been hoping you had some good news."

Isaiah didn't look all that hopeful as he removed his black jacket.

"I think we should get everyone together before we talk," he said, following her through to the kitchen.

She wondered if Sheen had decided to recant his confession. Maybe he'd been paid to keep his mouth shut? He had a talent for self-preservation, and had already demonstrated he was morally corrupt when payment was involved.

Isaiah stood at the end of the island while she poured him a cup of coffee. Axel, August and Nick gathered in the kitchen, each taking a seat.

"Did you manage to find him? I hope he had a good

excuse for not showing up this morning," Nick said, pissed Sheen had wasted their time.

"I did," Isaiah said, and Phoebe felt like all the air had been sucked from the room. "We sent someone to his apartment to do a welfare check. Unfortunately, he was found deceased."

They all stared at Isaiah like he had two heads.

"He's dead?" Phoebe asked, unable to process what he was saying.

"The cause is suspected insulin overdose. He was a type one diabetic, and the medication was in his name." Isaiah sipped his coffee.

"Do you think it was intentional?" Axel dared to ask. "Suspicious that he died just before he was about to confess."

"Right now, it's being ruled as accidental. There was no forced entry or sign of a struggle. There is no evidence to suggest that someone else was in the apartment," Isaiah said, but it felt like there was something he was leaving out.

"What are the chances of a type one diabetic accidentally overdosing?" Phoebe asked.

"Guilty conscience?" Nick countered.

"Given his attitude last night, suicide doesn't make sense. He didn't want to die," Phoebe said, recalling how he was afraid of the person behind all this.

"I wish I had more answers, but there's something else I want to show you," Isaiah said, opening some photos on his phone. They all leaned in. "Sheen's apartment was like a shrine to Brothers of Anarchy. Posters, fan art, signed T-shirts, photos, articles. There was a heavy focus on Cillian, even a couple of photos of them together and a napkin with Cillian's signature."

"This is intense," Nick said, swiping through the disturbing photos. Sheen was far more than just a fan.

August was the first to back away. "I feel like I need a shower."

"I believe Sheen was responsible for the harassment entirely," Isaiah said. "When you caught him last night at the gallery fire, he might have wanted to appear like the hero. When you weren't willing to fully accept his story, he might've realised he was never going to get close to you all like he'd hoped."

"What about the cash? Sheen said he was paid?" Axel asked, looking for any evidence of another person's involvement.

"I searched the room with the other officers. No one found any loose cash, and he'd made no recent bank deposits. However, we found a few burner phones in his desk drawer, and envelopes identical to the one he gave you. There were also packs of single razor blades in his bathroom."

"So that's it. It was just him. There really isn't anyone else?" Phoebe asked, needing certainty.

"We found no other evidence of another person's involvement. We checked the footage outside the Reid Gallery, and there is a hooded figure who is seen throwing a lit bottle through the front window and leaving. Only a few moments later, we see Sheen come down the same street and start busting in the gallery door." Isaiah told her. "He either passed the person responsible or did it himself."

Phoebe would've felt better if Lena had got the video footage from LouderTech, but given what she'd been through last night, she wasn't going to push for her involvement.

"That's it, investigation over?" Axel didn't sound all too relieved.

"We're waiting for the autopsy, but he sent an email to LouderTech telling them he was solely responsible for the break-in at the studio, and that he was sorry for the destruction he caused and the harm he did to both Phoebe and the company's reputation."

"It all seems too easy. I don't like it," Axel said, pacing.

"He wasn't a criminal mastermind," Nick said. "Sheen was an obsessed fan who didn't get what he wanted and gave up."

"What do you think?" Axel asked, looking to Phoebe.

"I want to believe Sheen was working alone, and that he'd been manipulating us last night. But the overdose, the confession, and all the evidence feel too good to be true."

"I'll keep digging," Isaiah said, "but don't let Sheen get into your head. I don't want any of you looking for shadows that aren't there."

"So that's it?" Axel said. "We return to normal?"

"I don't see why not. Just be cautious until we get the final results from the evidence we found and the autopsy."

"Thank you for everything." Nick shook his hand.

Axel sat down solemnly, and Phoebe could hear his mind going a mile a minute.

"I'm sorry I couldn't get to him sooner so I could get you a real confession," Isaiah said, and it was obvious he wasn't too happy with this ending either.

August started washing the dishes to self-soothe, and Nick grabbed a beer from the fridge.

"You've done more than enough. Thank you for helping us," Phoebe said, walking Isaiah to the door.

He pulled on his jacket. "I'll be in touch with the results. Look after each other, and call me if there is anything else you need."

He left with a quick goodbye, and she couldn't believe it was over, just like that.

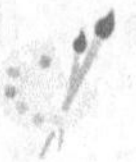

WHEN SHE GOT BACK to the kitchen, Nick and August didn't look like they were in the mood to chat about the new development, and Axel was gone.

"He's down in the basement," Nick told her. "We're going to take Bart for a walk."

Phoebe guessed they wanted to give Axel and her some space.

"Are you okay?" she asked.

She knew they'd suspected that Cillian's death wasn't an accident. If there was some maestro behind the curtain targeting all of them, then they had hope that Cillian wasn't responsible for what had happened. Isaiah had quashed that hope with reality.

"It's over, like Isaiah said. Let's not look for shadows," Nick said, resting a hand over hers.

She nodded, not wanting to put doubts into their heads. After so much going wrong, maybe she just couldn't believe this because it felt too good to be true. But seeing Sheen's shrine in the photos had confirmed all she needed to know. It made sense that he'd targeted her; there was no phantom orchestrating everything. Cillian's accident was an accident, and Sheen was just an obsessive fan who blamed her for Cill's death and resented her close relationship with the rest of the band. He'd fed on their fears to try and get close to them.

Phoebe hesitated at the basement door. After everything Axel had done for her, she felt a surge of guilt and wasn't sure whether to disturb him or give him some space. The news about Sheen was a lot for them all to digest; going down to the basement to play was code for "Axel needs space", but she wanted to make sure he was okay.

She turned the doorknob and figured that since the door wasn't locked, he wasn't too opposed to visitors. Padding down the steps, she heard him curse as he made a mistake.

"Are you going to hide down here, or do you want to talk?" Phoebe asked, playing with the long sleeves of her black dress.

His head snapped up before he started again.

"I'm not hiding, I just needed some time to process." Axel's shoulders relaxed as she approached him. "Playing is the only way I can get my mind to stop racing."

"Do you want me to go?" she asked, even if leaving was the last thing she wanted.

"Don't you dare. Come over here." Axel reached out for her, bridging the gap between them.

She handed him the small towel from the amplifier beside her. Watching the beads of sweat run down Axel's chiselled torso only reminded her of how his body had felt against hers, and she didn't want her desire distracting her from their conversation.

"I can't seem to forget that Sheen won't have to suffer for what he put you through, but having you beside me is a much more effective distraction." He put down his sticks and wiped the sweat from his brow with the towel.

"I'm sorry so much of this has landed on you," she said, running her hands down his bare chest. "I know how worried you've been about all of us. I wish Sheen was still alive so I could kick his arse into jail for making these past few weeks so much harder."

He pulled her close until her head rested on his bare chest. His lips hit the sensitive skin on her neck.

He held her waist. "You never have to apologise to me for someone else's actions. None of this is your fault. Though I will admit you're sexy when you're mad," he teased, and she rolled her eyes.

"I'm trying to be serious," she said, swatting at him.

In one quick motion, he placed her on the stool, trapped in by his drums. She thought he was going to kiss her, but he pulled back.

"I'm serious when I say I can't breathe when I don't know if you're safe or not." His hands gripped her hips. He pressed his body against hers, and when she arched to get closer, he inched away, furthering her frustration.

"I'm serious when I say I love how stubborn and protective you are about those you care about," he said, his lips teasingly close. Her breath quickened as his fingertips brushed beneath her T-shirt, and all thoughts of their conversations drifted away.

"Axel," she groaned as his lips trailed down her neck, increasing the ache within her.

"I thought you wanted me to be serious," he said with a smirk, and she resented how much his proximity intoxicated her.

She reached for the buttons on his trousers and saw a wicked grin appear on his lips. Phoebe unzipped his trousers, her eyes never leaving his. Stroking the length of him, she could feel how ready he was. She gripped him tighter, and delighted in his sharp intake of breath.

"I'm serious about how much I want you," she said, struggling against him, but he held her still.

Removing her hand from him, he pinned her hands to her sides.

"Keep squirming like that, and I'll fuck you on the floor."

His mouth claimed hers, the sweet taste of his tongue driving her wild. He released her hands only to stand her up, and before she could touch him again, he ripped through her button-down black dress.

"That was my favourite dress!"

He quickly silenced her as he wrapped her legs around his waist. The feel of him against her core only increased her desire, and she forgot about her ruined dress.

"I'll buy you a new one." Axel dropped her onto his bed, and she landed with a thud on the duvet. Her laughter silenced as Axel towered over her, a demanding look in his eyes. She could feel the aching pulse between her legs.

He watched as she rose in her underwear. Kissing his chest, she trailed down his chiselled stomach until she reached his belt. He grabbed her chin, and she whined as he ended her exploration.

"Keep your eyes on mine, and hands on my chest," he ordered, and she nodded, eager to please.

His hand went to her waist, sliding over the curve of her ass, and she tried not to squirm. Phoebe dug her nails into his chest and cried out when his fingers slid over her lacy black underwear.

"I told you not to move." Axel spun her around, pressing her back against his firm body as his fingers brought her closer to the edge, the other hand massaging her breast. The heat of his body only heightened her desire to move with him.

"Stand still," he said against her ear. His lips trailed down her spine as he shifted her underwear down her legs.

Before he could issue any more orders, she straddled him on the floor. She loved the surprised look in his eyes; his need for her only increased her insanity. He sat up, and slid his lips along her collarbone as he freed her from her bra.

"What do you want?" His teeth clamped down on her hardened nipple as he began to stroke between her legs.

"You." Phoebe stilled and kissed him gently. "I need you," she rasped.

His hungry gaze disappeared, and gentleness took its place. He groaned as she slowly rocked against him. All she heard was their laboured breathing as she finished pulling his trousers off.

"I'm serious when I say this is mine." Axel lifted her onto him, easing inside her. He groaned, and she remembered how good he felt stretching her, filling her in a way that made her lose all sense of self until there was only them.

"God, I love you." His rough words brushed her ear so quietly she thought she'd imagined his confession. She wanted to reply, but he started to move. Gripping his shoulders, she met his thrusts. She brought her lips to his, and his calloused hands dug into her hips as he moved deeper into her. She felt herself tightening around him, getting closer. She arched her back, allowing him to take her deeper. He groaned, biting her neck, and she erupted around him. The sting of his teeth only heightened the ecstasy until they were both left out of breath and clinging to each other for support.

"I love you too," she whispered, and she met his smile with a kiss.

Phoebe

A fortnight passed without incident, no booby-trapped fan mail or threats in graffiti. Once it was reported that Gunther Sheen was the culprit behind both the studio break-in and fire, the media started to back off since they had his unhealthy attachment to the band to focus on. LouderTech reached out to apologise for believing his lies and for trying to accuse Phoebe of setting up his schemes.

Knowing he couldn't hurt her anymore brought Phoebe some relief, but it didn't make up for the hurt he'd caused by destroying her remaining work. Instead of wallowing in self-pity, though, she focused her energy on building her next collection and decided to reopen her studio as a free space for financially struggling and disabled artists to come together, using the money that Cillian had invested without her knowledge. Struggling with her injured hand had made her feel alone, and she hoped this new space could help others from feeling the same way, as they expressed themselves without worrying about judgement, or paying for materials. Lena helped her get it all organised, and they'd plenty of time to plan since the band were busy promoting the new album and rehearsing for Cillian's six-month memorial concert. They all needed time to heal, and they were finally getting it.

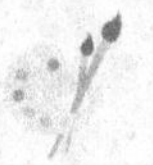

Almost there! A text came in from August as Phoebe rocked back and forth on her heels, trying to keep warm outside Abrams Pub in the cold night air. Spotting August and Nick at the end of the street, she hurried inside through the crowded entrance. They were just about ready; Lena gave her a thumbs up as she finished helping one of the bar staff hang up the last 'Happy Birthday' banners behind the bar.

"They're coming!" Phoebe squealed to Anita, who was waiting at the bar.

Anita gave the signal and Susan, one of the pub's owners, flicked off all lights except for the old neon signs. Phoebe lit the giant sparklers on the cake.

The old couple who owned Abrams had given the band their start by letting them perform on Fridays before they got signed, and they'd been regulars ever since. Staffed by the owners' friends and family, the pub was the perfect place for Nick's surprise birthday party without the media finding out. They'd kept the guest list to a bare minimum so there would be no risk of it being leaked.

Nick had refused to let them celebrate given what happened at the house party, but Sheen was gone, and Phoebe wasn't going to let her brother let a year pass without celebrating. Losing Cillian had taught them every year was precious. She'd also wanted to do something special for him, since he'd handled her new relationship with Axel surprisingly well.

"Surprise!!" they cheered as Nick walked in.

August smirked, nudging his frozen friend. Phoebe hugged him, hoping this wasn't a terrible idea.

"I can't believe you did all this. I said no party!" Nick whispered. "Isaiah warned us all to be careful."

"Susan kindly closed the pub for the night, and everyone has been sworn to secrecy. I only invited close friends and family." Phoebe glanced over her shoulder to their parents. "They asked about Sheen, but I told them it's over. They don't need the details. This is your birthday, you only turn thirty once, and we are going to celebrate."

"Thank you." It was great to see him smile; it was rare these days.

Everyone hollered and cheered as he blew out his candles. The music and lights turned on once the sparklers burnt out. Nick's laughter echoed around the room as he was tackled by friends from his school days. Seeing him so happy made the effort of keeping the secret worth it. The remembrance concert was weighing on him, and she wanted to give him one night without grief and hurt.

"Shots all round!" Nick cheered over the music.

"Coming right up!" Susan said, with a bright, red-lipped smile as she racked up the small glasses.

Nick joined their parents, and it was nice to have her family all in one place. It brought back memories of when all their friends and family would gather in Abrams for the band's performances.

With the guests distracted, Phoebe snuck into the back kitchen to cut the cake. Shots on an empty stomach wasn't a good idea. Axel snuck in through the back door, and she looked up to find him unashamedly running his eyes over every inch of the short red dress that hugged her hips. She'd worn his favourite colour on purpose. Since he'd been busy rehearsing with the band, and she'd been doing physio to help her get back to painting, they hadn't had much alone time recently. She smirked when he shook his head to stop himself staring.

"Sorry I'm late," he said, coming up behind her as she cut a slice of cake. "I didn't think I'd ever get out of the studio. Three days and I'm still trying to put together the setlist for the concert. I thought about adding some of Cillian's favourite songs, and Nick and August loved the idea, but now I've made the job even harder."

"Don't be sorry, you're here now." She turned to stuff the small slice of cake in his face. She got most of it in his mouth but smeared the rest when he tried to kiss her.

"You've got icing on your face, don't you dare," she said, trying to wrestle herself out of his arms, but he held her firmly against his hard body.

"It's too delicious not to share." He kissed her, smearing the icing and crumbs on her lips and cheeks.

Phoebe tried her best to wipe away the icing without smearing her make-up. "How was that?"

"Tasty." He winked.

"I wasn't talking about the cake," she said, not wanting to return to the party looking like he'd ravaged her in the kitchen.

"Neither was I." His lips brushed her ear, making her shiver.

"I don't have time for your seductive antics, I have a cake to bring out," Phoebe warned as his hands teased the hem of her dress. "Go join the party, you are distracting me." She turned around to face him as his fingers brushed the inside of her thigh.

"I apologise for distracting you from your very important birthday duties." He raised his hands in defeat as she pointed the knife at him playfully. She lowered it when she realised how he was dressed.

"You're wearing a shirt," she said, surprised he wasn't in his usual favoured T-shirts with one or more holes.

He shrugged. "I wanted to look my best, have to make a good impression with your parents."

"You've met my parents a dozen times," she said as he pulled at the end of his sleeves like the cuffs were too tight. Given that it was big on him, he must have borrowed it from August.

"True, but I want them to think I'm worthy of their precious daughter," he said, kissing her hand like the gentleman he wasn't.

"They don't know about us yet, and they like you well enough," she said, not wanting him to overthink it. She wasn't sure what her parents would think of anyone she dated; it wasn't like she'd dated anyone other than Cillian before.

"How's the cake coming along? We've got some hungry guests," Anita said, joining them in the kitchen.

Axel cleared his throat and stepped away from Phoebe.

"Almost finished, but you can take out the first couple of slices," Phoebe said calmly.

"Axel, could you take the first lot? I'll grab the second. Need a snack to soak up all the shots Nick is buying every-one," Anita said, and Axel saluted and left without discussion.

Anita didn't snack; Phoebe knew this was just an excuse to talk to her. They hadn't spoken much since Italy.

"You should end it before you ruin them all," Anita sighed, once Axel was out the door with the first tray of plates.

Phoebe tried to remain civil. "I appreciate that you want to protect the band, but it's not your job to get involved in our personal relationships."

"Don't say I didn't warn you," Anita scoffed, and

followed Axel out with the second tray.

Phoebe had the overwhelming desire to pick up the rest of the cake and hurled it after her, but it would be a waste to ruin such a delicious chocolate cake. Instead, she let the velvety rich frosting soothe her anger. If her brother and August supported her and Axel, she didn't care what anyone else thought.

For the rest of the night, Phoebe kept her distance from Anita's disconcerting gaze.

"I don't think she's listening to us," Nick said, sipping his drink as they stood around the pool table.

Axel was talking to one of Nick's school friends, a startlingly beautiful blonde, at the bar as he ordered a round of drinks. Phoebe jumped when August placed a hand on her shoulder, startling her out of her jealousy.

"She has nothing to worry about," Nick said to August. "Axel isn't shy about telling anyone he's already taken."

"What were you saying?" Phoebe quickly focused her attention on the conversation, only to realise they were making fun of her.

"Nothing. I was just asking August if he could get you a knife," Nick said, smirking at his friend.

"Why would he need a knife?" Phoebe asked, eating the pineapple from the umbrella on her drink.

"To cut the tension," August chuckled, and stifled his amusement with a sip of his drink.

Phoebe ran her hand over her glass, collecting the droplets to flick at him. He grimaced, and she erupted into laughter.

"We were coming to say goodbye to the birthday boy." Phoebe and Nick's mum interrupted them, and Phoebe hoped her parents hadn't heard the playful mocking about Axel. She didn't think tonight was the right time for them to discover she was dating another rockstar.

"We really are so proud of you, darling," Mum said to Nick, handing him a card.

"Please do your best not to make trouble for the boys while you're staying with them," she said, patting Phoebe on the shoulder. "We spoke to your agent, Lena, about your cancelled shows, and if you need to come home for a little while your brother and his friends are rehearsing for the concert, please don't hesitate to call."

As always, the boys were the light of her life and Phoebe was the burden playing with paints. She bit her tongue, not wanting to get into an argument.

"Sorry, Mrs Fletcher, but Phoebe can't go home," Axel said, setting down the round of drinks on the table beside them. "She's the glue that holds us all together. We even have an art studio all set up for her at the house. Having made so much progress with her physio, it won't be long before she's ready for more shows." He stepped close enough to make Phoebe flush, and her mum eyed him suspiciously.

"I'm glad to hear your hand is doing better," Mum said with a forced smile. "We'll have to come back up to town when you put on your next show."

Dad gave her a reassuring nod, not wanting to get involved as usual.

"Look after each other," he said, and gave Phoebe a tight squeeze.

Mum shot one last troubled glance at her and Axel, before kissing her brother's cheek and saying their goodbyes.

"Sorry to interrupt, but can we steal the birthday boy?" Meghan, one of the back-up singers from the last tour, fluttered her long lashes at Nick, while her friend made intense eye contact with August.

"It would be a pleasure to be stolen by you," Nick said,

offering his arm to her.

August put his arm around the other woman, who giggled. Phoebe looked between them and wondered if they were having some silent conversation. August didn't even need to say anything for women to swoon. Phoebe figured that he just didn't want to be a third wheel with her and Axel as he and Nick followed the women away.

"And then there were two," Axel said, racking the balls for a new game. "Ladies first."

"Such a gentleman." Phoebe pulled the pool cue back to strike, but he leaned over only inches away, stopping her. She glanced at him, wanting to be irritated, but his serious expression was adorable.

"You'll get more power with your fingers in this position," Axel said, adjusting her hand position.

She took the shot, and instead of the balls clustering in one spot like before, they shot around the table. She concealed her smile, not wanting to admit he'd helped.

"See, I won't lead you wrong," he said, and Phoebe watched his face light up as he moved around the table.

"Your turn," she said.

He was winning, but seeing his tensed muscles through his shirt, she didn't care. Before he took the shot, his eyes lingered on the wrap of her dress where the crossover exposed her cleavage. Messing with him, she leaned forward, and he missed the shot entirely. He clenched his jaw.

"You did that on purpose." His dark eyes sent a rush of heat through her body.

"Maybe you shouldn't be so easily distracted." She straightened, and chalked the cue.

"You were wearing that dress the first night I saw you," he whispered as she lined up the shot.

"Was I?" She tried to think back, but all she remembered was that they'd met at a show. "Refresh my memory?" Acting innocent, she bent over in front of him.

"A dangerous game you're playing." Axel whispered in her ear, brushing her hair from her neck as he pretended to adjust her grip again.

"Winner takes all." She widened her stance and felt his hand brush her thigh; a gasp escaped her lips. "You were refreshing my memory?"

Phoebe loved the confidence he brought out in her.

Axel's fingers gently caressing her thigh made her miss the final shot. She stood, needing to catch her breath as he explained, unfazed:

"Right, you were standing in the front row of our concert. It was the first time I saw you since I'd joined the band. You had bright pink hair and dried paint on your hands, and this soul-captivating smile as you danced and sang along to every song. I couldn't take my eyes off you, and then I found out who you were, and it killed me that you were off-limits," he told her, melting her heart.

"When I went backstage, you ignored me. You didn't even introduce yourself," she said, taking his hand. She wanted him alone, and his sly smirk told her he knew exactly what she wanted as they headed down a narrow hallway to an office.

Axel closed the door behind them. He rested his back against the closed office door, taking in the sight as she lifted her dress to the tops of her thighs.

"Because if I got too close, I was afraid everyone would see the truth." His gaze darkened as he followed her to where she sat on the desk and stood between her legs.

"What was that?" Phoebe slipped her arms around his shoulders and arched her back as he rested his hands on her hips and pulled her against him. He brushed his lips against hers, teasing her mercilessly. Their tongues intertwined, silencing her moans as he deepened the kiss.

"That I wanted to make you mine." His hands drifted to her inner thighs, the overwhelming pulse at her core. Phoebe sighed in delight as she felt him harden against her.

Kissing his neck, she moved her hands to the button of his black jeans, but he gripped her wrists and placed them firmly on the desk. His hungry eyes met hers, and she went still. He pulled the tie on her dress, exposing her lacy bra.

Phoebe's breath caught as his demanding lips trailed down her neck to the swell of her breasts.

"Don't stop," she groaned as he started to pull away.

"You want me to bend you over this desk, but you'll have to be quiet, because we wouldn't want anyone to hear us," he said, and Phoebe leaned over the desk teasingly.

He pulled her hips sharply against him, and she squealed at the rough sensation of his trousers against her bare skin.

"Be quiet, or I'll stop."

The sensation of his touch caused her to shift. She chewed her lip and nodded, then felt his lips on the back of her thighs. She rose on her tiptoes as he moved aside her lacy red underwear to taste her. A rough moan escaped her when she felt the sharp tear of her underwear.

"Not a sound," he reminded her, and she nodded. She glanced to her side to see him lay the underwear beside her. "It's a pity I can't tear this dress to pieces. I think it would look excellent on the floor," he said, and his fingers caressed her. "Good girl," he rasped as she bit her lip, trying to stay silent.

She heard his belt clink, and she smiled back at him as she watched him undo his zipper.

"Hold on to the edge of the desk," he ordered, and her

insides clenched excitedly.

"Tell me you want me." He fisted her hair.

"I want you," she pleaded, arching her back against him.

"What do you want?" Axel teased the inside of her thighs, the frustration growing deep inside her.

"You. I want you!" Phoebe panted, and she cried out as he slipped his finger inside her.

She ground against his hand while he circled her. Axel reached up with his other hand, caressing her breasts.

"You're so ready for me," he groaned, bringing her to the edge.

Pleasure coiled inside her as she gripped the table.

"On second thought, I want to see those beautiful eyes." He turned her over, and she squealed happily; he was standing between her legs, facing her.

He kissed her so tenderly it was almost painful. He slid his hand down her body, his fingers grazing her throat, breasts, down past her navel. As his teeth grazed her pebbled nipple, she wrapped her arms around his shoulders. The pressure built up, and she bit down on his shoulder, shaking with need.

"Don't stop," she pleaded as she rode the wave.

Reclaiming her mouth, he removed his fingers, and she lay back on the table. Just as the wave started to subside, he sank inside her, and she gasped as she took him inch by inch. His hand gripped her thigh causing the most delicious pain.

"Fuck, I love how you feel." She dug her nails into his hips.

Ecstasy built between them as her walls clenched around him. He released her thigh and moved her arms above her head, intertwining his fingers with hers. He sank his teeth into her breast, and a whimper escaped her lips.

Phoebe couldn't take it as he took possession of her body; she could feel his heart beating across her chest. Axel released her hands and she gripped his hips begging him to move faster. He smiled at her, and Phoebe nearly exploded looking at his dimples. She bucked her hips, meeting every thrust, enticing him until she exploded around him, calling his name as her walls contracted around him and pushed him over the edge.

"That was…" she stammered.

He rested his forehead against her as she caught her breath. She couldn't believe what they'd just done, and with the party only down the hall.

"I know," Axel panted, closing his eyes. She felt him trembling, and loved that he'd lost himself as much as she had.

Phoebe slid off the desk while he fixed himself up, her legs like jelly as she adjusted her dress. They needed to make themselves presentable before heading back to the party.

She picked up her ruined underwear. "They were expensive," she chuckled.

"I can afford to replace them. It won't be the last pair either."

His lips brushed hers, and—

A sudden bright white flash filled the room. Phoebe cursed, as Axel's eyes shot open, the whites exposed. He bolted into the hall to chase whoever had taken the picture. She wanted to call after him, but he reappeared seconds later.

"Whoever they were, they're gone," Axel said, his brow furrowed.

Phoebe hoped this wasn't the end of peace time, but when they re-joined the party, they found they weren't missed. Nick was with the back-up singer, while August had found a guitar to entertain himself with.

It wasn't long before karaoke started. Axel stayed by her side until Nick made him get up and do an ABBA duet —even August joined them with an impromptu guitar solo. Watching them do a terrible rendition of 'Super Trouper' helped her forget her worries. Seeing them on stage together again, happy and almost whole, brought a warmth to her heart that told her everything was going to be okay again. She hoped that wherever Cillian was, he was at peace, and comforted to know his death had brought his friends together instead of tearing them apart.

"Penny for your thoughts?" Lena asked, taking a seat beside her.

"Just enjoying the show. It's nice to see them on stage again," Phoebe said, but she couldn't stop eyeing the guests and wondering who might have taken the photo. There were some faces in the pub she didn't recognise, and she worried some might have snuck in. Maybe she was being paranoid, and someone had just taken a photo out in the hall. Just because they'd seen a flash didn't mean it had anything to do with them.

"I don't think pop is going to be in their future," Lena said as they moved on to a Backstreet Boys song Phoebe recognised but couldn't remember the name of.

"You have to love them for trying," Phoebe said, just happy to see them enjoying themselves.

All their rehearsals were paying off—Nick looked comfortable being front and centre.

Lena nodded, twisting the stem of her wine glass. It wasn't like her to fidget.

"Is there something wrong? Phoebe asked, and she stopped twisting.

Lena leaned in a little closer so the people gathered

around them wouldn't hear. "I didn't know whether to mention this now that Sheen is dead, but a security guard from LouderTech reached out to me. They were fired recently after the incident in the parking garage."

"What did they want?" Phoebe asked.

"Apparently the security guard's boss instructed him to record over any footage that you could use against them or Sheen if there was a court case. He did as he was told but made a copy in case it was worth something. Once he completed the task, management told him they were downsizing and he reached out to me," Lena explained.

"And you have the footage?" Phoebe asked, eager to have some closure.

"He wants five grand for it."

"Is there even anything on it?"

"He said he wouldn't have reached out if he didn't have something worth giving." Lena topped up her wine glass with the open bottle of white on the table.

Five grand for closure didn't seem like a bad deal.

"I'll transfer you the money tomorrow," Phoebe said, finishing her drink for some liquid courage.

"Are you sure?" Lena asked, but Phoebe needed to know the truth. Even the guys were still suspicious as to whether Sheen had truly been behind all the chaos, and this footage could silence their unanswered questions.

"Is she sure about what?" Axel asked, appearing in front of them. Phoebe hadn't even noticed the song end.

"About whether to get another round?" Lena said, covering quickly with a bright smile.

"You're right, I've probably had enough," Phoebe said, putting her hand on top of her glass.

"Then how about you get up off that fine arse and join us for a song?" Axel asked.

She wasn't going to tell him about the security footage

now, not when he was having fun. This was Nick's night, and all the footage would do was confirm that Sheen had lied about someone leaving an envelope on his desk. It was the last piece of the puzzle. Right now, what scared her most was having to get up in front of a crowd and sing.

"Absolutely not." Phoebe shook her head in protest. Nothing could drag her up on stage.

Lena tried to contain her amusement.

"Are you kidding? Have you heard her sing?" Nick chuckled, appearing behind Axel.

Axel shook his head.

"I got the artist skills, and he got the musical talent," Phoebe explained. "Unless you want to clear this place out, I'm going to sit out the karaoke."

Axel sat down beside her. He leaned in close, his hand brushing her thigh beneath the table where no one would see. "So, you can write beautiful lyrics, but can't sing?"

"The gods are cruel." She shrugged. "But hearing you sing my lyrics makes up for such cruelty."

"Lena, would you care to join us?" Nick asked, offering her his hand.

"Are you sure?" Lena squealed, trying to act like she wasn't a big fan of theirs.

"More the merrier, you can even pick the next song."

Phoebe rolled her eyes at her brother trying to enchant her friend.

"Are you okay by yourself?" Lena asked her, and she waved them away.

"Go. I'll be right here cheering you on!"

"I can keep you company," Axel teased, and she nudged him away.

"Go, all of you, your audience is waiting!" Phoebe said with a grin, not wanting the night to end as she watched everyone she cared about gather on the small stage.

As they sat around the dining room table, hungover and nursing an unhealthy amount of energy drinks, Phoebe helped Axel, Nick and August pack up all their new signed albums and merch for the concert. They had a nice assembly line going when they heard the harsh clacking of heels coming down the hall.

"Are you insane?" Anita stormed into the room like she was ready to deliver bad news and ruin their good streak.

"Hello Anita." Nick greeted her as he passed another pile of CDs to Axel. "How's your day going?"

"How's my day going?" Anita crossed her arms over her chest, and Phoebe thought steam was about to come out of her ears. "Swimmingly. We finally get rid of that creep Sheen, and foolishly, I thought all my problems were solved. Then, your sister and Axel get photographed intimately at your birthday party. Do you know about their little sordid affair?" She directed the question at Nick and August.

"You can relax. They told us about their relationship. It's not their fault that someone took a photo of them." Nick acted as cool as a cucumber, though Phoebe doubted he was happy about where the photo was taken. "Has it been leaked?"

"No. I've paid the photographer for the photo. If you don't want this to keep happening, you two should keep away from each other in public," Anita warned them, like they were teenagers to be scolded. "First Italy, and now you can't even be bothered to be discreet about your fling."

Phoebe was going to lose her mind if Anita kept referring to their relationship as a fling.

"It's not a fling." Axel voiced her thoughts, looking up from his signing stack. "You can tell the person threatening to leak the image that they can be persecuted for taking and distributing an intimate image. The most they got was us kissing; the only thing that'll happen is our relationship will be outed."

Phoebe recalled the flash. "He's right. There is no way they got anything exposing."

"How did a photographer even get into the party?" August asked as he folded the band shirts.

"We had security," Phoebe added. They'd been so careful, and discussed the guest list with Olivier.

"Someone could've brought a friend along, and they took the opportunity to make some money," Anita said. "Do you want the world to know about this? The sea has just started to settle, and you want to cause another storm. I knew you never should've moved in," she snarled at Phoebe.

"Don't speak to my sister like that," Nick cut in. "We all understand that the timing isn't perfect, but we've all been through a hell of a lot worse over the past few months, so I think them dating is nothing to cry over."

Phoebe resisted the urge to squeeze her brother tight for supporting her without question. Anita glared at her, but she refused to shrink.

"We aren't going to make some grand announcement or hide our relationship. Their music has nothing to do with our relationship, and real fans will feel the same," Phoebe reasoned. Axel leaned over and kissed her cheek.

Anita rolled her eyes. "I know how this will end."

"Are we paying you extra for your psychic powers?" Phoebe asked.

"I'm only trying to protect all of you because I care," Anita argued, but her tone sounded anything but caring.

"The photo isn't getting out, and Axel and Phoebe are free to do their own thing, so can we all shut up and watch the interview?" August said, eager to see the news about Cillian's concert selling out in record time. Not only that, but they were interviewing the head of the charity for disabled artists who they'd decided to donate the profits from the concert to. They'd all watched Phoebe's struggle to adjust to her new normal, and they wanted to help other creatives going through similar challenges.

Phoebe flexed her hand. Her strength was slowly returning, even if the pain refused to ease.

"Turn it up," she ordered, excited for the charity to get some airtime.

"Is that...?" Nick said with a frown, as August turned it up.

Cillian's girlfriend, Helen, looking very pregnant, was sitting across from the chat show host. They all stared, slack-jawed.

"What the hell is Helen doing?" Nick asked, only for Phoebe to shush him.

The perky host smiled. "Thank you for joining us this evening."

"Thank you for having me." Helen fidgeted with her top, pulling it over her bump.

Was this why she was doing this? To reveal the news of her pregnancy? None of them had heard from her since the will reading. Nick had tried to check in on her, but she said she didn't want to hear from any of them. It wasn't like she needed the money, and outing herself as the late, beloved rockstar's secret lover wasn't going to play in her favour.

Phoebe forced herself to focus.

"My producers were surprised you were so willing to do this interview. I'm sure what you have to say will be a great shock to the fans of both Brothers of Anarchy and Phoebe Fletcher." The host in her brightly coloured shirt was loving every second.

"I came here to tell you all a rather salacious story," Helen started, and the host sat forward, eager for the scoop. "With everything being said in the media about Phoebe and Cillian, I wanted to set the record straight."

"How will you do that?" the host teased, and the camera zoomed in.

Helen, visibly shaken, took a deep breath.

"I was having an affair with Cillian Hunt for six months before his death. It was Cillian driving the car when he crashed with Phoebe. She wasn't driving, and that video of her being pulled from the driver seat was edited." She rattled off the confessions in quick succession.

"How can you know all this about the crash?" The host pressured her for more.

"Because the band's manager, Anita Harding, paid me to do this interview."

A shiver ran down Phoebe's spine. Axel reached for her hand, but no one dared say a word.

"That's quite the accusation. Anita Harding, who's been with Brothers of Anarchy for nearly a decade, paid you to confess to an affair with her client?"

"Ms Harding paid me to do this interview, not to

confess to the affair, or to stand in defence of Ms Fletcher being a victim of Cillian's drunk-driving. Instead, Ms Harding paid me to tarnish Phoebe's reputation further by revealing that Phoebe was having a love affair with Axel Adler while she was with Cillian and that it was that discovery that led to the car accident. This couldn't be farther from the truth. I was to say I witnessed this affair while I worked with the band as their lead make-up artist." Helen straightened in the seat as though finding her courage as she spoke.

"That's one hell of a story. Just to clarify, did you witness such an affair between the drummer and Ms Fletcher?" the host challenged.

"No. I only mention it to out the lies being spread. Without Ms Harding's knowledge, who I'm sure will be very upset with me, I agreed to do this interview to set the record straight. I believe someone else was meant to be in this seat today, but Ms Harding had the power to swap us at the last minute. Ms Fletcher has been tormented these past few months, and I'm sorry to say that my actions have caused her much hurt, and for that I'm so very sorry." Helen looked at the camera, talking directly to Phoebe.

Is she looking for sympathy? Phoebe wondered. *Or am I being paranoid because of all that's happened recently?* She hated how jaded she was becoming.

The interviewer frowned; clearly this wasn't the interview she'd been expecting. "Why are you coming forward?"

Phoebe had the same question.

"Because I'm tired of seeing all the hate. I loved Cillian and I've worked with the other members of the band for the past few years. I once considered them friends, and Cillian would've hated to see his friends, his family, hurting. We all deserve peace. Cillian wasn't perfect, but we all loved him, and I feel like we've all lost sight of that. We all lost him, and no one is to blame, least of all Phoebe," she said, and the emotion in her voice sounded genuine.

They were all stunned into silence. August turned off the TV. No one knew what to say, including Phoebe.

Could Helen be telling the truth? It doesn't make sense, why would Anita do this? Why would she want to destroy me like this?

All turned to look at Anita at the end of the table.

"Why are you all looking at me like that?" Anita said. "You can't believe her."

Nobody said anything. They looked to Phoebe, waiting for her reaction.

"You can't believe a word she's saying. She's a liar out for money and trying to come out of this situation as a saint," Anita added, but no one was listening to her.

"Why defend us, me, if she was out to stir trouble?" Phoebe asked calmly.

"How could I know the reason for her doing this?" Anita acted stunned, but there was a hesitation in her gaze, a recalculation as she looked around the room. "She's probably out to make a name for herself."

Nick rose from the table. "Cillian left her a home, and plenty of money for her and the baby. Putting herself in the spotlight only puts her at risk."

"I'm not a mind reader, I can't possibly know what her reasoning is."

"How did she get the interview spot?" Axel challenged.

"She probably promised the producers a great story, which she provided. A *story*."

"Did you put Helen up to this?" Phoebe asked. "You knew Axel and I have been together since Italy. Did you want to ruin any chance for us with rumour and specula-tion? Have the world blame us for Cillian's death because he found out about an affair that never happened?"

"I would never do anything to hurt you," Anita said, gawking. "I've dedicated the last ten years of my life to you all."

"And made plenty of money doing it. Was this your way of trying to break us up?" Axel asked coldly.

"I would never want the band to break up. You can't believe any of this," Anita said, but there were no tears, no pleading, only a smug dismissal that felt anything but genuine.

"With Sheen gone, there was no one left to torment us. Did you want to finish what he started?" Phoebe pressed.

"Can you blame me for wanting to get rid of you? The closer you get to them, the bigger the mess you make."

There it was. The truth.

"I've been with them longer than you, and I'll still be by their side long after you. Get out of this house and don't come back," Phoebe barked, and no one tried to intervene.

"You can't tell me when to leave," Anita snarked.

"Yes, she can, this is her house," Nick said sharply. "Get out, and Olivier will be informed that you are no longer welcome."

"Firing me? You can't be serious. It was one interview; your relationship was going to come out eventually."

"You wanted us to be painted as the villains, for our relationship to have caused the death of our friend!" Phoebe exclaimed.

"Anita, leave before we have Olivier escort you from the grounds," Axel ordered, getting between them.

As Anita left, the interview replayed in Phoebe's mind on a loop. Anita had tried to use Helen against them, but failed to understand her connection with the band. Helen had loved them all, not just Cillian. Anita underestimated her—but what else had she orchestrated? Could she have been behind Sheen? He'd been desperate for any connection to the band, making him easy to manipulate.

Phoebe shook off the thought. *There is no way Anita would've worked with Sheen. She might want me gone, but dead feels too far of a stretch.*

Phoebe was painting a one-eyed blue alien with a guitar when she heard the studio door open.

"I'm surprised to find you in here," Axel said. "I thought you'd be too sore to work after physio?"

"Painting after the sessions helps me maintain my mobility, otherwise my hand gets too stiff. The thicker brushes I found are helping, and even if I'm too sore to hold a pencil and sketch out new work, I can finish painting up this little guy. It's a present for August's birth-day," she said, sitting back to admire the adorable guitar-wielding alien sitting on Mars. Even in pain, being surrounded by the colours and the smell of the paint helped her find some relief.

"Space, guitar and an alien with a mohawk, he's going to love it," Axel said, admiring the canvas. "Speaking of gifts, there's something I want to give you."

She turned on her stool to face him as his tone turned serious.

"It's not my birthday for another month." She wiped her stained hands on a cloth on her easel.

"It's not a birthday present," he said, avoiding her gaze as he sat on the arm of the couch beside her. "With everything happening with Sheen, I put off giving this to you. Now that things have calmed down, I thought it was time."

"You're making me nervous," she said, and then she recognised the journal he took out from behind his back. She'd looked for it herself after Helen's TV interview. "Why do you have Cillian's journal?"

"I found it when I picked out his funeral clothes. I was afraid to give it to you in case the answers inside hurt you, but I don't want there to be any secrets between us, and I've no right to decide what you can or can't handle."

"I thought it was probably sent with some of his other stuff to his mum," she said, flicking through the first few pages. Seeing Cillian's handwriting stirred up her grief, but it didn't cut like it used to. "I tried looking for it after Helen's interview. Thought it might have some answers, to see what was going on in his mind during those last few weeks, or months. Without knowing whether we could really trust if Sheen was behind the harassment, I think I was looking for closure in some form or another."

"I'm sorry I kept it from you," he said, brushing his lips against her cheek.

"Don't be. If you'd given it to me back then, I probably would've burnt it," she said. She still wasn't sure if she really wanted to know Cillian's secrets.

"And I wouldn't have blamed you. I'll be down in the studio if you need me," he said, kissing her hair before closing the door behind him.

She closed the lids of her paints, staring at the journal on the stool beside her. Flicking through the pages, she skipped to the last half-finished entry.

I FUCKED UP ROYALLY. PHOEBE IS NEVER GOING TO FORGIVE ME WHEN SHE FINDS OUT. SOMEONE ALREADY KNOWS, AND IT'S ONLY A MATTER OF TIME BEFORE SHE LEAVES ME FOR GOOD. I THOUGHT PROPOSING WOULD FIX EVERYTHING, AND IF WE COULD HAVE JUST ELOPED LIKE I WANTED WHEN WE WERE IN ITALY THEN SHE MIGHT BE MORE RELUCTANT TO LEAVE ME, BUT NOW THAT HELEN IS HAVING MY BABY, I'M GOING TO LOSE EVERYTHING. NICK WARNED ME THAT IF I DIDN'T GET MY ACT TOGETHER HE'D TELL HER ABOUT THE CHEATING, AND I WOULDN'T BLAME HIM. HE ALREADY LOOKS AT ME DIFFERENTLY NOW, LIKE I'M A WALKING DISAPPOINTMENT, AND WHEN HE FINDS OUT ABOUT THE BABY, I'M AFRAID THEY'LL KICK ME OUT OF THE BAND. I DON'T WANT TO LOSE THEM, I CAN'T LOSE PHOEBE AND MY BROTHERS...

PHOEBE TURNED the page to keep reading, but a couple of sheets of paper fell out from the back of the journal. She picked them up, only to find they were printed-out messages from Anita.

Anita: How could you do this to the others? You're going to ruin everyone and everything they've built for your own selfish desires.

Anita: I know what you've been doing with the make-up artist. If you don't end it, then I'm going to tell Phoebe. She doesn't deserve to be treated this way, and I don't like to see you so unhappy.

Anita: Drinking isn't going to solve your problems. You're just making life harder for yourself. Everyone would be better off without you!

THE SOUND of barking told her Axel had probably got distracted by Bart in the garden en route to his studio session. She wanted to show him the texts, and see if he knew Anita had treated Cillian like this.

When she stepped out into the sun, there was no sign of Axel.

"What are you doing out here?" she asked, seeing Bart chained up against the wall.

He was trying to pull himself out of his collar, barking at her.

"Where's your dad?" she asked as he lay down at her feet, whining until she undid the chain.

It wasn't like Axel or any of the others to chain him up —Bart was well-behaved in the studio. They only attached the long chain to his collar when the gardener came because he hated the lawnmower.

Her phone buzzed. It was an email with a video file from Lena; Isaiah was also CCed in. Bart jumped up on her, and she nearly tripped over him as she tried to watch the video. The quality wasn't great; she suspected the security guard had recorded the screen on his phone. The LouderTech logo on the wall revealed the location, but judging from the lack of people in the office and the dim lighting, it was filmed after hours.

Phoebe stopped at the door to the studio when she saw a hooded figure walk through the cubicles and leave the same generic envelope Sheen had given them on Sheen's desk.

"We can play later after I've talked to your dad," she said to Bart, trying to calm him.

A message from Lena came in.

> Sorry about the footage being so rough! I should have checked the quality before paying him. There is no face, but Sheen WAS telling the truth about someone leaving the envelope on his desk. From the silhouette, I think it could be a woman! This was left on his desk on Thursday, the day before the accident!!!!!

Phoebe wanted to reply, but she rewatched the video instead, desperate to see if she could make out any other details. The person never looked up, but then, when the culprit left the cubicle, she saw them. The red-bottomed breakneck heels. Her stomach dropped.

"Anita." The name caught in her throat.

Sheen was telling the truth. If she'd had breakfast, the rose bushes would have got some extra nourishment.

"Axel?" Phoebe called out as she opened the studio door, even though it was a waste of time with the sound-proofing in the booth.

Had Anita planned the accident because she thought Cillian was ruining the band? She had sent him those threatening messages; she felt sick at the thought that Anita had been the one to identify Cillian's body.

She doubted Axel had seen the messages at the back of the journal, or they would have fired Anita long ago. She scrolled through her phone to find Isaiah's number, wanting him to find Anita before she made a run for it—if she hadn't already. Now it made sense why Cillian was drinking so much—he was being intimidated and harassed, and who'd feel sorry for him, considering what he'd done? Anita played a great game.

"Please answer," she begged as Isaiah's phone rang out.

She turned down a small hall to the production room and opened the door, only to drop the phone when she saw Anita standing over Axel in the booth. His hands and neck were bound with thin wire, and he had a gash on his eyebrow. She crouched down, not wanting to be seen, and fumbled with her phone again, only to get Isaiah's voicemail.

"Anita, help, studio," was all she managed to send before she heard the click of the booth opening. She didn't dare look up.

Anita found her anyway.

"Like a coward hiding, while the man you claim to love has a gun to his head." Anita fisted her hair and smacked her head against the floor.

Disorientated, Phoebe tasted blood as she bit her tongue on impact. She glared at Anita, her blood chilling as she saw the gun in her hand.

"You don't need a gun," Phoebe fretted.

"I needed to protect myself, and this is just a little extra motivation to get you to listen."

Anita dragged her into the booth, and she could only hope that Isaiah would see the message and come to the house as she asked. She wondered where Anita had even managed to get a gun, but it was her job to be resourceful.

She just hoped Isaiah would hurry. The burning pain of her scalp distracted her as Anita shoved her down beside the piano.

"How did you get in? Did you hurt Olivier?" Axel's voice helped Phoebe focus, but he sounded groggy. She looked up to see a thin trickle of blood dripping down his neck.

"Don't fret," Anita said, resting her hand on Axel's shoulder and taking a seat on his lap. Axel tried to pull away, but she tightened the cords when he tried to speak. "Olivier is out with Nick and August, I've got no reason to hurt him. Maybe I should have considered punishing him. He never changed the gate code, or the security camera app password. He is supposed to be keeping you safe." Anita kissed Axel's cheek, and Phoebe could see the hate in his eyes. "I don't want to hurt you. I only wanted to help you see the truth."

"What truth is that?" Axel asked, remaining calm.

"That Phoebe doesn't love you. She only cares about herself. She got Cillian killed. He started to drink, stopped writing because of her." She turned to Phoebe. "You made him reliant on you, so he could never leave you!"

"If this is about Cillian..." Phoebe swallowed as the gun shook in Anita's hand. "...why don't we let Axel go? He didn't do anything to you. It's me you hate. I saw the messages you sent to him. You cared about him, wanted to protect him. You loved him..." She just wanted Axel out of the room. The cords were like razors against his throat, and she feared one aggressive tug would take him from her.

"I don't love Cillian," Anita snapped, and gave a tortured laugh. "Cillian was in the way. He ruined every-thing with his pathetic little love triangle. Because of that stupid make-up artist, you were going to break up with Cillian, and I wasn't going to let you get your claws into Axel—I had to get rid of you!"

"Get my claws into Axel? What are you talking about? There was nothing going on between Axel and me back then. Are you starting to believe your own lies that we were having an affair?" she asked, reminded of what Anita had wanted Helen to confess during her interview.

"Do you think I'm stupid?" Anita's nostrils flared. "I heard Axel buying your paintings; he even sent one as a gift to his family. I couldn't stomach how devoted he was to you when you didn't even care about him! So I thought while we were in Munich, I'd teach you a lesson in appreciation, and have Sheen destroy your studio. I had to get rid of you, because if you were single, I knew Axel wouldn't be able to contain his feelings for you—and I was right! You both moved on before Cillian's body was even cold."

"Get rid of us? You really wanted us both dead? Did you hate us that much?" Phoebe asked, not buying into her game. She wasn't going to explain herself to Anita. "You knew Cillian was with Helen in the dressing room that night—you even directed me to the damn room! Did you plan the crash to get rid of us?"

"Not exactly. I didn't expect Cillian to die, that was just a bonus. I thought a drink-driving charge would ruin Cillian's image. Add in his cheating, and his failure to produce the songs he had promised, and he would've had to leave the band to save their image."

"You've lost your fucking mind. How could you do such a thing? Cillian thought of you as a friend," Axel rasped, trying to get her off his lap. Phoebe used the distraction to move closer, but stilled when Anita slapped him.

"He was my friend, but he refused to get his act together! I had no choice."

"No choice?" Phoebe said. "You had nothing but choices."

"Shut it." Anita planted a heeled boot into Phoebe's ribs. "You also had a choice, and you chose to get into that car with him! So what if I told Cillian you were staying with Axel in the tour bus? You should have seen what a wreck he was that morning. Riddled with guilt, and remorse, but he refused to come clean about the pregnancy and I knew what I had to do. I gave him something to take the edge off."

"You drugged him?" Phoebe asked, holding her ribs.

"There was so much in his system, I doubt a few Xanax even made a difference. I didn't make him drive. When I told him Nick wanted him to drive you home so you could clear the air, he decided to get behind the wheel because he was so desperate to believe Nick wasn't angry with him. That he was being given a chance to make things right. Again, why would you let Cillian drive? He smelt like he'd taken a bath in vodka. Maybe you're the one who wanted him dead."

"I don't believe you; the coroner would've known if you drugged him," Phoebe countered.

"I identified the body. He was a famous rockstar with a reputation for partying. All I had to do was tell the coroner about his Xanax problem and that we would appreciate it if he left it off the report. Drugs in his system wasn't a surprise. I didn't even have to plan the accident; it was just a happy coincidence. Two birds with one stone—too bad I only got one, but I still managed to clip your wing."

"Is that why you sent the razor blades? Because you wanted to hurt my hands even more?" Phoebe asked, wondering if Anita had been behind everything or if Sheen had helped. She needed to keep Anita talking so that Isaiah would have time to get her message.

"I only did that because you cut Axel at the studio. Again, he was trying to help you, and you cut him!" Anita snarled. "If you were really worried about them then you would've left the house."

"I get it—you wanted to hurt me, you want to protect the others. But why set the gallery fire? Lena has nothing to do with this, and she could've been killed!"

Anita moved away from Axel. "You were supposed to be there! It's your fault she got hurt. In Italy, when I saw you together at the beach and I saw that tattoo…

Matching tattoos! You really made me sick with that one. I knew you were worming your way into Axel's heart, but that was overkill. You weren't going to give up. You even had Axel defend you—he threw me out of the villa like I was nothing. After the reports about the break-in, another attack on a gallery wouldn't be a surprise, and all that paint went up so fast. Sheen was the perfect cover, but he ruined everything when he busted open the door. And then he had the nerve to turn up here! When I saw him on the cameras, I knew he couldn't be trusted, and I couldn't let him meet with Isaiah and Nick."

"You killed Sheen for trying to help us." Phoebe's heart raced as she realised Anita's delusional love had turned her into a murderer.

Anita tapped the gun against her thigh. "You shouldn't be worried about him, he was a threat. He was so eager to get close to all of us; he opened the door for me once I told him Nick sent me to talk with him. Then I saw the state of his apartment, and yikes, obsession would be an under-statement. There are some real crazies out there—you can't blame me for wanting to protect the band. In fact, you should be thanking me, but you couldn't think of anyone but yourself. Your wants, your needs, your reputation."

"You're right, the police told us that Sheen was obsessed," Phoebe said. "You only wanted to protect them. I'm sorry I didn't see that."

"You're lying—you don't care about anyone but yourself." Anita kicked her again, knocking the breath out of her. She recoiled to the piano, trying to protect herself, as Anita turned to Axel and stroked his cheek. "No matter what I did, Axel never looked at me the way he looked at you. The first time I saw him on stage, I knew he was the one. He was a nobody with more talent than anyone knew.

I got him into the band, I made them into stars, I gave them everything they could've wanted, but it was never enough. You did nothing but add misery to his life with your drama, and yet he couldn't stay away. I won't let him destroy himself."

Axel's cheeks reddened as she tightened the cord around his neck. It hurt Phoebe more than anything Anita could do to her.

There was no way they were going to get out of this alive without playing along with her delusions.

"You're right, I don't love Axel," she rasped, clutching her chest. "I was only using him to get back at Cillian's memory. To get even. And I drove a wedge between you to get what I wanted."

Anita studied her, and Phoebe feared she wouldn't believe her. But then she smiled. "Finally you're telling the truth."

"But you're wrong about one thing—"

"Phoebe, don't," Axel interrupted, and Anita tightened the cord around his neck.

"Let her talk."

Phoebe felt herself go cold but forced herself to continue. "You don't need to pretend, Axel. I know you love Anita, and I know you were only with me because you felt guilty about letting me go with Cillian that morning," she said, before turning her attention to Anita. "Axel cares about you, and I'm the one who made him fire you. I was jealous." The flattery tasted like ash on her tongue.

Anita started to lower the gun, and Phoebe stepped slowly toward the piano to get closer to Axel. If Anita fired, she'd be able to shove him off the stool.

She tried to hide her hope. "I don't want you to do something you'll regret. You love him, you don't want to hurt him. All you've done for him over the past few months, years—I'm sure he can see how much you care about him."

"Even if that's true, he won't forgive me now. You got your claws in too deep." She turned to Axel, stroking his cheek while pointing the gun at his temple. "We could always go together—maybe we'll get the chance to spend our next life together. I can't make you see how much I truly love you, and you are so blinded by your guilt that you won't give in to your feelings for me."

Phoebe wanted to scream but no sound escaped her. She struggled to stay calm.

"No, he's only upset because I lied. I used him to get back at Cillian. You've done all this so you can be together. He can't speak with the cords around his neck, he doesn't need those—"

"I only put them on because he wouldn't listen, and I didn't want him to try and protect you," Anita reasoned, and Phoebe let out a long exhale when the gun left his temple.

"But he wouldn't protect me now, not now that he knows all you've done to show him the truth. Right?" Phoebe said to Axel, trying to fight back tears.

A growl distracted them all, and Anita turned to see Bart charge into the studio and leap on her. With a snarl, he chomped down on her hand with the gun. Anita screamed in agony, and the gun went off. The shot rang off the drum, but Bart refused to let go, no matter how Anita struggled.

Phoebe used the distraction to rush to Axel and unravel the cords.

"Get away from him!" Anita screamed, and Bart whined as she kicked him off.

He scampered under the piano behind Phoebe. Anita pointed the gun at their four-legged protector, but Phoebe refused to move. Blood dripped down Anita's arm and her eyes were black with rage. Axel froze when she locked eyes with him. Phoebe wasn't going to let Anita take anyone else from her.

"Anita… please…" Her pleas were silenced by the sound of shattering glass, the sharp shot of the gun, and she dropped to her knees. Phoebe waited for the pain, but none came. She looked up from the carpet to see Anita hunched over the piano. The keys trilled as Axel pushed her from his lap.

The door opened and she looked to the shattered studio window. Isaiah burst into the room as Phoebe scrambled to her feet. She didn't care about Isaiah looking after Anita, who'd fallen to the ground. She just wanted to get the cords off Axel's neck.

"I'm so sorry I didn't get here sooner. I'm so sorry," she cried, removing the tight cords carefully.

The thin cuts caused him to hiss, and she checked him over for any other injuries, but he grabbed her and wrapped his arms around her.

"I'm okay, and I wish you hadn't come at all. It wasn't me she wanted to kill," he said, holding her so tight she could barely breathe.

A team of medics followed Isaiah in.

"She has a pulse," Isaiah told them. "The bullet clipped her shoulder. She's bleeding, and she hit her head on the way down."

Axel pushed the medics aside when they tried to get a look at him. Thankfully the cords hadn't cut too deep.

"You should go to the hospital," she said, but he shook his head.

"Not a chance." He smirked, but his hand went to his neck, which was sure to be hurting.

The promise of treats finally got Bart out from under

the piano. His teeth were bloody as he padded over to Axel and sat at his feet.

"Thank you for saving us." Phoebe crouched and rubbed his ears. If Bart hadn't managed to get in, Isaiah could've arrived to find a room full of bodies.

They strapped Anita to a gurney, and a satisfied smile crept across her face as she was handcuffed to the side.

"I could have pulled the trigger at any time. You'll never be able to move on from me. You're alive because of me," Anita rasped, tugging at her new chains.

"We'll live in spite of you." Phoebe leaned in close, despite Isaiah's warning. "You'll spend the rest of your life in a jail cell knowing you lost everything and everyone."

"Get her out of here," Axel said, not even giving her a second look.

The paramedics wheeled her away as Nick and August burst into the studio.

"Olivier saw her arrive on his phone and we got here as fast as we could," Nick said, panicked. He reached for the bump on Phoebe's head. She winced, and he backed off.

"Sorry, we'll follow you to the hospital," August said, already ushering them to the door.

"We don't need to go to the hospital," Axel argued, holding Phoebe close.

"We aren't giving you a choice," Nick said. "You're both bleeding."

"Just scrapes and bruises." Phoebe winced as she brushed her bruised ribs.

Axel kissed the side of her head. "The paramedics already looked us over, we're fine."

Nick and August gave up on their attempts to convince them and joined in on the group hug, suffocating her.

"We're all going to be fine."

T he sound of the crowded stadium reminded them they didn't have much time before they had to be on stage. Right now, they were all gathered backstage with Isaiah, talking about their deranged ex-manager. They had been waiting for an update since Anita had been refused bail until trial. Cillian's memorial concert wasn't the best time for legal discussions, but they were all desperate for news. None of them wanted a drawn-out media trial; none of them wanted Phoebe and Cillian to be dragged through the mud, again.

"So, there isn't going to be a trial?" Phoebe asked, gripping the back of Axel's T-shirt as he held her close.

They no longer concealed their relationship, and now the world knew the truth about all that had happened, the fans and media had turned in their favour. There were still one or two trolls, but that kept them humble.

"Everything Anita confessed to you in the studio booth was recorded since she'd interrupted Axel's recording, so her lawyer convinced her to plead guilty and took the plea deal. She'll get fifteen years, without a chance for parole. At trial she could have got longer, but since we can't prove she played a role in Cillian's death, it's the best the prosecutors could hope for." Isaiah's words were music to their ears.

"Prison is too good for her." August was the first to speak, and Nick placed a hand on his shoulder.

"Least we don't have to go to trial, none of us wanted that. This way we'll never have to see her again," he said, fidgeting with his earpiece.

"I hoped it would be longer, but she can't hurt us in prison," Phoebe said, running her thumb over her scarred wrist. It had become a tick of hers. "Thank you for telling us."

"I wasn't sure if tonight was an appropriate time to tell you, but I couldn't see all of you and not tell you what I learnt this morning," Isaiah said.

"No, it's perfect," Nick assured him. "It's like Cillian is with us, and he'll be happy to know she'll go to prison for what she's done."

"Thank you for helping us," Phoebe added, grateful to have him in their corner.

Isaiah shook his head. "No need to thank me—you've made me uncle of the year with the tickets for tonight. I should get back to my nephew before he wonders where I've gone."

"Anytime you need tickets, give us a shout. It's the least we can do," Nick said, shaking his hand.

"I really just did my job. And if you ever need me in the future, please don't hesitate to call," Isaiah said, and Phoebe hugged him goodbye before returning to Axel's side.

There was so much he wanted to say to Isaiah. If he hadn't arrived when he did, he might not have Phoebe with him today, and he could never repay that debt.

Lena came around the corner wearing Phoebe's trainers. They'd swapped, given the size of the stadium and the amount of running around Lena had to do.

"Sorry to interrupt, but you all need to get your butts on stage before I murder all of you."

The group stared at her.

"Too soon?" Lena winced, and August wrapped an arm around her shoulder and dragged her out of the back room playfully.

In the time between Anita's case and the concert, trust levels were low, so Lena had volunteered to help manage them until they found someone else. Seeing how comfortable August was with her meant they were never going to let her go. Axel had been nervous of whether Phoebe would mind them stealing her, but they'd agreed to share.

"You better get out there," Phoebe said, staring up at him.

"If I have to." Axel brushed his lips against hers, needing some good luck before heading out on stage.

"Enough of that, she'll still be here when we're finished." Nick grabbed Axel, who didn't resist.

Together, they followed August to the stage. Lena guided Phoebe into the wings as planned. He made sure he could see her as he sat at his drums on the raised platform at the back. The smoke machines announced their arrival, and the crowd cheered as they started to play. Axel had missed this rush of adrenaline; the heat of the stage lights and the cry of the crowd was exhilarating. He caught sight of Phoebe singing along as her brother stood front and centre like the natural leader he was. The echo of the crowd singing back at them was his second favourite sound on earth—the first being the way Phoebe said his name.

As they finished their last song and the crowd chanted for more, Nick gestured to him. Axel nodded and jumped down from his drums as August led Phoebe on stage despite her protests. The crowd started to quieten down, wondering what was going on.

"What are you doing?" Phoebe said, panicking. Axel and August stood by her sides so she couldn't make an escape.

"Don't worry, dear sister—we aren't going to make you sing," her brother teased, covering the mic.

He turned back to the crowd. "Before we say our good-byes, we have one more surprise for all of you. Tonight, I know we are meant to be celebrating Cillian, but I don't think he'd mind sharing the spotlight with someone close to his heart," Nick said into the mic while Phoebe glared at Axel.

"Just watch the screens," Axel whispered, and her expression softened.

All the screens around the stadium no longer displayed their image; instead, they showcased images of Phoebe's paintings that had been destroyed by Anita. Phoebe froze, speechless, watching as one painting faded to reveal another.

"As many of you know, my sister Phoebe is an exceptionally talented artist, and though her works were maliciously destroyed, we thought it was only right to try and give her the exhibition she deserves," Nick said, and the crowd roared her name.

The waves of applause never got old.

"How did you all do this?" Phoebe beamed at them, and tears filled her eyes. The last thing Axel wanted was to make her cry, but he hoped they were happy tears.

"Lena found the pictures she'd taken when you put together your first exhibition, and we had them turned into prints and projected them onto the screens. They aren't perfect, but we wanted you to have your exhibition," Nick explained, and Axel winked at her as she stood with them, stunned by their secret plan.

"I think my dear sister has something she wants to share with all of you." Nick stepped aside, giving her the mic.

She took a deep breath as the audience cheered her name. To have been criticised by so many but still have the courage to face such a large crowd made him love her even more.

"Hi, I'm Phoebe, and I can tell you that I had no idea he was planning this. I don't know what to say, other than thank you for all the love you've shown everyone on this stage over the past decade." Phoebe shifted nervously, glancing at them as they stood beside her. "I know you've all heard some things about me, but I want you to know how much I loved Cillian, and you should know he loved all of you very much. More importantly, I want to thank you for loving him. Thank you for being here with us to remember him. I'm sure he is watching over us now, and he'd tell us to stop being so sappy and get on with the next song. All that's left is to thank you for indulging my brother's mad scheme, and I'm sure they'd be happy to play an extra encore," Phoebe said, and she handed Nick the mic as the crowd cheered and begged for more.

Axel watched her in awe as she took a final bow. He wouldn't have judged her for holding a grudge against their fans who had berated and judged her, but instead she had thanked them for all their love and support. He had seen the tear in her heart Cillian had caused, and he planned on spending the rest of his life healing it.

They shared a quick group hug, basking in the moment. After so much uncertainty, they'd all made it here.

Phoebe exited the stage as they started the encore.

Once they said their final goodbyes, and gave Cillian the proper send-off he deserved, Axel ran to the wings and scooped Phoebe up in his arms. Even though they ached from hours of playing, she was the perfect balm.

"I can't believe you all did that!" Phoebe said to the group as he put her down.

"Don't blame us, it was Axel's idea," Nick said, and August held up his hands in defeat.

"Those paintings deserved to be seen," Lena added, hugging her friend into submission.

"Thank you. Seeing them again, standing up there with all of you, was the best moment of my life." Phoebe teared up again and Axel wrapped his arms around her.

"Let's promise each other that we'll make many more great moments in the future," Nick said, and everyone agreed.

"Promise," they all echoed.

"A group hug to seal the deal—I missed the one on stage," Lena said, and they all squished together as the sound of the cheering crowd echoed around them.

Axel stared at his family, and couldn't help but think that Anita had helped him find them. He'd always be grateful to her for that, but he'd never forgive her for threatening to take them away. Tonight was their chance to say goodbye to Cillian and start again, and as Phoebe's arms circled around his waist, he was never going to let them go.

"Penny for them?" Phoebe whispered.

Axel stared down at her. "I was just wondering how long we have to hang around here before we can be alone," he said, wanting to bring her home for the real encore.

"You guys go, I'll distract the others," Lena chimed in. Axel chuckled at her shameless eavesdropping.

"Have I told you how much I love your friend?" Axel asked Phoebe.

"Not as much as I do," Phoebe said, and Lena winked at them.

"August, Nick, you've got a meet-and-greet to get to," she ordered.

"What about them?" Nick asked, looking at Axel and Phoebe.

"Don't worry about them." Lena ushered Nick on. "Move it, or I'll add a five a.m. interview to your schedule."

"I like it when you're bossy," Nick teased, and Lena rolled her eyes.

"You'll like it less when I follow through."

August sighed as they all put up with their flirting.

"I think we should make a run for it," Phoebe said over their bickering.

Axel nodded, and took her hand.

"Ready?" Phoebe asked, already walking backwards towards the emergency exit.

"Lead the way." He winked, ready to follow her for the rest of his life.

Did You Pre-Order Not Another Rockstar?

Scan the QR code below
and fill in the form to claim
your bonus content.

Thank you so much for pre-ordering Phoebe & Axel's story. I hope you love the exclusive chapter.

Acknowledgements

Thank you for reading Phoebe and Axel's story! This is the second romantic suspense novel I've written, and I'm so grateful to you for letting me explore new genres. I've lived with chronic pain for years, so Phoebe's character truly came straight from my heart. My hope is that any readers facing pain—whether physical, emotional, or both—feel seen and heard in her character. You all deserve a happily ever after.

I also want to give a massive thank you to Ellie, who did a fabulous job editing Axel and Phoebe's story. She helped me put those final touches on their love story (insert round of applause!). She truly deserves a medal for putting up with my half-finished paragraphs and out-of-sequence sentences in bold.

A special thank you goes to my editor, Emma, who introduced me to Ellie. While we didn't work on this book together, for nearly five years, you've been that voice in my head—cackling over mistakes in my spicy scenes and debating all my "Kate-isms."

To my readers: you have my heart and always will.

Thank you so much for all the love you've shown Axel and Phoebe from the moment I first introduced them. On days when I struggle mentally and physically, your support inspires me to keep going and creating. I couldn't do what I love without you. Every share, comment, review, fabulous video, or photo brightens my world. Thank you for letting me live my dream. I don't take a single one of you for granted.

2025

The Deeper You Sink, The Darker It Gets.

The Situation Ship

KATE CALLAGHAN

The Situation Ship

Pop star Poppy Roe's glittering life of fame takes a sinister turn when she finds herself trapped in a nightmare aboard a luxurious cruise ship. As her every move is monitored by a sinister stalker, the ship becomes a hunting ground for a relentless predator. In a desperate bid for survival, Poppy turns to enigmatic detective Isaiah Rivers, also a passenger on the ill-fated voyage. Haunted by his own demons, he never expected to get caught up in a web of danger on the high seas. Determined to protect Poppy, he joins forces with her, seeking to unravel the twisted secrets that lurk beneath the ship's glamorous façade. Amid the horrifying murders, a thrilling romance blossoms, intertwining their fates in a dangerous dance of trust and vulnerability.

As danger lurks on every deck and passions ignite, Poppy and Isaiah must navigate a treacherous sea of suspicion and desire. Will they unmask the killer before the final note of their haunting melody? Prepare for a pulse-pounding tale of romance and suspense that will leave you breathless

Join The Mailing List

Sign Up To Be The First To Hear About:
- Advanced Release Copies
- Cover Reveals
- Teasers & More

Scan Me

About The Author

Kate Callaghan released her debut YA dark fantasy trilogy, *Crowned A Traitor: A Hellish Fairytale* in 2020. She loves dark tales, villains and happily-ever-afters—something you will find in all of her books. Chatting with readers and getting to share many different stories is her favourite part of being an indie author. Currently she lives in Dublin. She loves dramas with subtitles (to silence the characters), coffee, and reading too many mysteries and romances. If missing, please check your local coffee shop. You will find her with her computer and an iced beverage.

Follow the links below if you want to know to learn more about future stories! Signed copies are also available on the author's website.

www.callaghanwriter.com